EXORCIST FALLS

WITH THE BONUS NOVELLA
EXORCIST ROAD

JONATHAN JANZ

SINISTER GRIN PRESS
MMXVII
AUSTIN, TEXAS

Sinister Grin Press

Austin, TX

www.sinistergrinpress.com

March 2017

"Exorcist Road" © 2014 Jonathan Janz

"Exorcist Falls" © 2017 Jonathan Janz

Cover Art by Matthew Revert

Book Design by Travis Tarpley

ISBN: 978-1-944044-51-0

Exorcist Road was originally published by Samhain Publishing, Ltd. in 2014 in digital format.

Author's Note

The book you are holding is actually two books. The first is a novella called *Exorcist Road*. It was published in late 2014 and appears here with some minor revisions. If you're holding the paperback copy, it's the first time the novella has appeared in print. The second book is its sequel, a brand-new full-length novel titled *Exorcist Falls*. The two stories are highly dependent on one another. Though you *can* read *Exorcist Falls* as a standalone novel, you'll likely want to read the books in order.

Lastly, before you begin, you should know that this tale falls under the category of "religious horror." Being a spiritual man myself, I understand how sensitive people can be about the topic. Please remember that this is a work of fiction. I don't condone the ghastly events that occur in the novel, and I'm not my main character, Father Jason Crowder. If you want to find more of me in a protagonist, check out Joe Crawford from *The Nightmare Girl* or Will Burgess from *Children of the Dark*.

At any rate, like William Peter Blatty's *The Exorcist* and *Legion* (incredible novels that influenced this series in fundamental ways), the book you're about to read ventures into some horrific and unsettling places. I don't apologize for that because I follow where the characters lead. Do know, however, that I have a deep respect for the Catholic faith, a strong love and sense of protectiveness toward children, and am simply telling a tale.

It is, nevertheless, an exceedingly dark tale.

Acknowledgments

First, I want to thank Don D'Auria, who has been a constant champion of my work and a good friend. I also want to thank Brian Keene for believing in me before anybody else did. Without Don and Brian, none of you would be holding this or any other of my books.

Thank you to Sinister Grin Press for their continued support. Thank you also to artist Matthew Revert for creating such outstanding covers.

My agent Louise Fury was the one who suggested I write *Exorcist Road*. I'm very thankful for her enthusiasm and guidance. My fans were the ones who suggested I write *Exorcist Falls*. Their support is deeply appreciated. And as always, my pre-readers, Tim Slauter and Tod Clark, contributed a great deal to these stories. They're both indispensable parts of my team.

Thank you to William Peter Blatty. No one who writes in this subgenre can do so without owing a debt to its master. Mr. Blatty passed away recently, but he left a mark on the literary and cinematic landscapes that few ever leave. He will be missed.

I thank God for the opportunity to write, and even more importantly, for blessing me with such a wonderful family. My wife and three children mean everything to me. They love me, support me, and remind me to laugh every day. I'm eternally indebted to them for filling my life with joy.

Exorcist Road

Jonathan Janz

DEDICATION

This novella is for my Aunt Letha. You passed on before my first book was published, but during those long, hard years of rejection and frustration, you believed in me and had faith in me. Your smile, your quiet kindness, and your positive attitude always made me feel good about myself. Thank you for all you did for me, Aunt Letha. I think of you every day.

"And I think—I think the point is to make us despair; to reject our own humanity, Damien: to see ourselves as ultimately bestial, vile and putrescent; without dignity; ugly; unworthy. And there lies the heart of it, perhaps: in unworthiness. For I think belief in God is not a matter of reason at all; I think it finally is a matter of love: of accepting the possibility that God could ever love us."

~ *The Exorcist*, William Peter Blatty

Before

They called him the Sweet Sixteen Killer.

At least I assumed the killer was a man. To inflict that kind of damage on the human body a person would have to possess a hell of a lot of strength. Especially the fifth victim, the Harmeson girl.

It requires a fair amount of pressure to rip a person's head from her body.

Forgive me. Father Sutherland always chided me for my gallows humor, the flippant comments I'd make when a situation demanded gravity. I guess it's a coping mechanism, though that doesn't excuse it. Especially not in a priest.

So before I talk about the worst night of my life, let me tell you my name, my age and my greatest fear.

Jason Crowder.

Twenty-nine years old.

Having people discover what a coward I am.

Men enter the priesthood for all sorts of reasons. Many are called by God. Others feel the need to atone for some long-ago sin.

I took the vow because I was scared of the world.

I've always been frightened of women, particularly. And before you make any assumptions, let me just say that I am attracted to them. It's simply that they're too capricious, too wild. Their breath always seems to smell of summer rain, their skin like some dewy tropical fruit. They make me feel dizzy. Powerless. Therefore, the vow of celibacy seemed a natural step to take.

How was I to know being a priest would only make things more difficult? How was I to know how tempting a married woman could be, how beguiling, despite the terror she made me feel?

I'd like to tell you about Liz now. I'd like to tell you about her mesmerizing green eyes, about the way her clothes hugged her body.

But, because I don't have much time, I need to tell you how it began that storm-swept night. I need to tell you about the cop who roused me from a deep sleep a few minutes shy of midnight.

I need to exercise the patience that has kept me alive this long. The discipline. Perhaps it was my discipline that caused Danny Hartman to select me that night, for him to show up on my doorstep and drag me unknowingly into a nightmare beyond my darkest imaginings.

Or perhaps it was something else that chose me.

PART ONE
PRESENCE

CHAPTER ONE

Picture Danny Hartman as I saw him the night he awakened me:

Average height, handsome in a sad way. Eyes that darted away before you could discern the pain in them. Lean, but possessed of a tensile strength. Forty-one. A dark-brown goatee that matched his short hair, though the hair was sheltered by his navy-blue policeman's cap as he stood on the stoop of my cottage at the rectory.

The rain was coming down in freshets, pelting Danny as if in punishment for some ghastly sin. And though doing so soaked him to the bone, he removed his waterlogged cap and clutched it to his stomach out of respect for me, despite the fact that I was only a lowly junior priest. I inhaled the faintly metallic scent of the rainfall and waited for him to speak.

He smiled apologetically. "Sorry, Father. I know it's late, but I need you to come with me."

I nodded. Danny was a parishioner at St. Matthew's, and though he was a quiet man who kept mostly to himself, he had always treated me with more reverence than I was used to being shown.

I took a step away from him but hesitated. "Should I bring anything, Officer Hartman?"

He chuckled. "It's Danny, Father. I only get called Officer when I'm being reprimanded." He sobered. "I'd bring a Bible if I were you. And anything else you might use in an emergency."

That stopped me. "Do you mind if I ask what sort of emergency this is?"

He gave me an appraising look. For the first time I saw myself through his eyes and imagined how ridiculous a figure I must make. Blond hair sticking up in jackstraw tufts. Faded blue robe hanging cockeyed on my bony shoulders. Unshaven, though that hardly made a difference. I never could grow much of a beard.

Danny said, "Look, Father, I don't know where to begin, so I'll just say this: Bring whatever you guys use in a special situation. When things could be dangerous. Spiritually, I mean."

His words chilled me more than the cool April air blasting through the doorway. I nodded again, sure my disquiet was etched plainly on my face, and hurried to the bedroom.

I was back within a couple minutes, taking time only to throw on a T-shirt, jeans, socks, and tennis shoes. My robe and the rest of the stuff I grabbed were crammed into my duffel bag. Danny, I realized with self-reproach, had been waiting patiently on the front stoop, being doused by the storm because I hadn't invited him inside. I muttered an apology on the way to his police cruiser, and soon we were pulling out of the rectory parking lot and onto the deserted parish road.

"Where is this emergency?" I asked.

He made a face like he'd tasted something rotten. "Rosemary Road."

I was surprised. Rosemary Road was in one of the nicest areas of Lincoln Park and one of the most affluent neighborhoods in all of Chicago. Several of our largest donors lived on Rosemary Road. It wasn't the sort of place where you'd expect trouble.

I said as much to Danny Hartman.

He drummed his fingers on the steering wheel, passed a trembling palm over his cheek. "Father—"

"Jason, please. At least for tonight."

He nodded, though he looked disquieted by the prospect of addressing me by my first name. It was one of the many things I disliked about being a priest. Rather than feeling honored by my position, I felt distanced, set apart from normal society in often unpleasant ways. I wasn't just a guy sitting next to another guy I happened to like and respect. I was a different species of creature, one who made others uncomfortable by my presumed judgment of them.

"Like I said, Jason, I don't really know where to start. My mind's spinning from what I saw, and, honestly, I can't make any sense of it."

"Just start talking, and I'll stop you when I need clarification," I said, falling naturally into my role of confessor.

He swallowed. "I've got a brother. Ron. You never met him. He isn't the religious type. Lives over on Rosemary. He's got a wife, a couple kids. Works at the Mercantile. Makes a hell of a lot of money— Forgive me, Father."

I nodded, thinking Ron must indeed make a good deal of money in order to afford a house in Lincoln Park.

"He called me earlier tonight—actually, that's wrong. It was Liz who called me. Ron got on the phone because she got choked up talking about it, but it was Liz who called me first."

I knew Liz Hartman, though I didn't mention it. Instead, I asked, "Were you on duty?"

Danny nodded. "I was with Jack Bittner, my partner."

I knew Bittner, and though I wasn't surprised they were partners, I couldn't help thinking that the higher-ups at the CPD couldn't have chosen a more mismatched pair than Danny Hartman and Jack Bittner.

While Danny was a faithful parishioner and the kind to stay for fellowship after Mass was over, Jack's visits were infrequent, and when he did attend, he invariably sat in the back row with a forbidding look on his face. Truthfully, Jack had always intimidated me.

Danny sighed. "My brother, when he got on the phone, he told me to come quick, that they'd locked Casey—that's their son...he's fourteen and one of the nicest, most unassuming kids you'd ever want to meet—he said they'd locked Casey in his room."

"That seems a mite barbaric."

Danny considered a moment. "See, this is where it gets crazy." I watched him chew on the inside of his mouth and decided to give him time to get it all straight before he spoke. Though I'm not naturally a patient person, I've learned the importance of the trait in my duties at St. Matthew's.

Danny said, "I guess the only way to say it is to say it, right?" He shook his head ruefully. "I just know what I'd be thinking if I were you. Someone came to me with a story like the one I'm about to tell, I'd laugh in their face.

"Ron says to me, 'Get over here fast. Something's wrong with Casey'. I was driving, so I did as I was told, and maybe because I was so distracted I made my first mistake right then. Right at the beginning."

Careful to keep my tone neutral, I said, "Mistake?"

"Taking Jack along with me. I should've never done that." He gave me a miserable look. "How was I supposed to know what would happen?"

"What did happen?"

He grimaced. "See, before I get to that, you really need to understand the mood everybody's been in. You know, all this Sweet Sixteen business?"

I nodded. I'd sensed a change in the entire city over the past three months. It was one thing to have a serial killer loose in Chicago. It was another thing entirely for the madman to prey exclusively on sixteen-year-old girls. A few years ago I did some reading about a notorious serial killer named Albert Fish. A cannibal and a child molester, Fish's case was the most horrifying thing I'd ever read. The Sweet Sixteen killings weren't carbon copies of that horrible business with Albert Fish, but there was a kinship there. Kids were supposed to be off-limits. And though the Sweet Sixteen Killer's victims were a good deal older than most of Fish's victims, the six young women who'd been slain were far too young to die.

Making matters even worse were the similarities to Jack the Ripper and the sexually violent nature of the murders. Not only did the Sweet Sixteen Killer fixate on teenage girls, but the depravity of his crimes defied comprehension. Thinking about the monstrous things I'd heard, I tried to distract myself by focusing on the sound of the rain pelting the roof, the relentless sweep of the wiper blades providing us just enough visibility to not sideswipe a parked car or drift into the oncoming lane.

"The whole thing is a terrible business," I said, and decided to leave it at that.

"You're not kidding, Father. Jason, I mean. And while it's been rough on everybody, it's been especially hard down at the station. No one wants to talk to each other. Or even look at each other. It's like we've all taken the killings personally. Like we've failed the city. Especially the victims."

"A certain amount of ownership is laudable," I ventured. "If you all feel a sense of duty, that means you care. It also means the killer will be less likely to slip through your fingers."

Danny's expression went hard. "Oh, he'll kill again, a scumbag like that. Don't kid yourself, Jason." A look of anxiety flitted across his face. "I'm sorry, but…can I just call you Father?"

I smiled and nodded, understanding the awkwardness of addressing me by my first name. I also thought there might be some deep-seated need that could be fulfilled by calling me Father. Even policemen need comfort.

Danny looked relieved. "So like I was telling you, we've all been frustrated. Moody. Guys snapping at each other, pulling long shifts. Getting paranoid and…" he shrugged, looking embarrassed, "…maybe even fantasizing about being the one who catches him."

"Nothing wrong with that," I said.

"I mean, we're human, right? We want to bring this monster to justice. This guy… this guy's worse than Gacy."

I thought of John Wayne Gacy, the serial killer who'd terrorized Chicago back in the seventies, the man also known as the Killer Clown. I said, "Gacy was an interesting case. There were several factors that contributed to his homicidal urge, particularly his troubled childhood."

24

Danny didn't comment, but pressed on with his narrative. "Like everybody else, I've lost sleep, brooded, that sort of thing. But no one's taken it as hard as Jack."

I waited, thinking—perhaps uncharitably—that Jack Bittner did not seem the type to take his work personally.

I asked, "Is there any reason why Officer Bittner would take a more-than-ordinary interest in the Sweet Sixteen killings?"

Danny gazed at me bleakly. "His daughter turns sixteen next week."

I looked at Danny, a bit astounded at this news. I couldn't imagine Jack Bittner being a father.

Danny nodded. "Most people don't know about Celia. But you can't assume anything about people. Bittner used to work on the South Side—that's where he was born and raised. He had a hell of a rough childhood, Father. His dad ran out. His mom committed suicide. Jack always used to talk about that, how he imagined his mother burning in hell." Danny sighed. "Anyway, when Bittner's wife left him for another guy, he moved up here to put some distance between them. I don't think I've ever seen a man hate his ex-wife as much as Bittner does. At least, short of the ones who kill their ex-wives."

I'm afraid I must have betrayed some of my displeasure at this sentiment, for Danny seemed a trifle flustered. He rushed on, "Reason Jack stayed in Chicago rather than pulling up stakes and starting his life somewhere else was Celia, his little girl. He wanted to be close enough to visit her, but not so close he'd have to see his ex. Or her husband."

I mulled it over. "It sounds like there's more to Jack than I thought. But what has this to do with your brother's family?"

"I'm getting to that. We showed up at Ron's place at around... oh, it must have been around eleven o'clock. I couldn't believe what we found. Liz looking beat up. Ron limping around like he'd been mauled by a bear. Even little Carolyn..." He smiled sadly. "I guess she's not so little anymore. She'll be ten in a few months. But she's still my little Carolyn."

"What happened to them?"

"Casey attacked them."

I glanced at Danny, an unease growing within me.

"I got this from Ron, okay? He was freaked out, but I think he was relatively coherent. According to Ron, one minute everything's going along like normal—Carolyn in bed asleep, Liz reading a book, Ron downstairs doing something, probably checking his investments—when they heard noises coming from Casey's room."

"Can you be more specific?"

Danny took a right on Rosemary Road. "A loud thumping sound. Like a giant drum being struck at intervals."

"You heard this?"

"Uh-uh. By the time we got there, things had become too chaotic, but the first thing they heard were the drum sounds."

"Go on."

"Liz got there first. Ron said she was standing frozen in the middle of Casey's room staring at their son. Casey was on the floor at the foot of the bed, sitting on his knees. Ron said Casey was smiling in their direction, but not a nice smile. Not Casey's normal one." Danny looked at me with that same desperate expression I'd seen earlier, like he was afraid I wouldn't believe him. "Casey really is a good kid," Danny explained. "I've known him since he was born. I'm his godfather. He's never been in any kind of trouble. Excellent grades. In fact, I've always worried he was a bit too...I don't know, passive? Like other kids might take advantage of his kindness?"

"What was Casey doing, Danny?"

"'Like the devil' was how Ron put it. He said his son looked just like the devil." Danny shook his head. "Jesus, the kid's own father."

"I'm afraid I don't—"

"The sound they'd heard was Casey's fists beating the floor in that steady, merciless rhythm. He's a skinny kid, not really grown into his body yet. But he was striking the floor so hard the windows were rattling. The stuff on his dresser was jumping. The wood—" he licked his lips, "—the wood floor was dented and bloody. I saw that when we got there.

"Liz was the first one to go to him. You know, this is her baby boy. She tried to grab his hands so he wouldn't hurt himself anymore, but before either Ron or Liz knew what was happening, Casey had lashed out, torn a gash along his mother's hairline. Liz was too stunned to react, but Casey never hesitated. He belted her in the face. By that time Ron was over there too—so was Carolyn; somewhere along the line, she'd come in—but Ron was no match for his son. Casey heaved him across the room. Then he got on top of Carolyn. He was..." Danny trailed off, and I saw tears in his eyes, "...Casey was hitting her, but he was fumbling with her…he was trying to do something no brother should do to his sister."

My mouth was dry. There was a painful, steady throb in the base of my skull.

"Liz saw what was happening and went over there right away." Danny smiled admiringly. "She's a hell of a woman, Father. I have no idea why she married that brother of mine. I guess it could be the money, but that doesn't seem like Liz."

"Was she able to get Carolyn away?"

"Thank God. She pulled Carolyn out from under Casey, but not before Casey smacked Liz in the face again. Anyway, that was about the time Ron was shutting the bedroom door."

I shot a look at Danny. "Shutting them in?"

He looked at me meaningfully. "Not according to Ron. But I've got my suspicions. At any rate, they all three got out and were able to keep Casey contained until we arrived."

"Then what?"

Even though the only illumination in the cruiser was the blue luminescence of the dash and the occasional sodium streetlight on Rosemary Road, I could see the blood drain from Danny's face. "Then…" His eyes shifted to something on our right. He signaled. "Here's Ron's house. Maybe it's best for you and Father Sutherland to see for yourselves."

My heartbeat quickened. Father Peter Sutherland was the best priest I'd ever met. And my mentor. "He's here?"

Danny nodded. "Any minute now."

"I'm not sure I understand."

Danny glanced at me as we pulled to a stop. "The only way I could persuade Bittner not to take Casey to jail was by telling him we needed to have the boy examined by a priest first."

"Danny," I said. "Are you saying you believe this is a case of demonic possession?"

He shut off the cruiser and sat there a long moment without answering. When I was about to abandon it as a lost cause, he said, "I don't know what it is. I'm no expert at that sort of thing. All I know is what I saw in that bedroom, and it was the scariest damned thing I've seen in my whole life. The growling and the roaring and the... My God, Father, it was like a horror movie in there. If I hadn't been there, I'd have said Jack used excessive force. But I was there. I saw Casey going ballistic. It took everything we had just to get him restrained. Then we went to fetch you guys."

"How did Bittner get to Father Sutherland's house?"

"He took Ronnie's car. The Mercedes. It's the car Ron drives when he wants to go slumming."

"Why did you have Jack drive your brother's car?"

Danny smiled. "First off, I figured you for a tougher sell. Father Sutherland has experience in these matters."

"He'll be skeptical."

"Secondly," he went on as though I hadn't spoken, "I didn't want Jack changing his mind and radioing in to headquarters." Danny tapped the mouthpiece dangling from the dash. "If he was in Ron's car, he couldn't use the radio. And Jack doesn't carry a cell phone."

I frowned at Danny in the gloom. "But you just said it yourself—I don't have any experience. Why was it important for me to get here first?"

Danny shrugged, not meeting my eyes. "I wanted to make sure I was here to protect Casey when Bittner got back."

"Why would you need to protect him from your own partner?"

"Oh that," Danny said, and I could see he hadn't forgotten it at all, but had rather been hoping I wouldn't ask. "I guess I didn't tell you."

"Tell me what?"

"Jack thinks my nephew is the Sweet Sixteen Killer."

CHAPTER TWO

We entered without knocking and were faced with nothing more phantasmagorical than a sprawling, stylishly decorated historical home. The foyer looked thirty feet tall, and I could see a baby grand piano to our left, its sleek black lines dominating what looked like a parlor. To the right there was another room, though the door was shut. As we scuffed our sodden shoes on the welcome mat, Liz Hartman appeared from the second doorway on the right.

Examining her blonde hair and her careworn expression, I did my best to keep my expression neutral.

"Did you bring them both?" she asked Danny, her striking green eyes flitting to me and back to her brother-in-law again.

Danny shook his head. "Jack went to get Father Sutherland." He gestured toward me. "Liz, meet Father Jason Crowder. Father, this is Liz Hartman, my brother's wife. And, um... Casey's mother."

"We know each other from church," she said. "Hello, Father Crowder."

I nodded and ventured a smile, but I could tell right away that Liz scarcely noticed me. Her forehead was creased, her eyes red-rimmed and wet. She had on a snug-fitting, light-blue T-shirt and equally snug jeans. I put her at about forty. She was a stunningly attractive woman. I'd often caught myself staring at her during Mass, and on several occasions, I'd lingered on the front steps so I could to talk to her before she and Casey left. And while our interactions were usually nothing more than polite, I'd always sensed a deeper connection between us. Or perhaps that was simply wishful—not to mention dangerous—thinking.

She nodded for us to follow her and disappeared through the doorway. I trailed after Danny, suddenly conscious of my bedraggled appearance, my cheap, damp clothes and my messy blond hair, which was plastered to my skull in several places from the downpour. On the way into the kitchen, I did what I could to tame it, but with no mirror and no comb, I fear I made a poor job of it. But when we reached the doorway all thoughts of my wardrobe and hair scattered.

The kitchen was the largest I'd ever seen. There were custom cabinets on all four walls, two islands. I thought of a gourmet restaurant in Paris, or perhaps Venice. Whatever kind of people the Hartmans were, they were rich. The pleasing aroma of freshly cut lemons permeated the room, which was meticulously clean. The appliances were stainless steel. On the fridge I saw kids' drawings and family pictures. One of the photos showed a boy in a baseball uniform. He was smiling at the camera, his bat poised for a swing. Casey Hartman, I thought, remembering how polite the young man always was at Mass. Likeable. Sincere. Not a child capable of violence. Certainly not a serial killer.

A man I presumed to be Ron Hartman stood between the granite-topped islands, his hands planted on either side of what looked like a stiff drink. His black hair was shaggier than I would've guessed, and the forearms protruding from his red Blackhawks jersey were larger than I would've assumed, given his white-collar profession. He reminded me of a bigger Al Pacino, though there was none of the actor's sardonic good humor in Ron's dark eyes.

Across from the man and off to his left sat a little girl I assumed was Carolyn. She had tousled brown hair and wore a violet nightgown. Ron neither spoke to the girl nor seemed to notice her. Before her on the island lay an open coloring book, though the pages and the crayons sat untouched. The little girl's morose face was downturned. Her hands lay in her lap.

As we entered the kitchen, Danny made the introductions. Ron took a long drag from his glass, eyeing me steadily. I returned his appraising stare with forced civility.

In the silence, Liz said, "Thank you both for coming." She gave Danny a grateful look and took a post behind her daughter. I could tell Liz was fighting back tears, but she began to rub her daughter's slender shoulders anyway, perhaps for something to do.

Ron placed his drink on the speckled countertop and said, "Carolyn, it's time for you to go to bed."

Liz's face stiffened, but she didn't stop massaging her daughter's shoulders.

"Do I have to?" Carolyn asked without looking up.

"Now," Ron said, eyeing me again.

Liz said, "She's scared, honey."

Ron had lifted his drink halfway to his mouth, but at his wife's remark he froze and stared at her. Liz didn't seem as intimidated by her husband as I was.

Ron was about to say something to her—whatever it was going to be was clearly not affectionate—but at that moment Danny moved up next to Carolyn and said, "Hey, kiddo, let's head to the basement, okay?"

She looked up at him with large eyes. "It's dark down there."

"Then we'll light that place up like Wrigley Field," he said, grinning.

He grasped her under the armpits and scooped her easily out of the chair. She was nine and probably about average size for her age, but Danny lifted her as though she were a newborn. I also noted how she allowed Danny to handle her, the two of them obviously having reached a level of comfort few children accord people who are not their parents. My respect for Danny rose another notch.

Once he'd carried her out of the kitchen, Liz said to me, "Father Crowder, did Danny tell you what happened?"

I folded my hands before me. "He gave me the general idea."

"What do you make of it?"

"Mrs. Hartman, I don't think I should speculate about Casey's condition until I see him. And certainly not before Father Sutherland examines him."

Ron said, "But he told you what Casey did."

"He told me some of it, yes. Enough to know the child needs attention."

He chuckled mirthlessly and glanced from Liz to me. "What the hell's that supposed to mean?"

"Again," I said, in a mental frenzy to capture the tone and words I thought Father Sutherland would use, "it would be irresponsible for me to speculate. I haven't seen the child yet. While we can't rule out anything, we must first investigate all the potential causes. Some sort of seizure, maybe. A previously undetected psychological condition."

"Psychological condition," Ron repeated.

"It's one of many possibilities," I said.

Ron leaned forward and raised an index finger toward the second story.

"He threw me across the fucking room."

Liz frowned. "Please be nice, Ron."

"Mr. Hartman, I'm not discounting anything. I'm merely saying we should reserve judgment until examining your son. One of the greatest mistakes a priest can make is to attribute a medical or psychological issue to the supernatural. For centuries people have suffered unduly— have even died—because their conditions were misdiagnosed. It's entirely possible the only thing your son needs is the proper medication."

"Medication?" Ron arched an eyebrow at me and began to pace. "With all due respect, Father," he said and paused for what I was certain was dramatic effect, "you're what, twenty-five? Twenty-six?"

I told him my age.

He nodded as if he'd expected that. "You're still very green, Father. In fact—and I'm not trying to be unkind here—but it's sort of hard for me to address you as Father."

I waited, not bothering to comment or return his condescending grin.

"When you get my age," he went on, "and have seen a bit more of the world, you begin to understand people better. Their ways, their idiosyncrasies. You know?"

Again, I didn't bother to answer. I was sure this was part of a canned speech he gave to his interns and underlings at the Mercantile. Ron was probably used to eager nods and bright eyes, but I'd be damned if I was going to give him either of those things. I had already decided that Danny's brother, though obviously skilled at playing the stock market, was a first-rate jackass.

He patrolled the area between the granite islands like a practiced lecturer. "When someone is as young as you—again, no disrespect intended—and especially when he's led a..." he glanced at Liz, who I noticed wasn't regarding her husband with any more warmth than I was, and gestured vaguely, "...well, what would you call it? A *cloistered* lifestyle?"

Trying to keep my cool, I said, "I don't see what my profession has to do with this."

Ron laughed again, the kind of laugh that declared I was even dumber than he thought. He took a big gulp from his glass, wiped his mouth. "Jesus Christ. I'm glad there are two of you then."

I opened my mouth to answer—I had no idea what I was about to say, but it would have almost certainly aggravated the already unhealthy dynamic between us—when we heard the front door open and a pair of male voices echo down the hallway.

"That'll be Bittner," Ron said, something different penetrating his belligerent expression.

Liz offered me a drink while we listened to them tromp down the hallway, but I demurred. Frankly, I was afraid I'd be unable to keep anything down. She nodded, chewing her bottom lip. I wanted to say something soothing to her, but my eyes caught sight of the laceration along her hairline, her bruised jaw. A chill whispered through me.

I moved deeper into the room to accommodate Father Sutherland. He looked every bit as composed as I'd expected him to be, the priest wearing his sable cassock and purple stole as naturally as another layer of skin.

What I didn't expect was Jack Bittner.

Danny had implied that Bittner had a nasty temper, but what he didn't mention was Bittner's sheer size. His unnervingly imposing presence. I guess I'd never really registered how enormous the man was because every time I'd seen him in the sanctuary, he'd been sitting down, and by the time I made my way to the lobby, he was already gone. But now I saw him all too well. Bittner easily dwarfed me and Ron Hartman and would have dwarfed Danny too had Danny been in the room. His shoulders as broad as a bookcase and his arms as thick as church pews, Bittner looked like an aging ex-professional football player, the kind who'd gambled his money away on women and alcohol. Bittner's unshaven cheeks were speckled with salt-and-pepper stubble. He neither wore nor carried a hat, and though his black crew-cut hair was as wet as mine, he did not appear to notice. His ruddy cheeks were pockmarked, his nose a bit mashed and crooked, like it'd been shattered in some violent brawl. His vast jaw reminded me of some long-ago sea captain, his burly chest of some battle-scarred gladiator. On his saturnine face was what I first mistook for dour courtesy, but what I soon realized was an unwholesome species of eagerness.

Neither Liz nor Ron looked at Bittner, instead focused on Father Sutherland, on whom whatever hopes they retained were clearly riding.

Sutherland nodded at me, then turned to Ron. "Is Officer Hartman here?"

Something momentarily curdled Ron's features— Derision? Contempt for his little brother? —then he nodded. "In the basement. Have you ever performed an exorcism?"

Bittner grumbled something I couldn't make out, but the only word discernible sounded like "bullshit".

While Father Sutherland was not a small man—he was about six feet tall and according to some at the rectory had been quite an athlete in his youth—he looked like a child next to Bittner. Yet Sutherland spoke with an authority that awed me. "The worst error we can make is to rush to judgment. This is a child we're talking about, and while it seems certain there is something abnormal about this situation, we must remember to respect the sanctity of his life."

Liz favored Sutherland with a grateful, teary-eyed smile, but Bittner only glowered as if the priest had just insulted him.

Sutherland addressed Liz with that same soothing tact. "I understand Officers Hartman and Bittner restrained young Casey."

In a small, thin voice, Liz said, "He's handcuffed to his bedposts."

Sutherland's bushy eyebrows rose. "Both hands?"

Liz nodded then raised her arms, demonstrating. She looked to me like she was signaling a touchdown. "Danny bound his legs too so he wouldn't hurt himself."

"I see," Sutherland said.

Danny Hartman reentered, his hat in his hands. He nodded at Sutherland and murmured to Liz with a small grin. "She's okay. She's watching *Tangled.*"

Liz touched Danny's arm. "Thank you."

He shrugged. "I didn't do anything. She just needed to blow off steam, so I let her talk a little bit."

"It's nice to be listened to," Liz said with a sour look in Ron's direction.

Ron didn't seem to notice.

Jack Bittner's booming voice broke in, "Are we waiting for something?"

Danny glanced at me. "I think we're ready. Do you two need anything else?"

I nodded deferentially at Sutherland, who glanced at Ron Hartman. "If you don't mind, I think we should have a word of prayer."

Ron shrugged like he couldn't care less what we did. Father Sutherland bowed his head. Closing my eyes, I heard Sutherland begin, "Dear Lord, we pray you help us take refuge in the truth, for it is the antithesis of evil and Satan's greatest bane. We pray you endow us with the resilience to face whatever awaits us with pure hearts and open minds. We pray you shield us with the truth, so that whatever afflicts young Casey be removed from his mind and body. We pray most of all that you guide us through the darkness, through the forest of lies and deceit that Satan uses to ensnare his victims. In your name, Amen."

Swallowing, I looked up and saw that the rest of the group looked unchanged:

Jack Bittner hostile.

Liz desperate and teetering on the edge of uncontrollable tears.

Ron embarrassed and dubious, the look of a man plainly inconvenienced by some vexing development beyond his control.

Danny as solemn and aggrieved by all of this as any caring family member would be.

Father Sutherland placid and benign.

Everyone was the same.

Except for me. I had changed during the prayer. Far from comforting me and imbuing me with steely resolve,

Sutherland's words had injected a black stream of dread into my being. I realized that this was not a dream, nor was it some performance to which I would be a disinterested observer. Far from spectating from a safe distance, I was to be involved, perhaps in some central and fundamental way.

Father Sutherland said, "Then let us help this young man." Moving toward me, he reached into a side pocket of his robe and came out with a second Bible.

I opened my mouth to tell him I'd brought my own, but he anticipated my protest. "This one," he said, patting the aged brown cover, "is a combination of the King James version and several others. You'll notice that parts of it are handwritten to coincide with the version I now hold."

I'm afraid I showed my apprehension. I did not like to think of any Bible as having been tampered with.

He favored me with his knowing smile. "I understand your misgivings, Jason, but let us not forget that the Bible itself is an amalgam of an incredibly diverse group of sources spanning many centuries."

Somewhat reassured, I accepted the book he proffered.

Sutherland turned to Liz. "Please show us the way, Mrs. Hartman."

Liz nodded and moved through the doorway.

Feeling like an unprepared understudy who'd just been thrust into a leading role and was now withering in the torrid heat of the stage lights, I followed the others out of the kitchen, up the stairs, down the second-story hallway, and toward whatever awaited us in Casey Hartman's room.

CHAPTER THREE

We entered the bedroom in silence.

When Liz and Ron and the two officers moved aside to allow us passage, I got my first look at Casey Hartman.

My first impression was that he looked like a sleeping child.

Father Sutherland and I stepped closer, and then, with a slight bow, Sutherland extended an arm, making it clear I was to take a position at the boy's bedside.

"What do you notice?" Sutherland asked me.

I studied the boy. He had his mother's delicate features but his father's shaggy, black hair. There were no blankets or sheets covering him. I wondered fleetingly if they'd been torn or even bloodied in the tussle. I studied Casey's body. The bare feet. The long, spidery legs. The red boxer briefs and white T-shirt. The arms were long and willowy. I took a step closer and noticed blood on the boy's knuckles. I realized I was having trouble breathing, a fetid warmth having pervaded the bedroom.

I looked at Liz. "Is this room normally so hot?"

She shook her head.

"It was like this earlier," Danny said. "I don't know if it has something to do with what's happening or not."

I didn't either. In all my studies, the temperature changes that accompanied demonic possession resulted in frigid temperatures, not tropical ones. I realized I'd begun to sweat.

"Father Crowder?" Sutherland said beside me.

I cleared my throat. "His knuckles are bruised, abraded. That seems to dovetail with the account we've been given by Officers Hartman and Bittner, though I expected the injuries to be more severe."

Bittner mumbled something, but I went on. "Casey appears to be sleeping, though his expression is troubled. His respiration seems labored too." I frowned. "One of his eyes is puffy. And his bottom lip is busted open."

I glanced at Bittner, who rolled his eyes in irritation. "You weren't here, Crowder. It was all I could do to stop the kid from killing us."

Sutherland took out a handkerchief and mopped his forehead. "Do you mind if I have a look at the child, Father Crowder?"

I receded from my place at the child's bedside, secretly relieved to have some distance between us. Because the sight of the unmoving child on the bed so disturbed me, I took a moment to study the young man's bedroom. Tan walls, ivory trim. Two large windows with light-blocking curtains. A red baseball-bat bag leaned in the corner; three aluminum handles jutted out. There were posters of sports cars flanking the bed. A cloth reproduction of the Beatles' *Abbey Road* album cover over the ivory headboard. I decided the boy had good taste in music.

There was what appeared to be an autographed picture of LeBron James hanging on the wall between Casey's bedroom windows. Ron noticed me studying it and grunted. "Season tickets to the Bulls, and the kid roots for LeBron. You believe that?"

Father Sutherland moved closer and placed his thumb and forefinger on either side of the boy's wrist. "His pulse is slow but regular. Whatever caused him to behave the way he did earlier seems dormant now."

I thought this a terribly obvious statement but kept the opinion to myself.

"Aren't you going to do any tests?" Ron asked.

Without looking up, Sutherland said, "Of course we are. But I wonder if you and your wife should remain in the room...should things go unexpectedly."

Ron folded his arms. "I'm not going anywhere." He nodded at Bittner. "Not with this gorilla in here. You ask me, he was twice as rough as he needed to be with Casey."

Before Bittner could contradict this, Danny said, "It's okay, Ronnie. I'll make sure Casey's looked after."

Ron gave his little brother a dead look. "Forgive me for not being reassured. You don't exactly have the best track record."

Danny looked stung.

Ron eyed his brother without pity. "You know, I'd have expected more from you, Danny. After we open our house to you, let you stay with us."

"Stop it, Ron," Liz said.

"Am I lying?" Ron demanded. "Guy says he needs some time to dry out—"

"You don't need to bring that up in front of—"

"Why not, Lizzie?" Ron asked, nodding at Danny, who appeared to be studying the floor. "He brings Bittner here, makes the whole situation escalate... I think everybody's got a right to hear why Danny's judgment might be a little clouded."

"I haven't had a drink in a month," Danny said.

"You don't have to explain yourself," Liz said. She glowered at her husband. "Can we focus on Casey?"

Ron grunted but didn't say anything more.

Liz turned to me, her eyes pleading. "Should we stay, Father Crowder?"

With Liz so close to me, my mouth went dry. Mustering as much composure as I could, I said, "Perhaps you should join your daughter, Mrs. Hartman. She needs you now as much as Casey does."

Liz didn't look totally convinced, but after a couple seconds she nodded and moved slowly out of the room.

Bittner waited for Liz to go, then closed the door and said, "Good. Now we can drop the bullshit and find out what all this kid knows."

Sutherland looked disapproving, but it was to Danny he addressed his question. "What's he talking about?"

Danny colored, looking like he'd rather be anywhere but where he was. "I was hoping he'd tell you on the way over, Father Sutherland. Jack here has this wild theory about Casey being the Sweet Sixteen Killer."

A thunderstruck silence seized the room. The only sound at all was the raspy susurrus of the boy's breathing.

Ron was the first to speak. "What the hell did you just say?"

Bittner's lip curled in a snarl. "You heard him."

Ron wheeled on Bittner. "Get the fuck out of my house."

"You called us here," Bittner said. "You invited us in. The only reason this little bastard's not in jail is because he's Danny's nephew."

Ron stared up at Bittner in disbelief. "What did you just call my son?"

Danny moved toward them. "Why don't we all calm down until Father Sutherland takes a look at—"

"Why the hell didn't you say something?" Ron barked at his little brother. "How can you let him into this house knowing what he thinks about my boy? He's your goddamned *nephew*. Don't you care about Casey at all?"

"Of course I do," Danny said in a hoarse voice.

"Then tell this stupid ape to—"

But before Ron could finish, Jack Bittner had him by the throat. Danny looked as shocked as I was, but he grasped Bittner's arm in an attempt to intercede. Faster than I would have thought possible, Bittner shoved Danny aside and slammed Ron one-armed against the wall. The picture of LeBron shattered on the floor.

"Officer Bittner!" Sutherland called, moving toward the pair.

I could see the striations of Bittner's forearm as he squeezed Ron's throat. Both Ron's hands were grappling with Bittner's flexing wrist, but he was having no luck at all breaking Bittner's iron grip or apparently drawing a breath. Ron squirmed, his face a livid red, his eyes huge with fright.

"You wanna see how strong this ape is?" Bittner growled into Ron's flabbergasted face. "I'll show you strong. If you'd been a better father, monitored your freak of a son a little bit, there might be six other sets of parents whose daughters were still alive."

As surprised as I'd been by Bittner's flare of violence, I was even more taken aback by the way his voice cracked when he spoke of the dead girls. Danny and Sutherland had reached the struggling pair, Danny shouting something to Jack about letting Ron go. My trance breaking, I joined them, and after a momentary struggle, Jack did let Ron go. The wheezing stockbroker tumbled to the floor, the ass of his gray sweatpants landing on the broken glass. Ron emitted a high-pitched yelp and pawed at his rear end. I thought to myself that Ron might have some difficulty explaining the stitches he'd likely have to receive in the morning, but then Bittner began raving, and the thought was swept away.

"I'm arresting this little shit," Bittner declared. "I should've done it earlier."

"Casey's not going anywhere," Danny said. "Let's just see what these guys can do before we go throwing fourteen-year-old kids in jail."

"I heard him, Danny. He was using the girls' names, talkin' like they deserved it. He knew stuff no kid his age should know."

"But he only started acting like this tonight," Danny persisted. "The murders have been going on for months."

"Then you tell me, Danny. You're so clever, you tell me how he knows so much."

Sutherland was on his knees helping Ron recover. I stayed where I was, watching with some awe how composedly Danny spoke to his enraged partner. "It's been everywhere, Jack. On the Internet, the TV…they even discussed it the other day in his Current Events class."

Bittner scowled. "And how the hell you know a thing like that?"

Danny shrugged. "Kid's gotta have someone to talk to beside his mother."

"What's that supposed to mean?" Ron asked.

"You know what it means."

Bittner nodded and favored Danny with an unpleasant grin. "See, that's the problem. You care about the kid too much to see the obvious. I've never met a person yet that believes someone he loves could be capable of killing."

"Casey is not a killer."

"Then how does he know so much?"

Ron glared at Bittner incredulously. "He's fourteen, for Chrissake!"

"Like that means anything," Bittner said. "I've seen younger ones than that kill people for the fun of it."

A scowl on his face, Sutherland asked Bittner, "The burden of proof is on you. On what do you base your theory?"

"Joy Smith."

Sutherland's scowl deepened. "What about her?"

"They go to the same school." Bittner nodded at the boy on the bed. "Little Casey here had a crush on her. He told Danny about it. Even wrote her love notes."

We looked at Danny, who sighed miserably. "Casey was saying all sorts of things earlier on, talking about Joy in particular. I could see what Jack was thinking right away, so I told him what I knew—that Casey and Joy were classmates—you know, thinking that would explain things for Jack." He regarded Bittner balefully. "Obviously, I made a mistake."

"Goddamn right you did," Bittner agreed. "This little son of a bitch had a thing for Joy and finally took it out on her the only way he could. Then he got a taste for violence. Started killing other girls for the pleasure of it."

"That's your proof?" Ron said. "That Casey had a crush on one of the victims?"

Bittner took a step toward Ron, who looked instantly alarmed. "That's not all Casey said. You woulda heard the rest, but you were nursing that bump on the head he gave you."

Ron muttered something and moved away, but Bittner was not to be put off. He tailed Ron, a vicious edge to his words. "That's right, *Ronnie*. The kid manhandled you like you were a toy. He beat the shit out of his mom, even smacked his kid sister around. Why don't you tell us more about what an angel he is?"

"Officer Bittner," I said, surprised by the authoritative sound of my voice, "what is it that Casey said that makes you so certain he's the killer?"

"I said," came a deep, ghastly voice from behind us, *"that the sound of Joy's pussy ripping open made me come in my pants."*

We all turned and stared.

"Oh Jesus," Ron said in a hollow voice.

Casey Hartman was gazing up at us, a look of unmitigated evil contorting his face.

PART TWO
BREAKING POINT

CHAPTER FOUR

Father Sutherland would not confirm it for another hour or so, but at that moment, when I beheld the depthless evil carved in that formerly innocent countenance, I knew beyond a doubt that Casey Hartman was possessed.

His eyebrows were hideously arched, the forehead above them deeply wrinkled. The eyes had gone a blazing scarlet hue, the skin a pallid white. But it was the leer stretching his lips that did it, the soulless, mocking grin that erased all semblance of humanity from that horrid face.

In a voice nothing like a child's, the thing on the bed said, *"Mary Ellen Alspaugh howled like a mongrel when I took a hacksaw to her tits."*

"You fucking monster," Bittner said and made straight for Casey.

"Stop it," Danny hissed, somehow managing to lunge between Bittner and Casey before Bittner could tear the boy's limbs off.

Though I knew I would do little good against the behemoth struggling to attack the boy, I joined Danny in holding him back. We succeeded for only a few seconds. First, Bittner cast me aside as though I were a yipping puppy. I hit the floor and heard a peculiar squelching sound. A downward glance showed me I'd landed where Casey Hartman had savaged his fists on the wood floor earlier that evening; there was a sticky patina of blood all around where I lay. Scrambling to my feet and slipping several times, I caught a peripheral glance of Danny and Bittner, who were still grappling. But Bittner was too big, too inexorable. He pivoted and heaved Danny toward Ron, who I noted with disdain hadn't lifted a finger to protect his son from the berserk cop. Bittner stalked toward Casey's bedside and encountered the boy's last line of defense:

Father Sutherland.

Far from seeming intimidated by the approaching hulk, Sutherland merely remained where he'd been, perhaps daring Bittner to physically assault a member of the clergy. For a moment it seemed Bittner would do just that. He advanced to within a foot of Sutherland, his broad jaw looming toward the older man like the prow of some haunted barge.

But Sutherland's gambit seemed to work. Bittner neither laid hands on the priest nor made a grab for Casey.

"Get out of my way, Father," Bittner said in a dangerously low voice.

"You brought me here tonight, Officer Bittner. I've sworn to uphold certain beliefs, just as you and Officer Hartman have. I need to examine this child, and I cannot have you threatening him while I do so."

Bittner didn't move, but his eyes flicked irresolutely from Sutherland to the boy.

Sutherland continued, "He is restrained. He poses no danger to you nor anyone else. Whether or not he has anything to do with the murders you so commendably want to solve is an issue we'll address later tonight. For now, Officer Bittner, I implore you—let us do our jobs."

At this last he nodded at me, and I made sure to reflect in my bearing and expression the same aura of dignity that Sutherland projected. I fought an urge to wipe my hands on my robe. The blood on my fingers felt slimy.

Evidently satisfied by my look, Sutherland said, "You shall respond to my reading, Father Crowder. Are you ready?"

"Wait," Ron said. "You're not going ahead with it, are you?"

Looking impatient but demonstrating what I considered admirable restraint, Sutherland said, "How Casey responds to the reading will be one of the indicators of his true condition. Now, *please*, Mr. Hartman."

"You wanna hear how Ashley Panagopoulos's head sounded while I bashed it on the floor of her bedroom?" the croaking voice from the bed asked.

"Motherfucker," Bittner said, his lips drawn back.

The Casey-thing leered at Bittner. "Or would you rather know what your daughter's squeals will sound like when I sodomize her with a carving knife?"

Bittner pounced.

I couldn't believe how easily he bulled through us, swatting us aside like rotten saplings in his eagerness to get his hands on Casey.

"I could just take you in," he said, grasping the boy by the T-shirt, "but I'm not gonna let you off that easy."

Danny grabbed at Bittner, but with a single jab Bittner sent Danny reeling toward the wall.

"I'll rape your daughter, Bittner," the Casey-thing said. "I'll make her beg for mercy before I disembowel her."

"You'll be dead first, you bastard."

The monstrous face on the bed changed, a new idea occurring to the presence inhabiting Casey. "Maybe I'll make you watch while I do her!"

Sutherland tried to intervene, but Bittner thrust him roughly aside. Bittner cocked a fist.

The awful grin on Casey's face split wider. *"Give it to me, Jack. Give it to me hard."*

Bittner complied.

The boy's head whipped sideways with the blow, a splat of blood stippling the ivory headboard.

"Don't touch him!" Sutherland shouted.

But this time Bittner's rage brooked no interruption. He grabbed Casey by the shirtfront and began shaking him, the boy's head thrashing up and down in crisp, brutal arcs.

"Leave him alone, Jack!" Danny shouted, but the moment Danny reached for Bittner, the big man whirled, seized Danny by the shoulders and head-butted him. The sound made me ill, like a blunt ax chunking into an oak tree. Danny staggered back, a crimson starburst of blood glistening between his eyebrows.

Sutherland made for Bittner again, and while the older priest did not succeed in wrestling the giant cop away from Casey, he was able to deter him long enough to allow Ron and me to join the fray.

Grabbing hold of one of Bittner's railroad-tie-sized arms, I marveled at Sutherland's ability to keep the man at bay so long. Likely attracted by the cacophony, Liz had joined us too. She was gamely hauling back on the collar of Bittner's coat. Danny lay in a heap near the wall, apparently knocked insensate from Bittner's attack.

The four of us had just begun to achieve a measure of progress in our attempts to move Bittner away from the boy when Casey spoke up again in a new voice, one that chilled me with its wheedling cruelty.

"Oh *my*, Jack," the voice said in a tone so derisive and full of revelation that we all turned and looked at the boy, "I never would've guessed it of you. You love your daughter all right, but you *lust* after her friends."

Bittner's eyes flared. "You son of a bitch."

"You dream of bending them over, of punishing them, of—"

I lost the next part in the melee that ensued, which was just as well. The things Casey was saying were some of the vilest I'd ever heard. And coming from a priest who has taken thousands of confessions, that's saying a great deal.

Bittner slugged Sutherland in the gut. Sutherland went down, and without him there to aid us, I knew our resistance wouldn't last long.

Ron shouted something about brutality, but whatever it was only served to incite Bittner further. He grabbed Ron by the face and bounced the back of his head off the wall. Ron slumped to the floor, looking like he wouldn't get up anytime soon.

With Liz and me still clinging to the huge cop like barnacles, Bittner waded toward Casey.

"Tell them!" Casey crooned, the sour odor of his breath making my eyes water. Casey laughed, the smell of rotten eggs and dead insects wafting over us. "Tell them how you dream of deflowering your daughter's friends! How you imagine them spreading their legs for you and writhing in pain while you rut away your frustrations!"

"Shut your sick mouth," Bittner growled and backhanded Casey in the face. Blood squirted from the boy's nose, drenching his already blood-spattered T-shirt so that it now looked as if Casey were wearing a red bib.

Liz and I struggled with Bittner, but our attempts had little effect. I'm ashamed to say I was the next one to be discarded. The mad cop half spun and cracked my underjaw with a cudgel fist. My jaw aflame, I collapsed and watched in dismay as he tossed Liz toward where her husband lay against the wall.

"Oh, Jack," Casey moaned in a voice eerily like a young woman's.

"Stop it," Bittner muttered. Another backhand to the boy's face, this one sounding like a mallet striking a deer carcass.

But Casey went on. *"Oh, Jack, oh, Jack. Please give me your big cock!"*

"Goddammit," Bittner muttered. He walloped Casey in the face again, this time with a closed fist.

I attempted to intercede, but Bittner anticipated me, aiming a vicious, blunt elbow that caught me flush in the cheek. The pain was exquisite. I sagged to the floor.

I looked up in time to see Bittner fumbling for his gun. I doubt he would have been so clumsy under normal circumstances, but his rage was too great to allow sure-handedness. He'd just freed his firearm from his hip holster, with the apparent intention of shooting the child, when a voice behind us bellowed, *"Don't you dare!"*

I glanced up and beheld Danny Hartman holding a gun on his partner. Danny's feet were planted wide, his arms extended. The barrel of the pistol was six feet from the back of Bittner's head.

Bittner didn't turn, but he seemed to realize what was happening. He didn't make a move on Danny, but he didn't holster his weapon either. His back to Danny, he said, "You really want to do this, partner?"

Danny's face was slick with blood, and he looked distraught. But there was resolve there too. "I don't want any of this. But I'm not gonna let you kill this boy."

Bittner turned, on his pitted face a look of ruthless irony. "This *boy*? You mean this killer of children? This rapist? This monster who speaks filth about my daughter and her friends? Who for all we know has been casing them to pick out his next victim?"

"Put the gun down, Jack."

"Why should I?"

Danny licked his lips. "Because we don't know he's done anything wrong."

"He attacked his family. He beat up his little sister. He knows everything about the murders. How the hell can you say he hasn't done anything wrong?"

Bittner's gun was rising.

Danny's voice was taut. "Last warning, Jack."

I don't know what would've happened had Bittner raised his gun high enough to shoot Danny Hartman. Maybe Danny would've shot him. Maybe Bittner would have slaughtered us all. At that moment he looked crazy enough to do it.

Good thing Sutherland hit him first.

All I saw was a flash of silver over Bittner's head. Then he dropped soundlessly to the floor as though struck dead by divine judgment.

Father Sutherland lowered the aluminum bat, looking like the holiest man to ever win the Triple Crown.

"Thanks, Father," Danny said. "I sure didn't want to shoot him."

"That's because you're a good soul, Danny. Now let's put Officer Bittner in some place safe."

"How about jail?" Ron suggested. He was on his feet, but he looked groggy. Liz, too, was rising.

Danny brought up a trembling hand, massaged his forehead. "That won't work."

Ron turned to his little brother with an expression of slow-dawning amazement. "Wait a minute. You're telling me I'm supposed to keep him in the *house*? After what he did? After he beat up my Casey? Threatened to *kill* him?"

Danny's voice was level. "You turn Jack in to the precinct—that is what you're proposing right? —you do that and how long do you think it'll be before he tells them everything that's gone on here tonight? How long do you realistically expect them to wait before they take Casey in too?" Danny glanced at the thing on the bed, which watched them with a sardonic gleam in its eyes. "You really want my bosses to see your son in this state? You think they're gonna know what to make of it? Or be sympathetic to a kid who talks about the killings the way he's been doing, not to mention beating up on his own family?"

Father Sutherland moved around and got his arms under Bittner's back. With an effortless heave, he had Bittner hooked under the armpits. Nodding, he said, "Get his legs, Danny. Jason, you get the door."

As Bittner's motionless body was muscled across the room, Ron threw up his arms in exasperation. "Isn't Danny gonna stay here and guard my son? Casey's already shown how dangerous he can be."

I said, "Your son needs help, not an armed guard," and Liz favored me with such an appreciative glance that my belly somersaulted. Then I was opening the door for Father Sutherland and Danny.

But Ron was not to be put off. Stalking after our slow-moving group, he said, "Where are you taking him?"

"The cruiser," Danny said. "I'll make him comfortable in the back and lock him in."

Ron groaned. "Hey, I don't know if you've noticed, but this isn't exactly Humboldt Park around here. What'll happen when this gorilla wakes up and starts wailing? You think my neighbors are gonna go for that?"

"How large is your lot?" Sutherland asked. As he and Danny lugged Bittner down the hallway, I could finally start to hear the strain in his voice.

"What's that got to do with it?" Ron demanded.

"Two acres," Liz said.

Struggling to support Bittner's considerable bulk, Sutherland said, "With all the trees and the distance...not to mention the storm raging outside...there'll be very little chance anyone will hear Bittner's cries. He'll be inside the car, remember."

"Can't you gag him?" Ron asked.

Danny shook his head. "Don't like to do that if I can help it. Some guys are mouth breathers. Or maybe just congested. Put a gag in the wrong person's mouth, he could asphyxiate."

"Wouldn't be much of a loss," Ron muttered.

I watched Liz shut the door to Casey's room and stand there a moment, clearly overcome with anguish and sorrow. I waited for her, and as she approached, I murmured what comforting words I could. Without acknowledging me, Liz went down the stairs after the others.

I descended a few moments later, but only after I gazed at that six-paneled door for a long moment. I didn't want to go back in there.

But I knew we had to.

CHAPTER FIVE

"What do you mean you don't have enough proof?"

Despite the aggressive way that Ron had approached him, Father Sutherland did not seem abashed. Standing beside the grandfather clock in the foyer—he and Danny and I had finally managed to arrange Jack Bittner's hulking form in the back of Danny's cruiser—Sutherland stood with his hands folded politely before him, looking for all the world as though he were about to deliver a sermon on the perils of greed.

Sutherland said, "There are many requirements that must be fulfilled before we perform an exorcism, or even pronounce the child possessed."

"Requirements," Ron repeated. "You're telling me you can't see it already?"

"I will not rush to judgment. The only evidence I have is the child speaking in an unnaturally guttural voice—speaking in English, I might add—and a secondhand account of anomalous strength."

"What do you need? The kid's head to swivel on his neck and spit pea soup all over you?"

"That's not funny," Liz said.

"Shut up," he muttered without taking his eyes off Sutherland. "Whatever that thing is, it's endangering my son. What if it kills him? What if Casey doesn't recover?"

The words were out of my mouth before I knew it. "Are you sure it's Casey you're worried about?"

Ron rounded on me, and for a flickering instant I was convinced he'd punch me. "You got a mouth on you, you know it? You gonna do anything other than contradict me tonight?"

"Maybe you should get a grip," Danny said.

"Screw all of you," Ron growled, his voice echoing off the soaring foyer ceiling. "I should've taken care of this myself."

"Allowing Danny to contact us was the one correct thing you did," I said.

"Listen, I know I may not be anything as impressive as a priest or a cop—" he threw his brother a stony look, "—and I know you guys probably resent me for my venial lifestyle—"

"Asshole," Danny muttered.

"—but I think you're all overlooking the obvious here."

"And what is that?" I asked.

"That Jack Bittner might have a good motive for claiming my son's the butcher who's been hacking up all those girls."

Liz's pretty face twisted with distaste, but Sutherland asked, "What motive?"

Ron spread his arms in amazement. "Bittner's the killer."

We were all silent a moment as that sank in.

"Wait a second," Danny started.

But Ron overrode him. "Think about it. The guy's a beast. You all saw him up there. It took every one of us to bring him down—"

"Father Sutherland brought him down," I reminded him.

Ron shot me a surly look. "The point is, the guy's got the brute strength and then some. Secondly, he's a cop. Who'd know better than a cop how to murder someone and get away with it? Hell, he might even be working it from the inside, planting false leads, putting them off his trail..."

"You're forgetting something," Danny said.

"Enlighten me."

"I'm his partner."

Ron shrugged. "So? You had trouble passing shop class, Danny, so forgive me if I don't place much faith in your deductive abilities."

Liz was twisting her crucifix necklace, her thumb and forefinger on the silver body of Christ. "He did seem quick to blame Casey."

"That doesn't make him a serial killer," Danny pointed out.

"Doesn't make him innocent either," Ron said.

Danny used a wet paper towel to dab at the cut between his eyebrows. "I know Jack was crazy up there, but you guys don't know him like I do. He's not a bad guy."

Ron uttered a harsh laugh. "'Not a bad guy'. God, you're gullible."

"We can't all be pricks."

But Ron was shaking his head. "So goddamned sensitive...such a bleeding heart. Always have to be buddies with everybody, always trying to play nice."

"There's nothing wrong with that," I said.

Ron ignored me. "Hell, Danny, it's no wonder you never married. Got your heart broke once, and now it's like you don't even notice girls."

"It sounds like Bittner notices them too much," I said.

Everyone looked at me.

"What about that, Father?" Liz asked. "How could Casey know Bittner's thoughts?" She shivered. "Those awful things he fantasized about his daughter's friends."

"Let's be fair," Danny said, "Casey could have been making that up. It doesn't mean Bittner really thinks those things."

"Clairvoyance is not uncommon in cases of possession," Sutherland said quietly.

Liz shook her head. "But how—"

"You saw how Casey's face changed," Sutherland said. "The moment Officer Bittner touched his skin, he seemed to surmise what was in Bittner's mind."

"You believe it then?" Danny asked.

"I believe nothing yet," he said, "which is why we must go upstairs and perform the tests necessary to confirm or dismiss demonic possession."

My stomach plummeted.

"Finally, someone sees the light," Ron said. "I guarantee Bittner's place is full of evidence."

But Sutherland turned a pitiless eye on him. "Jack Bittner is not the Sweet Sixteen Killer."

Ron scowled. "How the hell can you know that?"

"Because the killer visited my confession booth three days ago."

It was as though someone had unleashed the gates of a spillway and doused us all in freezing water.

Looking thoroughly displeased with himself, Sutherland went on. "I am bound by my vows to maintain secrecy in these matters. However, as this case is proving extraordinary, I will say this much: Based on what the man in my booth told me, I suspect very strongly that he is the individual responsible for the atrocities. He shared with me many specifics that have not been in the papers...items he'd collected from his victims and hidden in his home."

"Why didn't you go to the authorities?" Danny asked.

Sutherland met Danny's accusation with neither defiance nor asperity. "I didn't know what to do," he said simply. "People look to me for guidance, for wisdom, but so many times I am as bewildered as they are. I don't know the correct course of action any more than any other man. All I can do is beseech God for His guidance, for His wisdom."

Ron's mouth twisted into a sneer. "And I suppose God told you to sit on the information while that madman impaled girls on meat hooks—"

"Don't," Liz said.

"—while he mutilated their faces and skinned them alive."

"That's enough, Ron!" Danny snapped.

Ron spun on him. "And you're just as bad as the Father here. You're charged with protecting this city, and all you do is drink yourself into oblivion—"

"Stop it," Liz said. She put a hand on Ron's arm, but he flung it off.

"—and when I call you for help—the one fucking time I make the mistake of relying on you—you let that idiot of a partner attack my son."

Danny's voice trembled. "Shut up, Ronnie."

But Ron laughed, his expression vicious. "Hell, I remember when Liz said we should make you Casey's godfather. I said to myself, 'Why not? Danny surely can't find a way to screw that up.' Boy, was I ever wrong."

Danny looked for a moment like he might lunge at Ron, but before he could, Ron stalked off toward the kitchen, mumbling obscenities.

Liz said, "Danny, don't listen—"

But before she could finish, Danny averted his eyes and said, "I'm gonna check on Carolyn."

Leaving the three of us in uncomfortable silence.

"We'd better go to Casey," Father Sutherland said.

We'd started toward the stairs when Liz asked, "How do you know it wasn't Jack Bittner? The man in the confessional?"

Sutherland regarded her a long moment. "The man spoke Greek with a very specific dialect called Tsakonian, one that only people in the Peloponnese region still use. Earlier, Danny told us that Officer Bittner was born and raised on the South Side of Chicago. He could hardly have acquired such an accent in that environment."

Liz was standing very still, a troubled look on her face. I was about to ask her what was wrong, but before I could, Father Sutherland grasped my shoulder. "We must go to Casey now, Father Crowder. In one way or another, he needs our help."

I nodded and started up the stairs, but I cast one backwards glance at Liz, who was staring up at me with a look of dread.

My skin crawling, I followed Father Sutherland to Casey's room.

◆ ◆ ◆

The next hour passed in a haze of nightmarish vignettes. Because I must record my story quickly, I will forego most of the details and will include only what is essential to my narrative. But imagine if you can...

Sutherland asks, "Can you tell us your name?"

"Malephar," the boy says.

Sutherland tenses. "Where did you hear that word?"

No answer.

"Casey," Sutherland says, "do you want me to believe you're possessed by a demon?"

The boy leers, his light-brown irises darkening, going muddy. Then...spreading. Tiny threadlike tendrils of murk squirm over the whites like fast-growing roots. Soon Casey's eyes are pure obsidian.

"How did you do that, Casey?" Sutherland asks.

"Touch me," the creature says in a hushed voice.

Sutherland does not.

♦ ♦ ♦

Twenty minutes of questions, holy water, rites, and crosses. The boy alternates between lewd ridicule and enigmatic whispering. At Father Sutherland's request, the boy speaks in Latin. In ancient Hebrew. In Aramaic. In tongues I've never heard before. Even Sutherland looks baffled.

The boy falls silent and unresponsive.

♦ ♦ ♦

Sutherland says to me, "Put your hand on Casey's forehead."

I look uncertainly from the boy to Sutherland and back to the boy. Casey, whose black eyes are now closed, that hideous leer no longer contorting his face, appears to be sleeping. I place a tentative hand on the boy's forehead, and the black eyes shutter open; a monstrous, chortling laugh gusts out of a mouth that reeks of pestilence, of sulfur, a mouth now lined with daggerlike fangs rather than his mother's perfectly straight teeth.

The thing that no longer resembles Casey stares up at me with a look of measureless knowledge. The thing that isn't Casey says, "You'll never master your fears, Jason."

I resist the urge to bolt from the room, am held in check not only by my desire to impress Sutherland, but by my terror of the thing on the bed.

"So much discipline," the thing says, its voice an ode to suffering, to malice. "So much self-control, yet so much fear. Was it your mother that twisted you so, Jason? Was it the way she walked around the house naked that so transformed the female body into an unknowable goddess? Something to be worshipped and feared?"

"Don't listen, Father Crowder," Sutherland cautions.

But I listen. Oh, do I ever. I listen with a mixture of horror and self-loathing.

The thing on the bed goes on, "Something to flagellate yourself to in the small hours of the night. Something to fantasize about while you squirt your pitiful seed onto your pristine white sheets, sheets that grow yellow and crusty and stained with fear sweat. Your foreskin so chafed and red you can see pinpricks of blood as you stare at your emaciated body in the mirror, hating yourself and craving punishment for your fantasies."

"Jason!" Sutherland shouts. But I am doubled over beside the bed, weeping.

Delighted, the thing crows, "You've already imagined it haven't you? Already fantasized about Liz Hartman, a vulnerable woman who needs your help. What will she say when she learns of your pathetic carnal imaginings? Fantasies in which you cease to behave like a castrate and seize her from behind, knead her mounded breasts and thrust your miniscule phallus into her sex as she moans out her want. As if you had the audacity to commit adultery…as if you were man enough to seduce a woman so libidinous."

"She's your mother," I sob.

"She's *Casey's* mother," the thing says, its voice suddenly deepening.

"And where is Casey?" Sutherland demands.

"Burning," the thing says and begins to laugh.

◆ ◆ ◆

Forty-five minutes in, the room smells of feral dogs and feces, of spoiled yeast and brimstone.

The thing on the bed is levitating.

The hips are three feet off the mattress. The body is splayed, arched like a dome, the chained limbs straining against their bonds. Even the fingertips are several inches above the mattress.

◆ ◆ ◆

The thing on the bed thrusts its wrists against the handcuffs again and again, the hands pumping heavenward in spasmodic mockery. It is leering at us, its mouth frozen open in a salacious intaglio. The sound the flesh makes soon becomes a gruesome squelch. Sutherland demands that the thing stop. The thing does not stop. Its staccato jabs persist, the sound becoming wetter. Squishier. I cover my mouth and look away. The thing gloats at my revulsion. Its guttural voice challenges me to look. Sutherland orders the thing to cease its mutilation of Casey's body, but the thrusts continue, crimson gouts of blood pelting the sheets. I retch at the sound of flensed bones, of pulping meat. I plead for it to stop. But through it all, the thing on the bed grins with rapturous sadism. A smell of sheared copper mingles with the rank odors of sulfur and diarrhea. Soon I can see one of the thing's wrist bones. I gag.

♦ ♦ ♦

Five minutes later Sutherland too is coughing into his handkerchief, yet he is still attempting to recite the passages marked in his Bible.

"Touch me," the thing commands.

The young body has lowered to the bed, but it is now writhing in a most disturbing way. Undulating like windswept water. The bones as malleable as a serpent's. Black ichor has begun to seep from the thing's mouth. Its rapier teeth grin savagely through the viscous liquid, which reeks like boiling sewage.

Sutherland proceeds with his incantation, but the thing shouts, *"Touch me, you craven old woman!"*

But Sutherland does not.

♦ ♦ ♦

After the endless hour had passed, I staggered out of the room and stood for a long time in the hallway. I felt nauseated. Moving with my hand over my mouth, I gained the nearest bathroom and leaned against the closed door.

When I'd successfully fended off the urge to vomit, I shambled to the sink and stood panting in front of the ornate, gilded vanity. Clutching the sides of the white basin, I took stock of myself in the mirror and decided I didn't look nearly as wretched as I felt. In my mind echoed the damning words the thing on the bed had uttered. Father Sutherland termed it *clairvoyance*, and I supposed that was right. But to me it felt like the worst sort of torture. Laying bare my soul and ridiculing my most private thoughts and deeds in front of a man whose opinion I valued over all others, a man who was like a father to me. How could I face Sutherland again? How could he ever look upon me without embarrassment after learning of the depravity lurking within me?

I splashed cold water on my face and decided I looked presentable, if a trifle unkempt. The welts on my face, coupled with the damp hair darkening my forehead, added five years to my appearance. I reached into my pocket, found a stick of spearmint gum and popped it into my mouth, wanting my breath to be inoffensive should I bump into Liz.

So my surprise was great when I opened the door and beheld her standing in the hallway.

I smiled weakly and said something about not feeling well.

She nodded, studying my face in a way that both excited me and made me nervous. "I passed Father Sutherland on the way up. He said he needed to discuss Casey, but that he wanted you to be there too."

I nodded, made toward the stairs.

"Don't go," she said, a hand on my chest.

Gazing down at her, I felt suddenly weightless.

"I know you're not used to this sort of thing," she said, "and I want you to know it's okay for you to be scared."

I decided clairvoyance might run in her family.

She moved closer to me, our faces perhaps eighteen inches apart in the dim hallway. "I want to thank you for coming tonight. You've been very brave, especially for someone so young."

I'm afraid my tone was churlish. "I'm not that young."

"Don't be angry," she said, smiling. "I think you're more mature than my husband in most ways. You have a much better personality."

"Mrs. Hartman..."

"Liz," she said. "You're more handsome too. Please don't think badly of me for saying that."

My mouth worked for a moment, my throat emitting a dusty click.

"I've never cheated on Ron," she said, and there was a fervent, imploring look in her green eyes. "He's stepped outside the marriage. Lots of times, I'm sure." She grunted bitterly. "He doesn't make much of an effort to conceal it anymore. Like it's his right as a man or something. The breadwinner enjoying his dalliances." Her eyes brimmed with tears.

"He's an idiot," I said.

She wiped her eyes, sniffed. "Thanks for saying that."

"It's true, Liz. He... he doesn't know what he has."

She looked at me wryly. "And what is that? A woman who married for money? Who deluded herself into thinking she really loved a man who wasn't all that nice to her even when they were dating?"

"You mustn't be so hard on yourself. There must have been other reasons—"

"He bought me things," she said flatly. "Took me to nice restaurants. I acted like it was a fairy-tale romance. But it was only him buying me off, date by date." She shook her head. "And I liked it. How's that for shallow?"

"At least you see him for what he is now."

Her face clouded.

I mistook her expression for offense. "I'm sorry for being so forward."

As though I hadn't spoken, she said, "Ron was born in Greece, near Mount Parnon. His parents met when his dad visited the region to explore the caves. He was an anthropology professor at Northwestern. He met Ron's mother there. They married and remained in Greece until Ron was nine. He spoke their language as fluently as English."

I could feel my pulse throbbing in my temples. "He still speaks it?"

"I asked him to say a few words when we were dating, and he did with little trouble then. Now..." She shrugged, a deep indentation between her brows.

"Do you know where he was during the killings?"

"I thought I did."

"I won't let him hurt you," I said.

She gazed deeply into my eyes then, and I felt my hands closing on the crooks of her elbows, drawing her toward me. The swells of her breasts pushed against my robe, the subtle, delirious smell of her deodorant drifting up to me.

I might have kissed her then. Would have kissed her had it not been for the flawlessness of her lips, which my eyes happened upon at that moment. They were a deep pink, sculpted and full. Her son had the same lips, had nearly all of her features.

Casey.

I let go of her arms, angry with myself for doing so, but even angrier for having forgotten about Casey. He was the reason I had come tonight. Not to commit adultery. Maybe Liz needed to be kissed at that moment, and I just happened to be the man into whose arms she'd landed. Maybe she viewed me as a protector, a sanctuary from the horror that had gripped her family.

I suppose it was precisely this notion that forbade me from doing what I so longed to do. I couldn't take advantage of her need now. Later, I told myself. If given the opportunity. She was the kind of woman you could give up the priesthood for, a woman so warm and good and lovely you doubted God would blame you much.

But for now... there was Casey.

"We better join the others," I said.

Liz nodded, but she looked disappointed. I watched after her as she walked away, the sight of her firm buttocks tantalizing me.

Coward, I told myself as I followed her down the stairs.

CHAPTER SIX

Danny reentered the kitchen where we were all gathered around the outer granite island. At Liz's questioning look, he said, "Carolyn's fine. You sure you don't want her to stay with a neighbor or something? Maybe a friend?"

Ron glared at him. "And explain the bruises on her face? Have them think I smacked her around or something? No thanks."

"It is not your well-being we should be worried about," Sutherland said.

Liz looked at Sutherland. "You think she should stay somewhere else?"

He appeared to consider. The worry lines on his forehead were more pronounced than they'd been earlier. Or perhaps it was just the lighting. "The area of the disturbance appears to be limited to Casey's physical reach."

Danny leaned forward. "You called it a disturbance, Father?"

Sutherland nodded grimly. "I did."

"Does that mean…you're sure he's possessed?"

"I am," Father Sutherland answered.

Liz exhaled a shuddering sigh, and I put a comforting hand on the small of her back. It was an involuntary movement, instinct really. But I saw the look on Ron's face and decided to let go of her. If Liz noticed, she didn't let on.

"What will you do?" Liz asked.

"With your permission," Father Sutherland said, "we will begin the rites of exorcism."

The words hung in the air between all of us, thick as a fog.

Danny said, "Don't you guys have to...you know, contact the Vatican or something? Or maybe the local diocese?"

Father Sutherland regarded Danny gravely. "Not in cases like these, Officer Hartman."

Ron arched an eyebrow. "What the hell does that mean?"

Sutherland hesitated, looking uncharacteristically reticent.

I said, "If the host's life is in peril, an experienced priest is given the discretion to take what measures he deems necessary."

"You think there's a demon in my son, Father Sutherland?" Liz asked in a hoarse voice.

Father Sutherland sighed and nodded.

"Jesus Christ," Ron muttered. "Just like the goddamn movies."

Sutherland's face tightened. "I would appreciate your avoiding the utterance of blasphemy until we're finished."

"Amen," Danny said.

"And this bears no resemblance to the movies," Sutherland continued. He paused. "Danny, would you please check on Casey? Make certain there is no change in his condition?"

"Sure thing," Danny said, and was off immediately.

Liz said, "Do we need to sign something, Father Sutherland?"

"In this day and age, I should probably have you fill out some sort of release form, a disclaimer perhaps. But I fear taking the time to draft a legal document would be to Casey's detriment."

Ron asked, "What do you mean, 'his detriment'?"

"I've been present at four exorcisms, Mr. Hartman, one of which I believed to be a case of an untreated personality disorder, another a scenario in which a child was play-acting as the result of an unquenchable yearning for attention and her parents' religious zealotry. In both of those cases, the exorcisms wrought disastrous results. The woman with the personality disorder—she was in her thirties and had for years gone untreated—sank into deeper mental and emotional turmoil and eventually died in an institution. Branding her disorder possession only exacerbated her condition. The child who faked demonic possession injured herself badly, soon became resentful of her parents' mania, and descended into drug abuse. She overdosed on heroin at the age of nineteen."

Liz's voice was scarcely more than a whisper. "But you think Casey's situation is different."

Father Sutherland nodded. "In the two other instances, the affected parties fulfilled all the conditions of demonic possession. In one case, I assisted the officiating priest. In the second case, I performed the rites myself. In both situations, the victim of the evil spirit made a complete recovery."

I felt a rush of relief at Sutherland's words, but Liz, perhaps cannier than I was, only regarded him with trepidation. "My son's case is worse, isn't it?"

"I'm afraid it is, Mrs. Hartman." Sutherland crossed his arms, his eyes downcast. "In the two authentic cases to which I've been witness, the spirits in question were formidable. The risks in these cases were severe, and though I entered into those ceremonies with a reasonable degree of confidence, I could not guarantee the hosts' safety."

We waited in edgy silence. It seemed the temperature in the kitchen had risen by ten degrees, as though the heat emanating from Casey's bedroom was flooding through the rest of the house.

Sutherland said, "Mr. and Mrs. Hartman, I have never encountered such a fearsome, malevolent presence as the one attacking your son. It uses languages not uttered for centuries, perhaps millennia. It displays unsettling mental abilities; its ability to penetrate the minds of others is nothing short of remarkable."

Ron, who stood on one side of the island by himself, paced back and forth and looked like he might soon be sick. "So maybe we should wait then, huh? Call your bishop or cardinal... pontiff, whatever the hell you call your bosses? Maybe they could assist you."

"We could wait," Sutherland allowed.

Liz moved closer to Sutherland. "But you don't think we should?"

"This is all surmise, Mrs. Hartman. There are no absolutes in cases like these. We can only act with good intentions and hope our decisions are the correct ones."

"But what could happen if we wait?"

Liz gazed into Sutherland's profound eyes, and from the way she began to tremble, it was clear that Sutherland didn't need to say it. I again went to comfort her, and this time I didn't pull away. If Ron didn't care enough about his wife to reassure her during this crisis, I'd compensate for his failure. Compensate with pleasure.

Ron's voice was as sarcastic as it was resigned. "Well, that's it then, right? If it's a matter of life and death, we do the exorcism."

Sutherland eyed him closely. "You give your consent?"

"Of course I do. I want my boy back."

"And you?" Sutherland asked Liz.

"Yes," she said, wiping the tears from her eyes.

"Then let us pray," Sutherland said, motioning us closer.

"What if we're not Catholic?" Ron said, joining hands with me and Sutherland.

I glanced at him. "Then say a prayer to your mutual funds."

Sutherland frowned at me, and I looked away, chastened. My tongue has always been too sharp for my vocation.

We had just bowed our heads when a loud, rapid thudding erupted from upstairs. We stared at each other with dread. Sutherland was the first to move. Liz and I trailed closely after him, with Ron bringing up the rear. We had just begun ascending the staircase when Danny appeared at the top. His face was alabaster, his handsome features contorted by fear.

"You guys better get in here fast," Danny said. "I've never seen anything—"

His words were lost in the ungodly roar that billowed down the hallway.

When we burst through the door, we were met with a sight that defied description, though I will do my best to capture the horror of the scene:

I mentioned earlier the manner in which Casey—or rather the thing inhabiting Casey's body—had repeatedly thrust against the handcuffs encumbering movement.

Evidently, the spasmodic thrusting and jerking had recommenced at some point since we'd vacated the bedroom—and had done so with renewed vigor.

For now, one of Casey's hands had torn free of its restraint, but it had done so at a terrible cost. What jutted from the end of Casey's left arm was a sickening branch of bones and glistening cartilage—a bloody horror. The thing had wrenched against the steel cuff so violently that a good bit of the hand had been peeled away. Flaps of filleted skin lay on the floor and the bed like slaughterhouse offal. Evidently, finding his hand liberated, Casey had proceeded to gnaw off the ends of his own fingers.

The exposed bones of the Casey-thing's fingertips shone a lusterless white. The Casey-thing was using these pointed tips as instruments of masochism, digging slow, meaty grooves in the flesh of his pale thighs, of his belly. What remained of its shirt hung in scarlet tatters, its boxer briefs stained a deep burgundy. It was jerking at its remaining three fetters with maniacal violence, with each tug a new seepage of blood splurting from its wrist and its ankles. If the violence didn't cease soon, I decided, Casey would expire from blood loss.

For the first time since the ordeal began, I realized how negligent we'd been with regard to Casey's physical well-being. In retrospect, I know now we should have called a doctor earlier that evening. But how were we to know how violent the spirit inhabiting Casey would become, how severe Casey's injuries would be?

Something flashed past me on the right. I had halted at the foot of Casey's bed, and I realized with alarm that Liz was wrapping her arms around her son, obviously thinking to restrain him by force. Unceremoniously, the Casey-thing rammed an elbow at her face and cracked her a glancing blow in the temple. Liz was hurled against the interior wall hard enough to crack the plaster with the base of her skull.

I felt the first kindling of rage within me. I strode around the bed, and without tarrying further, flung my arms around the Casey-thing's waist. The bony frame immediately began to buck and writhe against my grip; I was unsurprised to hear the Casey-thing shriek with mocking laughter. It called me a eunuch, a pedophile, several hateful epithets associated with homosexuality. But the sight of Liz's motionless body was newly burned into my consciousness, and I was resolved to subdue this vindictive creature at any cost. Beneath the cackling taunts of the Casey-thing, I heard Father Sutherland's raised voice reciting the Apostles' Creed.

I had succeeded in corralling the left side of Casey's body, but the right arm—though still cuffed to the bedpost—was near enough for the fingernails to gouge my cheeks and neck. The free arm, which I'd pinned between our writhing bodies, was like a bloody boa constrictor, wriggling against me in a ceaseless campaign to break free.

"Help me!" I shouted to Ron, who was gaping at Casey from several feet away, and though I'm loath to assign Ron Hartman credit for anything, he did respond to my entreaty. Clumsily but resolutely, he seized Casey and helped me drive the thrashing body against the mattress. As I clutched the boy, the febrile heat radiating from his flesh conjured fears of brain damage, of fatal fever. Surely Casey couldn't withstand much more of this trauma.

"Tie him!" I shouted to no one in particular, but in the next instant Danny was beside us, wrapping a green extension cord around Casey's savaged wrist and looping the rest of it around the mahogany bedpost. I realized that Casey was talking again, though in a voice as ancient and deep as a fairy-tale dragon's. Further, he was staring avidly at his father.

"...lying in your reports and keeping it all for yourself..."

"Someone shut him up," Ron said.

"...and used it to buy that condo for your mistress," the voice croaked.

"Shut your mouth!" Ron demanded, but there was something naked and raw in the man's voice I'd never heard before.

"Another child," the Casey-thing went on, staring up at Ron with those venomous black eyes. *"Another child, another woman, another house. A very expensive mistake, Ronald. Very expensive indeed."*

"Stop it, you little shit," Ron hissed.

I realized with alarm that Ron had his son by the throat.

"Mr. Hartman," Sutherland said.

"You stole from your clients. But even that wasn't enough," the voice went on. *"Your mistress wanted more, more, and what could you do? If your wife found out, she'd leave you, and then she'd take half of all you had, but your concubine kept wanting more, more—"*

Both of Ron's hands were on his son's throat, throttling the boy.

"Damn it, Ronnie!" a voice shouted, and in a flurry of limbs, Danny tore his big brother away from Casey.

Aside from the livid red fingermarks on the boy's throat, Casey looked undaunted by his father's assault. *"Wait'll she wakes up,"* the Casey-thing said, flinging a glance at Liz's prostrate form. *"Wait'll she hears about all the hookers you buy, all the drugs you do on your business trips. But it was the waitress of all people who got her tenterhooks into you, wasn't it? The cute, flirtatious waitress who waggled her ass at you."*

Ron yelled at the Casey-thing, gesticulated wildly for it to stop, but Danny would not relinquish his grip on his brother.

"You rutted with her in your bed, didn't you? Your wife was shopping with the kids, and you took a long lunch and impregnated that harlot in your marriage bed."

Ron was weeping now, his struggles weakening. I glanced at Liz, unconscious on the floor, and I must concede that the basest part of my nature wished she were awake for this revelation.

"You urged her to have an abortion...you pleaded. But she had the child anyway, and now you're chained to her forever. Eighty thousand dollars the first year. Now it's a hundred, plus the condo. How much more next year? How many diamond rings? How many— Well hello there!"

The Casey-thing had swiveled its foul countenance toward the open doorway, and when we discovered who stood gaping at us, I believe we all lost the ability to speak.

"Little Carolyn!" the Casey-thing said. *"Come hear how your daddy sired you a half sister! Come hear how he plays dress-up games with his waitress whore, how he loves for her to piss on his face, how he..."*

◆ ◆ ◆

I need not record the rest of the thing's abhorrent diatribe.

Ron shouted something at Carolyn, and looking shell-shocked, she exited the room. With my help, Danny was able to secure Casey's bonds. Together, we carried Liz from the room and made her as comfortable as possible in the master suite. She was breathing evenly, and though she had two new bumps on her head, Danny and I agreed that she would recover from her injuries with nothing worse than a concussion.

Yet we refrained from calling an ambulance. Because when we returned, Casey's wounds appeared to be mending. When I commented on this, Father Sutherland only shook his head in wonderment. But there was little doubt of this miraculous improvement. For though his wrists were still bloody, in no place was the bone denuded.

With Casey lashed more securely to his bed and Liz resting peacefully, Danny took Carolyn back to her room and endeavored to calm her and to palliate—if such a thing were possible—the effects of the monstrous freak show she'd just witnessed on her young psyche.

We were in the hallway when Ron said, "You know, maybe Bittner could help."

Danny stared at him in amazement. "He pulled a gun on Casey."

"At least he tried to do something," Ron said. "All you do is talk. And forgive me for saying so, Danny, but what you say rarely exhibits much intellect."

Danny ignored the dig. "You want your son in jail? That's what you're saying. Because that's where he's gonna be if we let Bittner out now. And that's best case."

Ron waved a dismissive hand.

"You saw him," Danny persisted. "He damn near shot Casey. I can't believe you'd let him within a hundred feet of your family."

Ron shook his head distractedly, and as he did, a horrible thought occurred to me. I was about to give voice to it when Danny said, "Maybe you should take some time to cool off, Ronnie."

With a muttered oath, Ron disappeared. Looking disgusted, Danny soon followed.

Perhaps it was just as well that no one witnessed what Father Sutherland and I soon saw.

CHAPTER SEVEN

It started with Casey's knees.

I once witnessed an injury in a pickup basketball game that is indelibly inscribed on my memory. The young man—the brother of an acquaintance, I've long since forgotten their names—had driven toward the basket on a fast break and was attempting to jump stop with the evident intention of faking out the defender giving chase from behind. The young man did evade the defender, who leapt into the air to block a shot that never came. But the ball handler's left knee, rather than planting solidly on the hardwood and allowing him to gather himself for an uncontested shot, hyperextended in the most unnatural manner, the sight of it almost as grotesque as the protracted popping sound his knee made in giving way.

That incident, as terrible as it had seemed at the time, was a mere sprain compared to the ghastly contortion occurring on the bed.

The alteration in Casey's legs coincided with the beginning of a familiar rite. Father Sutherland read, "Deliver us, Lord, from sin."

I answered, "Deliver us, O Lord."

Father Sutherland: "From your anger."

"Deliver us, O Lord."

"From unexpected death."

Casey's extremities, as I have stated, were securely bound to the four ivory bedposts by handcuffs and extension cords. Once his parents and uncle had departed the room,

Casey had seemed to relax to some degree, as if it had been the presence of his blood relatives that had agitated him. At this point, I tested each of Casey's bonds to make certain he would not attack us. Then I rejoined Sutherland's reading. "Deliver us, O Lord."

"From the snares of iniquity," Sutherland read.

"Deliver us, O Lord."

"From fury, prejudice and enmity."

"Deliver us, O Lord."

At the continuance of our words, Casey grew very still. This wasn't the stillness I had witnessed upon first arriving that night, but was rather an alarmingly portentous posture, the alertness of his expression somehow gravid with anticipation. I realized at once it was not Casey who was now present in the room, but rather that diabolical *other* who reveled in torturing its host and frustrating our efforts to free the boy. The creature's mouth was slack in a parody of a grin, the look in its eyes far away, almost dreamy.

I had a nasty vision of a mentally challenged person nearing orgasm and shooed the notion away, though it seemed revoltingly apt. Drool was leaking from the corners of the creature's mouth, the teeth apart in that foolish, infuriating grin. And as paradoxical as it might sound, despite the creature's idiotic expression, the impression its features conveyed was as ancient and knowing as any I had yet beheld.

That was when Casey's knees began to crack.

My first worry was wholly irrational—perhaps conditioned by countless films about demonic possession and Satanism, I worried the walls themselves were groaning and preparing to give way. I cast a feverish glance at the ceiling, the floor, but found these surfaces as solid as before.

"From vulgarity and carnal thoughts," Sutherland read.

I stared openmouthed.

"From vulgarity and carnal *thoughts*," Sutherland repeated.

I remained dumbstruck, terrified by the groaning, cracking noises that filled the room.

"Father Crowder!" Sutherland yelled.

I jolted, realizing I'd ceased responding to his invocations. But I couldn't find my voice and didn't even bother locating my place in the Bible. I was too fixated on Casey's legs.

They moved at first as though someone had snagged the skin of his kneepits and was hauling steadily downward. Then the movements became convulsive, erratic, the knees somehow grinding deeper into the mattress and then causing the mattress to creak.

The rapture on the creature's face grew more obscene. I noticed with distant revulsion that its phallus was engorged, made tumid by the damage it was inflicting on its innocent host.

The knees continued their descent into the creaking mattress, and now became audible the discordant twangs of snapped mattress fibers, the force of the sinister gravity actually causing the mattress to split open.

The scrawny legs formed unnatural Vs now. The sounds of tearing cartilage and cracking bone were dreadful. Blood squirted from the distressed flesh. Jagged shards of bone punctured the skin. His patellas, drawn downward into a space unable to accommodate their platelike width, first domed the whitened flesh sheathing them, then exploded in purplish geysers, spewing bone fragments and gristle into the air.

I would like to claim I maintained some vestige of decorum despite the grisly scene playing out before me, but I have set out to record events faithfully, and must therefore admit to vomiting then. Thankfully, I was able to thrust open a window before I lost control. I saw, as I gave up my supper to the tempestuous April night, that below Casey's window there was a precipitous drop-off of three stories onto a stone patio that lay at basement level.

Suddenly fearful of tumbling out the open window and fairly confident my bout of vomiting had ended, I rammed shut the window and turned to find the awful contortion still in progress. Now, though the knees were so far buried in the mattress that I could no longer distinguish their gory ruins, a new, atavistic fear arose in me that the boy would simply be devoured by his own bed. For that was what appeared to be happening. The creature's bonds, I noticed with crawling dread, were serving now not to contain the creature, but were rather inflicting harm on Casey's body. Blood flow seemed to have ceased utterly to his hands and feet, which were now bleached of color.

Panting, my hands planted on my knees, I managed to say, "Hospital. We have to get him to a hospital."

"He'll be dead by then," Sutherland said. "His only hope is our intervention."

Don't you mean God's? I thought but did not say. I could scarcely say anything, so great was my horror.

Sutherland seized me by the back of the shirt. With an effortless tug, he straightened my bent back and jerked me closer so that our noses almost touched. "It is an illusion meant to break our will."

I glanced at the ruins of Casey's knees, the spatters of blood and the molted flesh. These were no illusions.

As if reading my thoughts, Sutherland shook me, spoke directly into my face. "I have witnessed these marvels before, Jason. They seem real. Our senses accept the deceit completely. Until the trance is shattered and the truth is revealed."

My eyes again drifted to the macabre vision on the bed, but Sutherland dropped his Bible and grabbed me roughly by the chin. "Look at his wrists—you can't deny they are healing! Look at his fingertips. They are covered over with flesh. You are deceived by its wiles, Jason. Have you learned nothing in our years together?"

This finally broke through the veil of terror that had been suffocating me. I didn't totally believe his claims that the gruesome scene on the bed was chimerical, but I did have faith in Father Sutherland's wisdom. I nodded, licked my lips, and said, "Deliver us, O Lord."

Sutherland retrieved his Bible. "From lightning, thunder, and tempest."

"Deliver us, O Lord."

What was left of Casey's knees began to emerge from the bed.

"From famine, pestilence, and war."

"Deliver us, O Lord."

Before my eyes, the flesh seemed to knit, the rills of blood that sluiced from the wounds diminishing to narrow trickles.

"From everlasting death."

"Deliver us, O Lord."

Sutherland's voice swelled with greater authority, "By the mystery of your holy strength."

"Deliver us, O Lord."

"By your presence."

"Deliver us, O Lord," I said, and the tremor in my voice was no longer audible.

"By your birth and baptism."

Casey's legs were whole again, the only sign of damage the blood darkening the bed around his knees.

"Deliver us, O Lord."

And now even the look of lunatic sadism had vanished from Casey's face and had been replaced by a drowsy expression, one I was certain Liz would recognize. Casey looked like a child ready to drift off to sleep.

Together, Father Sutherland and I finished our rites, and by the end, Casey appeared to be dozing tranquilly. The older priest placed a hand on my arm and led me away from the bed.

"I'm sorry for losing faith, Father," I said.

He didn't acknowledge my words, instead kept his eyes trained on Casey's slumbering form. "I need to check the boy's heart rate," he said in an undertone. "I don't want to rouse the presence, but I must make certain Casey is out of danger before we leave the room."

"Maybe if we sedate him…"

He shook his head emphatically. "Precisely why I want to avoid doctors and paramedics, Father Crowder. The first thing they'll do is administer a sedative, and that might prove disastrous."

I thought of the boy's knees. It hadn't been a vision, I knew, but rather an incredible act of violence followed by some inexplicable regeneration. But it *had* happened, of that I was sure. "Father Sutherland," I said, "if you're worried about his heart—"

"Only one of them lived."

I stared at him, uncomprehending.

"I lied to the Hartmans, Jason. I'm not proud of it, but it was necessary to gain permission for the exorcism."

I frowned and opened my mouth to speak, but he went on briskly.

"The exorcism in which I was lead priest, that one was successful. The one on which I assisted was not. Like you, I was convinced medical attention was necessary. I had seen exorcisms end badly before and was wary of the entire process. My mind was very much in keeping with our modern system of beliefs—that religion is an enemy of science and should never inhibit scientific logic."

He looked at me with those profound blue eyes. "But these are not matters of science, Father Crowder. They are matters of faith. And when the lead priest—a good, rational man who felt the same as I did then and as you do now— failed to drive the demon out of the host swiftly and decided to take refuge in modern medicine, the results were catastrophic."

"What happened?"

"The host died," he said simply. "And the malevolent presence overcame the officiating priest." Sutherland's eyes filled with tears. "He was my mentor, my shepherd. He had handpicked me from the seminary and nurtured me for more than a decade. He wasn't a good man; he was a *great* man. A legend in the eyes of many and an individual whose gentleness and piety were renowned throughout the Catholic Church."

Sutherland's voice broke. "And he nearly strangled me." With a fierce tug, Sutherland tore away his collar and the top of his cassock, revealing to me a familiar wormlike scar that spanned the right side of his throat all the way to the collarbone. The scar had long been a mystery to those of us who knew Sutherland. "His thumb and index finger punctured my skin," he explained. "The fingers burrowed into me and ripped a bloody trough through my flesh. Had he attacked the other side, he would have severed my jugular. As it was, he still perforated the carotid artery, and the doctor who arrived to administer aid to the afflicted child was able to apply sufficient pressure to save me from bleeding to death."

To fill the terrible silence that followed, I asked, "Did your mentor die too?"

"Not immediately. It took several paramedics and two policemen to bring him down, but eventually he was cuffed and taken away. He died at the hospital that night."

I gazed uneasily at the sleeping figure on the bed.

"And that is why, when I was permitted to lead an exorcism," Sutherland went on, "I was determined not to allow the same catastrophe to occur a second time. It was a decade later. I was older, wiser. I remained steadfast in my faith. And the demon was driven from the host."

I frowned. "Did you really need to lie to the Hartmans?"

"Maybe I shouldn't have. I understand why you might be bothered by my misleading them, but I wanted them to take refuge in the Lord."

"Aren't you worried they'll call an ambulance?"

He favored me with a singularly cynical grin. "And have Ron risk the exposure of his bad deeds to all of Chicago? He'd sooner permit his son to die than face such mortifying publicity."

I asked, "Do you think Casey..."

"Is the Sweet Sixteen Killer?" Sutherland finished for me.

I waited.

"I doubt it, Father Crowder, but who can know? Perhaps Bittner is correct. Or Bittner himself is the killer. I've seen enough tonight to make me question everyone. There's Danny...he's a bit of a loner, and he's saddled with an alcohol addiction. And then there's Ron, who has proven to be amoral. Who better a killer than a man who thinks of no one but himself?"

I considered this. "Ron doesn't have the stomach for it. Danny...he'd never do those things."

"Perhaps you place too much faith in man's goodness."

I exhaled a tremulous breath and tried to clear my head.

"Now," Sutherland whispered, "quietly."

I followed him back to the bed and saw that the beatific expression still lingered on Casey's face. It was difficult to believe that only minutes earlier he'd been grinning horribly while his legs were being mangled.

Father Sutherland produced his white handkerchief and, careful to keep the cloth positioned between his hand and the skin of the boy's wrist, he probed for a pulse. Finding one, he gazed down at his watch, silently counting the beats against the revolving third hand. A single bead of sweat formed at the corner of his eyebrow and dripped onto his cheek, but Sutherland didn't move at all, only maintained his concentration on the watch.

Casey's hand clamped down on Sutherland's wrist.

Sucking in air, Sutherland dropped the handkerchief and attempted to pull away, but Casey's grip was implacable. And when the eyes opened, revealing glassy orbs as black as fresh pitch, the legs beneath me went

95

rubbery with terror. The Casey-thing's face split into a nasty leer, and its abominably sharp teeth moved as if the creature were preparing to speak. Then a look of stupefaction spread over the malign features, as if some stunning revelation had just been imparted from its contact with Sutherland's flesh.

"Let... me... go!" Sutherland grunted as he struggled with the creature. None of the priest's normal self-possession remained. Whether it was the shock of being seized or the fear of having his deepest secrets revealed that had done it, the panic Sutherland now exhibited frightened me worse than anything had thus far.

I joined in the struggle, but in moments the creature relinquished his hold on Sutherland. Both of us stumbled a little from this abrupt release, and at once Sutherland contrived to usher me from the room.

"Don't go, Father!" the creature said in the same wheedling growl it reserved for its most scathing taunts. "Don't leave before you tell the eunuch here about your little hobby!"

I paused six feet from the door. Sutherland bade me continue forward, but I turned and listened as the creature said, "Told the diocese you wanted your own home for privacy and learning, didn't you, Sutherland? How astonished they would be to find the souvenirs you've hidden under the floorboard of your study!"

"What's he talking about?" I asked.

"Lies," Sutherland said, dragging me toward the door.

"What souvenirs?" I asked, and the creature on the bed began to cackle.

"Wants to know what his hero's been up to!" the demon laughed. *"Wants to see the little ladies' keepsakes!"*

"What keepsakes?" I shouted as Sutherland hauled me out of the room and slammed the door behind us.

"What's he talking about?" I demanded.

"He's planting doubt in you, Father Crowder." He patted his forehead with his purple stole. "Frankly, I'm astonished you were taken in so easily."

"But who was he talking about? What little ladies?"

"There *are* no little ladies, don't you see? He wants to divide us, for together we are invulnerable. You saw how we subdued the demon with Scripture. You bore witness to the power of faith."

"Why were you so afraid to touch him?" I asked, aware now that Liz had materialized beside me. She looked frazzled and drawn, but there was a vitality in her eyes that I admired. My attention, however, was on Sutherland.

As if to himself, Sutherland said, "We've been rash."

"Father?" I asked. "Why were you so afraid to touch Casey?"

"It isn't Casey," he said, teeth bared. "Can't you see that? It's a pestilence. A foul intelligence whose only skill is duplicity. It's using the terrible scandals associated with the clergy to induce doubt in your mind. Is your opinion of me so abysmal?"

"But it was so specific."

He flapped a dismissive hand. "This is absurd."

"What happened in there?" Liz asked.

I said, "May I use your phone, Mrs. Hartman?"

Sutherland shot me a sharp look.

"They aren't working," she said.

I swallowed. "Maybe the storm is affecting the signals or—"

"It knocked out the landlines too," she said. "None of them are working. Not even a dial tone."

Freezing tendrils of dread slithered down my spine.

But Sutherland seemed not to notice. He touched his forefingers to his lips and nodded. "We've been fixated on trying to exorcise the demon, but we've failed to ask the most important question."

Liz frowned. "I don't understand."

"Why?" Sutherland said.

I opened my mouth to press him, but he stilled me with a glance. "Why, Jason? Why here? This house? Why Casey specifically?"

His words acted on me like a galvanic shock. My misgivings were swept away in the light of some new realization.

Liz's voice was fierce. "Will one of you please tell me—"

"One of the most important questions relating to demonic possession," I said, "is that of selection. Very seldom—in cases deemed to be authentic—is the inhabiting spirit random in its choosing. Ordinarily, there's some logic behind the selection of a host."

She seemed to withdraw from me. "Are you saying Casey did something to deserve this?"

Father Sutherland spoke gently. "He's not saying anything of the sort, Mrs. Hartman. There are myriad reasons why one might become host to a demon."

She massaged her throat. "Such as?"

"Sometimes the host has dabbled in the occult. Ouija boards, séances, any manner of spiritualism."

But Liz was shaking her head. "Casey doesn't get involved with any of that stuff."

"Perhaps at a friend's house?" I ventured. "At a sleepover maybe?"

She thought about it. "I can't imagine any of his friends being interested in the occult. Or their parents allowing it."

"There are other causes," Sutherland said. "Sometimes the house itself is responsible for the manifestation. On these occasions the demon takes up residence in a home and preys on someone vulnerable. Typically a child going through adolescence."

"Do you know the history of the house?" I asked.

She frowned, thinking. "We're only the third owners. The people we bought it from, they were very nice. Simple people. Ron couldn't imagine how people so unostentatious could afford such an expensive property."

"And before that?" I prompted.

"I don't know," she said. "Ron probably does, but I've never bothered to ask."

We fell silent, pondering. Then, his voice scarcely audible, Sutherland said, "There is another possibility, Mrs. Hartman."

She waited with a look of naked dread.

"In some of the worst cases," Sutherland began, "in some of the most violent cases recorded in the annals of the Catholic Church, the cause of possession was neither a conscious invitation from the host, nor was there a history of supernatural disturbance in the property." He sighed, plainly unhappy to utter the possibility. "In these cases the possession occurred as a result of some terrible sin."

Liz looked at him wonderingly. "What could Casey have possibly done?"

"In most instances," Sutherland explained, "it was not the host who transgressed. It was a member of the family."

Liz's eyes widened.

Unable to keep silent any longer, I told Liz what the demon had revealed about her husband while she was unconscious. Sutherland didn't interrupt me. Perhaps he also desired that she know the truth. To Liz's credit, she didn't seem surprised by anything I said.

"Mrs. Hartman," Sutherland went on, peering deep into her eyes now, "how well can you account for your husband's whereabouts over the past few months?"

Her voice was little more than a whisper. "You're talking about the murders."

Sutherland's intense scrutiny never wavered.

I waited for Liz to tell Sutherland what she'd told me about her husband's childhood in Greece. I waited for Sutherland to ask her if he could search the premises. But neither of those things happened.

Because a shrill cry reverberated down the hall and made us stare at each other in shock. It hadn't come from Casey's room.

It had come from Carolyn's.

◆ ◆ ◆

"Help me with her!" Danny shouted.

Liz bolted toward the bed right away, with Sutherland and me close on her heels. Danny was struggling to hold Carolyn down, but she was whipping from side to side, her head thrashing back and forth on her slender neck hard enough to snap her spine. We grabbed hold of the girl to prevent serious injury. Liz had both hands on the girl's shrieking face. Danny clutched Carolyn around the waist. I fought to maintain a grip on her scissoring ankles. But, heedless of our attempts, the girl continued to whip from side to side and up and down as if she were being shaken by an immensely powerful man.

"When did this start?" Sutherland shouted.

Danny shook his head, his eyes huge. "Twenty seconds ago?"

Liz pleaded with the girl to stop, as if, I thought wryly, it were in Carolyn's power to prevent the abuse being visited upon her.

"What was happening when it began?" Sutherland asked.

"Nothing," Danny said. "We were just talking. I was stroking her forehead. You know, to calm her. And then she just..." He looked away, clenching his jaw with the effort of stabilizing her movements.

Carolyn wailed and begged us to make it stop, and though the abject terror in the girl's voice deepened my concern, I took it as a hopeful sign that the girl still retained the power to speak in her own voice. The demon, I decided, had not taken control of her the way it had Casey. Which meant...

Sutherland seemed to be on a similar wavelength. "Father Crowder, please go to Casey's room. Verify for me that—"

But I was already pushing away from the bed and racing toward the bedroom door. For once I was excited, determined even. I had a task that I was capable of performing. Further, I found, I wanted to perform it, wanted to verify that the demon was still inhabiting Casey. If it wasn't, I wondered, could I possibly smuggle the boy out of his room and away from the house? Was it feasible to sneak the demon's host away while its attention was diverted toward the boy's younger sister?

I didn't know if it was possible, and as I dashed down the hallway to Casey's room, I had a terrible vision of the demon taking up residence inside Carolyn. At least Casey was a teenager, able-bodied enough to perhaps sustain such a dreadful assault. Carolyn was a mere child, with a mind and body incapable of withstanding such trauma. I burst into the room, my anger rising. How dare this abomination lay siege to this family? Despite their father's sins, these children were guiltless. Innocent victims of a fathomless evil. Nor did their mother deserve to be plunged into such a nightmarish ordeal. Wasn't being married to Ron punishment enough?

Casey's door was ajar, and I entered without wondering why. Had I paused to consider the fact, who knows what might have happened next. But such questions are pointless now. Since we had vacated the room and closed the door, it had somehow reopened. As if beckoning me inside.

As if inviting me to venture closer.

I got halfway to Casey's bed and stopped, my airway constricting as though invisible fingers were clutching my neck. I stared at what lay before me.

The extension cords had been torn apart.

The handcuffs had been snapped.

The bed was empty.

I whirled, thinking to escape before the creature could attack me.

Then the door slammed shut.

And the room went black.

PART THREE
CLASH

Chapter Eight

There was a sense of being caged. And like a trapped thing, I immediately began to panic. Not only was the room as stygian as a tomb, but the atmosphere enveloping me was as humid and thick as an unaired closet. The odors that had assaulted my nostrils earlier now swarmed over me like a shroud. Wild-animal musk. Sweaty, oily hair. Dog excrement. Hot sperm squirted over a prostitute's heaving stomach.

I grew nauseated, but the nausea was as nothing beside the mind-shattering fear that gripped me. To my left I could hear the storm raging outside, the wind buffeting the solid brick exterior, the rain machine-gunning the double-paned windows. I was, I judged, only seven or eight feet from where I'd entered the room, yet that expanse suddenly seemed impassable. I took a step in the direction of where I believed the door to be.

I paused, my flesh crawling. I fancied I could hear breathing in the room with me, but strove to dismiss the sound as nervousness. There was no denying how overtaxed my faculties were at that moment, how beleaguered my emotions. Even my body, unaccustomed to the physical punishment it had sustained at the hands of the insidious presence, seemed to flag as I took another step toward the door. I believed I would reach it. I'd actually extended my right hand to grasp the knob when the toe of my shoe encountered some object. My blood froze.

Something touched my ankle, my shin. I realized there were fingers caressing my calves through my robe. Then *under* my robe.

"Jasonnnn," a female voice whispered.

Sexual yearning such as I had never experienced swam over me like warm, jasmine-scented water. I could feel the delicate nails tracing the backs of my knees, my hamstrings. Instantly erect, I was assailed by images of Liz, nude, beneath me. Her succulent body was warm and unresisting, her skin supple, her face an exultant pout. As I rammed into her, her bare feet juddered in the air, her molten breath drowsed into my ear.

In the darkness of the bedroom, the fingers curled under my buttocks, then snaked over my thighs. They found the underside of my scrotum, applied pressure, and a wave of arousal so powerful rippled through me that I feared I might faint. In my mind I was still thrusting into Liz's warm sex. She was offering herself up to me, begging me to give her more, more. She was moaning, and the hands in the darkness found me, began to stroke me. The citrusy scent of her skin was intoxicating. I swayed on my feet. The silky hands kneaded up my body, slithered over my shoulders, and in the dense, sultry air of the bedroom I heard Liz's voice whispering to me, cajoling me. I realized I'd closed my eyes at some point, and now I opened them, and when I did I let loose with the wildest shriek of horror I have uttered in my life. It was the *thing* that had aroused me, the demon that had possessed Casey, but now the boy's face was a goblin-like nightmare, the heavy eyebrows arched above eyes that were a lambent, hellish red, the pupils narrow and vertical, the pupils of a cat.

Lightning strobed in the tenebrous bedroom and I saw the demon's maw was stretched wide, the hot slaver dripping off its bared incisors. It was about to sink its killing teeth into my throat, and by instinct I jerked up my right hand to ward it off. It lunged at me. Fire erupted in my hand. When I brought it to my face for inspection, another triple flash of lightning revealed the jetting stumps of my pinkie and ring finger, both torn off by the demon's razor-like bite.

Backpedaling, I clutched my hemorrhaging hand. I heard it chewing, watched the unblinking red eyes drifting nearer in the gloom. The backs of my legs connected with something, and I realized too late it was the footboard of the bed. I toppled onto it, kicking at the demon despite the fact that I had lost sight of its infernal scarlet eyes. I did hear it laughing at me though, and the effluvium that filled the bedroom was so powerful that the urge to vomit nearly surpassed my terror. Dread of the demon reduced my movements to feeble twitchings and ineffectual kicks. I was drowning in the odors of shit and fur and sex and death and my own spraying blood.

With a fresh surge of panic, I realized I was lying on the exact spot Casey had occupied earlier, and with the realization came the sensations of moist sheets, cold and clinging to my flesh like sluggish parasites. There came the briefest hint of quicksilver through the windows, and in the attendant rumble of thunder I caught a shadowy glimpse of the figure striding around the bed for me.

Rolling sideways, I hit the floor, and in my childlike fright, I scuttled under the bed to put something between me and the presence.

The darkness under the bed was greater than any I had ever experienced. Though the space from floor to bedframe was at least a foot, it was as though the bed itself possessed some light-eating quality that ensured absolute blackness. I felt blind, and though I continued to hear rumbles of thunder, no shimmer of light reached me where I lay.

I listened for the laughter of the demon, for the creaking of a floorboard. So great was my terror that I actually expected the thing to compress the whole bed on top of me, thus smothering me while I let loose with one final soundless shriek.

But other than the sounds of the storm, there was nothing. I wondered vaguely where the others had gone. Were they still with Carolyn? Was she still being attacked? I didn't know, but I confess here that any concerns I had for the child were as secondary as they were ephemeral. In my childish dread, I even flirted with the notion that the demon had forgotten me.

Until I heard my mother's voice.

Had my mom not died when I was twelve years old, the sound of her voice would not have been so disconcerting. But she had. Just a senseless traffic accident. Coming home from work. Black ice. A loss of control, her little car veering into the oncoming lane and hitting a semi head on.

I never knew my father. Nor did I know the men my mother used to bring home. After she died, I went to live with my uncle, but though he was a decent person, the damage had already been done. I associated men with meanness, with drunkenness.

It was with a man named Joe Wilson that I discovered my mom one night many years before her accident. I've since blocked out most of the memory, but as near as I can tell, I was five years old. Just five and completely naïve about men and women. So when I awoke that night and heard my mother's and Joe's voices calling out together, I automatically hurried to her room to make sure they were okay.

When I stepped through the doorway, they were locked together, my mother sitting on top of Joe, a man whose hairy body reminded me of a werewolf movie I'd glimpsed on cable TV when my mom didn't know I was watching.

She didn't know I was watching now either, but I was. And, what was more, I was so transfixed by the appalling sight of her straddling Joe that I grew dizzy. I swayed on my bare feet as Joe reached up and fondled my mother's breasts. I became nauseated as my mother moaned out words I knew were bad words because I'd heard Joe holler them when he watched football.

I felt no excitement at the sight of those writhing bodies, no inchoate sexual thrill. There was only a dismal sense of betrayal. And the nausea. At some point I threw up, the creamy acid bubbling out of my mouth and painting the front of my pajamas. It must have been the splattering sound that drew their attention because they looked at me then, my mother with surprise, Joe with unconcealed disgust.

"Go back to bed, honey," my mom said.

I started to cry.

"Jesus Christ," Joe muttered. "Get him the fuck out of here."

I thought my mom would defend me, but she just scowled. "Go to *bed*, Jason."

I cried harder, wanting my mom to hold me.

"Get him *out* of here, Linda!" Joe demanded.

She scrambled off of Joe, whose glistening member made a slurping sound as it left her body. The sight of it made me want to puke again, but then the sight of my mom's milky flesh filled my vision. She was yelling at me, her fingers biting into my shoulder. She drove me from the room and into the bathroom across the hallway.

I plopped down on the closed toilet seat and waited for her to clean me up, but she flipped on the light and continued berating me, shouting that she'd be able to find a man if she didn't have to worry about me all the time, telling me what a good guy Joe was, what a great provider he would be. But I scarcely heard what she was saying because I'd noticed her black nest of pubic hair—it was difficult not to notice as I was sitting on the toilet and her midsection was at eye level.

As I watched, something pearlescent began to seep from between her legs. At first it reminded me of the cold medicine she sometimes fed me from an eyedropper. But as I watched, the drooping stream of mucus-like liquid grew longer, attenuating, then plummeted to the pale-green, tiled floor with a quiet splat. I threw up again, spraying orange liquid all over my mother's legs and the white shower curtain beyond.

Then she was shrieking at me, railing at me for ruining her night. I heard Joe cursing in the hallway, his heavy footfalls retreating toward the door. My mom left me sitting there. She implored Joe to stay. But he didn't, and when my mom returned, she bellowed at me as she never had before, sobbing and screaming and occasionally slapping my cheeks. She left the bathroom after that, and I heard her weeping in her bedroom. I thought of going to her to apologize, but I was too afraid of getting smacked again.

Eventually, I returned to my bedroom and lay on top of the covers. The vomit stank, but it had dried to a moist crust on my chin and the front of my pajamas. At some point, despite the bitter taste in my mouth, I must have fallen asleep.

◆ ◆ ◆

Lightning strobed in Casey's bedroom, and I sucked in air, realizing I'd been lost in the suppressed memory. I turned to the left, half expecting to discover the demon or my mother or even Joe Wilson lying beside me under the bed. But there was no one there with me, just empty space. I began to wonder if the demon had left the room, perhaps to prey on someone stronger, and I resolved to escape a space that had begun to feel like a dusty coffin. Moving slowly, careful to make no sound, I wormed my way sideways toward the down-hanging corner of a sheet. At every moment I expected a face to appear in the gap between the floor and the bed, an inverted face with glowing red eyes and a malicious smile.

But no face appeared. Nor did I hear anything other than the storm. Had the demon really moved on from me? I knew the thought should have filled me with concern for the others, but I promised at the outset to record the events of that night as faithfully as I could, and so I will.

It is therefore with deepest shame that I admit to experiencing a gust of relief at emerging from my hiding place and finding the room barren. The door was closed, but that meant little. The demon could have easily gone out noiselessly and shut the door behind it. Or perhaps it had opened a window and leapt into the night in pursuit of new victims. Such a feat of physical prowess would not have surprised me. For now I was convinced that the demon was none other than the Sweet Sixteen Killer. Its knowledge of the crimes, coupled with the strength and ferocity it displayed, made it easy for me to imagine it doing those terrible things to the six dead girls.

At thought of the victims, I remembered my severed fingers and realized that I'd neglected to keep the blood flow staunched. I endeavored to stand up, but the loss of blood defeated me. Swooning, I flopped sideways onto the bed, and doing all I could to tend to my bleeding hand, I lay on my back and closed my eyes.

I decided that if I survived the night, I'd see a therapist about the memory this experience had just dredged up. I knew psychology wasn't a linear subject and understood the folly of attributing all my difficulties with the opposite sex to a single traumatic event involving my mother and Joe Wilson. But I thought the experience at the very least germane to my troubles and wondered if I might not enter my thirties with a healthier view of women and maybe even explore the possibility of entering a relationship with one. The night had certainly revealed my lack of fortitude, so it would be no great loss to the church if I left the priesthood. Perhaps it would be a relief to Father Sutherland. At least he wouldn't have to fire me.

Thinking of Sutherland, I opened my eyes and beheld the figure glued to the ceiling above me, the red eyes glaring at me in triumph.

The demon fell. As it swooped downward, its splayed limbs groped for me as if eager for my blood. Forgetting my injury, I brought up my hands to fend it off, but its snarling body slammed against me, setting off a conflagration in my mangled hand and pounding the wind from my lungs. Its head rose, the mottled fangs catching glints of pale light, and I jerked up a forearm a moment before it could chomp into my face. The scimitar teeth punctured the flesh of my forearm, pierced the surface of my ulna. The pain was excruciating, but I was barely conscious of it. The demon crunched down harder, its black tongue flicking at the blood that gushed from the wound.

I shot a knee into its crotch, but if anything this only whipped its bloodlust into a more violent frenzy. Its talons harrowed my shoulders, shredding my robe, my T-shirt, and carved deep slashes in my deltoid muscles. I bellowed in terror and agony, implored someone to intervene, and as though one of my prayers had at last been answered, I heard footsteps in the hallway. There were shouting voices, the sounds of a struggle. What sounded like a man screaming.

The beast gave off the attack to stare over its shoulder at the door. My angle afforded me a glimpse of the doorway just as it burst open. I muttered a mental prayer of thanksgiving, thinking Father Sutherland or perhaps Danny Hartman had arrived to save me.

But it was neither Sutherland nor Danny who came through that door.

It was Jack Bittner.

◆ ◆ ◆

The question of how he'd gotten out of the cruiser did not occur to me at that moment, though I would learn how later. The only thoughts I had at that moment were the desperate hope that the demon would release me and a sudden fear of being shot.

For Jack Bittner had not only escaped the cruiser, he had managed to arm himself. He strode toward the bed with the gun trained on us, a look of deadly calm on his pitiless face.

"This is for your victims," Bittner said. "This is for those poor kids you destroyed."

The door behind Bittner slammed shut, but he hardly seemed to notice. He lumbered inexorably on, looking intent on finishing what he'd begun earlier.

Bittner stopped just shy of the footboard, the barrel fixed on the back of the demon's head. I realized then that the beast hadn't even watched Jack Bittner approach, had instead watched me watch Bittner. And as I gazed into those lurid red eyes, I understood why. Its lips stretched into a sly grin. Bloody slaver drooled off its teeth and pooled onto my face.

I don't know now if it would have made any difference had I warned Bittner of the impending attack. My conscience says it would have. My reason, however, points out the appalling suddenness of the onslaught, the manner in which the creature sprang and spun at Bittner like some agile jungle cat.

Bittner fired once, and the plaster over the headboard exploded, showering me with grit and dust. I pushed onto my elbows to see Bittner windmilling his arms as he blundered backward, the demon affixed to his upper body like an inoperable tumor. I crawled forward on the bed just as Bittner landed on his back.

He was slapping at the demon—at some point he had apparently dropped the gun—and I could hear the demon's deep, throaty voice taunting him in some indecent-sounding language. I thought at first the demon would simply lean down and bite Bittner's face off, but that, I soon understood, would have been too quick.

The demon actually climbed off Bittner's supine form. Bittner scrambled to his knees and had just retrieved the gun when a new voice said, "No, Daddy."

Despite how bloody Bittner's face was, I could distinguish his eyes well enough. They were huge, starey. "Celia?" he said.

"No, Daddy," the voice repeated. "Don't leave me, Daddy."

Jack's face crumpled, the enormous man breaking down.

"Why are you moving away, Daddy?" the girl's voice asked, and when I turned and stared at the demon, I received another shock.

Though nothing at that point should have amazed me— not after all I'd seen—the vision of Celia Bittner standing there in the murky bedroom still took my breath away. She had long blonde hair tied into a ropy braid. She wore pink pajamas that emphasized her little potbelly. She looked perhaps five years old.

"I didn't wanna move," Jack said, and after all the man had said and done, I have to admit that I still pitied him. Never on a human face had I beheld such an expression of sorrow and longing. "Daddy didn't wanna move away, honey. It was your mother..."

"Mommy says you don't care about us anymore," Celia said. I noticed she was clutching a small beige teddy bear to her chest and had no doubt that this was the same stuffed animal Celia had carried with her when she was a young child. The demon, I felt certain, had mined these images,

115

this voice, from Bittner's memory. But the effect was uncanny. It was like time had reversed and the child Celia had been was standing in the room with us.

Bittner was up on his knees. "Honey, you've gotta believe me. Daddy would've never left if it were up to him. I love you—" his face crumpled again, his words coming in a ragged rush, "—I love you more than anything. I didn't want to go."

"Then why did you?" the voice demanded, and I fancied I could hear a hint of the demon's true malicious tone buzzing around the edges of the child's voice.

If Bittner heard it, he gave no indication. "It was your mom's decision. She...she didn't want Daddy anymore. She—"

Celia's face hardened, a cold, calculating intelligence permeating it. "Are you saying Mommy's a whore?"

It acted on Bittner like a slap. He actually recoiled and blinked for a moment. "Honey, please don't talk like—"

"Please don't talk like that," the voice mimicked, and though the pitch was still the same, the tone was eerily wicked, the buzzing darkness more pronounced. "You always want control."

I began to edge around them. The closed door was perhaps twelve feet away. Someone was on the other side of it, hammering. Yet the sounds were oddly muffled in here, as though Casey's bedroom existed in a separate reality, another dimension.

Bittner was on his knees, a hand extended toward Celia, or the thing pretending to be Celia. "I'm not trying to control you, Honey. Don't think that. I just want to teach you the right things, you know?"

116

Was there a flash of vermilion in the girl's blue eyes? The skin seemed to be tawnier, more aged. *"Control is all you want,"* the voice said, and now there was as much of the demon in it as there was the young Celia. *"You wanted to control Mommy, and you want to control me."*

If Bittner sensed the changes, he didn't let on. He walked on his knees toward Celia, the gun holstered now, both his hands extended. "No I don't, Baby. I only want to be near you. I just want to be—"

"No pierced ears, Celia!" the voice said in a vicious singsong. *"No going on dates!"*

Bittner's chest shuddered, his voice thick and weary. "I didn't say that. I only said I wanted to meet the boy before you went out with him. You know, so I could—"

"So you could intimidate him!" Celia snapped, and now there was nothing at all girly about the voice. It was all hornets and echoes, the demon's full-throated drone. *"So whoever went out with me could see what a tough guy you were, so he could see the gun on your hip."*

Something finally clicked in Bittner's mind. His face went slack with dismay. "You're not...you're not..."

"Celia?" the voice roared. The sound of it made me want to squeal in terror.

I was five feet from the door.

The Celia-thing was expanding, the demon no longer resembling a child, but rather a noxious, misshapen beast. Its face loomed toward Bittner's. *"Celia despises you. You abandoned her!"*

Bittner whimpered, his hand quivering toward the grip of the gun.

"Yeeeesss," the demonic voice said, nodding, the eyes a hellish red now, the vertical disks of pupil narrowing in

savage glee. *"Go for your weapon, Jack. See where it gets you."*

My hand was trembling so violently I could scarcely grip the brass doorknob, which was hot to the touch. Though we were only separated by a few inches of solid wood, the voices on the other side of the door sounded miles away.

"You're not Celia," Jack whispered, as if to himself. "You're not my baby."

"No, Jack," the voice rumbled. *"I'm not. But Celia's going to hear all about her daddy tomorrow."*

Something new came into Bittner's face, and his right hand finally seemed to steady. His fingers looking sure now, he drew the gun from his holster. But rather than imbuing him with confidence, this seemed to bring him only puzzlement and dread.

"Jack Bittner," the demon's voice said. *"Aged forty-six. Twenty-year veteran of the Chicago Police Department…"*

The gun rose, Bittner's hand as steady as a surgeon's.

"…died last night in an upscale Lincoln Park home…"

Bittner stared at the gun as if it had transformed into a deadly viper. "What are you doing?"

The demon's tone was celebratory. *"Time to join your mommy in hell!"*

The full realization of horror stretched Bittner's rough-hewn features. He uttered a breathless little moan.

The barrel drifted toward his open mouth, penetrated the barrier of his quivering lips.

Bittner's eyes were moons, his moan going shrill.

His lips wrapped around the slender barrel.

His trigger finger whitened.

I looked away a moment too late. I saw the finger squeeze. I saw the rear of Jack Bittner's head explode like a bloody firework.

The door swung toward me, its edge narrowly missing my face. Danny stumbled in. He stopped beside me, gaping at Jack Bittner's slouching form, which toppled sideways as we watched.

The demon, unmasked, turned and grinned at us. It was still Casey's body, but nothing in that face resembled human feeling. Or perhaps it was the horror we all wore beneath our carefully constructed masks.

"Jesus," Danny whispered.

"Run," I said.

CHAPTER NINE

Sutherland stood in the hallway, his forehead bloodied and gathered in a taut bump. I realized at once how it had likely happened. Bittner had somehow gotten back inside, overcome Danny, taken his gun and then subdued Sutherland too.

Liz and Carolyn stood adjacent to Sutherland and Danny, with Ron a little ways off.

Footsteps sounded within Casey's bedroom.

"Come on," Danny said, sweeping Carolyn into his arms. I put a hand on Liz's back to get her moving. Sutherland looked bemused, but he followed us anyway. From behind us somewhere, Ron was pleading for us to wait up.

But we couldn't wait. The demon was coming.

"We can't leave Casey," Liz said, her voice shrill.

"We won't!" Danny shouted over his shoulder. "But I'm getting Carolyn out of here!"

We sprinted for the stairs, but even before we got halfway there, I could see something was wrong. I heard a multitude of deep, cracking sounds. The spindles of the banister seemed to undulate in the meager light of the corridor.

"Wait a second," I called as we drew nearer, but Danny either didn't hear me or was too frightened to heed my words.

He and Carolyn were five feet from the top stair and running at full speed when the whole thing gave way.

There was an unearthly groaning noise, followed by a series of harsh staccato pops. Splintered wood and scraps of carpet twirled through the air like pinwheels. Danny skidded on the wood floor, and for a terrible instant I thought both he and Carolyn would go tumbling over the edge of what was now a ragged snarl of shattered boards and nails. His need for self-preservation evidently secondary to his desire to keep his niece safe, Danny hurled Carolyn bodily away from the yawning drop-off.

But Danny's momentum carried him over the abyss.

His feet went over, his legs and hips. I heard a terrible scraping sound as his belly raked the protruding barbs of broken stairwell. Just when I was sure he would plunge screaming to his death, Danny's left hand snagged one of the few remaining spindles. The narrow wooden cylinder groaned with the strain, but it held long enough for him to grasp the edge of a rug with his other hand.

The staircase had crumbled completely and now, I saw with a downward glance, lay in ruins in the formerly grand foyer. Not only would Danny's drop amount to a twenty-foot free fall, he would be landing on a nasty heap of jagged shards that would almost certainly prove fatal.

I let go of Liz and dove forward. I knew I wasn't powerful enough to support Danny's weight by myself, but perhaps I could supplement his strength long enough for Father Sutherland to arrive. I grasped Danny's right hand, the one with the poorest hold. Our fingers twined together. His eyes fastened on mine, and I could see how frightened he was. Without thinking, I seized his wrist with my mutilated hand. Despite the soul-destroying agony that erupted in the ragged stumps of my missing fingers, I held on and began towing him toward me. Danny gritted his teeth, and I realized that between us we were lifting him to safety.

Seconds later, a large hand seized the back of Danny's shirt and joined us. My peripheral vision told me it was Father Sutherland. With our pooled strength, we dragged Danny up onto what remained of the landing, but before I had time to catch my breath, my attention was arrested by Ron's raised voice.

"...any second now," Ron said. He was crouching next to the three of us, but his eyes were fixed on the hallway outside Casey's room.

I jerked my head around, certain the demon would be stalking toward us, but despite the dimness of the corridor, I could see well enough that the space was empty. Either Casey's possessed form was lurking somewhere else on the second floor, or it hadn't yet exited the bedroom. Either way, we had to think fast.

"What's down there?" I asked, nodding toward the sooty corridor beyond where Liz stood with Carolyn clutching her around the waist.

"The guest room," Liz said.

"Are there stairs leading—"

"No," she said. "This and the stairs at the far end are the only ways down."

We looked with crawling dread toward the corridor outside Casey's room.

Ron shook his head. "No way in hell I'm going that way."

"There's nowhere else to go," Liz said.

Ron nodded toward the missing staircase. "Let's jump down here."

We looked at him in disbelief.

"What?" he said. "Would you rather deal with that monster?"

Sutherland grasped Ron by the front of his Blackhawks jersey. "That monster has your son. Will you forsake Casey?"

Ron didn't say anything to that, but the look on his face suggested he would absolutely prefer sacrificing Casey if it would ensure his own survival. I glanced at Liz, who was regarding her husband with such dead-eyed loathing that I couldn't imagine the pair remaining married. If they survived this ordeal, of course.

Sutherland knelt over Danny, who sat clutching his belly. In the semidarkness, I could see how the front of his shirt had been shredded, the way the navy-blue material glistened. He looked like he'd been gored by a bull.

Liz joined our huddled group, fingers still cinched around her daughter's shoulder. "We need to get you to a doctor, Danny."

"I'm fine," he said, but the way he grimaced belied his words.

Ron paid no attention to his brother. "We gotta get out of here!"

"There's nowhere to go," Danny said.

Sutherland glanced about. "What about the windows? Is there a way onto the roof? Maybe a tree close enough..."

But Liz was shaking her head. "There's nothing. Not unless you want to fall two stories."

"There's only one thing," Danny said. He looked up at Sutherland. "You guys gotta do what you came here to do."

Sutherland returned Danny's gaze for a beat, then turned to me.

"Father Crowder?" Sutherland said. I looked at him, and though he appeared haggard and far older than his sixty-one years, the resolve in his face gave me hope.

"We have to save Casey from the demon," I said.

Danny nodded. "Goddamn right."

Sutherland permitted himself the ghost of a smile.

I took Liz by the arm. "You and Carolyn go to the guest room." When Liz started to shake her head, I said, "This is about keeping your daughter safe, not me trying to be a hero. The farther she is from that thing, the better." Whatever mistakes I'd made that evening, this seemed to be the right thing at that moment. Liz swallowed, reached up and touched my face. In her brimming eyes I saw gratitude and what might have been a deeper regard.

Ron seemed to catch it too because he stepped toward us. "Hey, what the hell—"

But he never finished. Because behind us erupted such an unholy blast of laughter that my flesh broke out in goose bumps and an icy chill raced up and down my spine.

We all peered down the hallway at the figure standing unmovingly outside Casey's bedroom door.

"Go," I whispered to Liz. Reluctantly, she took Carolyn's hand and receded into the guest bedroom. I heard but did not see the door close.

"Take out your Bible," Father Sutherland said.

But it was already in my hands.

CHAPTER TEN

Sutherland and I approached the waiting figure. Behind us were Danny and Ron. I trusted Sutherland and Danny to stand. Ron would abandon us shortly, I felt sure.

Sutherland began, "Save me, O God, by thy name, and judge me by thy strength."

I knew the psalm well enough to recite it by memory, but I kept my eyes on the Bible Sutherland had given me so I wouldn't be distracted by the demon's horrid countenance. "Hear my prayer, O God; give ear to the words of my mouth."

"You weak, puling cowards," the demon said. Far from seeming distressed by our reading, the demon's face was twisted in an attitude of scornful arrogance. *"Watch what faith has reaped."*

The objects on a table ahead of us began to rattle.

Sutherland pressed on. "For strangers are risen up against me, and oppressors seek after my soul: they have not set God before them."

"Behold, God is mine helper: the Lord—"

My words were drowned in a vortex of noise. The demon, its clawed hands outstretched, was levitating the objects on the table: a small Tiffany lamp, a silver candleholder with a cream-colored candle, an old-fashioned rotary phone and a carving of either a bear or a wolf.

It was difficult to tell with the objects rising and beginning to spin.

"Father Crowder!" Sutherland shouted.

My voice quaking, I finished, "—the Lord is with them that uphold my soul."

The demon roared and extended an arm, its fingers splayed toward us. Obediently, the carved figure rocketed toward my face. I whipped my head aside at the last moment and then groaned with regret as it crashed into Danny's forehead, lashing his skin and sending him flailing backward with his hands clamped to his wound.

"Holy fuck," Ron whispered. With a quick glance I saw that the crotch of Ron's sweatpants had darkened. The cloying odor of urine clotted the hallway air.

Sutherland went on as though nothing had happened, "He shall reward evil unto mine enemies and cut them off in thy truth."

The demon's grin flared in ghoulish delight. With a flick of its talons, it sent the lamp careening toward Ron. The racing object knifed through the air between my head and Father Sutherland's, and when it connected with Ron's face, there was an awful crunching sound—Ron's nose imploding—and then a boneless drop to the floor, the fragments of colored glass decorating Ron's body like strewn wild flowers.

Trembling, I stared at Ron's motionless form.

Sutherland gripped my forearm. "The response, Father Crowder."

I answered, my hands so palsied I could barely read the text, "I will freely sacrifice unto thee: I will praise thy name, O Lord; for it is good."

As Father Sutherland continued the psalm, the demon began to chortle.

"*Silence,*" Sutherland commanded. "For he hath delivered me out of all trouble: and mine eye hath seen his desire upon mine enemies."

"*Says* I'm *the monster,*" the demon rasped, its red, slitted eyes shifty and knowing. "*Says I'm the monster, but look at what* he *does.*"

Sutherland went on. "Give ear to my prayer, O God; and hide not thyself from my supplication."

"*Supplication?*" the demon said. "*Did you make Kate Harmeson supplicate before you raped her? Before you opened her belly like a Christmas present and ripped her earrings out for souvenirs?*"

When I didn't proceed, Sutherland said, "Attend unto me, and hear me: I mourn in my complaint and make a noise."

Did I detect the slightest agitation in Sutherland's voice? The strain of ignoring what the demon was saying?

"*And Joy Smith,*" the demon cooed. "*Her barrettes are under your floorboard.*"

"I said silence!" Sutherland yelled. "Father Crowder?"

"*Under his floorboard, Jason. You'll find a pair of panties belonging to Ashley Panagopoulos. The waistband is torn from when the good Father ripped them off her.*"

"Don't listen, Father Crowder."

But I was listening. Listening hard.

"*Mary Ellen Alspaugh. He took her brassiere.*"

"Lies, Father Crowder. 'Because the voice of the enemy, because of the oppression of the wicked—'"

"*Shelby Farnsworth's promise ring. It had belonged to her grandmother.*"

Sutherland didn't miss a beat. "For they cast iniquity upon me, and in wrath they hate me."

"Oh they hated you all right, Sutherland, and who can blame them?"

"Lies," Sutherland said, teeth bared.

"Like Katie Wells," the demon went on. *"He snipped off her middle finger and added it to his collection. Despite the fact that it's beginning to rot, he sniffs it every night before bed. The good priest jacks off to it while he replays the murder in his mind."*

I was staring at Sutherland, who kept his eyes studiously trained on the demon. When it became apparent I wasn't going to join in the reading, Sutherland seized my arm, shook me. "I told you the demon would lie," he said. "You're playing right into its hands. Now, when it matters most, you're weakening—"

"But when it grabbed you—"

"It read my thoughts, yes," Sutherland interrupted. "And where do you think those thoughts originated? The man in my confessional, Jason. He told me everything. Have you no faith?"

"Faith in God, yes. I have less and less faith in man."

"Read the psalm, Father Crowder."

"Why would the man in your confessional talk about all the things he took from the victims?"

The demon was grinning at us.

"Because he was proud of them," Sutherland said. "The man was a monster, can't you see that?"

"So much detail," I said, more to myself.

"The Scripture, Father Crowder."

"Did you do it?"

Sutherland was breathing hard. His teeth were bared, and his silver hair hung in lank, sweaty strips on his pink forehead. "You're letting the demon divide us. You have known me for eleven years, Jason. Must I give you a detailed account of my whereabouts on the nights of the killings?"

I didn't answer. The demon was laughing softly.

An iron grip squeezed my forearm. I stared at Father Sutherland, at the creased, sweaty forehead, the fierce blue eyes. Could this man be the murderer of six innocent young women? Could this be the defiler of their bodies, the rapist who violated each of them both in life and in death?

I wanted to believe he was not. I wanted to believe Peter Sutherland was the man I'd always revered. But try as I might, I could not. I didn't know whether he was the Sweet Sixteen Killer or simply a man who'd heard too much, whose mind, in absorbing the confession of a diabolical killer, now contained the poisonous seeds that had taken root in his mind.

The demon's laughter swelled.

And I realized that my belief in Father Sutherland's guilt or innocence mattered little. For whether Casey had anything to do with the killings or not, he—the boy in the baseball cap I'd seen on the refrigerator downstairs, the boy who liked the Beatles and LeBron James and who was always polite and cheerful to me on Sunday mornings despite the earliness of the hour—did not deserve to die, nor did he deserve to be usurped and tortured by a presence beyond human understanding.

Casey Hartman was a good kid. He deserved to be manumitted from this filth.

I rose. Opened the Bible Sutherland had handed me. "I rebuke you, accursed serpent, by the power of God," I said. "And I demand that you depart from this child's body."

The demon's eyes narrowed.

Sutherland continued with me in unison, "I order you by the might of the Holy Spirit and the name of Christ to depart from this innocent flesh."

For the first time that night, a flicker of uncertainty entered the demon's eyes. *"He'll kill again,"* the demon told me. *"The blood of more children will be on your hands if you permit him to escape this house."*

I faltered, but only for a fraction of a second. "The power of Jesus Christ compels you. Tremble before His mighty hand."

The demon snarled, took a backwards step.

Sutherland joined me. We advanced on the demon. "Jesus Christ orders you to abandon this flesh. God Himself demands your departure from this house."

The demon took another backward step. *"I'll destroy his body. I'll leap from the window."*

"You'll do no such thing!" I shouted. "By the power of the saints, I demand you leave his body!"

The demon staggered, but did not fall.

Sutherland moved apace with me. "Jesus Christ casts you out!"

The demon lurched through Casey's doorway.

We hastened after it. I experienced a moment's terror that it would make good on its promise, that it would hurl Casey's body through the window, because if it did I couldn't imagine the boy surviving. The fall was precipitous, thirty or more feet down to merciless concrete.

We passed into the doorway and entered what appeared to be an empty bedroom. Recalling what had happened earlier, when I lay on the bed in enervated shock, I cast a panicked glance at the ceiling. But this time the demon was not clinging there, waiting to pounce on me.

This time the demon was hidden behind the door.

It hurtled from its hiding place and crashed into Sutherland. In a flash the Bible had tumbled out of his hands and was skidding across the floor, the demon grasping both sides of Sutherland's head and dashing his skull against the unyielding wood floor. Precisely the way, I thought with a sense of fatedness, the Sweet Sixteen Killer had staved Ashley Panagopoulos's head in.

Impulsively, I strode forward and aimed a kick at the demon's head. My sneaker connected with its chin. Its head whipped back, its teeth clicking together, and as it turned toward me, its face contorted in a rictus of fury and enmity, I ripped the crucifix from my necklace and thrust it into its face.

Squalling, it tumbled backward, calling me all manner of names as it fell. A foul gust of breath assailed me, the withering odors of flyblown meat and spoiled milk. But I ignored these smells, ignored the fearsome rage stamped on the demon's features.

I felt the power of the crucifix in my hand, the simple silver object seeming to vibrate in my grip, the power coursing up my arm, thrumming through the muscles of my upper body, endowing me with a power and faith such as I had never known. Unthinkingly, I leapt atop the demon and pinioned its arms to the floor with my knees. I shoved the crucifix against the sodden T-shirt, meaning to expunge the demon from the boy without searing his flesh. I had seen the demon ravage Casey's body and restore it to its former state, but something told me any damage inflicted by the crucifix would be permanent.

The wet fabric of the shirt began to hiss as the crucifix seared into it, the demon writhing and baying in agony. But despite the terrible strength surcharging its limbs, I managed to keep it pinned to the floor, my voice bellowing above its frightful din, "Depart, Seducer! Depart, Transgressor!"

"No!" it shrieked, its red eyes incandescent, its black tongue darting in and out of its purple lips. *"Don't make me—"*

"YES!" I roared. "Be gone, you foul pestilence! Depart from this innocent flesh!"

The demon bucked beneath me, a torrent of blood gushing from one of its flared nostrils. The crucifix began to sizzle the flesh beneath, the smell of the scorched T-shirt now tinged with the aroma of frying bacon.

"Get...off...me..." the thing demanded in a deep, insectile voice. It sounded a thousand years old, ancient and fueled with the outrage of a besieged king.

"I will not release you," I shouted, "nor will I have done with you until you release this boy."

Sutherland was beside me, dazed but undaunted. "Our Father," he said, "who art in heaven."

"No!" the demon yowled. Lightning blazed outside the window.

"Hallowed be thy name," I continued. The whole house shook with the roar of thunder.

"Enough!" it said, but beneath the bass rumble of its voice I could hear another voice, a feeble, pleading note. The sound of a child who has been adrift at sea for days and is in his extremity. A boy who desperately needs saving.

"Thy kingdom come," Sutherland said.

The demon thrashed its head. One of its eyes had ceased to glow.

"Thy will be done," I said.

Blood drizzled from Casey's other nostril, but his struggles were abating.

"On earth, as it is in heaven," Sutherland and I said together.

The demon opened its mouth, but the tongue within looked human again. And when Casey's eyes fluttered open and shut, the lambent, red glow was gone, replaced by a stark white.

"Give us this day our daily bread..." we went on, and as the prayer continued, Casey's struggles grew less and less violent. His upper lip and the sides of his cheeks were slick with blood, but his features were no longer pale and contorted like they'd been. The demon's monstrous voice was gone entirely, the only noises issuing from the boy frail moans that sounded like he was experiencing nothing more dangerous than a particularly bad dream. The stench of roasted flesh still hung in the air, but smoke no longer rose from where the crucifix touched Casey's skin.

"For thine is the kingdom," we said, "and the power, and the glory, forever and ever."

Casey ceased to struggle.

"Amen," we finished.

In the silence that followed I was sure we had killed the boy. In exorcizing the demon, we had accomplished the very thing the demon had promised to do—destroy its host.

As I knelt over Casey, my face at his lips and my hand over his heart, I thought of Liz, deprived of her only son. How could we ever tell her what happened? How could we possibly inform her of her son's death? There was no way to relay that sort of information to any parent, especially one as devoted as Liz. It would ruin her.

I heard a cough and jerked my head around, thinking the demon had somehow escaped from Casey's body and managed to ambush us. But I saw that Danny had crawled into the doorway and now leaned against the jamb, the bloody scar gleaming dully in what light filtered in through Casey's windows. Danny looked battered but strong enough to recover. Maybe he'd be able to help us break the news to Liz, I reflected. At least he was family.

I jolted as Casey's body twitched beneath me. I scrambled to retrieve my Bible, which I'd laid on the floor, but as I prepared to resume my battle against the demon, I discovered Casey's eyes were riveted on mine.

They were normal again. The boy watched me, his brown eyes wide with uncertainty.

I fear I smiled then, for I realized how I must look to the child. I was bloody, my clothes and hair wild and sweaty from a battle of which he likely had no recollection. All he knew was that I'd pinned him down, and he no doubt felt the pain from his various wounds.

Feeling strangely guilty, I climbed off him. He sat up on his elbows, made to scuttle away from me, then winced in pain. He clapped a hand over his chest, where the crucifix had burned him, and whimpered. I wanted to help him, but at that point I wasn't even sure he knew me. After all, the Father Crowder with whom he was familiar was a skinny but presentable young priest who greeted him with warmth and formality each Sunday morning at St. Matthew's. The man staring at him now resembled a deranged scarecrow.

Thankfully, Danny saved us both the embarrassment of an explanation. With a tenderness I admired, he gathered Casey into his arms, and with a nod in my direction, carried the young man out of the room. Toward his mother and sister, I assumed. Liz would get her son back. Smiling, I sat back and tried to restore my heart rate to something approximating normalcy.

A voice at my ear said, "Are you all right, son?"

I swiveled my head and gazed into Father Sutherland's solicitous face.

My smile shrank.

"We did it, Jason," he said. He squeezed my shoulder. "You did it."

"Don't touch me."

He frowned. "Jason, you've had a—"

"I know the truth," I said, pushing to my feet.

He only stared at me uncomprehendingly. Then he took a step toward the door.

"You're not leaving here," I said.

He turned, and his expression began to change. I fancied I discerned more than surprise there. I was sure I saw rage. And something infinitely cunning. "After all that's happened tonight, you would deign to question my honesty?"

"Show me what's under your floorboard. Right now. You and I and Danny will go to your house."

His eyes burned into mine. "I will do no such thing. How...*dare* you accuse me of such atrocities?"

"You hide it very well," I said. "No one would ever suspect a man your age of such prodigious physical strength."

He shook his head slowly, circling me now. "You ungrateful, *gullible* boy."

"I'm not a boy," I said. "Not anymore."

His hands knotted into fists. He brandished one at me, stepping closer. "I *made* you, Jason. Can't you see that? Just a quiet, backwards, neurotic child in seminary who'd never had a decent family—"

"That won't work, Sutherland."

"That's *Father* Sutherland, you impudent boy. You had nothing when I found you—"

"How did you choose them, Sutherland?"

"—brought you into my church, trained you. I was patient with you despite your awkwardness. I counseled you—"

"Were they girls you saw around town, or were they all connected to the church?"

"—and never asked a thing from you. Not a thing. I gave you money, told my superiors that you were improving. I helped you through your fear of women—"

"But you don't like women, do you, Sutherland? Just nubile girls."

"I did not kill those girls!" he shouted, his face inches from mine. "I've made mistakes, dammit, but that's the lot of every man!" His face was a deep crimson. Spittle flew from his lips. "How dare you believe the word of that fiend…that *monster* over the word of your mentor? Are you such a fool to be taken in?"

I shoved him.

He stumbled back several paces, likely because he wasn't expecting me to lash out. But when he regained his balance, he glared at me with an expression of blackest mockery. "So you've made your decision. You've chosen to side with evil."

"You're not leaving this room. My conscience won't allow it."

"To hell with your conscience!" he bellowed. Then a look of awe came over him. "Maybe you're the killer. Where were you the night of the first murder, Father?"

I took a step toward him, mindful of avoiding Bittner's motionless body. The huge man's brains lay on the floor like the pulpy remains of a beached jellyfish. Sutherland was near the foot of Casey's bed, and I had a fleeting moment of recollection, the first time Sutherland and I had approached the possessed boy. It seemed a lifetime ago.

"Nothing to say?" he asked, smiling bitterly. "Were you the one who tortured and raped those girls, Father Crowder?"

"You've blamed everyone but yourself," I said, edging closer. "Me, Bittner, Ron. Even Danny."

He shook his head wonderingly. "Fool."

"You were the reason we didn't take Casey to a hospital. You were the one who wouldn't touch him."

He exhaled loudly. "I've heard enough of this." And made to move past me.

I barred his way.

Nose to nose with me, he clenched his jaw. "Out of the way."

"Get back!" I thundered and pushed against him with all my might.

He flew backward, his legs tangling, and only saved himself from falling by clutching the footboard of Casey's bed. I advanced on him, thinking to subdue him and perhaps use Danny's handcuffs to prohibit his flight from the house.

But he surprised me by pivoting toward me and springing out of his crouch with a violent, right-fisted blow.

It caught me flush on the jaw, sent me spinning toward the interior wall.

Sutherland was on me before I could recover. He rained blows on me, grunting words like *betrayal* and *satanic* and *deceiver*, and though I soon grew numb to the bludgeoning of his hard fists, my alarm grew and grew. I knew a loss of consciousness could mean death. If Sutherland was the Sweet Sixteen Killer, that meant he was a seasoned murderer. If he'd tortured and executed those girls, why would he scruple to take the life of a man who could lead to his ruin? And what of Danny, Casey, and Carolyn? What of Liz? Would Sutherland trust them to believe his story—that he'd beaten me to death in self-defense—or would he silence them too and thus ensure his flight to safety in some faraway place?

Perhaps it was the thought of this, the image of Father Sutherland preaching before a new congregation somewhere else, that brought me back to myself, brought me back to the brutal onslaught taking place in that bedroom.

My fingers curled into fists. I timed Sutherland's blows. Just when he was about to clout me in the back of the head again, I rolled sideways and came up with my fists raised.

He was breathing heavily, but when he saw my boxing pose, his face broke into a caustic grin. "So you're still convinced, eh? Still think I'm the killer?" And he unleashed a haymaker at my face. Prepared as I judged myself to be, the blow nevertheless connected, and when it did, something within me changed. The scent of my own blood was suddenly intoxicating, a pleasing scent rather than a disquieting one. I palmed blood off my forehead. The sight of it on my fingers, black and oily in the gloom of the bedroom, incited me. I looked up at Sutherland.

Whatever he saw made him suck in air and retreat, his arms thrown up in a warding-off gesture.

I followed.

Apparently realizing he'd committed a tactical error, he pushed away from the window and lunged toward the door.

I caught him. Caught him and slammed him against the wall. The base of his skull crashed against the hard plaster, and he rebounded toward me.

I opened my jaws wide and bit him in the throat. He howled out an inarticulate cry and slapped at my ears. Ripping out a chunk of his flesh, I spat blood in his horrified face, set to throttling him, his head whipping forward and back like a road sign in a violent storm.

"Please!" he said in a choked whisper.

I balled a fist and hammered him in the face. He went flailing back against Casey's window, his head shattering a large pane and letting in the maelstrom that raged outside. As the wind began to swirl through the opening, a stronger need surged through me. Sutherland would have killed me, I realized, had I not fought back. The others in the house weren't coming to my aid. Only one of us would leave the bedroom alive.

Grinning, I lifted Sutherland off his feet and smashed his upper body against the damaged window. This time the whole thing gave way. The room churned with icy wind and stinging rain. Sutherland was pleading with me now, and I reflected grimly that he'd at last taken refuge in the ideas he'd so hypocritically espoused in his years as a priest. He begged for mercy, for forgiveness, for one more chance.

Snarling, I cast him out of the window.

I stumbled forward onto the jagged aperture, glimpsed Sutherland's form plummeting toward the Hartmans' concrete patio. The priest landed face-first, his skull shattering on the unforgiving surface, a plume of blood spouting from his mouth like vomit. His broken body lay unmoving, the rains washing his blood away like a remorseless tide.

I gazed at Sutherland's shattered body for perhaps a minute. Then I turned and discovered Danny Hartman watching me from the doorway.

CHAPTER ELEVEN

Danny stood there blinking at me. The wind rocketing from the west conjured fierce eddies in the bedroom, worrying Danny's already disheveled hair and pelting both of us with a fine spray of rain. In the scant bluish light, he looked like a kid just out of high school, not a battle-scarred veteran police officer. But if the light had been better in the bedroom, I suspected he'd look far older than his forty-one years.

I eyed the gun in his holster. I couldn't help it.

"I don't figure you'll take me at my word," I said.

Danny was quiet so long I thought he wasn't going to answer. Or was going to train the gun on me. Had he done that, I'm not sure how I would have responded. I likely wouldn't have. After killing one man—a man who'd been a father figure to me, after all—my taste for conflict had pretty well evaporated.

But Danny didn't do that.

"Tell me why," he said.

I glanced at the shattered remains of the window. "He knew too much."

"About the dead girls?"

I nodded.

Danny reached up, touched the bloody swath gouged in his forehead, then regarded his wet fingertips. He didn't look like he was in any condition to pull a gun on me, but so great was my guilt at that moment that part of me felt I deserved a bullet.

At length, he said, "Let's get Casey and the girls."

I took a step toward him, then hurried to his side as he lost his balance. I grasped Danny around the shoulders, supporting him until he regained his equilibrium.

"Thanks, Father," he said, slowly straightening.

"Listen, Danny," I began, "if you need to take me in, I won't—"

"You're no killer," he said. "I wouldn't have thought it of Father Sutherland, but I started to wonder earlier."

"Earlier?"

Danny frowned. "I don't know. He was just so emphatic about not going to the police...not calling a doctor...I wondered why he'd be so afraid to bring others into this."

I had shared the same concerns, of course, and was about to say so when a voice from the corridor startled us.

"You guys okay?"

Danny and I both looked up and saw Casey standing in the doorway, an arm wrapped protectively around his little sister's shoulders. Other than a couple scrapes and bruises, he looked much as he always had—a healthy, guileless fourteen-year-old boy.

Liz appeared behind him and looked at me with apprehension. I realized with a start that I hadn't cleaned my face after my battle with Sutherland. Turning away, I used my robe to mop some of the blood away.

Danny said to Liz, "Father Sutherland didn't make it."

I heard Liz's sharp intake of breath and knew this was the moment of decision. Would Danny consign me to a life in prison? Illinois no longer executed those convicted of murder, but the prospect of living out my days in a cell did not excite me.

"Where is he?" a small voice asked. Carolyn, I realized.

I faced the others, ready to tell them the truth and have them condemn me, but Danny said quickly, "He jumped out the window."

Liz covered her mouth.

"Why?" Casey asked, looking like he might cry.

"It's not your fault," Danny said. "That's the important thing. Whatever reasons Father Sutherland had for doing what he did are between him and God."

And me, I thought. *His executioner.*

Danny put a hand on Casey's shoulder. "You okay?"

Casey nodded, but he looked troubled. For a moment I forgot all about Father Sutherland and my new existence as a priest killer. I wondered what kind of memories Casey retained from his nightmarish ordeal. None, I prayed.

"Can we go?" Carolyn asked.

Danny chuckled, ruffled Carolyn's hair. "You got your mother's brains, you know it, kiddo?"

And for the first time that night, I saw the girl smile.

◆ ◆ ◆

The lights came on less than a minute later.

We had made our way out of the bedroom, moving with the uneasy silence of war-weary refugees, and had turned away from the ruined staircase in the hopes that the rear staircase was still intact.

Ron was in the bathroom, sobbing. I thought at first Danny would pass by the closed door, so it surprised me when he stopped and called, "Ronnie."

No answer.

I had an arm around Casey's shoulder. Liz was beside us, Carolyn clutched protectively to her side.

"Ronnie," Danny said with more force. "Open the damned door."

Ron continued to sob.

Danny tried the knob, but found it locked. Without hesitating, he brought up a foot and slammed it sideways into the door. The heavy door banged open, a bit of the frame splintering.

Ron glanced up at us. He looked seventy years old. There were bloody cotton balls jammed in both nostrils.

"I didn't know Bittner would try to kill him, Danny, I swear it."

"How'd you get him out of the cruiser?"

Ron's mouth worked weakly—mentally fumbling for some sort of lie, I was sure. Evidently unable to think of one, he said, "I used a rock."

"Bet you had to hit the window a few times."

Ron didn't answer.

Danny nodded. "So you'd rather turn that mad dog loose on your son than risk anyone finding out about your other family. The money you took from your clients."

Ron muttered something unintelligible.

Danny crossed his arms. "I always knew you cared too much about money, Ronnie, but I never thought you'd do the things you've done."

Ron hung his head lower, his fingers threading through his thick, greasy hair.

Danny went on. "Say Bittner did shoot Casey. What then? We still would've known about your thieving. I would've known. Father Crowder here would've known."

Ron regarded his little brother with a look that I found chilling, even after all I'd witnessed that night. "I didn't think that far ahead. Maybe Bittner would have killed you

146

guys too. Maybe one of you guys kills Bittner, and nobody remembers what was said about my business dealings."

Danny tapped his own chest. "*I* would've remembered."

Ron shrugged. "Maybe I could've bought you off." Ron nodded at me. "The Father here too. I notice he's not above coveting another man's wife. Maybe he's as enchanted by money as he is by a nice set of tits."

"Father Crowder's worth a hundred of you, Ronnie."

"Says the man who showed up tonight with a homicidal partner."

"That's right," Danny said. "And now he's dead, thanks to you."

Ron's voice rose an octave. "*You're* the one who brought him here. He was your partner; why didn't you keep control of him?"

"I did," Danny said. "I locked him in the back of the cruiser, remember?"

Ron buried his face in his hands. "Casey would've told; I know he would've. He was that kind of boy. Always black-and-white, no gray."

I had held my tongue up until that point but could hold it no longer. Making sure to keep Casey out of Ron's view, I said, "You're a wretched excuse for a father."

"Go to hell," Ron answered. "I didn't want him to die... I'm just saying a kid like that doesn't realize the pressures... keeping up a lifestyle..."

"Two lifestyles," Liz said from behind me.

Ron glanced in her direction. "Oh my God... Honey..."

Liz's expression remained impassive. "You selfish bastard."

"You're where he gets it," Ron said, an edge to his voice. "You're the reason he never listened to me..."

At that point, Casey limped into the bathroom.

Ron gawked at him. His expression would have been comical if the situation hadn't been so ghastly. "Casey! You're okay!" He rose unsteadily, his arms outstretched to embrace the boy.

Casey said something I didn't catch. Ron didn't either, judging from the look on his face.

Danny put a gentle hand on the boy's shoulder. "Case, you don't have to—"

"I remember everything," Casey said to his father. "I *saw* everything you've done...when it touched you."

Ron stared at his son, thunderstruck.

Without another word, Casey turned away and left his father standing there, still apparently hoping for a hug.

I thought Danny would slug Ron in the face then, or perhaps slap the cuffs on him for his white-collar crimes. But, instead, he said, "You can put your arms down now," and left the room.

CHAPTER TWELVE

The back staircase hadn't fallen. The demon either hadn't worried about our escaping that way or hadn't thought of it. At any rate, we made it to the first floor without issue. As we crept through the back hallway, through the kitchen and into the ruined foyer, I kept expecting some new menace to leap out at us. And why not? The whole night had been like a horror movie, and it was still pitch black outside. Navigating the wreckage of the staircase made me wish we'd gone out the rear of the house, but after a few uneasy moments we reached the front door.

A glance at the grandfather clock told me it was only three thirty in the morning, which didn't seem possible. The others' faces showed the same strain I assumed showed on mine. Casey and Carolyn had dark circles under their eyes. Danny looked more than ever like he could use a drink.

Liz still looked radiant.

Ron came scurrying out of the darkness behind us and said, "What, you're just gonna leave me here?"

No one answered him. Casey, I noticed, didn't even spare his father a glance.

Danny glanced at Liz. "You got somewhere you can go for a little while?"

"The Tomlinsons," she said. "They live up the road. Sarah's my best friend. She'll let us stay without asking questions."

Carolyn tugged at her mom's arm. "Can I sleep in Anna's room?"

Liz smiled. "I'm sure it'll be fine."

Ron said, "Should we pack some stuff?"

Liz's eyes swung up and came to rest on her husband's. "You're never going near these children again."

Ron's lips moved soundlessly. He hesitated, then made to put a hand on her shoulder.

Liz said, "And if you touch me, I'll have Danny arrest you."

Ron flinched. He cast an unbelieving glance at Danny, who said, "It's true, Ronnie. You don't deserve these three, not after the stuff we found out tonight."

Ron shook his head, put his hands on his hips. "So that's it, huh? Some crazy spirit says a bunch of shit about me and you all believe it. I'm guilty without even giving my side of the story."

"That's right," Liz said. "You're guilty, and you're a revolting excuse for a human being."

I resisted an urge to kiss her.

As we made our way out onto the covered porch, Ron said, "Hold on a second... Where the hell am I supposed to go?"

"How about your other wife's place?" Liz said. "I'm sure she'd love to have you."

The door closed, leaving Ron gape-mouthed in the foyer.

On the porch I glanced at Liz's lacerated forehead. "Those need stitching up."

"It's shallow," Liz said. "You're the one who needs a doctor."

I nodded down at my missing fingers. "I guess I'll never be a concert pianist."

"I'll take you to the hospital," Liz said.

"I'm okay to drive," Danny said.

"Okay to drive *safely?*" Liz asked.

Danny smiled wanly. "The Father and I'll go to the hospital once we get you guys somewhere safe, okay?"

Liz tilted her head. "Still trying to prove how tough you are, Danny?"

Danny chuckled, nodded at the kids. "I'll get 'em into the cruiser," he said, and hustled Casey and Carolyn toward the police car. "Back window's busted," Danny muttered, "so you two'll have to pile in the front."

"We get to sit with you?" Casey asked.

Danny opened the passenger's door for them, and they climbed in.

Leaving me with Liz on the porch.

"I'll let you sit on the side with the window," I said. I took off my robe and folded it. "You can put this under you in case there's any glass."

She smiled. "What about you?"

"I'm already so banged up a few more cuts won't make a difference."

She chewed her lower lip and touched my jaw, which was puffy from Father Sutherland's hard-fisted blows. Her hand lingered against my chin. She seemed to debate with herself a moment. "Jason... I want to—"

"You don't have to thank me for anything."

She gave me a wry smile, cute dimples forming in her cheeks. "That's not what I was going to say."

I closed my mouth, chastened.

"What I was *going* to say," she went on, "is how much I'd like to see you again." She swallowed. "I mean, in more than a professional capacity."

"I know what you meant."

She smiled again, and despite the fact that her husband might very well still be in the foyer and only separated from us by a wooden door and about eight feet of space, I felt a powerful urge to take her into my arms.

But I didn't, and this time my resistance had nothing to do with fear of women.

I said, "There might be a time when we can see each other."

She looked crestfallen. "But not now?"

"There are things that must be done."

She searched my face. "What kind of things?"

"It's better if I don't tell you. Not yet, at least."

She didn't seem satisfied, but she said, "All right, Jason. But when you finish with these—"

"You'll be the first person I call."

She watched me a moment longer. Then, I put an arm around her, and together we walked through the moonless night to Danny's police car.

◆ ◆ ◆

After dropping Liz and the kids off at the Tomlinsons, Danny drove us to the hospital. We rode mostly in silence, though occasionally Danny would remark on how the storm seemed to be letting up.

On the way to Saint Joseph Hospital, Danny and I got our stories straight. We kept it as simple as possible, deciding that we should tell the truth about the demon possessing Casey, about Bittner committing suicide. We'd claim that Sutherland killed himself after attacking me. The damage to my face certainly bore the tale out. Danny got out his cell phone, which unsurprisingly was working again, and called Liz. He told her our version, and she agreed to tell the same one. Since Ron hadn't been in the room with me and Sutherland, there was no need to let him in on the deceit. Anyway, I doubted Liz would call Ron even if we wanted her to.

Everything settled, Danny radioed in to the precinct, and we went inside the hospital.

◆ ◆ ◆

We were both discharged in the early afternoon. Despite the pain medication I was given, my hand was a shrieking holocaust, and my face ached nearly as badly. Danny had received stitches in half a dozen places, but though it was difficult for him to sit upright, he still managed to drive me home.

The story we'd told had been met at first with incredulity. But after a team had been dispatched to the Hartmans' home and the place had been examined, even the most skeptical investigators had to concede that our story was consistent with the state of the place. It was difficult to argue with the crumbled staircase.

Though I'd never been a believable liar, I felt I acquitted myself well. Of course, having Danny to corroborate my story helped a great deal. Many of his fellow officers acted almost apologetic as they asked him questions.

So it was at two o'clock that we headed back to the rectory. Neither of us said much on the way there, though Danny kept eyeing my heavily bandaged hand grimly.

He pulled up to the cottage and slid the cruiser into Park.

"I wanna thank you for all your help, Father."

I sighed. "I'm afraid we did more harm than good."

"You don't mean that. If it weren't for you, Casey would still have that thing in him."

I cocked an eyebrow. "And Liz wouldn't know about her husband's other family."

"Hey, man, you screw around on your wife, she's bound to find out."

"Liz deserves someone better," I said.

"That she does, Father. That she does."

We sat in companionable silence for a moment before he said, "You realize it isn't done."

I nodded, thinking about the deaths of Jack Bittner and Peter Sutherland. I had no idea if Danny's story about the priest would float, nor did I have the slightest clue what Danny would say about his partner. I knew he wouldn't want to incriminate Casey, but what else could explain the man's abrupt decision to blow his own brains out? I supposed we could claim that Bittner and Sutherland had made a suicide pact. Or were merely playing a high stakes game of truth or dare.

"What are you smiling about?" he asked.

I realized I had been smiling and briskly sobered.

He seemed to hesitate. "How much time do you need?"

I frowned at him, unsure of his meaning.

"Father Sutherland's," he explained. "We need to check his study."

I swallowed, but cringed when I felt how raw my throat was from all the shouting I'd done in Casey's bedroom.

But Danny was not to be put off. "If it's Sutherland, we need to tell my bosses. If it isn't... well, I suppose the investigation goes on."

"Do you think he's the killer?"

"You mean *was*," Danny said. He slouched in his seat, peered out the side window. "I don't want him to be the one, but at the same time, I do, you know? I mean, if he's the one who did all those terrible things to those kids...then that means it's over. It means you ended it. You did the dirty work. Stuff like that isn't pretty, but somebody's got to be willing to do it."

For some reason those words frightened me deeply. I didn't like to think about what I'd done to Peter Sutherland. I was already second-guessing myself, sure I'd made a mistake. Somehow the prospect of searching Sutherland's house was scarier than not searching. If we left it alone, I'd never know if I'd slain an innocent man. And if it had been Sutherland doing the killings, the city would soon realize the reign of terror had ended, and I could gradually return to a semi-normal life.

"Father?" Danny asked.

I met his gaze with difficulty, and after a time, I nodded. He was right, of course. We had to know. It was the only way.

Evidently satisfied by what he read in my face, he nodded.

"An hour," he said. "Get cleaned up, and I'll come back to get you then."

"An hour," I agreed.

I went inside already feeling like a condemned man.

CHAPTER THIRTEEN

I had been inside Father Sutherland's stately brick Queen Anne home perhaps a hundred times over the past decade, yet somehow the atmosphere within its aged walls already seemed different. As though the house itself understood that an irrevocable change had taken place and that its owner would not be returning. I was skittish on the way to Sutherland's study, and that sense of foreboding grew as we opened the door and switched on his desk lamp.

Danny fingered the bandage covering the gash in his forehead. Blood had already soaked through the white bandage. "You sure this is the room?"

"I'm not sure of anything," I said. I suddenly felt absurd, like a hapless gumshoe on some old television mystery show.

Danny eyed me in silence as I walked around, studying the familiar objects on Sutherland's shelves. I saw his hymnal, several books examining the dual nature of Christ. It was one of Sutherland's primary interests. I continued through the study, glancing at several pictures of the priest with important members of the clergy and various foreign dignitaries. There was a snapshot of Sutherland shaking my hand on the day I was appointed to my post at St. Matthew's. Looking at the faded picture, I felt a pang deep in my chest. I crossed the room, as if to escape the image, and as I did, the floor creaked.

I froze. Danny was staring down at my feet. He moved closer, placed a foot on the same board on which I stood and tested it with the toe of a sneaker. The board wiggled perceptibly. I stepped away from it and watched with apprehension as he produced a pocketknife, knelt and used it as a pry. Though the plank was thick and long, it took very little to unseat it. Very much as though someone had been removing the plank and replacing it on a regular basis for a good while.

I watched in speechless dread as Danny levered up the board.

We both gazed at what was inside.

I'm afraid I began to weep.

There were no souvenirs from six dead girls in the two-inch deep space beneath the floorboard. There weren't trinkets of any kind.

Just a pair of girly magazines—a recent *Penthouse* and a very old *Hustler*.

These, I realized, were Father Sutherland's great sins. For these petty crimes I had sentenced him to death. My mentor. My best friend.

Danny was watching me with sympathy. "Maybe there are...you know, other hiding places. It's a big house."

I nodded, but I knew before we resumed our search that we would find nothing. At least nothing to incriminate Peter Sutherland in the Sweet Sixteen murders. I had been deceived. The demon had used me to affect its revenge on the best man I'd ever known, the man whose love and faith made me what I was.

We scoured the house for more than two hours, and when we came together at the base of the staircase, Danny removed his hat and said, "I'm sorry, Father Crowder. I can't seem to find anything."

I shook my head. "There's nothing to find."

The silence drew out.

Into it I asked, "Will you arrest me?"

Danny compressed his lips. There were tears streaming down my cheeks, but I was very much in control of myself. Mine were silent, passionless tears. Danny lowered his eyes, perhaps in embarrassment.

"I won't resist," I said, offering up my wrists.

Danny's voice was gruff. "Put your hands down, Father."

"I've committed the worst sin imaginable. I took a good man's life."

"You didn't do it out of cruelty," Danny said. "You thought it was the right thing. And you saved Casey."

"That doesn't excuse—"

"You know what you did," Danny interrupted. "You know, and you'll have to live with that. I can see how it's weighing on you. I think Father Sutherland would have forgiven you."

Somehow, this made me feel even worse. The wet heat in my throat was unbearable.

Danny put his hat on. "There's been enough horror already. Our church will need you to help us through this. And there's still a killer out there. People will need you to help them keep the faith."

I knew there was truth in what he was saying, but I also knew he was letting me off too easily. Danny wouldn't meet my bleary eyes, but I could see he was choked up too, already mourning Father Sutherland and Jack Bittner. Even after everything that had happened, I was amazed at man's capacity for good. For forgiveness.

"Come on," he said, nodding toward the door. "Let's get out of here."

It was while we were leaving the dead priest's house that the idea first occurred to me. We were on the front porch, and though the yellow daffodils and white hyacinths had started to bloom in Sutherland's front beds, and the pink blossoms of the magnolia trees hung over the porch like grieving loved ones, there was a chill in the air that day, and while we'd been inside the house, an unbroken caul of clouds had smothered the pink light of dusk.

I locked the door with the key Sutherland concealed beneath a statue of Saint Francis in his backyard. Danny moved down the porch steps slowly, as if burdened by the weight of our shared secret.

But I stood on the top step, frowning.

Danny stopped and looked up at me. "Something wrong, Father Crowder?"

"I was just thinking of something you said to me last night."

Danny smiled his boyish smile. "Never assume anything about people?"

I looked at him, the corrosive taste of bile searing the back of my throat. "That's not it. It was something you said after I killed Father Sutherland."

Danny glanced uneasily up and down the sidewalk, scratched the nape of his neck. Coming up the steps, he said, "You might wanna keep it down, Father. I know why you did what you did, but others might not feel the same."

"When I murdered him, you didn't seem bothered by it. You acted like it was the right thing to do."

Danny shook his head. "It was, given what you knew about him."

I stared deep into his brown eyes, my thoughts racing. "But you weren't in the room when Casey said most of those things. How could you know about that stuff?"

Something guarded came into Danny's face, but he shrugged, glanced down at a couple strolling slowly past Sutherland's black wrought-iron gate. "Maybe I had my suspicions too, you know?"

I felt short of breath. "You were raised in the same part of Greece as your brother."

"So?"

"You would've spoken the language too."

"Of course I did," he said, laughing a little. "It was like a badge of honor for my mother's family. Doing our part to keep tradition alive, you know? We all spoke it. Jesus, Father, what are you trying to imply?"

"Sutherland said the killer spoke that language."

"Sutherland knows everything about everybody in the church," Danny countered. "You ever think of that? Maybe he was trying to fool you. Frame Ronnie or me."

"'Sometimes you gotta be willing to do a little dirty work.' That's what you said."

"What of it?"

"You were glad when I got rid of Father Sutherland."

Danny's smile was gone. "You must think I'm a hell of a bad person, wanting a good man like Peter Sutherland dead. And here I thought you appreciated my keeping quiet about what you did."

"Is that a threat, Danny?"

"It's Officer Hartman from now on, and, yeah, if you wanna take it that way, sure."

"You've got the physical strength," I said. "You were the one person Casey didn't touch."

"Christ," Danny muttered. "You're just like Bittner. You realize there are damned near *three million people* in Chicago? What are the odds of you finding the killer when the best detectives in the city can't?"

"Why put me through this whole charade? Searching Sutherland's house when you knew we wouldn't find anything?"

"You're delusional."

"And you were staying in the same house with Casey when the demon invaded him."

"What does that have to do—"

"Sutherland said demonic possession could occur as a result of some terrible sin by a family member. You're Casey's uncle, his godfather."

"So now you're blaming me for Casey too?"

"But why not get rid of me in Sutherland's house?" I asked. "Did you think I wouldn't figure things out?"

A change came over him. His eyes became hooded and absolutely cold. "Maybe I should do something about it now, huh?"

"But I'm not a girl," I said. "And I'm a lot older than sixteen."

His lips bunched together, trembling with what might have been rage. Then, as if dismissing me, he turned and stalked down the porch steps.

He was almost to the gate when I called, "Is that how old she was, Danny? The girl who broke your heart?"

He froze, his hand outstretched for the gate lock. For a time he stood there, motionless, and I took note of how broad his back was, how muscular.

He looked back at me then, and when he did, I suppressed a gasp of shock.

Gone was the affable policeman I'd known for so many years. Gone was the man who'd stood shoulder to shoulder with me in a battle against blackest evil.

In its place was a face so malign, so shot through with wickedness and depravity, that it took all I had not to faint at the sight of it.

Danny Hartman grinned a grin no less sinister than the demon's had been on Rosemary Road, grinned at me and said, "We all have our secrets, Father. I'll keep yours if you keep mine."

Turning away, he opened the gate and strode down the sidewalk as though he didn't have a care in the world.

AFTER

The next day the city was rocked by news of the seventh murder, the Sweet Sixteen Killer returning with a furious vengeance and his most sadistic atrocity yet. The victim was a black girl named Makayla Howell. She was, of course, sixteen.

Makayla had been a model student up until her sophomore year in high school, during which it seems she began spending time with the wrong sort of people. She'd taken to defying her parents and dating boys several years older than she was. It was one of these boys who'd gotten her drunk, attempted to take advantage of her, and when Makayla denied him, he kicked her out and forced her to walk home from his apartment.

Someone—authorities have no idea who—offered her a ride. For reasons inexplicable to the police and to her brokenhearted parents, Makayla accepted. The murderer had then driven her to a secluded park, somehow gotten her out of the car and then...done things to her.

The newspapers did not divulge all of the details, but the following facts appear to be true:

Makayla was tortured.

Makayla was raped.

Makayla was still alive when the killer began cutting on her.

Makayla was eviscerated in a way that recalled the worst of Jack the Ripper's crimes.

And after Makayla finally expired from her wounds, the Sweet Sixteen Killer raped her again.

◆ ◆ ◆

Officer Hartman is planning on framing me for this most recent killing. Perhaps for all the killings. I'm already a chief suspect in the deaths of Bittner and Sutherland, despite what Liz and her kids have said on my behalf. Maybe Danny means to link Father Sutherland to the earlier crimes and me to Makayla Howell's death. Maybe he has something in store for me even more horrific than the seven murders he has already committed.

But there is something Danny Hartman doesn't know. A secret that changes everything.

You see, there is something inside me. Something more intelligent, more bloodthirsty and infinitely more powerful than a thousand Danny Hartmans.

The most important question was one that neither Danny nor Liz nor her soon-to-be ex-husband Ron bothered to ask. A question more important than fallen priests and cheating husbands and homicidal cops.

It is the question of where the demon went after it was driven from Casey's body.

◆ ◆ ◆

And now I must conclude my narrative. I have much work to do. It is grueling, at times, maintaining control of my actions. It is even harder to master my thoughts. Last night I awoke at the bathroom mirror with a razor blade pinched between my thumb and forefinger. I had been about to slash my own throat.

I shall take pains to remove all lethal objects from my cottage at the rectory. Or place them where I cannot access them when my defenses are weak. My mind is teeming with impure thoughts, ideas that make me shudder. Images that make me grow pale.

Yet I am still in control.

And that is why the thing inside me wants me dead. It needs another host, one without such tremendous willpower, without my discipline.

But it will not usurp me. I am not a fourteen-year-old boy. I am a man on the brink of a new life, a man of faith. I plan on using my unique knowledge of evil to wage war on the powers of darkness.

According to one source, there are over a thousand exorcisms performed each year in the United States. A great many of these are conducted in error, cases in which medicine or a trained psychiatrist would be more effective.

Yet even if a fraction of these cases—say a tenth—are authentic, who better to do battle with these malevolent spirits than a priest who has thwarted one already? A man who has so overmastered the offending demon that he can bend it to do his will?

I aim to end the Sweet Sixteen Killer's reign of terror.

Danny Hartman will be coming to my cottage tonight. I've invited him.

He was pleasant enough on the phone, but I know what's in his mind.

But Danny has no idea what's in store for him. He has no idea what I'm capable of when I unleash the presence inside me.

And after Chicago learns of how a shy, boyish-looking priest brought to justice the most vicious serial killer in the city's history, they will revere me and accord me the respect I deserve. And during the warming light of day, I will gladly play the figurehead. I will lead my church. I will be a pillar of the community.

But at night, I shall sate the presence that dwells within my flesh. I shall use its unspeakable powers for good. I will only permit it to prey upon those who deserve its wrath.

The hour is growing late, and I must prepare. The presence within me is restless. Ravenous. And though it is difficult, I must maintain control of these urges. I must bide my time until Danny arrives. I will await his coming.

Await him in darkness.

EXORCIST FALLS

JONATHAN JANZ

DEDICATION

This novel is for my daughter Juliet. You've been with us for nine years, and I can honestly say that you've made every one of those days brighter and happier. You constantly look on the bright side of even the darkest of events. Your loving heart brings warmth and kindness to a world that so desperately needs both. I am honored to be your dad, and I consider every moment we spend together a blessing. I love you, Juliet, and I'm so proud of the amazing person you are.

"There it lies, I think, Damien… possession; not in wars, as some tend to believe; not so much in extraordinary interventions such as here…this girl…this poor child. No, I tend to see possession most often in the little things, Damien: in the senseless, petty spites and misunderstandings; the cruel and cutting word that leaps unbidden to the tongue between friends. Between lovers. Between husbands and wives. Enough of these and we have no need of Satan to manage our wars; these we manage for ourselves… for ourselves."

~ *The Exorcist*, William Peter Blatty

BEFORE

My name is Jason Crowder.

Until recently there was a *Father* before my name, and though I haven't been stripped of my title, it's only a matter of time before I am. Never before did I comprehend the depths to which Man could fall, nor did I grasp how precipitous his descent could be.

But fall I have.

Every good thing I once possessed is lost or in mortal danger. And though it is base selfishness on my part, I can't help but gaze with dread into my own abyss, an encroaching danger exceeding the flesh, a peril far bleaker than mortal harm.

I fear my soul is damned.

What's worse, I fear damnation is the only fate befitting my actions, actions I would have perceived as unfathomable only a couple nights ago.

My God, has it only been two nights?

Two nights since a kindly cop named Danny Hartman materialized at my rectory cottage from the stormswept April darkness? Two nights since I encountered an evil so monstrous I quail at the memory? Since Father Sutherland and I triumphed over the demon inhabiting Casey Hartman? Or believed we triumphed?

Has it been two nights since I committed murder?

I should have ended my life then! To cold-bloodedly rid the world of a man like Peter Sutherland, to thrust his screaming body through a third-story window into the howling, lightning-riddled night. To watch his body tumbling into darkness with a fiend's grin on my face, thinking in that moment only of the service I was providing mankind, foolishly believing I had expunged the scourge from our wonderful city.

But I didn't save Chicago from the Sweet Sixteen Killer.

Unwittingly, I emboldened him and tightened his grip on all of us by murdering a hero.

Yes, I believed the killer was Father Peter Sutherland.

But it was Danny Hartman after all. Danny Hartman who raped and tortured that poor girl. Makayla Howell. The seventh victim of the Sweet Sixteen Killer.

The killer who wore a policeman's blue.

The killer I invited to my cottage one terrible night.

PART ONE
THE SWEET SIXTEEN KILLER

CHAPTER ONE

My notion was to meet the murderer in darkness. The decision was not only a symbolic one—though I blush to admit there existed a strain of the poetic in my plan—but more importantly a strategic one. Despite Officer Hartman's unrelenting depravity, he was, after all, a man, and bound as such by human limitations. He relied on the same senses that all men rely on, and unless he wore night vision goggles, he would find himself at a disadvantage in the darkness.

Malephar, the demon inhabiting me, would suffer no such hindrances.

Yet despite my precautions, I soon realized the room in which I awaited Danny's coming was not that dark at all. Granted, it was murky enough to obscure my position on the couch from a distance of perhaps twenty feet, but for my plan to work, I would need to get much closer to Danny, and to do that I would need to cross several motes of light, traverse spills of moonglow that had managed to leak through the various blankets and towels I'd draped over the windows of my cottage. Even worse, I realized with incipient horror, once Danny's eyes adjusted to the semi-dark room the way mine had, he would detect any movement and would have ample time to parry an attack.

Or to mount one of his own.

I sat shivering on my ratty brown secondhand sofa as memories of Danny and his behavior that night on Rosemary Road strobed through my head. The night Father

Sutherland and I had exorcised the demon Malephar from young Casey—and had unintentionally driven the fell presence into my own body—Danny had behaved as nobly as any storybook hero could.

More troublingly, he had exhibited incredible physical strength. If, I now realized, my hands atremble on my black-slacked knees, any aspect of my plan failed to unfold as I'd envisioned, Danny would simply wrap those long, tensile fingers around my throat and throttle me until my windpipe collapsed.

Or worse, he would torture me the way he'd tortured his innocent teenage victims.

The abrupt gunning of a car engine made me jump. Though the noise issued from blocks away, in the silence of the cottage it sounded like cannon fire. It came to me then how very quiet our humble campus was, how watchful and silent the rectory. It was spring and the sky was cloudless, yet there seemed to be no life at all in the fragrant April air, no birdsong or cricket's chirp. Upon opening my front door, as I had instructed Danny to do over the phone, would he immediately detect my breathing, which grew shallower and shallower? Worse still, would he smell the fear on me, like a cowardly miasma, from his position on the stoop?

My heart thundered as a new revelation crashed over me. When the front door swung inward, a pale column of moonlight would illumine the foyer and a section of the living room beyond, the room in which I sat waiting. How far would that hideous rectangle of light creep? Far enough to expose the fishing line I had strung across the walkway? Far enough to reveal the toes of my black shoes, the ones I'd repeatedly scuffed to dull their polished gleam?

If you truly had faith in your plan, a voice in my head whispered, *you wouldn't have bothered with the tripwire.*

That was correct, I knew, but my rising panic made it impossible to focus on anything, even my debilitating self-doubt.

I wore no watch, and in throwing the main power breaker in my fuse box, I had disabled the various digital clocks scattered throughout my living quarters. Yet I knew the hour of my momentous encounter was at hand, knew it as surely as I knew my plan hinged on a theory, a theory as volatile as the sinister being around which it revolved.

Since the demon had entered my body two nights before, since Malephar—if that was indeed its true identity—had burrowed into me like a chortling pestilence, I had succeeded in thwarting its attempts to govern me the way it had governed the teenager Casey Hartman, the way I was certain it had controlled innumerable human hosts in its accursed history.

Once, I had awakened to find myself at the bathroom mirror, a razor drifting toward the soft flesh of my throat. Even at that moment, with every molecule of my being hyper-aware and thrumming with fearful energy, I could feel the savage intelligence, like some towering medieval siege engine, battering at my brain in an attempt to topple my defenses and possess me utterly.

Yet how could I be certain that, when the appointed hour arrived, Malephar would seize control the way I needed him to? And once the demon had possessed me and had perpetrated the brutal atrocity he yearned to commit, how could I be certain I could regain control of my own body?

Earlier that day, when I first read about Makayla Howell and the manner in which the Sweet Sixteen Killer had sexually abused and ultimately eviscerated her young body, I resolved that the killer should suffer the same unspeakable depredations.

Yet now that the moment was upon me, my courage waned. There was a ghastly logic to it. The one instance in my life during which I'd exhibited bravery—the exorcism—had been promptly undone by my execution of an innocent man, and my punishment was a reversion to my former state of abject meekness, a state in which I now quivered as I waited for Danny to fling open my door.

But at that moment I realized I needn't have worried about the front door at all.

Because the stirring of a kitchen curtain behind me told me Danny was already inside my cottage.

I had forgotten to lock the windows.

CHAPTER TWO

I waited for Danny's gloating voice, my pinwheeling imagination even scripting words for him: *Nice place you got here, Father. Too bad it's about to get so messy*. In my mind Danny sounded like Marlon Brando in *On the Waterfront*, calling me *Fadda* even though his dialect was Chicago through-and-through.

Or perhaps Danny would address me in Tsakonian, that almost extinct language of his Greek childhood home, the language in which he'd not long ago made his confession to Father Peter Sutherland.

Oh, how I wished Father Sutherland were with me now!

He would be, a raspy voice spoke up, *if you hadn't ended his life, you puling sodomite*.

As horrid as these words were, they sent a surge of excitement through me, for the demon had been completely dormant since my phone call to Danny earlier that evening. Now, the foul intelligence had awakened, and that meant my plan might still work.

If Malephar would come forward when I needed him to.

I strained to listen for Danny's footfalls. A floorboard creaked from my left.

I sprang to my feet, painfully aware of how empty my hands were, how bereft of bludgeoning weapons my living room table was. There were books, a glass of orange juice I supposed I could smash and use to stab at Danny. But nothing else. Unless I could smother him with a couch cushion.

Come forth, Malephar, I commanded.

No answering voice sounded.

A flicker of light from the kitchen arrested my attention. The same curtain that had alerted me to my intruder moments ago, I now saw, was swaying slightly in the chill night breeze.

No, I thought. *Focus on the bedroom. It's accessible from the back hallway. Danny entered the kitchen, stole through the back hall, and is now lurking in your bedroom preparing his attack.*

Or perhaps, I thought, *he's waiting for me to attack him.* It was I, after all, who'd requested this meeting. And though my tone during our conversation had been amicable, Danny knew why I had called. He knew I wanted to kill him. Just as he wanted to kill me.

So do it, I told myself. *You don't need the demon for that. This is your turf. You know this cottage better than he does. Use the darkness. Sneak into the kitchen, find a weapon, surprise him—*

"Hey, Father," a voice said at my ear. I whirled, gasping, and saw something glint in the shadows, something at the level of my abdomen. I went stumbling backward and was only prevented from falling by the living room wall. I became aware of a dull heat in my belly, but it wasn't until I pressed a hand to my midsection that I realized I'd been wounded.

Wounded grievously.

My palm was slimed with blood, my black sweatshirt split horizontally in a foot-long swath across the navel. I realized with numb shock that something was bulging out of my stomach. I tried to cram my entrails back inside my belly, but Danny was hurtling toward me, his bloody carving knife flashing in the gloom. He thrust a forearm under my chin, cracked my head against the wall, and flicked the knife at my face. My nose became a blazing heat, a gushing wetness. Like a man suffering through his blackest nightmare, I let go of my bulging intestines and pawed at my nose, which was gone. Just a ragged hole through which blood and mucus popped and bubbled.

Too aghast to fight back, I stared into the eyes of the Sweet Sixteen Killer.

Danny's face was inches from mine, as close as a lover's. "How's that feel, Father? We understand each other better now? Or you wanna mock me some more, make fun of my prom date?"

This last barely registered. I remembered goading Danny the day before, speculating about why he'd chosen sixteen-year-old girls on which to unleash his monstrous fury, but this seemed a lifetime ago. And immaterial anyway. Because I was dying, my lifeblood gushing from my stomach. And the ragged hole where my nose used to be.

"What I don't get," Danny said, still speaking directly into my face, "is why you thought you'd get away with it." He shook his head. "I mean, I woulda killed you eventually, but I woulda let you live a few more days." He grinned crookedly. "It was sorta fun knowing someone was out there who knew what I was doing. Kind of like a thrill? You kill for a while, you start to get bored with it. You need something to make your dick hard again."

I opened my mouth to tell him what a ghoul he was, but the only thing that escaped was a phlegmy cough. I began to choke on my own blood.

He slammed me against the wall, bashing the base of my skull on the plaster. Waves of dizziness rolled through me, the dark living room pixelating, becoming a starry orange-and-black tapestry. My knees threatened to unhinge.

"Stay with me, Father," Danny urged. "We're not done yet."

I am, I thought dimly. *When a man has to clutch his small intestine the way he would a colostomy bag, he is most definitely done.*

Danny seized me by the upper arms, shook me so hard my neck rattled. I realized I'd been drifting into unconsciousness. Despite my fading state I marveled at how strong he was, how effortlessly he supported my body despite the fact that my muscles had turned to gelatin.

"*Look* at me, damn you," he snarled.

Blinking, I did. Though my vision was filmy, distorted, I saw his face well enough. He actually chuckled. "Jeez, Father, I'm sorry for the profanity. Even now I can't get used to cussing in front of a clergyman."

"Not... not part of the clergy anymore," I croaked.

The lopsided grin. "Hell, I know that. I was just trying to be nice to you in your last moments. You're no more a priest than I am."

Some vestige of anger kindled in me, some dying ember flaring brighter at his insults. I heaved my arms up—they felt a hundred pounds each—and slapped weakly at his torso.

His grin broadened. "Ahh... you gonna do something about it, Father? That's what I was counting on. Not this pussy behavior. I hoped you'd put up a decent fight."

Fight. The word reverberated through my brain. *Please fight him, Malephar.* But if the demon was cognizant of my plea, he gave no sign.

I began to slide down the wall.

"Whoops," Danny said, hauling me up with a grunt. "Thought I'd lost you there, Father. I didn't mean to cut you so deep, but it's this damned darkness. What'd you do, take out all the bulbs?"

He glanced about, as if the dormant lamps would answer him. "Like bein' in a cave," he muttered. He glanced at me, saw perhaps how my eyes were glazing, and something like pity permeated his glittering brown eyes. "Okay, Father, I'll let you relax a little. I can tell you're cooked anyway." He released me, and I found myself slumped on the floor. My vision was grayer than ever, but I still distinguished the outlines of his legs.

My stomach had begun to throb. I coughed again, and though the pain in my gut was extreme, it was the gaping hole in the middle of my face that ached the worst. I imagined how I must look, and a new species of terror surged through me, the black dread of disfigurement. Even though I was about to die, the thought of how repulsive I must appear filled me with a mind-numbing horror.

Danny crouched before me, perhaps catching something of my emotions. "Sorry, Father. Definitely a closed casket for you. I'll be sure to tell Liz how hideous you looked. Like fucking Lon Chaney. She'll be thankful she never kissed you."

In spite of all that was happening, this still shook me to the core. Tears of rage burned in my eyes. "Can't," I tried to say. "You can't—"

"I *will*," Danny said. In the dark living room, his white teeth shone like incandescent tombstones. "I *will* visit Liz and her kids one of these nights, and I'll carve them up so badly you'll hear their screams in hell."

I couldn't even shake my head in abnegation, couldn't summon the strength to plead for Liz's life, for the life of her children. Before that night on Rosemary Road, I never would have believed a man would murder his sister-in-law, his nephew, and niece. But now I believed anything. And I could see in Danny's eyes he meant what he was saying. He would slaughter them, and he'd exalt in their screams.

Yet my body would no longer respond. My lips wouldn't even form a plea.

Kill him, I begged Malephar. *Stop him before he can hurt Liz, before he can harm Casey or Carolyn.*

My left hand shot up, seized Danny's wrist.

"*Jesus!*" Danny hissed, and made to jerk away. But that other intelligence had finally taken hold of me—five minutes too late, I thought ruefully. It was my fault for relying on such ghastly forces for aid.

My hand, compelled by the demon, clamped tighter on Danny's wrist. Through the undersea roar of my own gushing blood, I heard the bones in Danny's wrist crack. His fingers jittered, splayed wide. The knife clanked to the floor.

My whole body was consumed in a billow of flame. My lips moved, but it wasn't my voice that spoke. "*Ambitious wretch!*" the terrible voice buzzed. "*You have grand designs, Daniel!*"

Danny was staring at me with wide-eyed terror, his free hand beating at my fingers, his legs scrabbling on the floor in a frenzy to escape.

"*You've got 'em all lined up!*" the demon crowed. "*Gonna rape some teenagers this week, aren't you!*"

Danny writhed to escape my iron clutch. "*Get... the... fuck... off me!*"

Faces flashed in my mind, but they were unfamiliar, detached from any context. The images churned and pirouetted and morphed into others even more nightmarish:

Danny plunging the knife not into my stomach but into some teenaged girl's. She had a small scar near her left eye, and she screamed as Danny gutted her, the blood splurting over his knuckles as he grinned his maniacal grin... Another girl, another setting, the room squalid but bright, Danny goring her on a meat hook as her head thrashed, Danny masturbating as she flailed about, the blood and sweat and saliva flicking from her face and hair... Another kid, this one wearing some sort of school uniform and styling her hair in a pair of insouciant pigtails, sauntering down the sidewalk and giggling with a pair of friends... The same girl, spread-eagled on the floor, a blood-freezing view of her ravaged stomach cavity, the skin flaps opened like a tropical flower, the glistening guts and viscera purple and Valentine's Day red... A smiling Liz Hartman, taking Danny's hand and thanking him for being such a help, Danny's eyes crawling down her creamy throat and lingering on her shadowed cleavage... Quick glimpses of Danny's niece and nephew, Casey and Carolyn, smiling up at their uncle... A girl begging for her life, face down, Danny mashing her cheek against the aged floorboards, tributaries of scarlet trickling over her skin as Danny bit into her ear... A yearbook photo of a girl with glasses and braces, a girl who'd be a knockout once her awkward stage was over... Danny leaning out the window, talking to a black girl, Makayla Howell, Danny's eyes lingering over the muscular cocoa-colored quadriceps showing beneath a too-tight pink skirt... Makayla wailing as Danny's knife ripped a ragged trough from her navel to her sternum... a dishwater blond girl with too much eye makeup staring back at Danny with a more than healthy interest... A hand clamping on Danny's shoulder...

...and then Danny was sucking in air and scrambling away from me, his eyes vast and starey in the dimness of the cottage. I realized Malephar had also receded, and with that came the knowledge that, just for a moment, the demon had controlled me the way I'd commanded him to. And wasn't that another example of man's hubris? To believe he could manipulate the sinister forces that ruled the night? I deserved this fate. Danny would go on killing and torturing innocent kids, while I would die unmourned. Liz might miss me, but she wouldn't for long. Because Danny would murder her too, would slaughter her and her children.

I realized Danny had gone. Whatever he'd glimpsed in my face when Malephar had seized his wrist had spooked him enough to leave without confirming my death. He probably figured it was a foregone conclusion, and surely he was right. I was dying, could not believe I still drew breath. But it was getting harder and harder now, my respiration gossamer-thin, the choking death rattle more pronounced. Within minutes, I estimated, my life would be over. If I had minutes.

The back door banged open. Footsteps scampered down the sidewalk. Danny was getting away. No one would connect him with my death, no one would link my murder to the Sweet Sixteen. He was free to kill again.

I had failed.

I attempted to lift my head, but it cost an effort. Soupy blood lapped over my lips in a molten rill, and when I coughed, plump droplets scattered into the darkness. My gauzy vision unfocused, focused, then went bleary again. I glanced at my outdated black wall phone in the hallway. If I could crawl the ten feet I might be able to dial 911 and summon help. But what good would it do with my lifeblood already so depleted? And besides, I didn't think there was any chance I could reach the phone. I could barely lift my head.

I lolled sideways onto the sodden, spongy carpet. My plan had been so childish. I had thought to trip Danny on the fishing line and leap onto his back. This way, I'd reasoned, I wouldn't have to see his face as Malephar tore him to shreds.

But Malephar, the traitorous fiend, had abandoned me. I coughed again, and torrid air seared my exposed nasal cavity. The pain in my ruined nose intensified; it felt like ropes of nettles were sawing the delicate bones apart, splintering bone, grinding the raw lumps of tissue into gleaming burgundy divots.

I jerked my chin up, realized I'd been under for a time. There was no question about crawling to the phone now. I could scarcely open my eyes. Yet I fought against my growing torpor, clinging not only to life, but toiling to escape the nightmare reel in my head, the images that had assailed me when Malephar had seized Danny's wrist. I couldn't bear those screaming girls, that maniacal rictus on Danny's face as he masturbated to their death throes. I saw him thumping someone's head on the floor, heard the meat hook puncturing a girl's lung...

...saw him leering at Liz.

"Malephar," I tried to say, but of course my vocal cords had shut down, that function forsaking me as surely as all the others. I opened my mouth again—

Speak, craven, Malephar answered.

193

I jolted where I lay in my congealing pool of blood. I realized I need not speak aloud for Malephar to hear me. The demon resided in my head.

Why did I see Liz when you touched Danny? Why did I see Casey and Carolyn?

Malephar's diabolical chortle echoed in my brain.

Tell me! I demanded.

A pause. Then, the demon's voice: *You know.*

The muscles of my forearms hardened despite my dying state. *He can't hurt them! He can't—*

He will and you know it, craven.

No!

He will slay Casey and Carolyn quickly. But Liz…

Stop

…with Liz, he'll take his time—

Please

—he'll gag her, bind her, cut on her—

You can't

—rape her, sodomize her, FLENSE her—

You have to stop him

STOP HIM? the demon asked, laughing. *We serve the same master. I sacrificed my host tonight so Daniel could continue his butchery.*

A formless notion flitted at the periphery of my mind. *You need me.*

A pause. *I need no one, craven. Least of all a cowering, mewling afterbirth like you.*

You need a host.

Another can be found, he answered. But was there a hint of apprehension in his voice? I thought there was.

How? I challenged. *You transfer by physical contact. When I'm dead, you won't be able to latch onto anyone.*

It is possible.

But not likely, is it? Then what? A deep grave and the stench of decay? The oppressive soil bearing down on you while the maggots feast on my flesh?

A long silence, then, *The waiting is necessary.*

What if you don't have to wait?

Something altered in Malephar's bearing, as incorporeal as he was. An increased interest shot through with a wicked cunning. *You have nothing to offer me*, Malephar declared.

I'll do anything, I said. *And you'll remain inside a living body.*

No answer this time, but I could tell he was thinking. A body-racking cough took hold of me, giving me the sensation my insides were being shredded again. My time was nearly over.

Just let them live, I begged.

Who? The whore and her spawn?

Even in my extremity, the words enraged me. *Liz Hartman and her two children.*

No answer. I couldn't feel my legs anymore, nor the slit in my stomach. It was as though a heavy burden had been placed on the hole where my nose had been, a weight that crushed my face downward, downward, choking off breath, filling me with a languid, equatorial heat. I labored for air, spewed more blood.

Fallen one, the demon said.

Dimly, I listened.

How fascinating, the voice mused, *that in your last moments, you never even prayed, never beseeched your God for aid.*

I scarcely noted the past tense in relation to my life, focused instead on my lack of faith, my telling disregard for the Savior's grace. Only two nights ago I had experienced the prodigious and very real power of God in my body, and now, when faced with my own mortal trial, I had failed to enlist His aid.

Never had I been so ashamed.

Malephar said, *I will allow you to carry on your pathetic existence with the following stipulations.*

I'm afraid I was weeping, not with relief, but with hollow despair. I was damned. Irredeemable. Even if I lived, my eternal soul would roast in hellfire. A contract with a demon?

You must do nothing to brook the mission of your nemesis, Malephar said.

Let Danny kill? I thought. More tinder for the flames.

You must allow me to sate my appetites when I see fit.

Damned, I thought, shaking with sobs. *Utterly damned.*

You must continue the pretense of your profession. You must lead Mass, offer false succor in the confessional, you must—

And what will you give me in return? I demanded.

Life, Malephar said.

That isn't enough, I answered. *My life is worth nothing now.*

A pregnant pause.

Then, *I will protect them.*

I froze, too hopeful to ask him to clarify.

Malephar said, *Liz Hartman and her children will remain safe from the Sweet Sixteen Killer.*

There was a lump clogging my throat.

And if I don't agree?

The voice was flat, emotionless as an insect's drone: *They will die before night falls again.*

CHAPTER THREE

I knew nothing for a time. Perhaps it was mere minutes before I regained consciousness. Perhaps it was an hour. Whatever the interval between the sealing of the satanic pact and my return to awareness, I found myself lying in my bathtub, the shower spray assaulting the upper regions of my body. The water was scalding, yet I hadn't the strength to resist its onslaught.

But I was able to move my limbs again. I grasped the edge of the tub, started to push myself to a sitting position.

Be still! Malephar commanded.

Can't... breathe, I protested. *The water's too hot, choking me...*

You saw me heal Casey, did you not?

Reluctantly, the memory of the exorcism arose, of Casey Hartman's knees imploding, the patellas popping from the titanic inner gravity Malephar had exerted on them. I remembered Casey's wrists reduced to raw hamburger by Malephar's relentless jerks and thrusts. One of Casey's hands had become a bloody snarl of bone and gristle, yet it and every other wound in Casey's body had mended, the lone exception being the brand of the cross on Casey's chest.

The cross I had wielded to drive the demon out.

At thought of Casey's miraculous healing I glanced down at my flayed stomach and was stunned to find the incision all but knitted. Here and there the edges of the wound had yet to meet, but even these portions had turned pink with new flesh.

Gasping, I thrust a hand to my face and nearly wept with joy to find my nose restored. I realized, too, I could breathe almost normally. There was still pain in my wounds, but it had dwindled to a manageable discomfort.

I swiveled my head away from the spray to better breathe, but the demon within me flared again. *My ministrations do not prevent infection. You must allow the cleansing.*

Taken aback by the demand, I turned my face to the burning spray, allowed it disinfect my facial wound.

Minutes later, when the shower had grown tepid, Malephar said, *It is done.*

I made to stand but was steamrolled by a wave of nausea. My guts, healing though they might be, howled in protest. My nose throbbed incessantly.

Feel the agony, craven. Wallow in it, drown in it, you imbiber of semen, you defiler of infants.

As revolting as these insults were, I almost welcomed them. The role of nurse didn't suit Malephar. The universe made far more sense when he was spewing filth.

It didn't occur to me until I stepped out of the bathtub that I had somehow disrobed. Dreading the vision that would greet me, I raised my face toward the vanity mirror, but rather than a mutilated hole, I discovered the same nose to which I was accustomed. Whether the demon had somehow reattached my old nose or generated a new one, I had no idea. Nor did I care. I was simply thankful to look like myself again.

I crept closer to the mirror and stood on tiptoes to inspect my stomach wound. The movement exacerbated the throb along my incision, but the gash itself had closed. The livid ridge of scar tissue felt rubbery to my fingertips, the flesh around it sensitive. That was to be expected, I thought. It wasn't every day that one was gutted by a serial killer and healed by a demon.

I held up my hand and stared in amazement. The fingers I'd lost the night of the exorcism had regenerated as well.

I feared I was losing my mind.

All at once I realized what I needed, the only restorative that would prevent a complete mental breakdown.

I wanted to see Liz.

I *needed* to see Liz.

Staring into the mirror, I set to work on the blond, bedraggled scarecrow I resembled and began the job of making myself presentable.

It wasn't until later that endless night that I gave another thought to the pact I had made with the demon.

Or the serial killer still loose in Chicago.

CHAPTER FOUR

My sense of propriety reminded me to park down the road from Liz's home. Though no one seemed to be stirring at this dead hour of night, I still feared one of my parishioners might spot my rusty Honda Civic in the driveway of the Hartmans' estate.

I approached the front door of Liz's enormous house on Rosemary Road with some trepidation. The fact that she and her kids had moved back into the site of the possession not forty-eight hours after Father Sutherland and I had ridded Casey of the demon was proof, I felt, not only of Liz's courage, but of her obstinance. She would be angry with me, I believed, not for disturbing her at such a late hour, but because I hadn't returned her calls all day. At the time I had viewed my silence as noble, as a protective measure between the demon inside me and Liz's family. Yet now, as I reached out to depress the glowing doorbell, I realized there had been cowardice in my uncommunicativeness as well. After triumphing over the demon in Casey's bedroom, I had wrongly believed myself cured of my lifelong phobia of women. Walking Liz out of her house that night, I had fancied myself a virile, capable man.

But now, staring down the prospect of encountering the woman who mattered more to me than anyone in the world, the woman for whom I'd already decided I would give up the priesthood, my confidence evaporated, leaving me as fearful as ever.

I rang the doorbell and awaited Liz's wrath. Too soon, the front porch lamp spilled its sallow light over me, and the door cracked open a couple inches, a chain preventing it from swinging wide.

"Ron?" a voice asked. "That better not be you."

I mustered a grin. "Uh-uh," I said. "It's the guy you don't have a restraining order against."

"Jason?"

"Sorry for showing up unannounced."

"Keep scaring me like this, and I might sic the cops on you too." The door closed, the chain scraping, then opened. "What's wrong?" she asked, ushering me inside. "It's three in the morning."

I entered, did my best not to notice the way her voluminous white robe hung open at the throat. "Did I wake the kids?"

"Who knows?" she said, shutting the door. "I doubt they've slept much since..." She let the thought die, her pretty face pinching at the brows.

"Liz..." I faltered, glanced at the door. "May I?"

She didn't protest as I refastened the sliding chain lock, twisted the deadbolt.

She cinched the throat of her robe together. Not out of modesty, I thought, but from a quickening of terror. "Jason, what's happening?"

I stood there mutely for several moments. In my frenzy to assure myself that Danny hadn't attacked Liz and her children, I'd neglected to concoct a suitable explanation for my visit. Now that I was faced with her panicked gaze, I found myself unable to construct a suitable fiction.

"I don't know why I drove over here," I admitted. "I guess I've been worried about you since the exorcism."

It was the wrong word to utter. I realized that immediately. She shot a glance toward the second story landing, a landing without a staircase. The stairs had been destroyed the night of the exorcism, and though the rubble had been cleared away by workmen, the stairway had not yet been rebuilt.

"You don't think the demon will return, do you?" she asked. "Please tell me Casey isn't in danger."

Deep in my brain, the demon chortled.

I shook my head, arranged my features in what I hoped was a reassuring look. "He's completely safe. There's nothing—"

"Then why are you here?" she demanded.

Because I'm in love with you? "I—" I gestured lamely toward the door—"...I was having a nightmare. It was your husband."

"*Ex*-husband."

Though the dissolution of their marriage wasn't official, I didn't correct her. "Ron was trying to get in. He didn't have a key anymore, not one that worked—"

"That's weird. I had the locks changed this afternoon."

"—but that didn't stop him. He..." I looked around, struggling to complete the lie. "...he got in through the kitchen window."

"That window's fifteen feet off the ground."

"It was a dream, Liz. Anyway, he got in and he—"

"Do I want to hear this?"

"No," I said, relieved. "But it was vivid enough to wake me up. I thought of calling you, but that didn't seem like enough. I had to see you, make sure you and the kids were okay."

She sighed. A miserable, listless sound. "Honestly, I've been fretting about the same thing. Ron isn't a violent man, but he's persistent. I could see him trying to break into the house." She laughed mirthlessly. "He bought it, after all. Probably thinks he's entitled to live here despite the shit he's put us through." She glanced up at me. "Sorry, Father."

I arched an eyebrow at her. "We're beyond the stage where you need to watch your language around me."

She searched my eyes. "Are we?"

The old nervousness geysered up from the pit of my stomach, my paralyzing fear of women. Particularly beautiful women like Liz. "Of course we are," I said, dry-mouthed.

She stared at me.

I attempted a deprecating laugh. "After all, you've seen me at my worst. I wouldn't think you'd still believe me worthy of being called Father."

Something new came into her face. A strength and a breath-stealing certitude. "I've seen what you're capable of." She held me with her gaze. "Father."

"Liz..."

"You were magnificent."

This should have buoyed my spirits. Yet faced with that unwavering belief, that naked admiration, I felt less worthy of praise than I ever had. If she only knew what madness slithered inside me. If she only knew the diabolical bargain I'd made.

Liz took my hand, her eyes holding mine. "Come to the kitchen," she said. "If we're going to be up this late, we're sure as hell going to have coffee."

She gave my hand a squeeze and headed down the hallway. I noticed the pleasing mounds of her buttocks shifting beneath the plush white robe.

Want to lick that ass, don't you, Father? Malephar whispered.

Jolting, I followed her into the kitchen.

◆ ◆ ◆

The coffee was rich and black, yet a chill still clung to me, an acidic restiveness that ate at my composure, made it impossible for me to relax in Liz's presence. I wanted to be confident. I wanted to be suave. I'd always wondered how other men did it, appeared to give no thought to how they were being perceived. Perhaps they *didn't* care, perhaps they were so secure in their masculinity that worrying about how women viewed them never crossed their minds.

But I worried. I always had. Without a father, not particularly loved by my mother, I'd always felt unformed, incomplete in some way. As if God had neglected to include all the ingredients when creating me, and then, as some dreadful cosmic joke, endowed me with an acute awareness of those deficits, those missing ingredients.

Liz was staring at me, and in her gaze I glimpsed admiration, attraction even. It was as though her soulful green eyes were distorting mirrors that flattered rather than insulted. *But what you see,* I wanted to say, *is an illusion. If you knew what was beneath this skin, you would look upon me with disdain. Or*—I thought of Malephar—*you'd regard me with horror.*

From the other side of a kitchen island, eyeing me over her steaming mug of coffee, Liz asked, "Have you resumed your duties yet?"

I glanced at my own mug, which was broad and ivory and said WORLD'S BEST MOM. "I thought of stopping by St. Matthew's today, but decided I'd wait."

She nodded, but I could tell she wanted to push it further. I hoped she wouldn't. Because I couldn't reveal the true reason for my hesitation.

Just how would the demon that dwelt in my breast react to the church? To the crosses and the holy visages of the Virgin Mary and her only Son? Would the demon fall prostrate and screaming? Inflict damage upon his host for subjecting him to such images? Or simply burst into flames?

To fill the uneasy silence, I asked, "How is Casey?"

"Shell shocked," Liz said. "Like a soldier with PTSD. He walks around in a daze most of the time."

"Maybe he's just fatigued," I ventured. "An experience like the one he endured...that had to take a toll on his body."

Liz didn't appear to be listening. She gazed askance. "I worry more about his mind. His soul."

I wanted to say something helpful but deemed it best to keep silent. In truth, the annals of the Catholic Church chronicled very little of what occurred after a successful exorcism. True, there were footnotes claiming that hosts went on to lead normal lives, but there was precious little verifiable information. And what was normal? Not being infested with a monster? Not having one's body abused by a malevolent spirit? What were the dreams of those who had once played host to a demon? What were their memories? I had an acute interest in these questions on an academic level, but lately, my interest had become a good deal more personal.

"Jason?" Liz asked.

I looked at her, surprised by the terseness of her tone.

"Sorry," I muttered. "I was thinking about—"

"Casey," she finished. Her eyes lowered and her features went slack with amazement. "Your fingers..."

I'm sure color rushed to my cheeks. "They were able to reattach them. I... forgot to tell you."

She reached toward me, but I placed my mug on the island and leaned forward. "Have you thought of safeguarding your home?"

She withdrew a little. "Against what?"

When I hesitated, she asked, "You don't think it will come back, do you? Please say it won't."

"I was thinking more about Ron," I lied. "You said he was persistent."

"What else can I do? The papers were served this morning, but he still tries to call. Texts, emails. He might've come by, but we weren't here until after suppertime." She sighed. "But we have to sleep somewhere."

"Have you considered protection?"

"I've never fired a gun in my life."

I shook my head. "Not of that sort. I was thinking—"

"You could move in."

My mouth fell open. With something like amazement I realized she'd been building to this, working up the courage. I didn't know what was more astonishing—that she trusted me enough to make the offer or that she actually believed I might be of some help in keeping her and her children safe.

If she only knew.

She fixed me with an earnest gaze. "You helped my son."

"That was Father Sutherland," I said, staring down at my coffee. "I'm afraid you think more of me than you should."

"Father Sutherland died, Jason. He was overwhelmed by that... thing. It sent him to his death."

"Liz, I couldn't—"

"I'll tell your superiors that I requested you. That I *begged* you."

I shook my head, but she was stepping around the island. "I *am* begging you. I haven't slept at all since that awful night. And when I do it's fitful, full of nightmares. I wake up sobbing."

"Liz—"

She got between me and the island, her body deliriously close to mine. But her voice was frantic, her eyes watery and red. "You have to help us, Jason. I want you to think I'm strong, but I'm not. At least not that strong. I need help." She grasped my biceps. "From you. I need you to make sure that...that fucking *monster*...doesn't come back. Doesn't—" Her voice broke, tears spilled down her cheeks; she wiped them away angrily, "—doesn't haunt this house again. I can't let it get Casey."

I looked down at her, undone by her candor. It was surreal to hear her give voice to many of the same emotions I was experiencing. How much of our time, I mused, we spend attempting to appear strong. How much better our world would be if we would admit to feeling weak now and then.

"Will you?" she asked, her body very close to mine.

I felt a momentary echo of the power I'd experienced the night of the exorcism. I knew it was a fleeting sensation, but it was edifying enough to decide me.

"Okay, Liz. I'll go get my stuff—"

"In the morning," she said.

I hesitated.

"*Please*, Jason," she said, squeezing my arms. "I won't sleep if you're not here."

Maybe it was the heat of her body within the robe, the press of her febrile flesh communicating her need...but for the first time, I wondered what it was she was asking. Her face betrayed nothing, but I knew I'd never forgive myself for taking advantage of her when she was most vulnerable.

I cleared my throat. "Does your couch fold out?"

I detected a flicker of wry humor in her eyes. "There's a guest bedroom upstairs."

I'm afraid I blushed.

If Liz noticed it, she made no sign. "The bed's already made, and you'll have your own bathroom. There's even a TV in case you want to watch the news."

It was a throwaway comment, totally innocuous, but it splashed over me like a noxious tide. I remembered the Sweet Sixteen Killer. Remembered Danny Hartman. The reason I had rushed over here tonight.

Unbidden, the images I'd glimpsed when Malephar had gripped Danny swooped through my mind: Danny's eyes lingering on Liz's breasts. Danny staring at Casey and Carolyn in a way far less wholesome than any uncle should. Staring at them like slabs of meat. Like animals about to be slaughtered.

"Liz, you mentioned guns. Does Ron have any?"

A ripple of distaste crimped her pretty features. "Several. He keeps them in a safe in our—" She colored. "—in my bedroom. In the closet."

"Do you have the combination?"

She nodded. "It's on a post-it note in his nightstand. Do you think we'll need them? Ron's not the violent type."

It's not Ron I'm worried about, I thought. But I couldn't say that. And I certainly couldn't tell her about Danny. Not only would the divulgence of this revelation shatter the tenuous pact I'd made with the demon, but judging from Liz's fragile state, it might just drive her insane to learn that the godfather of her son was the most fearsome serial killer in the city's history.

I took care to keep my tone neutral. "I don't believe Ron means you or the children harm. But stressful situations bring out the worst in people."

She uttered a mirthless laugh, and though my words had probably dredged up more memories of that dreadful night, I could tell I'd hit my mark. "That son of a bitch," she muttered. "I still can't believe he'd let that animal get at Casey…"

There was no need for her to explain. When the demon Malephar laid hands on someone, he could read the person's innermost thoughts—or memories—in an instant. After revealing to everyone that Ron had been leading a double life with another woman, that he was heavily into aberrant sex and illicit drugs, Ron had been so frightened of having his secrets revealed to the world that he had released Jack Bittner, Danny's partner, from the squad car in which he'd been imprisoned. We had locked Bittner in earlier that night because he'd believed Casey to be the Sweet Sixteen Killer. And when Ron had unleashed the raging cop on his son, Bittner had come a hair's breadth from murdering Casey.

If that wasn't grounds for divorce, I didn't know what was.

"As I said," I went on, "I don't think we have anything to fear from Ron. But I'd feel better having access to the gun safe." *In case Danny breaks in and tries to kill us*, I thought but didn't say.

Liz clutched the edges of her robe. "What about the demon?"

"He's no longer a danger to you," I said, doing my best to sound convincing. "He... he died when Father Sutherland died."

She searched my face, hope and doubt warring in her eyes. "Can a demonic spirit die, Father Crowder?"

I noted the change in her manner of addressing me. She was questioning me not as a man in whom she might be interested, but as a spiritual advisor.

I knew I had to tread gingerly. Liz was an astute woman. She would research the matter on her own. Had perhaps already done so. A lie might very well cost me her trust and any relationship—platonic or otherwise—we might enjoy in the future.

"The demonic presence likely did not die, no—although such an event has been deemed possible by some experts. But when the host dies, most believe the offending spirit enters a dormant state, in which it might languish for many years. Even centuries."

Skepticism darkened her face. "So it just, what, leaves the corpse and floats around? Until it drifts into someone else?"

I smiled, grateful to find myself on solid intellectual ground. "You're thinking about the presence too literally. It isn't that tangible."

"But the demon worked by touch. Father Sutherland said it was physically clairvoyant. Wouldn't it make sense that it would transfer to the next body it came into contact with?"

I shifted uneasily, angry at myself for underestimating her. She was coming disquietingly close to unraveling my secret.

"Reading one's thoughts is a far cry from transferring bodies, is it not?" I argued. "The demon had many opportunities to inhabit a different host. A more physically developed host than Casey. It could have chosen Bittner, Father Sutherland..."

"Or you," she finished.

My throat went dry. "Or me."

"Why is *he* here?" a voice asked from the doorway.

We turned and discovered Casey watching us from the shadows of the hall. I had a terrible memory of the possessed adolescent's face twisted into a vulpine mask, but shoved it aside.

Liz stepped away from me. "How long have you been standing there?"

Casey shrugged with one shoulder, a gesture that seemed far more world-weary than any fourteen-year-old had a right to make. "Just now." His eyes shifted from his mother to me. "Why? Don't you want me disturbing you?"

Liz smiled guiltily. "Of course I want you here. So does Jas—so does Father Crowder. Don't you, Father?"

"Of course," I said. And despite our mutual discomfiture, it was true. I had been worried about Casey since our harrowing ordeal of two nights earlier. Seeing him now allayed all sorts of fears, even if he did seem more cynical than I had hoped.

But I wasn't, after all, his father. And despite the fact that he knew what a wretched person his dad was, the blood link still existed, as did their shared history. It was unreasonable to expect Casey to disavow the affection he possessed for his father, nor was it fair for me to hope for such a thing.

Liz moved briskly over to Casey and put an arm around him. He didn't resist her, but he didn't reciprocate, and he didn't take his eyes off me. I had a sudden recollection of a man to whom my mother was once engaged, an alcoholic named George who nearly became my stepfather. Had I regarded George with the same hooded, baleful look that Casey was giving me now? Had I viewed him as an interloper whose sole purpose was stealing my mom from me?

"Can I get you anything?" Liz asked him.

"Uh-uh," he said, still staring. "Unlike some people, I don't expect anything from you."

Liz glanced uneasily at me, then at her son. "We probably woke you up talking, didn't we?"

"It wasn't you," he answered. "It was Uncle Danny."

My legs nearly buckled.

Liz peered at her son, who was perhaps an inch shorter than her, whose features were almost as delicate, though his hair was dark like his father's. "Casey, what do you—"

"Uncle Danny called my cell," Casey explained. "Said he was sorry to disturb me, but he was worried and wanted to make sure I was okay."

Liz's cheeks dimpled in a smile.

My God, I thought, *she's moved by Danny's concern. If she only knew!*

"I'm so thankful for Danny," she said.

Casey ignored that. "He didn't believe me when I told him I was fine."

213

"He loves you," Liz said.

Not as much as he loves carving up teenage girls, I thought.

"Did he say anything else?" Liz asked.

Casey shook his head. "Just that he's on his way over here."

CHAPTER FIVE

I'd stood there in thunderstruck silence for perhaps three seconds before the doorbell sounded.

Though I'd always viewed myself as a weakling, hypersensitive and comically nervous, I had never until then suffered from hyperventilation. Yet my breathing had begun to heave in such shallow, unsatisfying waves that I feared I might faint. Liz noticed it and rushed over to where I leaned against the island, feeling vaguely foolish but far too overwhelmed with terror to don a manly posture.

"What is it, Jason?" she asked, an arm flung around me. I was scarcely aware of her physical proximity, though the warm pressure of her breasts against my shoulder still managed to send a spark of pleasure through me.

"I'm sorry..." I said, gasping. "I'm... it's just..."

"Flashback?" she asked.

I glanced sharply at her, my breath wheezing like an asthmatic.

"From the other night," she explained. "When you heard Danny's name, it brought back the memories of—"

"That's right," I managed. I looked up, wondering what Casey thought of my histrionics.

But the doorway was vacant.

"Where's your son?" I asked between breaths.

She smiled. "Answering the door."

"No. He can't—"

"Hey, Case!" I heard a voice call.

Danny.

It was too late to keep him out.

"Come on," Liz said, ushering me forward. "Danny will be delighted to see you."

The thought was so absurd that I almost brayed laughter.

I made my way out of the kitchen with Liz, ambled toward the foyer, saw that the entryway was empty but that the living room to the left was spilling out a warm buttery glow. As we neared the doorway, I heard Casey and Danny speaking in easy tones, with the comfort and familiarity that only years of trust can engender.

Six feet from the doorway I paused, my whole body shivering as if from an ague. The man on the other side of the wall had gutted me only three hours prior, had taunted me and sneered at me while my lifeblood splurted over my fingers. He had raped and butchered seven teenaged girls, had threatened Liz and her children. Yet I wasn't allowed to say a thing about it.

How woefully unprepared I was! Upon my miraculous—or infernal—healing, I had thought only of reaching Liz, of ensuring her safety. I hadn't considered how everything had changed because of my bargain with Malephar, nor had I any idea I'd be facing Danny again so soon. Would he let fall the kindhearted mask he'd so thoroughly cultivated and consummate the injury he'd done me earlier? Would he slaughter me in front of Casey and Liz before turning his blade on them?

"*Jason*," Liz said and placed a hand on my cheek, "you're so pale. Do you need to lie down?"

Though I was healed—or at least believed myself to be— the wound in my belly began to throb. The center of my face became a pulsing ache, as though a cudgel were steadily pounding my nasal cavity. *Oh God*, I thought. *I can't face him.*

Blanching, I turned away, and had taken a step toward the kitchen when the world went gray. I reeled against the wall, thrust out a hand, and only with Liz's help was I able to keep from crashing into a painting. As it was, my sweaty palm still bumped gracelessly against its gilded frame. Liz wrapped her arms around my waist for support, and with a glance I saw the painting was a Van Gogh print—"Starry Night." I nearly laughed aloud at the coincidence. One of us missing an ear, the other a nose. Of course, mine had grown back.

But Danny would hack up the rest of me if he discovered me in Liz's house.

As if hearing my thoughts, Danny called, "You alright in there, Liz?"

"We're fine," Liz answered over her shoulder.

My body went rigid. *We're fine*, she'd said.

We're.

Danny knew Liz wasn't alone.

She's not *alone*, an indignant voice broke through the wooziness, *because she's in danger. That's why you came, idiot! Remember?*

The bluntness of the voice snapped me back to my senses and reminded me of what a coward I was being. Of *course* I couldn't run. I'd raced over here to protect Liz and her kids from Danny. Now, for God's sakes, I needed to protect them. Here was the only place I belonged, however ineffectual a guardian I might prove.

Rustling from the other room, someone getting to his feet.

"Who's that?" Danny asked from behind me.

My breath congealing in my chest, I stood erect.

I turned to face him.

Danny stood in the doorway between the living room and the foyer. Half of his body was in darkness, half of it a golden yellow. When he realized who it was standing beside Liz, his affable expression slowly bled away, to be replaced by one of total disbelief.

I couldn't blame him. The last time he'd seen me, my intestines were oozing out of my belly, the hardwood floor under me a sticky crimson pond. My skin had probably been winter white then, though Danny's hue wasn't far from that color now. His mouth worked mutely, his face pinching for the briefest moment like a child working up to a good hard cry. Then he caught himself, his eyes flitting to Liz. "How long has he been here?"

Liz's voice was bemused. "I don't know... how long would you say, Jason? Fifteen minutes?"

"Give or take," I agreed, my eyes never leaving Danny's.

My resolve was growing. I didn't feel as imposing as I had when vanquishing the demon during the exorcism, but I no longer felt as gutless as I had only moments earlier.

It was something.

"Why so late, Father Crowder?" Danny asked. His eyes lowered to my stomach, as if he expected my innards to be drooling over my belt. "It's almost three-thirty in the morning."

"The same reason you're here, I expect. I was worried about Liz's wellbeing."

Danny didn't like that; he knew I was talking about him. But Liz didn't know that, not yet at least. And according to the bargain, I couldn't mention it to her.

What would happen if I did? Would Malephar destroy me from the inside out, make me explode in a detonation of blood and entrails? Or would he set upon Liz and Casey, ripping and tearing like the savage beast he was?

Liz's hand pressed my lower back. "Should we sit down?"

I nodded, walked abreast of her toward Danny, who stepped aside to let us pass. When we drew even with him, I fancied I could smell his fear sweat, like fried electrical wires and undercooked pork.

In the living room Liz offered me a seat beside her on a stiff red brocade sofa. Casey eased down on the glossy black bench of an antique Steinway grand piano. Danny selected a velvet green chair and sank into it, the arms of the chair high enough to give him a diabolical look. I half-expected him to offer to purchase my soul.

You've already sold it, I thought.

"Maybe I should brew some more coffee," Liz suggested.

"I'm great, kiddo," Danny said with his customary grin.

"Maybe you'd prefer something stronger?" I said.

His grin faded. He'd forgotten, I could see, that I knew of his alcoholism.

"What's so funny, Father?" Danny asked, his expression stony.

I opened my mouth to respond, but Casey broke in.

"Why did you come over tonight, Father? No one invited you."

I glanced at him, taken aback by his tone. I don't know what I expected from Casey—Respect? Gratitude for ridding him of the demon?—but the only emotions I read in his eyes now were mistrust and what might have been dislike. Just what did he remember? I wondered. And what might he now suspect? Could he sense the presence of Malephar within me? In one way, Casey and I were inextricably linked. We'd both housed the same demon, both experienced his debased thoughts and yearnings.

Yet Malephar had remained quiet for several minutes. Why? Was he biding his time, waiting until he could leap forward, seize control of me, and shock everyone with his filthy utterances? Or was he plotting something far worse, an orgy of violence that would leave everyone except Danny, his kindred spirit, a pile of unrecognizable offal?

"Father Crowder was worried about us, Casey," Liz said, her brows knitting. "We should be thankful he's here."

"Absolutely," Danny said. "The Father's a hero. He saved you from Sutherland, didn't he?"

Danny might as well have smacked me in the face.

"Did he?" Casey asked.

"Hell yes, he did," Danny answered. "You shoulda seen Sutherland's face when that monster wriggled inside him." Staring at me now. "That look in his eyes...that gruesome smile. He looked like he'd do the foulest things imaginable. I still shiver thinking about it."

Liz looked like she might be sick. "Maybe we should talk about something else."

"Of course, Liz," Danny said. "I don't know what I was thinking, so soon after all that terrible stuff went down." Again, his glance lit on me, and I saw he'd recovered from the initial shock of finding me alive. "Let's talk about Father Crowder and his plans. You going back to work, Father?"

"Tomorrow. I'm to meet with—"

"You might rethink that. I don't mean to be rude, but you don't look so good. Not sleeping much?"

My mouth was cotton dry. "Not tonight."

Danny nodded. "Yeah, I know what you mean. I tried to sleep earlier, but I kept having these crazy dreams about people getting cut open. Then I decided to get out of the apartment, drive around a little."

"You have any leads?" Casey asked.

He didn't need to explain. The Sweet Sixteen Killer wasn't just the biggest story in Chicago; after Makayla Howell's slaying, it was dominating national headlines.

But Danny didn't bat an eyelash. "Nothing yet, Case. Unfortunately. But we'll catch the bastard soon, I guarantee you that. I can barely rest knowing he's still out there hunting innocent girls."

And Danny regarded me with a look so smug that I longed to rend him to pieces.

◆ ◆ ◆

We sipped coffee and talked until, a few minutes later, Danny stood and announced he was going. Liz offered to walk him to his car, but he insisted she remain with me and Casey. She did venture as far as the doorway, and as they were saying their goodbyes, Casey turned to me and said, "I've seen you staring at Mom."

I attempted a smile. "Casey, you know I'm bound by my vows. And your mother is a married woman."

"But not for long, huh? Bet you're real torn up about that."

"I don't blame you for being cynical. Few have experienced what you have. You have trouble trusting people."

"I trust Danny and Mom," he said. "And my sister, but she doesn't really count."

"How is Carolyn?"

"None of your damned business."

I could only stare at him. This was a radical and unpleasant departure from the boy I'd known before that terrible night. He'd been kind, polite, almost—to borrow Danny's description of him—too passive.

Now he looked ready to unmask me for the fraud I was.

Did he suspect what was inside me?

Liz reentered and clapped her hands together softly. "What are you guys talking about?"

"Nothing, Mom," Casey muttered, rising. "I'm going to bed."

"Good night, Casey," I said.

He left without answering.

Liz regarded her interlaced fingers. "He's had a rough go."

"You don't need to apologize."

"I just wonder... maybe he associates you with what happened. With what was in him?"

"How could he not?"

She shivered, hugged herself. "Let's not talk about it, okay? I need to get you situated."

"You're sure you want me to stay?"

"Of course." She smiled a little. "Unless you have somewhere else to be."

My body tingled. I glanced through the window at Rosemary Road, which was steeped in darkness. I thought of Danny, out there somewhere. It was possible he would return tonight. Watching him with Casey and Liz, I couldn't imagine him hurting either one of them.

But I'd seen what was in his mind. I couldn't take that chance.

"I'm ready," I said.

She cocked an eyebrow. "For what?"

Heat rushed to my face. I felt my scrotum shrivel.

She laughed softly, took my hand. "I like it when you're bashful."

CHAPTER SIX

I don't know what I expected when I approached St. Matthew's Cathedral the next morning. Perhaps it was the movies I had watched as a child or the horror novels I had indulged in as an adult. Whatever the case, I feared some violent physiological reaction from Malephar as I approached the grand front steps and the venerable Gothic archway, some spiritual recoiling or even a tangible attack on me for subjecting him to a setting he must find abhorrent.

Yet the demon remained silent.

My sense of relief only lasted a couple minutes. There was a note on my office door instructing me to meet Father Patterson in his office immediately.

Feeling condemned, I made my way out of the reception area, down the stairs to the basement, and through the long, dim corridor that spanned the length of the cathedral. Father Patterson had always intimidated me. He was tall, powerfully built. Though he was a year or two past fifty, Patterson looked ten years younger. His brown skin showed no signs of aging, and his well-manicured black hair contained no strands of white.

Unlike Father Sutherland, Joe Patterson had never overlooked my many shortcomings. When I would participate in a metaphysical discussion, he invariably found the weak spots in my thinking, and when I dared to contradict him, he would mercilessly rebut me. On several occasions, Father Sutherland had played the role of intermediary and smoothed out the tension between us. But even then it had been patently obvious to all in attendance that Patterson regarded me and what he dubbed my radical views with contempt.

Drawing nearer to Father Patterson's wing, I eyed the flickering fluorescent overhead lights with dread. Father Sutherland, my protector, was gone. For the foreseeable future, Patterson was not only my superior, he was my direct supervisor, and as Sutherland's best friend, he would have an especial interest in the events of a few nights prior.

Would he discover the inconsistencies in my story? Would he read the lies in my face?

I turned the corner, tromped up the steps to his office. His secretary, a mousy girl with reddish brown hair and skin so pale she almost glowed, was watching me with unconcealed interest.

I nodded at her. "I'm here to see—"

"He's waiting for you," she said. Then, with a hint of apology, "He's a trifle grumpy. He thought you'd be here earlier."

Terrific.

Wordlessly, I opened the heavy oaken door and discovered Father Patterson glowering at me from across his burnished cherry wood desk. The desk looked like an antique, as did most of the furnishings in the office. Rather than the easygoing, eclectic décor of Father Sutherland's study, Father Patterson's office bespoke of propriety and order, efficiency and tastefulness. Whereas Sutherland had sometimes worn rumpled frocks, Father Patterson looked like a priest in a movie—not a hair out of place or a garment unpressed.

I closed the door behind me and gave Father Patterson what I hoped was a disarming smile.

He did not return it.

Nor did he offer me a chair. I folded my hands behind my back, but that seemed prideful, so I laced my fingers before me and glanced about the office. "This is a handsome room," I commented.

Patterson continued to appraise me. His brown eyes contained no warmth at all. I reminded myself of what Sutherland used to tell me whenever I shared my uncharitable opinions about Father Patterson. *He has seen much and lived through much. You must not judge him too harshly.*

Which would've been fine had Patterson not judged *me* so harshly.

Still, I would try. I owed Peter Sutherland that.

"Should I sit?" I asked.

He gave me the merest spreading of his hands, as if to say, *Well, get to it then.*

I got to it. The chair cushion was surprisingly deep. I felt like the dark leather seat might swallow me up.

I ventured another smile. "I was told you wanted to see me?"

"You're pretty cheerful for a person who just lost his mentor."

I flinched, not only at the hostility of Patterson's words, but at the boom of his voice. I had forgotten about that, was unnerved by that deep bass rumble.

I shook my head. "I'm not cheerful. I was merely trying to be polite."

"Polite," Patterson repeated.

"Yes, I..." I cleared my throat. "I'm very distraught over Father Sutherland's passing."

"You mean his murder."

My throat constricted. I pushed up on the armrests. "Have they changed their ruling? The last I heard, they called it a suicide."

The callous brown eyes watched me. "Who cares what 'they' called it? You were there, weren't you? You'd know better than anyone."

I squirmed in my chair, aware of how guilty the movement made me appear. I couldn't help it though. Patterson's eyes were hard, unblinking.

I said, "The demon went into Father Sutherland and—"

"Why not you?"

I squinted at him. "I'm not sure I—"

"Peter Sutherland," Patterson said, "had the spiritual resolve of twenty men. He was devout, his faith ironclad. He would never have been overtaken by whatever spirit you claim was in that house."

"In Casey," I corrected. "In the boy."

Patterson waited.

I'd begun to perspire. "I told the police everything I know."

A dour nod. "And I'm telling you to tell me."

"I don't know—"

"Yes you *do* know," he said, sitting forward. "This isn't like a verse of scripture you can twist and manipulate to serve your own bizarre agenda."

Oh my, I thought. *That.* I couldn't believe Patterson was going there in these circumstances. Whatever arguments we'd had about our interpretations of the Bible had nothing to do with Peter Sutherland's death, yet here was Patterson carrying on as though we were participating in a spiritual debate rather than discussing the death of a man we both loved and admired.

I did my best to maintain a level demeanor, but I was not about to be bullied. "We can quarrel about Leviticus on another occasion, Father Patterson. At the moment, I think we should focus on—"

"Oh you *think*, do you? You think we should look at things from your perspective instead of God's?"

I began to shake my head, but he overrode me. "Then let's do that, shall we?" Elbows on his desk blotter, open palms facing heavenward, he said, "On one hand, we have Peter Sutherland, whose record as a man of God was unimpeachable, who was trusted by mayors, Congressmen, bishops, and cardinals. Not to mention every single parishioner of St. Matthew's."

"I know who Father Sutherland was," I said, a heat building at the base of my neck. "You don't need to tell me—"

"I *do* need to tell you, Father Crowder. You need to be reminded. He was godly. A steadfast believer. A fisher of men."

"He was all those things," I agreed. Unexpectedly, a thickness formed in my throat. "He was like a father to me. He took me in and made me what I am."

"His only weakness," Patterson said. "I never understood what he saw in you."

"You can't—"

He silenced me with a raised hand. "I don't dispute his affection for you, Crowder. From a spiritual perspective, his willingness to prop you up with his faith was exactly the sort of generosity that made him so beloved."

I subsided into sour silence. I hated Patterson making of me a charity case.

He went on, nodding at an open palm. "So on this hand we've got Father Sutherland. And over here," nodding at his other hand, "we've got a junior priest who questions the authority of the Bible."

My cheeks burned. "It's not the authority of the Bible I've questioned, it's the veracity of its sources."

"The Good Book is the truth, Crowder. It's as simple as that."

"Weren't we given minds—by divine grace—to think? Aren't we supposed to question?"

"Sin, yes. Scripture, no." A mordant smile. "That's blasphemy, Jason."

"I call it utilizing the intelligence that God gave us."

Patterson's smile disappeared. "Are you questioning my intellect?"

The words were out of my mouth before I could stop them. "No, Father. I'm merely inviting you to use it."

The senior priest's jaw muscles flexed. For a moment I thought he might leap over the desk at me. "You're treating Sutherland's death as disrespectfully as you treat the Bible."

"One has nothing to do with the other."

"They certainly do," he said, sitting back in his chair. "There *is* such a thing as objectivity, you know."

"Fine," I said, my voice going thin. "Here's an objective fact: Father Sutherland and I—together—exorcised the demon from Casey Hartman's body. Then he attacked Father—"

"He?" Patterson's eyebrows went up.

"Malephar," I explained.

The curling of a lip. "The spirit told you its name?"

"Yes."

"Spirits don't have a gender, Father Crowder."

I fingered my Roman collar, aware I was on tenuous footing. "I got the impression the demon was male."

"And how did you come by that conclusion? Wasn't its host male?"

"Yes."

"Aren't you male?"

That stopped me. "Are you questioning my manhood?"

Patterson chuckled, a sound that made my fists clench. "I'd never question your masculinity, Jason. Big, strapping guy like you."

I sighed. "Why don't you come out and tell me what you think happened?"

Patterson's gaze was wintry. "I think you're responsible for Peter Sutherland's death."

◆ ◆ ◆

My heart thundered in my chest. "I don't know what you're talking about."

"Then why the overreaction?" Patterson pressed. "You look like you're about to swoon."

I gnashed my teeth at his word choice. *Swoon* made me sound like a maiden in a cheesy romance novel. Another deliberate belitting.

Patterson rose, crossed to a counter along the interior wall of the room, opened a cabinet, retrieved a glass, and filled it with water from a sink I hadn't noticed. He brought me the water, placed it on a silver coaster lined with green felt. I didn't accept the glass, instead took a moment to collect myself. While I willed my heart to stop racing, I noticed a gold, rather sharp-looking implement lying beside the coaster.

"I collect letter openers," Patterson explained, returning to his rolling chair. "You like that one? It was a gift from Peter, ironically. You look closely, you'll find an inscription."

I didn't want to do anything Patterson suggested, but so great was my fear of discovery that I welcomed any diversionary tactic, even one Patterson had suggested. With quaking fingers, I snatched the letter opener from the table and held it up to the lamplight.

TO JOE, it read. HERE'S TO MANY MORE MORNINGS AT THE FEELY CENTER.

"He was referring," Patterson said, "to our racquetball games at the fitness club down the road."

My throat was desiccated. "I know what he was referring to."

"I always wondered why you never took part in our morning workouts," Patterson said. "The last several years, we took up swimming too. I've become very comfortable in the water."

I examined the inscription, pictured Father Sutherland as he'd been only a week ago. Early sixties but as fit as most men in their twenties. Strong, virile. The kind of man others aspired to be.

Patterson's tone was reflective. "You see my point, don't you, Crowder? You see why it's so hard to believe that the 'demon,' as you call it, would overcome Peter rather than you."

"It wasn't a matter of physical strength."

"So you say."

"Did you plan this ambush?"

232

He went on as though I hadn't spoken. "Let's pretend for a minute your story is true. Even if it weren't a matter of physical strength, it *would* be a matter of spiritual strength. And let's be honest," he said, chuckling a little. "The disparity between you and Father Sutherland spiritually was even more pronounced than it was in the physical realm."

I tried to muster some indignation. "So that's why you called me here today. To insult me?"

"Stop feeling sorry for yourself, Crowder. It's unbecoming."

"You disliked me from the beginning. Now you're using this as an excuse to persecute me."

He laughed incredulously. "Persecute you? My best friend is dead."

"He was my best friend too."

"He was your *benefactor*, Crowder. Not your peer."

I had the sense of floating above my body. This was worse than I'd imagined. Infinitely worse. Did Patterson mean to press charges? Had he already shared his suspicions with the police?

"What are you doing there?" Patterson asked, frowning. "That supposed to be some kind of joke?"

I stared back at him, perplexed.

"I would think," he said, enunciating each word savagely, "you would strive to repair the damage you've done to your career instead of alienating your superiors."

"What are you—"

"Your *hand*," he snapped, nodding to where my hands rested in my lap.

Or where I thought they were resting.

I stared downward, completely at a loss for words. I'd thought I'd replaced the cruciform letter opener on the stand beside me. Evidently, I'd failed to do so. At some point in our conversation, I had begun digging into the skin on the back of my right hand with so much force that the letter opener had punctured my flesh, burrowed under the thick blue vein in the middle of my hand, and had punched through the skin on the other side.

Blood was spurting from the dual wounds.

Pain flooded through me.

Hissing, I jerked my hand up and stared in horror at what I'd done to myself. The gilded letter opener waggled as my injured hand jittered in the air. Blood streamed down my forearm.

Apparently realizing what he was seeing was no parlor trick, Patterson uttered a muffled oath and lunged to push the Call button on his phone. "*Tammy*," he barked, "send for a nurse!"

I scarcely heard him. The pain in my hand was worsening by the moment, whatever diabolical anesthetic I'd been under rapidly fading.

Tammy's voice came back, high and fraught with panic, "You want me to call the hospital?"

"The *convent*, Tammy. Send for Sister Rebecca."

Yes, I thought, *Sister Rebecca*. I'd seen her often but had only been treated by her once, a few years earlier when I'd come down with pneumonia. I had no doubt she'd be able to patch me up in the short term.

Yet what of the long term? The ramifications of what just happened assailed me, made my vision swim even more than the blood loss did. That Malephar could so cunningly access a weapon was disconcerting. What terrified me to a far greater degree, however, was the demon's ability to blunt the pain so thoroughly that I had no idea whatever that I had injured myself.

A rough hand seized my wrist. I glanced up at Patterson. The senior priest was even taller than I remembered. I was over six feet tall, yet Patterson dwarfed me, his sturdy shoulders twice as wide as mine.

He scowled down at my quaking hand. "Why on earth did you—" He compressed his lips. "Hold still. I don't know if removing it is the right thing or not."

"Maybe we should wait for Sister Rebecca," I suggested.

"You don't want that thing in your hand," Patterson said. "Hold still."

And before I could protest, he grasped the letter opener with surprisingly steady fingers. When he began to draw the dagger out, I sucked in breath and jerked involuntarily, but he clamped my wrist tighter, rendered movement impossible. His large brow creased with concentration, Patterson slid the blade out of my hand, my blood instantly spurting with renewed vigor.

I moaned, tottered to my feet. Patterson tossed the letter opener aside, slapped his free hand over the drizzling wounds. I crumpled and sank into the leather chair, only partially aware of the way Patterson loomed over me, endeavoring to staunch the flow of blood. I half-expected him to utter soothing words, to assure me everything would be okay, but Patterson remained grimly silent. At least he was trying to help me. A few minutes earlier, I wouldn't have guessed he'd make such an attempt. Perhaps it was akin to the Hippocratic oath; Patterson's devotion to his holy vows prevented him abandoning anyone to physical suffering, even a person he detested.

At some point, the mousy secretary entered, and after a few gruff words from Patterson, she exited and returned bearing a white towel, with which Patterson swaddled my hand. I glanced at her, noticed how her skin had gone an unhealthy green, and ventured a smile. She smiled back, looking not at all reassured. I couldn't blame her. With a cursory scan of my surroundings, I realized the area around me resembled a slaughterhouse. Or a violent crime scene.

My thoughts jumped to Danny Hartman.

Where was he right now?

Were Liz and the children safe?

The thought revived me. I bucked against Patterson who, though unprepared for my resistance, nevertheless kept me pinioned to the sodden chair with little effort.

"Keep still," he commanded.

After what seemed an age, Sister Rebecca bustled into the office and set about examining me. She tensed when she removed the dripping scarlet towel. Without looking at Patterson, she said, "Why didn't you call an ambulance?"

"Discretion is sometimes necessary," he said, moving away from us. "How would we have explained his wounds, Sister Rebecca? Claimed it was a gruesome accident?"

Her eyes flicked to mine. "How *did* it happen, Father Crowder?"

A wave of affection rolled through me. In truth, I'd always harbored a bit of a crush on Sister Rebecca. Though she was a decade-and-a-half my senior, she was a vivacious, attractive woman. Her curved cheekbones and full lips were at once motherly and beguiling. Her lustrous black hair, at the moment drawn back in a ponytail, made me thankful the nuns of St. Matthew's no longer wore habits. As she turned my hand over, bending each of my fingers in turn, I found my eyes drifting to her navy blue dress. She bent forward to get a closer look, and the dress yawned open. I could see her plain white bra beneath. Not particularly revealing, but the breasts it contained were round and firm.

"*Hey*," Patterson said, giving my shoulder a rough shake.

Flushing, I peered up at him.

"She asked you a question," he snapped.

I looked up at Sister Rebecca, whose cheeks now shone with faint maroon splotches. "I'm sorry," I said. "I didn't hear you."

Her tone was neutral. "I asked how this happened."

"I think I need to lie down," I said.

She glanced at Patterson, then to me. "Would you rather do that here or in the red room?"

"The red room," I said.

Patterson spread his arms. "Am I supposed to clean this mess up?"

Sister Rebecca helped me to my feet. As she did, she flashed what might have been an admonishing frown at Patterson. "I'll send a custodian over shortly. First, I need to make Father Crowder comfortable." She slung my arm over her shoulder, began shepherding me toward the door.

"Comfortable," Patterson repeated.

"You don't want him to be comfortable?" she asked.

Patterson looked like he'd scented something foul. "Take him."

I didn't look at Patterson again as I hobbled with Sister Rebecca out of the office.

◆ ◆ ◆

Sister Rebecca sat across from me on a rattan chair she'd drawn up in the red room.

"You're lucky you didn't sever this," she said. I followed her gaze, saw her examining the thick, wormy vein that threaded its way up the back of my hand. "Had you sliced it open," she explained, "you'd have lost a good deal more blood. As it is, you've almost certainly perforated it."

"I appreciate your help, Sister Rebecca."

She grunted. "Call me Rebecca. The 'Sister' ages me." She scrutinized my face. "How much have you slept since the other night?"

I wondered what she knew of the exorcism, or more importantly, what she'd heard. She certainly didn't project the same brand of belligerent accusation that Patterson had, but she wasn't her normal, cheerful self either. Willing to give me the benefit of the doubt, maybe, but not without a plausible explanation.

I wasn't in any condition to provide one.

I leaned against the couch back, blew out beleagured air. "I don't know. Maybe eight hours total? Probably less."

She looked disappointed, but apparently didn't think it prudent to press the issue. "You need rest. Would you like a ride to your cottage, or would you rather sleep here?"

The thought of my cottage reminded me of last night's near-death experience, and I realized with a jolt that I hadn't even cleaned the place up yet.

"I'll sleep here," I said.

She searched my face. "I suppose I can wait to hear your story. But I'll need to stitch this up before you begin sawing logs."

I glanced at her, surprised at the colloquialism. "Where are you from, Sister?"

She rose, stepped over to the end table at the foot of the couch. On it was a plain black bag that zippered down the center.

"Indiana," she said. "A small town called Lakeview."

"The one in the news last summer? The supposed werewolf outbreak?"

She pursed her lips. "Foolish sensationalism." She resumed her spot in front of me. "Now hold still."

She produced a small bottle of white cream, into which she dipped a cotton swab. She began to dab the cream around my twin puncture wounds, and though the contact made my flesh ache slightly, in short order the throb in my hand began to abate. As she extricated a needle and thread, I studied the red room, so called because of its lurid red paint. Located along the northern end of the basement corridor and illuminated by daylight windows and a trio of lamps, it had long been used as a sort of recuperation place for those who were too queasy to drive home or for others who simply needed a quiet spot. It had formerly, Father Sutherland had once explained, been painted the same drab gray as the other rooms in this section of the basement. But at Father Sutherland's request, it had been repainted in this gaudy scarlet because, in his words, "The color stirs the imagination."

Now, in Rebecca's intoxicating presence, I found his words unnervingly accurate.

Her legs, I noticed, had encroached on either side of my right thigh, so that my knee was nudging her skirt up a little. It was a modest skirt, but the combination of her seated position and the pressure from my leg had conspired to ruck up the hem past its accustomed reach. I couldn't help but note how firm and pale her thighs were. Muscular, smooth. She obviously shaved frequently, or at least she had in the past twenty-four hours.

I winced as the needle pierced my flesh.

She paused. "Would you like some more numbing cream?"

I suppressed a shudder, shook my head. "It's fine. The pain isn't that bad."

She eyed me impishly. "Liar."

"No really. I'll survive."

"Typical," she said, and continued to work. "Would you like something to help you sleep?"

I knew I should remain watchful, and I was eager to check in on Liz, but I'd instructed her earlier to be vigilant and to contact me should anyone stop by—especially Danny. That had stopped her, of course, but so emphatic were my entreaties that she agreed to call me before letting him in.

"Father Crowder?" Rebecca said, her voice tight.

I tensed. Looked down at my free hand.

Which was stroking Rebecca's thigh.

Sucking in breath, I jerked my hand away, mumbled an awkward apology. Her face had gone the same hue as the walls, but she nevertheless continued to sew up my wound. Soon, thankfully, she finished working on me, and I thanked her, apologizing once again.

Rebecca nodded, gave me a look I couldn't interpret, and slipped out the door.

I lay back, heart thumping. Malephar, it seemed, could seize control of me whenever he wished. Thank God I'd noticed my hand on Rebecca's leg before it delved any higher.

I lay back, mortified at what had happened. It took me a long time to drift off, but when I did, my slumber was so deep and dreamless that I didn't awaken until late afternoon.

Groggy and cursing, I hurried out of the red room and exited the church.

CHAPTER SEVEN

I hustled back to my cottage, furious with myself for my breach in etiquette with Sister Rebecca, and just as egregiously, for my lack of time management. It was approaching six PM, and night would soon descend on the city.

I had vowed not to go to the authorities about Danny, and I planned to remain true to that vow. Not out of allegiance to the infernal presence lurking in my breast, but because I yearned to protect Liz and her kids. According to Malephar, they would be safe as long as I abided by our pact. That the demon was the very incarnation of deceit was not lost on me, but what other choice did I have?

I ripped open my front door, twisted on the lamp. Surveyed the room and saw it was as I'd expected.

Blood everywhere.

I wasn't in the mood to clean it up, and besides, there was no advantage in undertaking the gargantuan task now. The blood had long since dried to an ochre crust, and it would take hours to remove all of it.

I didn't have hours.

Okay, I told myself. *Do what you've always done when you're overwhelmed by too many tasks: compartmentalize.*

I nodded, closing my eyes.

First, there's Liz. Is she safe?

Yes, I answered. *At least, she's safe for the time being.*

I believed Malephar would warn me if Danny moved on her and her children because if Malephar didn't, he and I would be right back to where we were last night. If Liz died, I'd have no reason to live—beyond stopping Danny from killing again.

Malephar must know this, intimate as he was with my psyche.

But was it in Malephar's power to prohibit Danny from making good on his threats?

This question troubled me greatly. Just how vast were the demon's powers? How far could his intelligence reach? Did he really know what Danny was doing at the moment? And if so, how could he stop Danny from killing Liz?

Maybe he can't, I reflected. *Maybe he doesn't have any idea where Danny is, and his promise to keep Liz and her kids safe is as empty as his soul.*

Dammit. I moved on to the next question.

What were my obligations now? Before my catastrophic failure in thwarting the Sweet Sixteen Killer, I had vowed to fight evil by harnessing my unique "gift." Yet the demon had triumphed over me, had proven his supremacy. Twice today I had been manipulated by Malephar. Now, Father Patterson—already an adversary—likely believed me insane. And Rebecca...

I didn't want to think about Sister Rebecca right now.

Because that would require thinking of other people, a nasty voice whispered. *You're worried about you, Liz, her kids—your own little circle. What about the rest of the city? What about the killer on the loose, the one who makes John Wayne Gacy look like a philanthropist? You're the only one who knows the Sweet Sixteen's identity, the one person who can put a stop to this madness. Are you really going to allow your allegiance to Malephar prevent you—*

It's not allegiance!

—from saving Danny's future victims?

I stood in the foyer of my cottage, the blood beating in my temples. The atmosphere here was oppressive, sweltering. I had to escape, if nothing else to clear my swirling thoughts.

I turned and grasped the doorknob to go outside.

Froze.

What if Danny decides to finish what he started? I wondered. *What if he's not interested in Liz at all?*

What if he's on his way over to kill you?

This, I realized, was far more sensible than anything I'd considered thus far. I was the only one who knew Danny's secret. What if he was on the porch, grasping a firearm this time rather than a knife? Yes, it was still daylight, and true, there were other cottages on the quiet rectory road. But if anyone had access to a silencer, it would be a policeman. All Danny needed to do was shove the gun in my belly, empty it into me, and no one would be the wiser.

So go out the back door.

You mean the door through which Danny escaped last night? The one you never locked?

Oh God, I thought, my terror escalating.

What if Danny was already in the cottage?

Crime-fighting priest indeed. You can't even defeat one man!

I fancied I could hear stirrings, imagined the ragged huff of the killer's breath behind me. In a panic, I tore open the front door, lurched outside, and smashed straight into a large figure—*Oh God! Danny!*—and then I was scrambling away from him, breath clotting in my throat, and nearly overbalancing on the porch. I leaped awkwardly into my yard, stumbled toward the road. What a fool I was, what a weak, hapless fool, and Danny was shouting at me now, his voice deeper than normal. Footsteps sounded behind me. I was nearly to the road, shooting glances left and right for some bystander, anyone who could rescue me from my murderer.

"Father Crowder!" the voice behind me shouted. "You gotta talk to me!"

I kept fleeing, in the road now. I'd bypassed my car even though I was clutching my keys. The voice behind me called again, closer this time, and I realized with confusion that the tone was pleading rather than threatening. In fact, it hadn't even sounded like…

I halted in the middle of the road, glanced over my shoulder.

It wasn't the Sweet Sixteen Killer.

It was his brother.

◆ ◆ ◆

Shoulders slumping, I ambled toward my Civic.

Ron Hartman was smirking and shaking his head, his wise guy routine already annoying the hell out of me. "You were really spooked, Father. I thought you were gonna keep right on going until you hit South Wacker Drive."

"Leave me alone, Ron," I said, completely enervated. Though I was glad it wasn't Danny, Ron was near the bottom of the list of people I wanted to see.

Ron approached my Civic from the passenger's side. "I know we didn't hit it off the other night, but we still went through a lot together, didn't we?"

I tipped my head at him. "Didn't hit it off?"

He stared at the ground, scuffed the gravel. His silence, I figured, was as much an admission as he could make. The fact was, he had behaved as shamefully as any human being could on the night of the exorcism. He'd been revealed as an adulterer, a drug user, and the architect of a sleazy double life. Yet far worse than these revelations was the decision to unleash Officer Jack Bittner on Ron's own son.

When Ron looked up at me, he must've read all of these memories in my face, for his eyes filled with tears, and his voice broke as he said, "Please talk to me, Father. I've got nowhere else to turn. Danny hates my guts, Liz slapped a restraining order on me. I can't even—" He choked back a sob. "—can't even see my kids."

"Don't you think that's best?"

He leaned forward on the Civic's lusterless gold roof. "I know I don't deserve mercy, clemency...whatever you guys call it."

"Absolution?"

"That either. But I'm still a person, right?"

"It's debatable."

He peered at me in the soft pink gloaming. "Can't you at least let me talk a little? I've got no one, Father."

"What about your other wife?"

He made a face. "Jesus, she wasn't my wife. Now she's worse than ever. Wanting this and that. You know how much she's asking for?"

I didn't particularly care how much his mistress was blackmailing him for, but I asked the question anyway.

"*Two hundred grand a year*," he said, eyes wide and aggrieved. "Two hundred Gs, Father, and that won't be the end of it. And it's not like I make millions at the Mercantile. Yeah, I do all right. Most guys would kill for the kind of income I've got. But that shit adds up. And she acts like it's nothing."

"It's a truly sad plight," I said and unlocked the Civic. I climbed in, rammed shut the door, and keyed the engine.

"Wait!" came his frantic plea. He hustled around the rear of the car, and some shadowy part of me—not the region governed by Malephar, I must confess—longed to wrench the car into Reverse and back over the bastard.

Ron was peering at me through the driver's window. I could feel his need, his pitiful desperation broadcasting over me in waves. I exhaled and slouched onto the steering wheel. Reached over, pushed the Unlock button.

Ron trotted around the front bumper, let himself in, and plopped down next to me. "Where're we going, Father?"

I jerked the Civic into Reverse, backed out, and guided us toward the business district. "The 7-11 on Clark."

"I gotta tell you, Father," Ron said as we cruised through the church-owned property, "it's nice to finally see a friendly face."

"I'm not your friend."

"Oh, I know that, I know that. But I was just thinking... have you talked to Liz?"

"Very little," I lied.

"That's interesting," he said, glancing out his window. "I'd have thought, after the other night... you know, you guys going through so much together...I figured Liz'd be really grateful to you for helping Casey. Beholden, even."

I looked at him sharply. "What are you implying?"

"Not a thing." He shrugged. "Only that... you know how traumatic experiences tend to forge a special bond. Soldiers in battle, that sort of thing." He whistled softly. "Craziest goddamned thing. Two men killed under my own roof. Right on my property."

I had a quick flash of Father Sutherland's broken body lying facedown on the concrete, the strobing lightning illuminating his splayed limbs.

"It was a nightmare," I said.

"But you haven't seen Liz?"

I shook my head, wondering where she was right now. I wished I were with her.

Alone.

"What about Danny?" Ron asked. "You two seemed pretty tight."

It took all I had not to bray laughter.

"What?" he demanded.

"Leave it," I said. "Where are you staying?"

"A friend's."

"Your mistress's."

Ron glared at me. "What about you, Father? I heard you were over there this morning. Over at my house."

I realized with dawning alarm that this might have been the true reason Ron had called on me this evening. To pump me for information about Liz. Or to learn if my relationship with her had evolved beyond the platonic.

I had no desire to reassure him.

"Your ex-wife got a restraining order for a reason, Ron."

"You mean my *wife*," he said.

"If you want to believe that. Either way, I don't believe it's my place to tell you what she's doing."

"Or *who* she's doing," he muttered.

I jerked the wheel and skidded to a stop. "Out," I said.

"Hey!" he said, palms up. "Don't go batshit on me. I didn't mean—"

"The *hell* you didn't," I snapped. "This is exactly the kind of crap that got you into trouble in the first place."

"It was my son getting possessed by a goddamned *demon* that got me into trouble."

"Your marriage was doomed anyway," I said, angry at myself for getting into this argument, but too full of rage to shut my mouth. "Liz married you for your money, she said so that night."

"Oh yeah? And what else did she say to you? 'Stick it in me, Father'?"

"I want you out of my car," I said. "Right the hell now."

"Yeah, you didn't look very priestly sneaking up my drive at three fucking AM."

I shot him a look.

"That's right, Crowder. I was there. Hell, you thought you were being clever, parking on the street like that. You parked right behind *me*. I watched you slinking into my house." His upper lip curled. "But I didn't see you leave."

I couldn't conceal my shock, but there was something else nagging at me now, something of even greater importance. "If you saw me go in..." I started.

"Yeah, I watched Danny drive up too. You guys were probably having yourself a threesome with my wife, weren't you? Goddamn perverts."

I barely heard him. "Where did Danny go when he left?"

Ron grunted. "That's a good point. I guess he didn't bone my wife, not unless he's a one-pump chump. Guy was in and out of the house in under fifteen minutes."

"That's right," I said, more to myself. "He left pretty hastily."

"I didn't say he *left*," Ron corrected. "I said he was out of the house."

I stared at him, bewildered.

Ron grinned nastily. "I thought you might not have known that. And here I thought he was just watching out in case I showed up." There was a speculative gleam in Ron's sharkish eyes. "Maybe it was you he was keeping tabs on. Making sure you weren't up to anything. You know, sneaking down the hall to Liz's room. Or one of the kids. I know you priests like 'em young."

The muscles of my forearms tightened. "Shut your mouth."

Ron smirked at me. "Or what?"

I forced myself to look away. "You're telling me Danny never left?"

"Not while I was there. I pulled out... Oh, musta been five in the morning."

"And Danny was..."

"Still in the side yard. Staring up at the guest bedroom. The one I'm guessing you spent the night in. Unless you got horny."

Bile tingled in the back of my throat.

Ron nodded. "Maybe Danny knows secrets about you, Father."

"You're a fool."

"Maybe. But if Danny thinks you killed Sutherland and Bittner, he's gonna arrest your ass any day now."

I reached across him, threw open his door. "Stop stinking up my car."

Ron giggled. "Sure, Father. I'll get out. I'll even accompany you across the street."

"What are you—"

"The 7-11," he explained, pointing at the building catty-cornered from us. "It's right there."

◆ ◆ ◆

To my chagrin, Ron was as good as his word. He moved with me across the street, making comments about the approaching thunderheads, and followed me into the convenience store.

I nodded to the clerk, a young Indian woman with a fetching smile. I'd never introduced myself properly, but we were cordial to each other and comfortable in each other's presence.

Or as comfortable as I could be around a pretty woman.

"This your favorite night spot?" Ron said, looking around. "I haven't been to one of these in years. Liz does our shopping."

I was sick of Ron's patter and didn't respond. Plucking a cherry-red basket from the stack, I crossed the entryway and ambled down an aisle populated by cookies and potato chips. I reached the refrigerated area, opened a glass door, and selected a couple microwavable meals, one of them lasagna, the other sweet-and-sour chicken. They weren't gourmet, but they were edible.

Ron eyed the frozen dinners with mock appreciation. "Nice choices, Father. You gonna wash those down with some good Irish whiskey?"

"Tired stereotypes," I muttered, moving down the aisle. "If you had any originality, Liz might've found you more interesting."

Ron hooted, drawing the stares of an older couple, a black man and a short woman who might have been Filipino. "That's the spunk I'm used to. The way you spoke to me the other night, I couldn't believe Sutherland let you get away with it." Ron's voice grew contemplative. "Maybe it was his lax attitude that got him into trouble, huh?"

I turned, the basket I grasped swinging so violently it almost knocked over a Gatorade display. "Don't speak of Father Sutherland. At least he tried to help your son. You wanted Casey dead."

Ron took a step back, as if seeing me anew. "So the gloves come off." His eyes grew shifty. "You still believe that stuff about my sic'ing Bittner on Casey?"

"I witnessed it, Ron."

I became aware of several sets of eyes on us. The couple a few feet away; a gaunt man to my left, whose wiry white beard gave him a vaguely homeless look. A pair of teenaged girls in the next aisle over, maybe sophomores in high school, who looked too innocent to be alone at twilight.

Ron crossed his arms. "What if I wanted Bittner there for Casey's protection, you ever think of that?"

"He wanted to kill your son."

"I told him to haul Casey in. I wanted my son out of that house. He was a danger to himself. Bittner was the only one big enough to handle Casey in that state."

"You're detestable."

"You're the one who needs to give answers. No one saw what happened between you and Sutherland—"

"It wasn't between me and Sutherland," I said, elbowing past him

"Sure it wasn't," Ron said, following. "It was the demon, right? The demon who hitched a ride in that priest's body and made him jump out the window? Just like the fucking movie."

I snagged a half-gallon of two-percent milk, shoved it into my basket. Ron's words had rattled me. The comment about *The Exorcist* was the same comment an investigating officer had made while taking my statement at the hospital. Had I time, I might have come up with a less derivative story to explain Peter Sutherland's death, yet it was the only one that fit the evidence.

Other than the truth, of course.

But I wasn't about to admit I'd thrown my mentor through that third story window. Or that Malephar had endowed me with the strength to commit murder.

"I was wondering," Ron continued, his breath hot and yeasty on my neck, "can priests get absolution when they screw up? Because you sure as hell need to spend some time in the confessional booth. Murder, coveting another guy's wife, telling lies so you can get in her pants—"

"Listen," I said, turning to stare him down. "You better shut your mouth before this goes any further."

(*Kill him*)

I tensed at Malephar's whisper. My rage must have awakened the demon—or coaxed him closer to the surface.

Ron's eyes went wide, his thick eyebrows disappearing under his shaggy black hair. "Tough words for a man of the cloth," he said. "You talk a big game, Father." A glance at the onlookers, Ron reveling in the audience. "You maybe want to do something about it?"

(*Kill him, Jason*)

"See," Ron went on, "I've been thinking about it a lot. You know, remembering how slick you were, how well you managed to insinuate yourself into my place."

The black man muttered something to the short woman, something about paying for their items and leaving.

Ron ticked off his points on his fingers. "You've been eyeing my wife on Sundays, and since I'm not one for

254

church, I had no idea you were hitting on her all those mornings."

Sweat was beading on my forehead, the eyes of the bystanders crawling over me like thirsty ants. "This is absurd."

(*Do it! Tear his throat out!*)

"And Casey. You come to his rescue, save him from the monster, and Liz thinks you're some big hero."

"Ron," I said, controlling my voice with an effort, "you and I have nothing to say to each other."

"Oh we don't, huh? When a man takes my place, sleeps in my bed—"

"I did not sleep in your—"

"—or maybe you were too busy boning Liz to sleep—"

"I did *not*—"

But I never finished. Because at that moment, three men in masks burst through the front door. They were shouting at everyone to get on the floor.

They were carrying guns.

CHAPTER EIGHT

"Open the goddamned register!" one of the gunmen shouted and leveled the gun through the Plexiglas at the Indian woman. She couldn't have been older than twenty-five, and seemed out of place working in a convenience store. I wondered if her parents owned it, then brushed the thought away as frivolous, considering the circumstances.

And the circumstances were dire. The other two gunmen had already dispersed through the store, bellowing at the horrified patrons to get the fuck on the ground, to put their goddamned hands on the backs of their heads, to not say a fucking word. And if anyone went for a cell phone, they'd blow a hole through his motherfucking face.

One of the gunmen stalked down the aisle toward me, his eyes blue and fierce under the black ski mask. "Are you a moron, Father? Do you fucking comprehend English?"

In the confused jumble of my thoughts, I wondered how he knew I was a priest. Then I remembered my Roman collar, and on the heels of that, my reasons for wearing one. The majority of the priests at St. Matthew's eschewed them. While I respected their decision, I had always aligned with Father Sutherland and Father Patterson's view, which was that a priest should advertise his vocation plainly. Not as a vain demonstration of pride, but as an outward expression of faith. "We need to show others that we care about pleasing God first," Father Sutherland used to remind me. "We need to make it clear that we're ambassadors of Christ, conduits through which His everlasting love can flow to those who will open their hearts to Him."

The gunman thrust his gun at my face. "I'm not gonna ask again, you fucking retard. Get on the goddamned floor!"

The next aisle over, a girl was moaning, and though she was shielded from my view, I was certain it was one of the teenagers. It appeared that the third gunman, a mountainous guy whose barrel-shaped torso stretched the black fabric of his hooded sweatshirt, was mashing his foot into her back, or at least that was my guess based on the way he was shifting every time she moaned.

"You think I won't do it?" the gunman in front of me demanded. I could see how puny his arms were, how the black hoodie drooped as though sodden. His blue eyes were very pale, the swatches of skin visible around them so white I was reminded of a skeleton bleached by the sun. "You think I give a flying fuck about your religion, Father? I was raised Catholic," he said, showing yellow, scummy teeth. "You think that shit helped my mom when she got sick? You think it helped me when I needed money for school?"

I gazed into his pale blue eyes. Lost, haunted eyes. "You believe that God makes people suffer?" I asked.

"I believe He doesn't give a shit," the young man said. "If He exists at all."

"He exists," I said. "And He'll never abandon you."

But the gunman wasn't listening. "You holier-than-thou bastards. You judge everybody and hide behind the Bible and tell people what they can't do and then you cut 'em loose the moment they mess up."

I understood his anguish, had wrestled with it myself. Very frequently, life wasn't fair. And God was the easiest scapegoat. If He was omniscient, the hurting heart demanded, didn't He know when something bad was going to happen? And if He knew, and He allowed the terrible thing to occur, wasn't He devoid of feeling? Or worse, wasn't He a cruel, pitiless deity rather than a loving one?

Yes, I understood this man all too well. But I had to try, had to do what I could for this lost soul. "God doesn't want to push you away. And he certainly doesn't orchestrate human suffering. His son showed us that love is the greatest power."

The gunman's eyes opened wide. "Are you telling me you *love* me? Are you really trying to peddle that bullshit now?"

"Yes," I said. "That's what I'm telling you. I do love you, and so does Christ."

He jammed the gun against my chin, the muzzle fitting neatly into my dimple. "I'm gonna waste you, you lying son of a bitch. So help me, I'm—"

"*Dylan!*" someone shouted.

The gunman's trance broke. He blinked, glowered over his shoulder. "We're not supposed to use names."

"When you're about to fuck up the whole thing," the massive gunman growled, "he's gotta get your attention, right?"

"Still shouldn't've used my name," Dylan muttered.

"Get 'em over there in one spot," the gunman at the front of the store shouted. "As far away from the door as you can."

"Sir?" Ron asked. He had his hands clasped obediently behind his head, his lips brushing the grungy floor as he spoke. "How're we supposed to move if we're laying on the ground?"

Dylan, the skinny gunman who'd threatened to kill me, chuckled. "Like worms."

Ron looked up at him, but before he could speak, Dylan's sneakered shoe flashed out, busted Ron in the cheek. Ron yelped and grasped his face, but the skinny gunman moved with him, aiming kicks at Ron's buttocks. "Move, Wormy! Move along, little Wormy!"

"You!" the gunman in the front of the store shouted at the young Indian woman. "Get your chunky butt out here and lock the store. I want all the lights out and the doors buttoned tight."

"Do you want me to hand you the money?" the young woman asked. Her voice was steady, not at all the way I'd expect someone to sound when she was staring at a loaded gun.

"Did I *ask* you to hand me the money?" the gunman demanded. "Do I look like I'm capable of walking around a counter and lifting a few bills out of a register? Now get your dumb ass out here and lock the fucking doors!"

Wordlessly, the woman began carrying out the gunman's directions.

"That's right, bitch. Kill the lights."

She did.

"And don't even think about triggering the alarm. I know you haven't yet because it's under the counter there." A nod. "That's right," he said, his voice oily and cozening. The young woman approached the door with a jangling key ring. "Good girl," the gunman said. "That's right...don't think about running for it..." The woman locked the doors, tested them, turned to face the lead gunman, who I noticed was shorter than the other two. "Now get your ass over there with the others."

She began to cross the entryway, but before she got far, the lead gunman moved up behind her, snaked an arm around her waist, and began stroking the front of her shirt. The woman resisted, but before she could break the gunman's hold, he dug the barrel into the small of her back.

"*Yeah,*" he said, moving the muzzle around to poke her in the ribs. He dragged his gloved hands over her groin, over the mounds of her breasts. "You like that, don't you, honey." He began pushing his pelvis into her from behind, grinding himself against her buttocks. "Uh-huh," he said, the woman shuddering with revulsion now, "you know you like it."

I looked away, sickened. I wanted to do something, but what could I do? I was nearly as scrawny as Dylan, and I wasn't equipped with the devil-may-care lunacy he possessed. I had to—

Possessed, I thought.

Malephar.

The idea slammed into me like a bonecrushing fist. What if I allowed Malephar to come forward?

(*Yes*)

What if I followed through with my original plan, that of combating evil with evil?

(*Yessss*)

Nervelessly, I began to crawl after Ron on knees and elbows, like some poorly-trained soldier avoiding gunfire.

Cries erupted from the corner area where everyone was being herded. I heard a muffled protest, then someone hushing someone else.

When I joined Ron in the corner, I saw what the commotion was about.

The largest gunman was sitting on a teenaged girl's legs. He had freed his huge paws of their black gloves and was now sliding his fingers up and down the girl's back. Her clothes were still on, but I suspected that wouldn't last long.

261

Bright rage flickered within me. I gnashed my teeth.

"Get the fuck on the ground," the lead gunman shouted, dragging the Indian woman around the corner and shoving her toward the group. He was rubbing his ribs. "Fucking bitch elbowed me. You believe that, Dylan?"

"Stop using my name," Dylan said, but his voice was toneless. I glanced up at him, saw how dead his eyes looked. They were battened on the massive gunman and the teenager he was fondling. The huge paws had graduated to the girl's lower back, were kneading their way toward her buttocks.

I was quaking with fury, my muscles bunching.

(*Let me out*)

I ignored Malephar. I couldn't tell whether the one named Dylan was watching the sexual assault with longing or dismay, but his next words clarified matters:

"Let her go, Fish."

The enormous gunman stared up at Dylan. "Hey! What the fuck? Just cuz they know your name doesn't mean—"

"It's a *nickname*, man. Take it easy." A glance toward the door. "C'mon, let's just take the money and go."

The lead gunman stalked over to Dylan, gave him a rough shove in the chest. "I decide when we're leaving, dickhead. And this bitch over here—" The gunman stepped over, and kicked the prostrate Indian woman in the arm, "—this *cunt*, she elbows me and thinks she can get away with it?"

"You need to stop that talk," someone said. I pushed up slightly and saw it was the black man, who, up close, was older than I'd at first guessed. Sixty-five at least.

But his expression was unblinking. "You need to stop messing with that girl," he said to the huge gunman.

"The dude's right," Dylan said.

But Fish only cackled, his hands now prying the girl's legs apart. "Old enough to bleed is old enough for me!"

Then something happened that I wouldn't have anticipated in a billion years.

Ron said, "She's just a kid."

So strained was his voice yet so raw was the emotion it contained that the huge gunman glanced at Ron. So did the assaulted girl, whose face had been mashed into the crook of an elbow, perhaps in an attempt to mentally escape from the degradation being inflicted upon her. She had big brown eyes, light brown hair, quite long, and a squarish but attractive jawline. She was gazing at Ron with something that fell just shy of hope.

The huge gunman glowered at Ron. "The fuck do you care? She your kid or something?"

Ron got swayingly to his knees, grimacing at the cracking sounds they made. "She's not mine," he said. "But she's somebody's."

Fish stared at Ron in astonishment, then his big gut began to jiggle. He glanced at the main gunman, who'd been watching the exchange, then they both began to gust laughter.

Ron didn't back down. "It's true. You three should get out of here before the cops show up."

"That's what I've been telling you," Dylan said. He was jittery now, bouncing on the heels of his sneakers. "We don't leave soon, we—"

"We *what*, Dylan?" the main gunman snapped. "We what? From the street it looks like there's no one here. The lights're off. If the cops do come by, they'll think the little Hindu princess here closed early for the night."

"We stay open twenty-four hours," the woman said. "My parents never close. The police will know that. They'll check on the store. They'll see you."

"She's right," Ron said. "You guys leave now, you'll have your take and nobody'll get hurt."

The main gunman, who'd been eyeing the Indian woman with a mixture of disdain and lust, now strode toward Ron. The way the gunman moved and talked had disquieted me. But now that disquiet blossomed into a full-blown dread. The man had staked a claim as the leader of this motley trio, which meant he'd asserted power not only over Dylan, but over the huge man as well. The lead gunman, I decided, must possess some amount of cunning, a caginess that the other two lacked.

In other words, he was a dangerous man. A man who has seen much and no longer cares about anything, least of all doing the right thing.

And the largest gunman? Fish? He was a sociopath who yearned to inflict harm upon others. Had probably already done so. I had little doubt he had raped women before, perhaps even killed them.

Let me out, Malephar demanded.

I swallowed. *No one deserves that.*

These wretches do. I'll leave Dylan alive if you'd like, but only if he doesn't interfere. These other two, however... they deserve to be gutted.

I couldn't argue with that. The massive gunman had resumed his sickening explorations of the teenaged girl's back. Her friend, lying beside her, was grasping her hand and whispering tearful words to her in an attempt to mitigate the horror.

"Yeah," the main gunman said, watching the assault. The leader's muddy eyes were glazed with sadistic pleasure, his mouth half-open.

Animals, Malephar declared.

"I told you to stop it," Ron said, and actually took a step toward Fish.

"That's it," the main gunman snarled, raising his gun toward Ron. "I'm shuttin' this cocksucker up."

"They'll hear you," the Filipino woman said. "If you fire the gun, everyone in the neighborhood will know there's a crime in progress. And you'll be a murderer."

A feral smile curved the leader's lips. "Maybe I'm already a murderer." He let that sink in. Nodded. "Maybe I came prepared, huh?"

With that he reached down, tugged up a leg of his black jeans, and unsnapped a large knife case on his ankle. When he stood erect, he grasped a Bowie knife.

"Hold on," Ron said, his palms up, but the leader moved closer, poked the tip of the blade under Ron's jaw, lifted his face with it.

I must admit to harboring the worst thought, the most selfish thought of my life at that moment. If Ron died, Liz would inherit a great deal of money and would be free to enter another relationship. With me.

Yet even as this thought tumbled through my head, it enkindled in me a feeling of such self-loathing that I feared I might vomit. No man, no matter how much he desires a woman, should sink to such emotional depths.

Servant of God indeed.

The gunman bared his teeth in a grin. "That's right," he told Ron. "You're gonna be the first to get it. I can tell by your clothes what a rich prick you are."

Ron started to speak, but then everything happened fast. The Bowie knife shifted higher, and Ron attempted to stand on his tiptoes. The knife tip pierced his flesh, the razor-sharp blade filleting the soft shelf of his jaw and unleashing a happy stream of blood. Ron let out a gargling, high-pitched cry.

I pushed to my knees, but a flurry of movement drew my gaze. The huge gunman was fiddling with the fly of his jeans.

"Jesus, Fish," Dylan whined. "You gotta stop it."

Fish unsheathed his erect penis.

"Let her go!" the black man shouted, up on his knees now.

Fish grabbed for his gun, retrieved it and aimed it at the black man. "You move again, you get this. I don't give a fuck who hears it." He grunted, reached up, peeled off his ski mask. "Fucking thing, can barely breathe in it." The enormous man's features were slack, formless. A scraggly beard the color of cinnamon reefed his ruddy round face. But when his eyes returned to the girl, his mouth curled into an indecent leer.

Several people were muttering oaths; Ron was still moaning that reedy moan and actually trying to grab the blade that pierced his underjaw. The knife hadn't gone deep, but a quarter-inch of it was slitting his chin in a delicate filigree, and the blood was splurting over both men's hands.

And as I watched the blood stream in rivulets down Ron's wrists, I remembered Ron's son, remembered Casey as he'd been the other night. Bound to the bed, the handcuffs gouging his wrists and the tender meat of his hands. I remembered Father Sutherland facing down the demon, recalled Sutherland's awe-inspiring courage in the face of evil.

Wasn't this evil just as unconscionable?

I thought of the Sweet Sixteen's victims, those poor girls butchered for no reason, save the satisfaction of a madman's whims. I looked at the teenage girl, sobbing into her elbow, the monstrous Fish about to tear her open and murder her when he was done.

Yet it was Ron that finally galvanized me, Ron who'd never to my knowledge done anything unselfish in his life, who'd brought others only misery and heartache. Even Ron had proven himself capable of goodness.

Was I so low that I couldn't still bring some good to the world too?

I closed my eyes, letting my body go limp.

Come forward, I urged.

This time Malephar did not hesitate.

◆ ◆ ◆

There was a sensation of weightlessness, of being propelled forward rapidly, as if strapped to some high-speed roller coaster. Yet with it came a singular sense of volition, one I hadn't anticipated. Far from feeling anesthetized and manipulated, as I'd felt twice that day at St. Matthew's, I now experienced the most exhilarating feeling of vitality. Malephar did come forward. He did seize control of my body. But I was not subverted or marginalized; to the contrary, I was rendered a willing, thrumming accomplice, my very will transformed into that of the demon. I *wanted* to spill blood. I *wanted* to rip flesh and inflict violence on these jackals.

I went for the main gunman first, not only because he was the closest, but because if the Bowie knife plunged any deeper, Ron would be mortally wounded.

One moment I was prone on the tiled floor. The next I was hurtling toward the leader. Yet I didn't take a step, didn't push to my feet. I was on the ground one instant, and the next I was flying toward the gunman and his Bowie knife. No creature of the natural world could have moved with such immense speed.

My body crashed into the main gunman's. At the same moment, I seized his wrist and jerked down, the Bowie knife leaving Ron's flesh with a wet *schlitt*. Peripherally, I saw Ron stagger back against the refrigerator door, both hands clamped over his bleeding underjaw, but my attention was lasered on the main gunman, who, Malephar's tactile clairvoyance instantly revealed to me, was an ex-con named Randy Connelly, a man who'd indeed murdered three people, one of them a delivery boy he'd crunched over in his SUV after drinking too much, his other two victims fellow inmates Connelly had been paid to kill. He had also, I realized as we crashed to the floor, sold drugs to children, not on street corners but from his own squalid apartment.

Which only enraged me further.

The force of my body slamming into his had knocked Connelly's wind out and completely disoriented him; the impact of our bodies on the hard tile was so great that the vertebrae at the base of his neck fractured, the crunching sound audible even above the shrieks and shouts around us.

I knew the scrawny gunman named Dylan would be too stunned at first to act, but the one they called Fish, the giant who'd been about to rape the teenaged girl, would not hesitate to shoot me. And though Malephar's powers were prodigious, I suspected there were limits to the wounds he could heal. If I were shot in the head or the heart, there'd be no saving me.

I turned, and just as I'd surmised, Fish had his gun trained on me, was even now in the process of squeezing the trigger. Though we were steeped almost entirely in darkness, I could yet make out the darker circle of the muzzle as it rose toward my face.

I lunged forward, my body sailing over Randy Connelly's, just as Fish fired. The bullet shattered a glass refrigerator door and sent a ghostly gout of milk spouting from its ruptured container. As the shards of glass and droplets of milk rose into the air, my agile body banged shoulder-first into the metal-walled corner. I knew Fish would be firing again, so I spun along the wall, swiftly flanking the massive gunman. Bullets split the thin layer of metal in my wake, but Fish's reflexes, though fueled by what I could only assume to be derangement, were no match for mine. I sprang off the wall, spinning toward him as I did, and in the instant before my body reached his, a new vista of sensory input revealed itself to me. I smelled everything in the store: the sour aroma of the rent milk jug. The fear-sweat hovering over the victims of this nightmarish robbery. The rancid stench of bad breath. And Fish, most of all, who reeked of bacon fat and crystal meth and unwashed armpits and unwiped ass. Beneath it I sensed an even more incisive odor, one I associated with Danny Hartman.

The unmistakable perfume of sadism.

I reached down as my body traveled over Fish's. My thumbnail wasn't especially long, but when it plunged into his left eyeball, the hard edge of the nail razoring into the tender cornea, Fish let loose with such a strident wail that one would've have thought I'd crucified him.

Though my momentum carried me over his kneeling body, I plunged my thumbnail deeper, grasping hold of his doughy red face like a bowling ball, and as we tumbled, I twisted his head unnaturally, hauling him off his teenaged victim, sending both of us crashing into a red wire rack full of hanging bags of candy. Our combined weight caused the entire rack to crumple, the metal prongs from which the candy distended gouging our bodies, the candy itself pinwheeling around as though a giant piñata had just exploded.

I didn't loosen my hold on Fish, whom I now identified as Marlon Meeks. Our bodies jounced on the overturned rack. My grip on his face was tightening, my fingers now compacting his temple, his left cheekbone, my thumb crushing his eye.

I reveled in his wails.

The girl Meeks had been assaulting was on hands and knees now, gaping at her dying attacker with disbelief. The Indian woman, I noticed at a glance, had leaped upon the injured form of Randy Connelly and begun battering his face with wild blows. Within moments, she was joined by the black man, the short woman, and Ron, who though he was still bleeding, appeared furious. Like a pack of wolves, they fell upon Connelly, the black man hammering his upflung arms, the short woman kicking him in the side. Ron was actually impeding the others by shouldering his way closer, evidently bent on exacting revenge on the man who had stabbed him under the chin.

But it was on Marlon Meeks I was focused. I beheld his life's work as I dug my thumb deeper into his eye socket. I

270

saw him raping multiple women, watched him torturing animals. But the images that floated to the surface and dominated my mind's eye were the ones that enflamed my fury the most, that whipped my dark passion into a frenzied blur: Marlon staring at his two-year-old sister as she slumbered in her crib, Marlon himself twelve years her senior and certainly old enough to know how unhealthy his thoughts were. Marlon reaching into the crib, one hand gripping his sex, the other rustling the bedsheets...

"*Die, pedophile!*" I growled, my voice unlike any that had escaped my lips before. "*Taste death, you defiler of children!*"

Meeks had gripped my forearm in an attempt to stave off my attack, and though his fingers were powerful—the flesh of my forearm was bloodmoist from his viselike grip—not even his panic strength was enough to wrest my steadily squeezing fingers from his head. Through the blistering sheet of hatred, I felt the cartilage around his eye socket give way, a hot burst of sclera, the tender bones of his nasal cavity splintering. My forefinger harpooned his temple, the flesh furrowing like sea-tender blubber. My middle and ring fingers caved in his cheekbone with a meaty crunch, even my pinkie finger puncturing the distressed skin of his cheek. My thumb was buried almost to the last knuckle. I could feel the gray mush of his brain squishing like hot porridge.

Meeks's big heels drummed on the candy-strewn floor.

I became aware of someone beside me recoiling in horror. But I was intent on my work, the demon in me reveling in the huge man's death throes.

"Mother... *fuckers*," Randy Connelly growled. Somehow, he'd broken loose of his attackers. Though injured, though the pain from his fractured vertebrae was etched on his sullen, whiskered face, Connelly was also enraged by the undoing of his robbery attempt.

Clutching the gun, he rose.

A ripple of rage swept through me. How could the group of onlookers—there had been no fewer than four of them attacking Connelly—have neglected to strip him of his weapon? It was unfathomable. Yet typical of human beings. All passion, no calculation. And now it was incumbent upon me to accomplish what the hapless group of fools had failed to bring to a close.

So be it.

The patrons nearest Meeks's convulsing body—the two teenagers and the white-haired man—were gazing at me with superstitious terror. I couldn't blame them. I had seen Casey's face when Malephar had possessed him: eyeballs swirling into bloodred marbles, teeth tapered to fanglike points, features angular and vulpine. An effigy of darkest evil.

Dylan had been transfixed by the sound of my demonic voice. He stood apart from the others, slack-jawed with fright.

I rose to my full height, stalked toward him.

"Your..." he whispered, swaying on his feet. "Your eyes..."

"Eat this, Father," a voice said from directly behind me.

Had I been in control of my body at that moment, I've no doubt my brains would have exploded out of my eye sockets. Connelly, the leader of the vicious criminals, squeezed the trigger less than a second after he uttered his crude valediction.

But I was not under my own power. I was governed by Malephar. And for the second time in twenty-four hours, the demon saved my life.

So quickly I could scarcely believe it, my head whipped sideways, though not crisply enough to escape the ear-splitting concussion of the gunshot, nor the slug's lethal trajectory. My eardrum was transformed into a pulpy goulash from the blast, the slug dug a messy trench through my hairline just above the ear, and Dylan, directly in the line of fire, cupped his throat, which began to gush blood.

Instinctively, I clapped a hand to the scorched wound in my head, fought off the spiraling vertigo that threatened to upend the room. As I staggered sideways into the refrigerated glass, Connelly said, "Dammit, Dylan, you shoulda moved!" and somewhere beneath my pain and disorientation, I sensed sorrow in Connelly's voice.

I knew this was my opportunity to disarm Connelly, yet my body felt sluggish, unwilling to comply with the rigors I was demanding of it. In some way, I realized, the gunshot had unseated Malephar, and the demon was struggling to regain control of me. Though doing so cost an effort and seemed like the sickest sort of compromise, I allowed my will to recede, and in its stead felt the immediate rushing forward of the demon.

Malephar's dire strength coursing through my veins, I turned, leered at Connelly, who had taken a step toward Dylan, who'd sunk to his knees, the blood dumping over his chest.

Connelly did not see me, only continued staring at Dylan, who clasped his gushing throat, whose face, even in the wan light, looked unnaturally pallid.

"Why didn't you move, Dylan?" Connelly whined. "I never meant to hit you."

I was three feet from Connelly, who seemed to have forgotten all about me. But I hadn't forgotten about him, about the men he had killed, about the children he had poisoned. All because of money. All due to base greed.

"You took my life," I said in Mandarin Chinese, my voice that of Huan Tseng, the twenty-one-year-old delivery boy Connelly had slammed into, drunk, with his black SUV. In a flash I saw Huan's startled expression, witnessed the glancing impact of the SUV as its grill pulverized Huan's body. Then the terrible crunch of the bike and the Chinese boy's bones as the SUV actually accelerated, Connelly too shitfaced to discern the pedals under his feet.

Connelly stared at me, his dingy hazel eyes huge and horrified. "The *fuck?*"

"I was just trying to earn money for college," I said in a tongue I'd never uttered before.

"I don't know what the hell you're saying," Connelly murmured, backpedaling.

"*The delivery boy,*" Malephar explained in his dark rumble. "*You murdered him and you never even said you were sorry.*"

Connelly passed a hand over his lips, retreated toward the front of the store. "I don't know what your problem is, man. Just get the fuck away from me."

I stalked toward him, marveling at his stupidity. He'd forgotten he was the one with the weapon. He'd also apparently decided his grief over the dying Dylan was immaterial when compared with his need to escape this growling priest who spoke Mandarin in a dead man's voice.

"Just get your...your weirdo shit away from me," he said, all traces of bravado absent from his voice.

I strode toward him, and as I did, a bar of spectral green light from the overhanging EXIT sign fell across my face. Connelly saw me and bellowed in terror, his fingers actually clamped on his cheeks, the gun he grasped striking him a rough blow on the side of the face. So ridiculous was the gesture and so deep was my contempt for him that I decided to prolong his suffering. *"Do what you did to those men in prison."*

"Prison?" he said.

"Kill me, you worthless piece of filth! Show these people what a brave man you are!"

Like someone who's taken a powerful sedative, Connelly raised the gun and aimed it at me. The muzzle bounced wildly, yet at such close range he couldn't miss. He squeezed the trigger. At the same moment I dove to his left, sprang to my feet, half-spun him so he faced the glass door.

"What are you—" he started, but I'd already buried my fingers in his brown hair. He opened his mouth, a yowling scream starting deep in his throat, but then I was bashing his face into the hard glass door, the impact so great that the thick glass shattered.

Had the concussion of his forehead on the door been the only injury Connelly sustained, he might yet have lived. But the shards of glass were of such a wicked sharpness that his face was carved up beyond recognition. A sheet of skin from his hairline to the bridge of his nose peeled down and hung in a flap over his lips, which were frothing blood. One eye was frozen in a permanent stare, the eyelid having been sheared off. A sickle-shaped hook of glass had slashed the other eye, so that ocular fluid was sloshing down Connelly's cheek.

I hauled his failing body close to me, Malephar's strength easily supporting Connelly's superior weight. I brought my face close to his, whispered, "*You're disfigured, Connelly. You've always been a sniveling, cocksucking shitstain, but now you're a freak. A hideous abomination. I should let you live like this. But instead...*"

I moved away from him, so that the onlookers in the rear of the store could see I had nothing to do with what was about to happen. The gun had been lost in our scuffle, but there were plenty of lethal objects strewn about Connelly.

He leaned down, and despite the fact that he was effectively blind, his fingers selected a crescent-shaped shard perhaps seven inches long. I delighted in the way the vicious edge sank into his fingers as he brought the shard nearer his throat.

"*Yes,*" I whispered.

"What are you doing?" he moaned. Perhaps he didn't realize what Malephar was forcing him to do.

The curved glass sank into his throat just below the Adam's apple. Then, as his scream devolved into a gurgling wail, the glass sliced a vertical line through his voicebox, continued through the soft tissue up to his chin. Then, with a flick, the shard completed the inverted cross in his throat, the severed jugular jetting all over the entryway.

I had a fleeting worry that Malephar would refuse to cede control, that he would turn his considerable powers on the innocent patrons. But almost immediately I felt the demon's grasp slackening, felt the diabolical power drain from my limbs.

Of course, I thought as Connelly writhed and choked on the floor. *Of course Malephar wants you to view it with your own eyes, wants you to feel the desolate guilt from killing Meeks and butchering Connelly.*

Someone was approaching from behind me, but whoever it was moved with a tentativeness that told me I was safe from an attack. Whoever it was feared me.

With good reason.

I turned and saw Ron and the Indian woman. The woman's face was a disbelieving mask, but Ron's expression was totally blank, as though he were studying a bare white wall rather than a mutilated criminal drowning in a pool of his own blood.

"Why did he do that?" the woman asked. "Why did he kill himself?"

I shrugged, tried and failed to keep the guilty edge off my voice. "He probably didn't want to live after he shot that Dylan guy."

The woman looked at me. "What did you say to him?"

I frowned.

"Just before he slashed his own throat, you whispered something to him. What was it?"

"Do we really give a damn?" Ron asked. "This piece of shit deserves exactly what he got. I'm just glad the Father here grew a pair of stones in time to bring this fucker down." He slapped me on the back. "You done good, Father. I didn't think you had that in you."

Far from feeling validated by Ron's words, the guilt only cored in deeper. It was God's approval I craved, not a sex-addicted stockbroker's.

Apparently reading the misery in my face, Ron said, "Look at me, Crowder."

I did.

He said, "They probably don't teach you this in seminary, but when shit like this goes down, there's two kinds of people: the predators and the prey. You either get your throat torn out, or you do the tearing. I don't know how you did what you did—hell, maybe it was luck, right? They were three of the dumbest fucks I've ever seen, but that's beside the point. The point is, you did it. You killed 'em. And everybody here's alive because of that."

"He's right," a male voice said. I turned and saw the black man with the short woman at his side. He had an arm wrapped protectively around her. "It was awful, but we'll testify that you had no choice. If anyone looks at that man's face..." He glanced toward where Myron Meeks lay. "...we'll just tell them the truth. He was trying to..."

"Rape me," a voice finished. We all turned and saw the two teenagers approaching. The one who'd been assaulted no longer looked like the same kid who'd entered the store. Her eyes were glazed hollows, her mouth downturned at the edges, not in despondency, I thought, but with the grimness of lost innocence. Outwardly, she was the same, but somehow she seemed thirty years older.

She gazed up at me. "Thank you for stopping him."

I nodded, having no words to express how I felt. Ron started to say something, but the whine of police sirens drew our collective gaze toward the shattered door and the flicker of red-and-blue lights.

"Fucking cops," Ron said. "Now they show up, right? But when you need one, the fuckers are never around."

The Indian woman squeezed my arm. "Who needs a policeman when you have a priest?"

Part Two
The Demon in the Dark

CHAPTER NINE

The aftermath went by in a haze of questions and hushed conversations. They'd shepherded me outside and provided a folding chair in which to wait. The police bustled about and kept casting glances in my direction. Perhaps they were considering pressing charges but wanted to build a strong case first. I had, after all, been responsible for one death and was at least partially to blame for another. One officer, a red-haired woman about my age, took my account but didn't offer praise or censure. Another policeman, whom I took for a detective, stood eyeing me from within the store, the glass between us having the effect of making me feel like some rare zoo exhibit: *Step right up and see the priest who mutilates people!* Though the detective wore a black, faded Goo Goo Dolls T-shirt and blue jeans with a rip in one knee, he appeared to be the one in charge. He was maybe forty, and several times the people taking pictures and interviewing witnesses came over to ask him questions.

He spent most of his time scrutinizing me through the window.

I sipped a bottle of Mountain Dew provided by the Indian woman, who was treating me with more warmth than I deserved. I watched them talking to her, and though I couldn't hear exactly what her responses were, I could tell from the earnest look on her face and the emphatic manner in which she gestured toward me that she was painting me in a favorable light. The detective in the Goo Goo Dolls shirt moved from the woman to Ron, who grew animated and appeared to enjoy recounting the tale far too much, given how ghastly it had been. The red-haired woman and the detective spoke to Ron for a while, and when they attempted to move toward the rear of the store, Ron followed them, clearly wanting to provide further details. I had no idea what he might be saying, but I put the odds at about ninety-nine percent that he was embellishing his role in the story. Finally, Goo Goo Dolls jerked a thumb over his shoulder to tell Ron to get lost. Ron exited through the fire door, which the police had propped open. The main exit, after all, was the site of Randy Connelly's apparent suicide and therefore part of the crime scene.

I didn't want to think about Connelly now. Or ever again, for that matter. Shivering, I took a swig of Mountain Dew.

"Don't worry," Ron said, coming over, his underjaw heavily-bandaged. "I had them call my brother. I know how tight you and Danny are."

He must have noticed how I paled because he said, "Hey, don't worry. He's got your back. If anybody can vouch for your character, he can." A pause, Ron studying my face. "Or maybe we should call my wife, huh?"

I squeezed the bottle in my hand, the plastic crinkling audibly. "If you're going to—"

"Okay, okay," he said, laughing softly. "We'll let that go for now. For *now*, mind you. I don't take kindly to anybody tapping my wife, not even a guy who saved my hide."

"I'm not tapping—oh, to hell with it."

Ron grinned, shook his head. "That mouth of yours. I still don't know how you became a priest."

"Neither do I," I said, for once in complete agreement with him.

◆ ◆ ◆

Ron tried to engage me in further conversation, but other than Danny, he was the last person with whom I wanted to spend time. I wandered over to the edge of the parking lot, sensed several sets of eyes on me. I turned and discovered the detective watching me through the window, his expression warning me not to leave.

So I'm a murder suspect, I thought. I had killed Myron Meeks, of course, but perhaps I'd been wrong to allow the affirmation of the other witnesses to lull me into a false sense of security.

How different this was than my expectations had been. Before, I'd harbored aspirations of becoming a crime-fighting hero, a priest endowed with the strength of God and the ability to harness the powers of darkness as well.

But rather than metamorphosing into a holy vigilante, I'd become a pawn, the unwitting plaything of an entity far more formidable than I.

Yet this wasn't the worst. I had long been accustomed to being dismissed by other men, to being invisible to women. No one, save Father Sutherland, had ever expected anything of me, and look where that got him.

But what dogged me as I drifted through the parking lot, a prisoner to Malephar's eruption of violence, was the renewal of my impotence, not of a sexual nature, but the overarching impotence from which I'd suffered since earliest childhood.

A hint of sewage reached my nostrils, and beneath that, something else. There must have been construction occurring in one of the nearby buildings, because I also caught a whiff of sawdust, the grit of broken plaster.

With a sinking feeling, I recalled an incident from my ninth year, a day I'd been looking forward to with the enthusiasm only a child can muster. My mom had been dating one of her long succession of boyfriends, a marina owner at the local lake. This man, Phil Garza, had been a do-it-yourself sort of guy, a carpenter on the side who made extra money purchasing run-down lake cottages, fixing them up, and flipping them for a profit. After dating my mom for several weeks, he made an effort to build a rapport with me. Since I desperately craved a father figure, I welcomed this interaction with an eagerness I now looked back on as heartbreaking. Phil asked my mother if I'd like to help him with a cottage renovation. My mom consented, hoping it would strengthen my bond with Phil. In the days leading up to that Saturday morning, I imagined myself driving a backhoe, wielding a sledgehammer, and engaging in other tasks beyond my abilities.

Of course, the reality had proven far more mundane. Phil enlisted me to hold his tape measure, to select the proper tools from his toolbox, orders that I invariably got wrong since I didn't know a wrench from a screwdriver.

Phil grew increasingly impatient with me.

The irony of this was that the very reason I didn't know how to do any of the things he asked of me was because I didn't have a father. So the lack of experience that came from not having a dad was preventing me from connecting with a man I fervently wanted to become my father figure.

Being nine, I had no idea how to express these thoughts.

The one thought I did express, incessantly I'm sure, was a desire to help knock down a wall Phil had marked for demolition. Situated between the small galley kitchen and the dining room, Phil had decided to raze the wall in an attempt to create a more open floor plan. Since the cottage had been built in the early fifties, the walls were constructed of plaster, which necessitated the use of the heavy blue-handled sledgehammer I'd spotted in the bed of Phil's truck. Maybe wanting to give me a chance to prove my worth, or more likely, to shut me up, Phil had finally agreed to let me strike the wall first and thus begin the demolition.

I knew I was in trouble the moment Phil hefted the sledgehammer and placed it in my hands. The weight of it made me stagger, though I did what I could to maintain a rugged demeanor. Cocking an eyebrow, Phil had instructed me to choke up on the sledge and to aim for a spot he'd marked with a penciled X. The spot, he said, was on a level with my face and should be an ideal starting place for the tear-out. Further, he explained, the electrical wires were situated about eighteen inches from the floor, which meant my aim would have to be, in his words, "worse than a blind man's" to miss my mark badly enough to do substantial harm.

Assuring him I understood, I strained to raise the sledge. Phil asked me if I needed help, and I shook my head no. When the sledge was about stomach-high, I realized I couldn't raise it any higher, but this, I decided, wasn't a problem. Once the sledge was in motion, I told myself, I'd be able to swing it in an upward trajectory and hit the large penciled X. But a third of the way through my swing, my muscles failed, that familiar impotence overwhelming me. I did what I could to redirect the heavy iron head of the sledgehammer, but my efforts were useless. In slow motion I watched it plummet lower, the force of my swing more than potent enough to punch through the plaster and crush the electrical wires lurking beneath.

The hole I'd made began to flash. Blue and gold sparks spat through the broken plaster. Growling obscenities and something about a faulty circuit breaker, Phil thrust me out of the way and grasped the sledge's handle. I went sprawling on a pile of nail-ridden boards, sustained an ugly puncture wound just below the elbow, and cried out. This was met with more obscenities from Phil, who'd wrestled the sledge out of the wall, but was now faced with an injured child and a potential fire. He disappeared through the doorway. Moments later, the sizzling and zapping sounds ceased from the severed wires, and Phil reentered the room, sweating and flushed.

He stood over me, heedless of the blood that dribbled between my fingers. "Goddamned breakers," he said, mopping his forehead. "Things shoulda tripped when you damaged the lines." He looked around, shook his head. "Whole damn place coulda gone up in flames, kid. You shoulda just told me you couldn't do it."

Those words resonated with me now. I'd wanted to help Phil, but I couldn't do it. As a teenager I'd wanted to enjoy all the things my peers were doing—dating, playing sports, making friends—but I couldn't.

And tonight, I had proven impotent again. Sure, I'd stopped Ron from being executed and prevented the teenage girl from being further violated, but it hadn't been Jason Crowder doing those things, had it? It had been the demon sating his warped desires. I hadn't actually done anything except relinquish control.

"Quite a mess you made here, Father," a familiar voice said.

I whirled and found myself face-to-face with Danny Hartman. I hadn't even heard him drive up.

He grinned broadly, relishing my surprise. "Relax, Father. From what Ron told me, you deserve a medal. Am I right?"

When I didn't answer, he said, "Sure makes me wonder though. I've been mulling over what's different about you since that night. You know, the night of the exorcism? I've been doing some reading on demonic possession and I've found some fascinating stuff." He pretended to consider. "Most sources claim you can't kill a demon. You can drive it out of someone, but it has to go somewhere. According to you, it went into Father Sutherland, no? But even if it did, he died when his head splattered on the concrete. Which means the demon would've been freed from *his* body."

"Not necessarily," I said, dry-mouthed.

Danny ignored me. "So I've been looking around for signs of demonic possession in my brother's neighborhood. Seeing if there's anybody speaking in tongues or barking at the moon. So far, I've got nothing." He gave me a meaningful look. "Nothing except a priest who crushed a guy's face tonight and somehow overpowered two other hardened criminals."

I couldn't endure that knowing smile. I turned away and saw someone else approaching from Danny's cruiser. This new policeman was younger than Danny, lankier. He had blond hair, a sunburned face, and wore the same dark blue uniform that Danny had on. I put him in his mid-twenties.

"Feels like it's about to cut loose again," the new policeman said, eyeing the cloudy black sky. "I've lived here all my life, and I've never seen a month with so much rain."

Danny nodded at the new cop. "This is my partner—my *apprentice*—as of yesterday. Father Crowder, meet Tyler Raines."

Raines nodded, offered his hand. "You really kill those bastards?"

I felt like I was going to be sick.

Danny whapped me on the back. "Father Crowder here's got a guilty conscience, Tyler. I'm afraid this business happened at the worst possible time for him."

Raines lowered his head in sympathy. "Yeah, Danny told me about that. Sorry about your friend, Father. He sounded like a great man."

"He was," Danny agreed. "It's a damn shame Father Sutherland died. Sometimes I wish it would have been one of us instead."

I shot Danny a look, but he only eyed me blandly.

"So," Raines said, swinging his arms a little, "you took down three dirtbags, huh?"

"Only one," a voice said. I turned and saw the detective in the Goo Goo Dolls shirt staring at me from a few feet away. I tried to control my galloping heart, but I feared I was coming undone.

"That's right, isn't it?" the detective asked.

When I didn't answer right away, Danny said, "Detective Ambrose asked you a question, Father."

I bit my lower lip. "I already told that other officer—" I nodded at the red-haired woman, "—everything that happened. I don't feel like reliving it."

"Relive it anyway," Detective Ambrose said. "Or you'll spend the night in custody."

So I recounted it again, down to the last gory detail. As I had earlier, I told the story as it occurred, the only omissions involving the role of Malephar. This wasn't difficult. Whenever Ambrose asked me why I did something, I explained that I was trying to save innocent lives.

When I got to the part about Myron Meeks, Ambrose asked, "How do you think God would feel about the way you mangled that guy's face?" A protracted pause, Ambrose staring. "You think He'd be proud of a priest who did that?"

"I won't speculate about God's feelings," I answered.

"You mean you don't *want* to," Ambrose said. He looked at Danny and Raines. "I don't blame him. You won't believe the carnage this guy left behind."

"I believe it," Danny answered.

Ambrose glanced at him, seemed about to say something, but I resumed my story hoping Danny wouldn't elaborate. When I got to the part about Connelly shooting himself, Ambrose waved his hands. "Hold on a second, Father. This is the part that makes no sense to me. You two are scuffling, correct?"

"That's one word for it."

"And you smash his face through a glass door."

I tasted acid on my tongue, tried to rid my mind of the way Connelly's face had molted off his skull. "Yes."

"Then you say something that nobody but you and Connelly can hear... and then Connelly just carves up his own throat?"

I didn't answer.

Ambrose shook his head. "I'm sorry, Father, but that doesn't wash. Why the hell would he fight you, then just decide to take his own life? Whatever you said to him must have been pretty bad to get a reaction like that."

I forced myself to meet Ambrose's shrewd stare. I was conscious of Danny and Raines watching me as well.

Ambrose uttered a little laugh. "You gonna make me ask the question, Father?"

When I didn't speak, he said, "Okay, fine. Be coy. I'll ask you: What did you say to make Connelly kill himself?"

And I repeated the lie I'd told the red-haired officer, the lie that made me despise myself to an even greater degree.

"I told him I forgave his sins."

This was met with silence. After a time, Raines said, "Well, at least there's that, right? I mean, at least Connelly got right with God before he bit the big one."

"You're forgetting something," Ambrose said. "Suicides go to hell, don't they?"

I swallowed. "Opinions vary."

Ambrose chuckled. "Whose opinions? I never heard of an alternative view, at least not among Catholics." He paused, scratched the skin beside his mouth. "And what I find most interesting is how this *same exact thing*, a man killing himself in Father Crowder's presence, happened earlier this week."

My muscles seized up, a new fear gripping me. All this time I'd been brooding about my soul, but I'd never really considered the possibility I'd be arrested.

Just how could I account for the similarity between Randy Connelly and Jack Bittner, both men taking their lives in my presence?

Irrationally, I found myself looking at Danny for help.

He eyed me in silence. Then he scratched his jaw. "The Bittner thing was different, Ambrose. I can tell you without question that Father Crowder had nothing to do with that."

"But Crowder was alone with him," Ambrose said. "Doesn't that seem like an odd coincidence to you?"

"Not really," Danny answered. "Not if you'd been with Bittner as long as I had. The guy was a time bomb. What his ex-wife did to him, taking his daughter away like that. It was only a matter of time before it all built up."

"But why that night?" Ambrose pressed. "Why when only the Father here was around?"

"Casey was there too." Danny frowned. "And whatever was inside Casey," he added quietly.

Ambrose sighed. "I'm sorry, Danny, but I still can't buy all that horror movie shit. I know you believe it, and I'm sure the Father here believes it, but...nope. Stuff like that doesn't happen. At least, not in Chicago."

There was another silence. I worried Ambrose would push harder to make a connection between the suicides, but Tyler Raines saved me.

"Should we tend to them?" Raines asked, motioning toward the onlookers who'd congregated along the yellow tape strung across the parking lot. I'd been so lost in my thoughts that I hadn't even noticed before, but there were maybe fifteen or twenty people rubbernecking at the 7-11.

"I'll stick around," Danny said. "Why don't you deal with that other business, Tyler?"

Raines began to protest, but Danny stilled him with a raised palm.

"Listen," Danny said, holding his partner's gaze for a beat. "You need to file that traffic stop. I can handle this.

You just go and get the paperwork done. I'd rather be out of the office anyway."

Raines nodded, but his expression was troubled. Was Danny throwing his weight around with the new guy?

I didn't know, and I didn't really care. Because the assaulted girl kept casting too-inquisitive glances at me as she sat there on the sidewalk, a blanket thrown over her shoulders.

Ambrose muttered something and drifted toward the store. Raines set off toward the police cruiser, leaving me and Danny alone.

His face only inches from mine, he nodded at the girl who'd been assaulted. "I understand how you felt, Father. Seeing those guys terrorizing that kid." He shook his head. "Makes you question mankind, you know? You wonder how evil like that can exist in the world."

The wound in my head began to emit a sharp pulse. I studied Danny's boyish face and marveled at how such monstrous thoughts could reside in such a seemingly innocent shell.

"Then again," Danny went on, "I get it, you know? The urge to hurt things? You look around at all the bad stuff going on, and part of you wants to go crazy too. Take those killings, the Sweet Sixteen business..."

My entire body had gone leaden. I couldn't breathe.

Danny let out an embarrassed little laugh. "If I was the murderer, I'd be getting pretty antsy. He killed that black girl the other day, but it was so good, he probably needs to indulge the urge again." Danny leaned toward me. "He's getting ready, Father. I think he's gonna kill another young honey."

As unstoppable as I'd felt when Malephar had commanded my actions, at that moment, standing under the orange-hazed streetlights with a serial killer, I'd never felt more helpless. If I revealed Danny for what he was, would anyone believe me? He'd gone undetected for months. Who'd take my word over his? If I went to the authorities with what I knew, would they investigate him, or would they arrest me for spurious accusations? If they gathered DNA from Danny, I'd no doubt they could convict him. But to get that deeply into the process, they'd have to cross-reference the murders with Danny's whereabouts on those dates, and I had no doubt he'd have alibis.

All this was moot, I knew, because of the deal I'd struck with Malephar. I'd sworn to allow Danny to continue his reign of terror, and if I opened my mouth to accuse him, Malephar would simply stop my heart.

Danny was eyeing me now, awaiting my reaction.

I said, "It's late. I need to get back to the cottage."

A glance at my hairline. "Funny thing," he said. "When we got here, that ear of yours looked like hell. Bunch of red-and-yellow crust glistening around it. Like someone had tried to make a sheet cake and botched it badly."

I began to walk away, cursing myself for refusing medical attention.

Danny called after me. "Then again, maybe I shouldn't be surprised, right? You're a hell of a quick healer, Father. Those fingers of yours grew back like a salamander's tail."

◆ ◆ ◆

After a few minutes of driving, I spotted a shimmering body of water far below and turned in that direction. I followed the downward-trending reservoir road until the asphalt leveled out. Then I guided the Civic into an open parking space, killed the engine, and climbed out.

The Jewel Reservoir was one of my favorite spots in which to ruminate and sort through my worries. The perfect place, I decided, to wrestle the complex issues facing me tonight. My eyes on the moonlight-spangled water, I thought about the carnage in the convenience store, the bloodcurdling pleasure I'd experienced while Malephar had murdered those men with my body.

I mounted the concrete walking path, began strolling along the rim of the reservoir.

From the perspective of the authorities, I had now been involved in two violent episodes in the space of a few nights. How long would they view me as a hero? How long would their good will last?

At what point would suspicion creep in?

Soon, I decided, if not already. My stomach performing a sick lurch, I stopped and leaned forward on the steel railing, my eyes lowering unseeingly to the Jewel Reservoir, which was part of Chicago's Deep Tunnel Project.

As always, the dark waters fascinated me.

Having lived in the city for more than a decade, I'd read often of the project, a colossal undertaking that aimed to prevent the flooding the city periodically suffered. Since it had rained a great deal over the past month, the network of runoff tunnels had surely been taxed to its limit.

I became aware of a dull roar. Peering out over the water, I saw, perhaps a football field away, a trio of huge cement openings from which gushed robust jets of excess rainwater. The tunnels were arranged like a stoplight. The lowest cylinder hung perhaps twenty yards over the churning surface of the manmade tarn, the middle cylinder thirty yards above that. The highest tunnel jutted eighty yards above the water.

Abruptly, the noise began to agitate me. I realized why. The reservoir was ordinarily dormant, the water level low. But tonight the surf was tempestuous and far too similar to my emotional state for me to find peace here.

I turned away and moved toward a dense thicket of trees, an area I typically avoided because I worried it was unsafe. But now, it seemed, I was the danger.

To escape the thought, I wandered through the thicket that comprised the eastern edge of Farris Park. Intrigued by the silent forest, I strode on, my unrest quickly dissipating. I gave myself up to the balmy night air, no longer concerned with the convenience store, with Danny Hartman, with anything.

I drifted through a grove of cedars, the path so lightless I could scarcely discern what lay ahead of me. Yet I moved forward, unperturbed. Aspens and willows brushed at my wrists. A squirrel chittered in the undergrowth. A piercing shriek split the night, but when I spun I realized it had only been an osprey searching for a mate. I closed my eyes, my arms outstretched, and in that moment the restlessness that had plagued me siphoned away, the park and the trees and the wildlife portending better times ahead, a life without murder and demonic spirits.

How long I wandered in the darkness, I had no idea. But when I again became aware of my surroundings, I found myself on an unfamiliar street surrounded by looming apartment buildings that were falling into disrepair.

I halted, my brow furrowing. Had I just experienced a fugue state? Had Malephar taken hold of me?

Pondering these questions and many others, I stuffed my hands in my pockets and continued down the shadowy side street. After a time, I discovered a path leading back to the reservoir road.

As I walked, I realized what I needed to do. I might not be able to escape punishment forever, but I could certainly keep an eye on Danny. He'd all but told me he was going to strike again in the next twenty-four hours. If I followed him, I might find a way to prevent—

You will die if you do, coward!

Though I knew the threat in Malephar's voice was real, part of me relished his anger.

I'm just going to tail him, I countered. *I never said I wouldn't do that.*

You promised not to impede his efforts—

And following him is not the same as stopping him.

If you so much as make yourself seen—

We'll worry about that when we get there, shall we?

A long silence, then: *You are meddling with a power beyond your comprehension, craven one.*

I didn't answer. But I did jog to my car and motor back to the convenience store, where I waited for Danny to leave the crime scene.

When he did, I followed.

CHAPTER TEN

My fears proved baseless, however. Despite his threats, Danny didn't go prowling for victims. He simply returned to his apartment around midnight, and though I waited until well past three AM, he never went out. It rained all night. I sat in the Civic, my head throbbing from the relentless drum of the raindrops, and watched Danny's apartment.

Finally, I returned home exhausted and slept until midmorning.

The staff members at St. Matthew's knew all about the 7-11 incident and proved surprisingly supportive. Many congratulated me for, in one secretary's words, "defending the innocent." I didn't encounter Father Patterson, which was a blessing. Sister Rebecca offered a muted smile when we crossed paths at the coffee station in the main office.

"Are you in much pain?" she asked.

I fingered the temple wound that had almost entirely healed. Feigned discomfort. "Pretty sore. I should have let them take me to the hospital."

"And the hand?"

I'm afraid I almost dropped the steaming cup of coffee I'd just poured. In truth, I'd forgotten about the back of my hand, had even forgotten to dress the non-existent wound this morning after showering.

Had she noticed?

"Much better," I said. "I still feel a twinge now and then, but the painkillers seem to be doing the trick."

Sister Rebecca studied me for an unbearably long moment, then nodded and filled her mug. "If you need anything, you know where I am." She turned to go, then paused and looked back at me. "The newspaper said the gun was fired less than a foot away from your ear. How severe is the damage?"

I gave a slight shrug. "Sounds are a little muffled. And there's a... um... ringing. I think I'll recover though."

"I'm sure you will," she said, going, "if it heals as swiftly as your hand did."

I gaped after her, feeling both exposed and impressed with her mental acumen. If I weren't so entranced by Liz...

Strike that from your mind, my conscience demanded. *If you care about either woman, you'll stay far away from them.*

That, however, proved difficult. For the moment I returned to my office, thinking only of holing up for the day and avoiding human interaction, my phone rang.

"Jason?" a voice I knew too well asked.

My pulse quickened. "Hello, Liz. Everything okay?"

"Is everything *okay*? Jason, why didn't you call me last night?"

"I guess I—"

"I've been trying to reach you at your cottage all morning. I even drove over there, but you'd gone to work."

I didn't know what to say.

She added, "I almost showed up at the cathedral, but I thought it might not be... you know..."

I did know. And the implications of her reticence made me deliriously happy. She was one of my parishioners, but she was becoming something much more. That she was mindful of how it might appear if she, a still-married woman, showed up at my office looking distraught about my well-being, made me very happy indeed. I knew my feelings for her were powerful, yet hearing her express a similar regard, no matter how indirectly, filled me with bliss.

"I appreciate your concern, Liz, but I'm—"

"Don't talk to me like I'm a stranger," she snapped. "Dammit, I'm worried about you. You could have been killed."

I closed my mouth, touched and chastened. I couldn't recall the last time a woman had shown so much genuine emotion toward me. Maybe never.

She pitched a weary sigh. "Just tell me when I can see you."

Goosebumps rippled my flesh. "I...I don't know."

Something new came into her voice. "Can you take a break? I can be at your cottage in twenty minutes."

I fought off a sweep of wooziness. "That would be fine. I—"

I jolted, remembering the blood I'd never cleaned up in my living room.

"Maybe it would be better if I came to your house, Liz."

"Casey and Carolyn are both at school," she said.

I couldn't speak.

"Will you?" she asked.

"Twenty minutes," I croaked.

"Sooner, if you can."

◆ ◆ ◆

I completed the trip in sixteen minutes, including the time it took for me to stop by my cottage to brush my teeth and comb my hair. My breath smelled fresh when I reentered the Civic, but my hair looked little better. Like some barn swallow's straw nest, my blond hair kept popping up where I wanted it to lie flat and remaining limp where I attempted to add a roguish spike or two.

After twenty-nine years of celibacy, I was overflowing with lust, but even more powerful was my regard for Liz, my desire to express my growing love for her. I pushed the Civic past the speed limit the entire way and navigated turns with a recklessness I'd never exhibited.

But when Liz opened the door, I knew instantly that something terrible had happened.

"What's wrong?" I asked.

"Come in," she said, casting a nervous glance toward the road.

I entered, saying, "If you're worried about my being here in the daylight, I could—"

"It isn't that," she said and led me to the living room. She was attired in a simple beige sundress, yet on her the garment was alluring, sultry even. It clung to her hips and buttocks in a way that augmented my attraction to her, and when she sat on the couch and beckoned for me to join her, the sight of her curvy bosom made me dizzy with desire.

"Can I help?" I asked, sitting next to her, our knees almost touching.

"Ron called," she said.

Wrecking things again, I thought. A dozen possibilities raced through my head, none of them pleasant: Ron had persuaded her to reconcile. Ron had decided to contest the divorce, thus drawing the process out. Ron had implicated me in an adultery accusation, and I would be publicly disgraced. Or worse, Ron had told Liz about what I'd done last night, had provided an unvarnished account of my savagery.

She said, "It happened again."

I stared at her. "I don't understand."

"The Sweet Sixteen," she explained. "He struck again last night."

Impossible! I almost shouted. "Liz, he can't have...he only killed the Howell girl a few days ago."

"It's the pattern. A serial killer's appetites get stronger, the murders more frequent." There were tears in her eyes. "It's on the news right now. Look if you don't believe me."

I sat there thunderstruck. Had Danny somehow slipped out of his apartment building to commit the atrocity without my knowledge?

Liz made a fist, tapped her knee. "They say it happened at around nine o'clock last night."

Another shock. Danny was at the convenience store from eight to ten. The authorities must have their times wrong, I reasoned. It was the only explanation.

I had to be careful. If I revealed too much, Malephar might murder me. Or worse, he might compel me to attack Liz. "Who was the victim?" I asked.

"Her name was Julia Deveroux. She was walking home from the private school over there, Saint Anthony's. Her play practice ran a little late. Her house is only a few blocks from the school, so her parents assumed she'd be—" Liz broke off, looked at me imploringly. "Father, why is this *happening?*"

Aware we'd fallen back into our former roles of parishioner and priest, I put a hand over hers, said, "We live in a fallen world, Liz."

She jerked her hand away. "Don't give me that crap. Don't tell me it's our fault or Eve's fault. Is that why my son was victimized by a demon?"

"I didn't—"

"Those girls should still be alive, goddammit."

"Of course they should."

"And Casey didn't deserve any of this! Don't you dare tell me he did!"

"I'm not saying Casey was at fault—"

She was on her feet, backing away from me. "Or Father Sutherland's theory? That a terrible sin brought this judgment upon our son. You still think Ron is the Sweet Sixteen Killer? That I was so stupid that I wouldn't have noticed something like that?"

"I don't think Ron's the killer."

"And what if he *is*, Jason? What if he *is*? Just what kind of a God does that to an innocent child? What kind of a God punishes a sweet, caring boy—"

"Casey *is* a good person, Liz. He's just going through a rough—"

"—for the sins of someone else? Are you going to throw scripture at me? 'The sins of the father'? Well that's *bullshit*, Jason!"

I rose, endeavored to close the distance between us. "The God described in the Old Testament can seem vengeful. Capricious even."

"Try bloodthirsty and sadistic."

I brought up my hands in a placating gesture. "Which is why I believe—as Father Sutherland believed—that we need to *interact* with the text, to examine it critically. To examine the *sources* so we can decipher the true will—"

"Follow me," she interrupted, starting past me.

"Where—"

"Just come on."

Bemused, I hurried after her. She led me through the living room, along a hallway, then down the basement steps. I detected an undercurrent of must and recalled the night of the exorcism, the torrential rains that accompanied the horror. Though the house was straight out of a magazine spread, it didn't surprise me that the basement would take on moisture in a storm. It was very old.

Liz hadn't bothered to illuminate the stygian corridor in which I now found myself. I extended my arms, going by feel and sound. I was about to call to Liz, my male pride be damned, when ahead a doorway lit up and Liz passed inside. I hustled after her, grateful for the light, even more thankful for the company. Being stranded in that lonely stretch of basement had been too much like being alone in my cottage with the Sweet Sixteen Killer.

When I burst through the doorway, I found Liz leaning against the wall with her arms crossed. The painted drywall against which she leaned was one of the few sections of the small room not festooned with corkboard bulletin boards. Of course, very little of the cork was visible because the boards were plastered with newspaper clippings, enlarged pictures. A Mac with a huge monitor sat atop a stylish desk with a light wood surface and spidery black legs.

"Well?" she asked.

I blinked at her, my eyes struggling to adjust to my new surroundings. The brilliant canned lights overhead were already making me sweat, though my anxiety and frightened dash through the basement might have played a role in that as well. "Well, what?"

She gave me an incredulous smile and flourished a hand at the bulletin board to her right. "*This.*"

I followed her gesture and at first felt nothing but puzzlement. There were large blocks of text, but no headlines. I moved closer to the bulletin board, squinting to read the tiny print. Different passages in the articles had been highlighted, though the colors varied. Pink, blue, orange, yellow.

Highlighted in pink, I saw…

"…taken Howell to a secluded spot in the park to sexually assault her."

The skin on the back of my neck prickled. My eyes flicked to a chunk of text highlighted in green: "Authorities initially suspected Panagopoulis's former boyfriend, until it was found that he was visiting relatives in Milwaukee on the night of her murder."

My heart dropped as the brutality of Ashley Panagopoulis's death arose in my memory.

"Are they color-coded by victims?" I asked.

"Theories," she said.

I glanced at her.

"So far I've got six possible explanations for the killings," she said. "The yellow highlighter suggests it's a homeless person committing the crimes. The light green one supports the notion the killer is a policeman."

With an effort, I kept my mouth shut.

"Two possibilities make no sense," she went on, "but the evidence is strongest for those theories."

"What are they?"

"Not yet. I want to hear what you think first."

I reached out, fingered the top of an article. I realized the headline hadn't been excised, but had rather been folded under and thusly obscured from view.

"I hate the headlines," she explained. "They're too lurid, particularly the Sun-Times. The article about Makayla Howell made me want to hurt someone." She gave me a half-hearted smile. "Poor choice of words, I suppose."

I scanned the bulletin board all the way to the next wall. More articles here, these from the first three murders. "Why the sudden interest in these crimes?"

"Who says it's sudden? I've been studying the case for months."

"But why?"

"The first victim was one of my son's classmates. Or have you forgotten, Father Crowder?"

The way she uttered my name sent a wave of desolation through me. I had driven over here believing my life as a celibate anchorite might finally be coming to an end; now the gulf between us yawned wider than ever. "I guess I forgot about the connection," I said in a small voice.

"Secondly," she went on, "do I need to tell you why I want to solve this case, Father? Why *everyone* should want to bring that monster to justice? I would think you, as a supposed man of God, would understand better than anyone."

Supposed man of God?

"Liz, I want these murders to end as much as you do."

For once I was telling the absolute truth.

She studied my face a long moment. Then, some of her ire seemed to bleed away. "I do have another motive," she said. "A couple more, actually. Since Ron was implicated in the killings the other night, I guess I've grown obsessed. All this," she made a sweeping gesture encompassing the entire room, "has gone up in the last forty-eight hours."

I cocked an eyebrow at her. "This is what you've been doing all day?"

"Would you rather I sit around and fret?"

I had to admit it made sense. If I were Liz, and my soon-to-be-ex-husband were implicated in a series of horrific crimes, I'd take a greater interest in the situation too. Despite the restraining order, their lives were inextricably linked. He'd fathered their children. He'd bought this house. Even now, his influence stained every room.

I perused the walls. "This is awfully thorough."

She gave me a rueful look. "I have a brain, you know."

"I know you do. It's one of the most attractive things about you."

Her eyes narrowed, but I could tell she was pleased. She looked back at the bulletin board. "What baffles me most about last night's killing is how the M.O. seems to have changed."

She reached toward a laser printer, came away with about a dozen sheets of printed paper. Studying the top sheet—the headline read SWEET SIXTEEN STRIKES AGAIN, the subtitle DEATH TOLL AT EIGHT AFTER LATEST ATROCITY—she said, "People are already calling last night's murder a copycat."

"They're saying it was a different killer?" I asked, though I was already convinced of this myself. I had no idea how the police had so firmly established the time of death, but if they were positive the crime was committed at around nine PM, it was impossible that Danny had killed Julia Deveroux.

A copycat crime was the only explanation.

"The first seven murders," Liz said, "kept increasing in intensity. The killer whipped himself—or herself—into a wilder frenzy with each successive crime."

I raised my eyebrows. "*Her*self?"

She nodded at the bulletin board. "You'll notice there isn't much highlighted in orange. That theory posits that there are two killers—a male-female couple, most likely. That would still explain why there was semen found in the bodies."

I kept my doubts to myself. She'd obviously invested a great deal of time in this investigation, and I had no desire for her to group me with Ron, who'd treated her with nothing but condescension. "You were saying last night was different?"

She nodded. "Last night's crime... it seems almost *shy* by comparison."

"Can't they test the killer's, um—"

"Semen?" she supplied.

I nodded.

"Oh, they'll perform DNA tests. But those take time."

"But in a case this important..."

"They'll put a rush on it, I'm sure. If it does come back different than the main perpetrator's, we'll know that the orange theory is possible—" She nodded at the bulletin board, "—or that the killing was a Sweet Sixteen wannabe."

The notion sent chills down my spine. That anyone would aspire to such depravity...

A thought occurred to me. "Why would a man and woman kill together? Or for that matter, why would two men?"

"Sexual thrills," she answered. "The man and woman like to watch each other sexually violate the girls. Or the men like to watch each other do it. In either scenario, there's the element of voyeurism. The fulfillment of forbidden desires."

I grew nauseated at the notion. "I don't understand why you're so obsessed with this. Isn't the fact of them bad enough? Why do you need to surround yourself this way?"

"Because I'm getting close, Jason. I think I can solve the mystery."

"But the police—"

"—aren't doing enough," she snapped. "Listen, it was the Alspaugh murder that changed things. Widened the net of possible suspects, so to speak. There were too many witnesses near the crime scene for the killer to have simply walked away. Security cameras everywhere. The killer had to have some secret way in and out to avoid being seen."

I opened my mouth, but she cut me off. "There's more, Jason. More no one is talking about. They think of the killer like some movie monster, but he isn't. He's a man." She paused, shaking her head. "I hate him, but... I think he's in terrible pain. Something from his past. I think that can be used against him."

I studied her face. "What's the real reason you're fixated on these crimes?"

She was thoughtful for a moment. Then she shuffled through the printed pages, found the one she'd been after, and handed it to me.

My stomach performed a queasy somersault. The photograph showed a girl in a school uniform. Julia Deveroux. The newest victim of the Sweet Sixteen Killer.

But I had seen the girl already. When Malephar had come forward during Danny's attempt to murder me, Julia was one of the faces I had glimpsed in the cesspool of

Danny's thoughts. Just a giggling schoolgirl walking with her friends. An innocent kid with no idea of the beast stalking her.

And now she was dead.

Could I have prevented it?

"For her," Liz said, tapping Julia's picture. She turned toward the wall to my left, the one I hadn't seen yet because I'd entered through that doorway. "And for them."

I beheld the faces of the seven prior victims of the Sweet Sixteen. Each of the girls was smiling, each excited about her future life. About a career, about friends. A family.

But now they were corpses, minor players in a greater tragedy, the macabre handiwork of a serial killer who sought to outdo even Jack the Ripper in infamy.

I despised Danny Hartman.

Yet even more, I hated myself for making the deal with Malephar, for agreeing to allow Danny to remain free.

I had to stop Danny, no matter the cost.

My eyes shifted back to the board above the computer, to the purple and orange highlighted text.

What if Danny *wasn't* the only murderer?

My body went motionless. My thoughts screeched to a ragged halt. The thought that had been clawing at me ever since Liz told me the Sweet Sixteen had struck again had finally stepped into the light.

"Where was last night's murder?"

"Farris Park," Liz said.

Oh my God.

She put a hand on my arm. "Are you okay? You don't look very well, Jason."

And I wasn't. Had, in fact, never been worse in my life.

Because there *had* been another person in Farris Park last night, a person with intimate knowledge of the Sweet Sixteen's habits, a person who had, for a moment, inhabited the depraved monster's mind.

Please, Jesus, I almost sobbed, *please let it not be true.*

It wasn't possible, was it?

Could I be the copycat killer?

CHAPTER ELEVEN

My mind spinning, I sped away from Liz's house.

No, I thought, my hands shaking on the wheel. *Please, God, no.*

From the depths of my bosom, I heard the demon's laughter.

My muscles tensed. *Tell me the truth*, I demanded.

More laughter.

Tell me, damn you!

Untoward language for a holy man, Malephar taunted.

Did you take control of me without my knowledge?

Are you worried you enjoyed it?

I nearly missed my turn, applied the brakes, and cut the wheel as a truck horn blatted its disapproval behind me.

I have to know if—

You delighted in the slaughter, Malephar said.

My hands gripped the wheel so tightly that, were I a stronger man, the whole assemblage would have snapped. *What slaughter?*

In the store.

I relaxed infinitesimally. *That wasn't me.*

You lying little shit, Malephar said.

I would not be drawn in. *I permitted you to seize control. I honored our agreement. I allowed you to sate your desires, and in doing so I saved—*

You're plotting to shatter our pact, you worthless cumstain.

I signaled a left turn onto the rectory road, my mind racing. Only twenty minutes earlier I'd resolved to unmask Danny as the killer, but I had clung to a feeble hope that Malephar would remain unaware of my resolution. How naïve that desire had been. The demon was part of me now, a constant companion. I could no more deceive him than I could deceive myself.

So I answered Malephar, *Thinking isn't the same as doing. You can't harm me for considering a course of action, only for taking it.*

I can and will do what pleases me, sodomite. I can harrow your puling face with razor blades. I can seize a pair of kitchen shears and snip your pathetic little penis off at the root. I can make of you a castrate, a disfigured abomination.

My hands were shaking again, not only at Malephar's words, but at the frightfully vivid images he projected while he uttered his threats. I saw my face as it would be when Malephar was done with it, the gory red-black hole in my abdomen, the shriveled rind of my member as it lay discarded on the kitchen floor.

No more, I thought, turning into my cottage driveway.

I'll decide when you've had enough, eunuch.

I climbed out of the car. I needed to clean up the cottage and return to work. Normalcy, or some semblance of it, might soothe the relentless clanging of my nerves.

I entered my cottage and beheld the blood-spattered living room.

Cleaning it would be a terrible job. One that would require hours.

Yet this, at least, was a mindless enough task to divert my attention from the dire question circling in my brain.

Had I killed Julia Deveroux?

Thrusting the thought away, I strode into the kitchen and prepared a bucket of hot, soapy water.

◆ ◆ ◆

It was well past two that afternoon when I finished cleansing my living room and bathroom of blood. I performed the task in the nude, deciding it would be best not to stain any more of my already spare wardrobe. When I'd completed my tedious and largely ineffectual ministrations, there still remained several dark splotches on the hardwood floor, an armada of indelible stains on the furniture and walls. But what could I do? Move? Commit arson? And after all, why should the presence of so much of my *own* blood unnerve me? I had been the victim, not the perpetrator.

With a tightening of the chest, I thought of the clothes I'd worn the night before. What if there were not three sets of bloody DNA there—those belonging to Randy Connelly, Marlon Meeks, and me—but four? What if the damning evidence were lying in a ball on my bathroom floor?

I rushed into the bathroom and snatched up my blood-crusted clothes. As I stood debating what to do, I caught sight of my naked body in the mirror. The vanity was situated high enough so that only the top of my pubic region was visible. From that perspective, I looked like the castrate Malephar had threatened to make of me, and all at once, a feeling of body-racking frustration gusted through me, a teeth-gnashing desire to prove my manhood, to assert my masculinity.

A white-hot flash of memory scorched my mind's eye. I saw myself from a distance, as though I were watching myself on a movie screen. My other self was grasping his penis in a dark, tree-filled setting. Farris Park, I realized. There was a savage grin on my other self's face, a rictus of cruelty, and I was telling someone to *Lick it, lick it.*

The brightly-lit bathroom disappeared around me, and I stood in the park with my other self, my vicious double, who now growled, *"Suck it, bitch. Gag on it."*

And not wanting to, I gazed down at the figure pinned beneath my vicious other self, and it was Julia Deveroux, it was that poor, unsuspecting girl, writhing in terror, unable to fend off her bestial attacker. That other me grasped his engorged penis, snarled at Julia to take him in her mouth, and then I was screaming *"NO!"* in my bathroom, screaming and weeping and thrashing my head.

The vision was gone, but my heart was thundering, my body lathered in cold sweat. I stared at my harried reflection and whispered, "It can't be. Please say it isn't true, Malephar. Please tell me you conjured that vision. It wasn't a real memory, was it?"

The demon laughed softly.

◆ ◆ ◆

To escape my cottage, which now felt like a torture chamber, I showered, dressed, and returned to the cathedral. I feared a confrontation with Father Patterson—would the incident in the convenience store provide further ammunition in his mission to defrock me?—yet of this confrontation, at least, I was spared. According to my secretary, Father Patterson had been called away on important business and would not return until later in the day.

I had been scheduled that afternoon for the confessional, but Father Richards, another senior priest, had entered the booth in my stead. I knew Father Richards to be a decent but lazy man who would no doubt welcome relief from confession duty, so I made my way to the upper wing of the cathedral and rapped softly on the booth.

"Yes?" came the voice from within.

It sounded like Father Richards, but I had become understandably paranoid in the past week and was beset with visions of Patterson opening the booth door, or even worse, of Danny Hartman springing forth to slash at me with his lethal carving knife.

I took a breath. "Father Richards, it's me, Jason. I've come to resume my duties."

A pause. Then the door opened and Father Richards peered out. "We heard about last night," he said, his watery eyes unblinking. He was sixty or so but looked a decade older. I'd always suspected him of drinking too much, but his haggard appearance could just as easily have been a product of inactivity. His indolence was legendary at St. Matthew's.

I stared down at my black loafers. They were old, a pair I only kept around for emergencies. Like when my better shoes were caked with blood.

"Last night was terrible," I said, which was true enough.

"Father Patterson is displeased, though I don't suppose that comes as a surprise to you."

"No," I answered. "It doesn't."

As though something had been decided, Father Richards climbed out of the booth and winced at the cracking of his backbone. "Need to get more exercise," he said with a hint of apology. "Quiet day. Only one penitent so far."

Despite myself, the antiquated word brought a grin to my face. Father Sutherland had always referred to those who frequented the confessional as *customers*.

"I can use the calm," I replied. Which was decidedly not the truth. My quieter moments lately had proved my worst. In them, Malephar seemed to sense his opportunity to wreak havoc on my emotions. Or to implant false memories of my sordid deeds.

Oh, how I prayed the scene Malephar had shown me in the park was false!

Father Richards hesitated. "You're sure you're okay, Jason? What happened in the 7-11 must have taken a toll on you."

"I need the distraction."

When Father Richards only continued to watch me, I assured him, "I'll be fine. This is the therapy I crave."

Though he didn't appear convinced, he nonetheless departed, and I stepped into the confessional and closed the door with a sense of relief. It wasn't long before I heard someone approaching up the stairwell. Then, the softer pad of footfalls on carpet. I readied myself with a prayer, secretly hoping my customer's sins would be minor enough to be forgiven with minimal fuss. I wasn't sure if I was ready to confront any weighty spiritual matters in my current state.

The door to the penitent's half of the booth opened, and whoever it was stepped inside and shut the door. I heard the deep clearing of a throat.

"Hello, friend," I said. It was the way Father Sutherland had taught me to greet parishioners. "Have you come for forgiveness, or would you rather just talk?"

A sigh. "Little of both, I guess."

The voice sounded familiar. I placed the man in his twenties, though he sounded a bit careworn for such a young person. Perhaps this would not be a simple matter of counting Rosary beads.

"Well then," I said, leaning forward with my palms on my knees, "whenever you're ready, I'm here to listen."

"Thanks, Father." A long pause. "I guess I should get to it, huh? No point in waffling."

I waited.

A soft chuckle. "I know how I'd feel if I was you. I'd think I was crazy. But you get like that, you know? The whole city's gone crazy this spring."

In the semidarkness of the booth, I frowned.

"But just because the city's going nuts," he went on, "that don't mean I gotta lose my mind too, right?" He laughed, but there was a strain in the sound. "At first, I told myself, 'You're imagining things. The thought you're thinking, it's just bonkers. No way in hell is it—forgive me, Father—no way in heck is it possible that...'" He trailed off, laughed his nervous laugh.

"I'm not sure I understand."

"I suppose I should tell you I'm a cop."

Ice water doused my spine.

"Relatively new to it, but not a rookie, you know? I got assigned to this new partner, a guy everybody loves. One of the most popular fellas in the precinct." A chuckle. "Hell, who am I kidding. He *is* the most popular guy in the precinct." A pause. "There's just one problem."

"And that is?"

"I think he might be the Sweet Sixteen Killer."

CHAPTER TWELVE

I clenched my fists at my wretched luck. How foolish I'd been to think I could escape my problems in this darkened booth! Was it possible Malephar had orchestrated this torture as well? I didn't see how, yet the coincidence seemed too great.

"Father?" the policeman who I now knew to be Tyler Raines said. "You still with me? Because I gotta say, if I just worked up the nerve to spill my guts and found out you'd nodded off on me, I'd be pretty peeved."

With an effort, I answered, "I'm here."

"You're there, huh. Well, that's something, I suppose. Could you maybe give me a little feedback? It's not like I just gave you a traffic report or something. This is serious stuff."

"Yes, it is."

"So say something, Father. I need some guidance. I don't figure out what to do soon, I'm gonna lose my mind."

My thoughts carouseled wildly. Could this be my way out? Could this be an opportunity to connect Danny to the murders without breaking my pact with the demon?

Deep inside me, I felt Malephar coiling into a furious knot. I heard, as beneath a thick layer of soil, his insidious voice raving.

Careful, I told myself. *Be very careful. You might nudge Raines in the right direction, but you have to do so in the natural course of your interactions. Give him the same counsel you'd give anyone who came to you with such an important problem. You'd encourage the person to do the right thing, would you not?*

"Let me get this straight," I said, choosing my words cautiously. "Your sin is the fact that you haven't gone to your superiors with your misgivings? You feel guilty for not having said something before last night's murder, and consequently, you feel like the most recent victim's blood is on your hands?"

He uttered a harsh laugh. "Man, Father. You don't mess around, do you? You're like everybody else in the city." He lowered his voice in a parody of mob justice. "'We want that bastard caught!'"

"I didn't intend to impugn your character."

"I wish the only thing I had to feel bad about was silence. If that was the case, I probably wouldn't even be here this afternoon."

"There's more you're not telling me?"

"Give the man a prize," he muttered. "Real Simon Freud, aren't you?"

I didn't bother to correct him. "Listen—" I froze, biting my upper lip hard enough to draw blood. I'd nearly called him Tyler! And in doing so I'd have given away my identity.

Heart thumping, I said, "Listen, friend. I need you to tell me everything. Only with a complete unburdening of your conscience can God's healing love do its work."

I felt a twinge of guilt at using God as a means to gain information. For perhaps the thousandth time since all this began, I contemplated what His opinion of me might be. After all, I still believed in Him. In a bizarre way, my faith had never been stronger. The existence of Malephar proved, unequivocally, the reality of supernatural evil. And didn't such a discovery render very likely the existence of a transcendent goodness as well? I thought it did.

But I quailed to imagine what He thought of my behavior, my consorting with a demon.

Most of all, my unholy pact.

A sly paranoia crept into Tyler's voice. "If I share this stuff, you're not allowed to tell anyone, correct? I need your guarantee on this, Father, or I'm not saying another word."

I leaned forward. "It's confidential. I would no more break my vows than I'd take my own life."

"Funny thing about that. I once heard priests have a high suicide rate. Sort of makes you wonder about things, doesn't it?"

It did, I decided, but I kept this opinion to myself. "You were saying..."

"All fired up to hear something juicy, huh?" An ugly laugh. "Well, I don't blame you. You probably get sick of hearing about husbands looking at porn and wives lusting after the cable guy."

I waited.

"Like I said," Raines went on, "if it were just about my partner and what he was doing to those girls, that'd be one thing. It'd be cut-and-dried, right? Just go to the chief and spill my guts. Popular guy or not, if my partner's the killer, he deserves to pay."

"The best scenario would be your partner—if he is indeed the murderer—experiencing a crisis of conscience and turning himself in."

A derisive laugh. "Yeah, right, Father. 'Crisis of conscience'? A guy's gotta *have* a conscience for him to have a crisis about it. And Danny don't have a single shred of—

aw, hell. You're sure you aren't gonna go to the police with this?"

My pulse raced. "I am bound by the highest possible authority to honor your privacy."

"That ain't exactly a yes, though, is it?"

"I won't tell a soul what you're saying."

I heard him sigh. "Okay, where was I? Oh yeah, my partner. See, we've only been together a couple days, so it's not like we know each other all that well. He had a different partner, but that guy committed suicide."

I thought of Jack Bittner, and for some reason, the image of the big man just before Malephar had forced him to shoot himself awoke a different set of memories in my head. Something about that wicked newsreel of images that had unspooled when Malephar had grabbed Danny's arm...

"Nothing to say?" Raines asked. "I guess I get it. I mean, what *is* there to say? People off themselves all the time. Life goes on for the rest of us. But the point is, I didn't know Danny very well beforehand."

"But now?"

"Now I know him a little too well."

I gazed at the iron grate, through which only the vaguest outline of Raines's face was visible.

"How do you mean, you know him 'too well'?" I asked.

"It's just...you ever hear the phrase 'kindred spirits'?"

I waited.

He sighed. "Well, I hate to say it, but that's me and Danny."

"I don't take your meaning."

But I thought I did. Far too well.

A self-conscious laugh. "I need to spell it out for you? Fine, I guess I will. I mean, I've come this far, right? It's like this..." The sound of fingertips tapping. "...when Danny starts talking about what it's like to kill someone, I find myself getting excited."

Only with an effort did I keep my tone level. "He actually told you about killing those girls?"

"Oh, no, not like that. At least, not at first. At first, I just asked him if he'd ever had to shoot anybody. He said, 'Yeah, of course I have. You don't put in nearly twenty years without using your weapon now and then. Not in this city you don't.'

"So I asked him, 'Who'd you shoot?'

"He laughs and says, 'Half a dozen people at least.'

"I say, 'Bullshit,' and he says, 'Several of them were fatal.'

"Well that got my interest. Big time. See, I'm sorta fascinated by death. My friends think I'm a little morbid, but my favorite shows are about murder. Serial killers and stuff. So I asked Danny about it, and he starts giving me details about the people he shot." A pause. "Only the details he gives, they don't sound like shootings at all. They sound like torture killings. Like sex crimes.

"I stop him and say, 'Hey Danny, what the hell we talking about? I thought this was line-of-duty stuff, defending yourself from some thug who pulls a gun on you.'

"Danny kind of looks away and stares out his car window."

Raines lapsed into silence. I forced myself to be patient with him, to avoid pushing. That was the quickest way to shut down a confession. *Don't pressure the customer*, as Father Sutherland was fond of saying.

At length, Raines went on. "Danny says, sort of smiling at me, 'You wanna hear something fucking crazy?'"

"That got my attention, cuz Danny never cusses on the job, or at least he hadn't around me. 'Sure,' I says. 'Let's hear what's so fucking crazy.'

"Danny gets a crafty gleam in his eyes and says, 'What if I told you I knew who the killer was? What if I told you I've got a source who knows everything about the Sweet Sixteen?'

"The way he said it meant Danny wasn't the actual killer, that his source knew someone who was." A pause. "But I could tell, Father. Anybody not in my line of work would think it's a load of shit, but I'm telling you, a cop develops another sense, one that goes deeper. And I'm not just talking about intuition here, I'm talking about knowing things on a *gut level.* Something primitive. It starts to get more honed the more you do this work. And on that level I knew Danny was talking about himself."

I asked, "What did Danny tell you?"

"Everything," Raines said. "Every detail you can imagine."

I felt like I was going to be sick.

"He told me something else too," Raines added.

I waited, my stomach churning.

Raines said, "He told me about last night's murder. He told me before it happened."

◆ ◆ ◆

The confession booth around me dropped away. Was Danny the killer after all? Or if Danny wasn't, and the worst-case scenario was true and I was the murderer of Julia Deveroux, was there some sort of psychic link between Danny and Malephar? Or—and this possibility was so

324

monstrous that it took my breath away—had Malephar purloined the identities of Danny's future victims and then used me to kill one of them before Danny could?

I said, "He talked about the Deveroux girl?"

"Bingo, Father. He told me he was going to do some surveillance on her because his source had tipped him off. Said she was going to be the next one to get hacked up."

I scowled at the silhouette on the other side of the screen. Raines's choice of words had been, at the very least, wildly inappropriate. What was more...

I shook off the thought. "Danny told you he was going to kill her last night?"

"He might as well have. Talked about her looks, about her...you know, her breasts. That sort of thing. He even made mention of this necklace she always wore, an emerald-lined crucifix. It was a sixteenth-birthday gift from her folks. The stones run up the sides of it. Thing's probably worth some money."

"Emerald-lined crucifix," I murmured, thinking of Danny's habit of collecting a precious object from each of his victims. Was the crucifix even now residing in Danny's apartment?

"Any other details?" I asked. "Think hard."

The silhouette swiveled its head. "You're pretty keen on hearing about this. Any particular reason you're so interested? Or are you like me? You know, kind of spellbound by this stuff?"

"These crimes are national news. Everyone is interested in seeing the killer brought to justice."

A soft chuckle that froze my blood. "'Brought to justice.' People love to say that. But you know what? This isn't

Hitler we're talking about. Not Bin Laden. It's just...people get urges, you know?"

The thought I'd had moments earlier resurfaced, but this time it refused to be displaced. "You're telling me you can relate to the killer."

"Something wrong with that, Father?" he asked, his tone drumskin tight. If I said the wrong thing, he'd bolt.

I took a breath. "There are darker regions within all of us, Officer. Places in our hearts we're not proud of. Shadow sides." I hesitated, then added, "Priests are no different."

"You're not kidding there, Father," he said with an ugly giggle. "I've heard things about priests that make the Sweet Sixteen look like Santa Claus."

I suppressed an urge to punch him through the screen. What I did do was ask, "How do you relate to your partner?"

From his silence, I feared I'd overstepped my bounds. After a time, he said, "How do I relate? Now that's a hell of a question, Father. That's a cut-the-bullshit, get-down-to-brass-tacks question. Am I right?"

I listened.

He stifled a yawn. "Well, I've told you this much. Maybe it won't hurt to tell you a little more. I can promise for sure Danny didn't kill that girl last night."

"But you said he'd identified her. You said—"

"I know what I said, Father. What I'm telling you is Danny didn't do it. At least not that one. He was busy with that thing at the 7-11. You might have heard about it." A sharp intake of air. "Hey, I bet you even know the priest that was involved! He's a friend of Danny's, Father Crowded or Coward or something like that. I met the guy last night."

Which erased one of my niggling worries. I had entertained, several times during our session, the notion that Raines knew who I was and was taunting me by showing up today. But from his tone I could tell he hadn't connected me with the vigilante priest he'd met last night. After all, a city this large, what were the odds?

"You were saying that Danny committed the other murders," I prompted, "but not yesterday's."

"So who did, huh?" The silhouette nodded. "Yeah, that's the million-dollar question, Father. If the Sweet Sixteen didn't do it, who did?"

"Perhaps a copycat?" I suggested.

"Perhaps," he repeated in a mock-proper tone. "Or perhaps it was somebody else, someone who knows Danny."

One of my temples started to twitch. Did he, after all, know who I was and believe me to be the murderer of Julia Deveroux? Had he come to arrest me?

I began to reach for the door handle. I grasped the cool iron surface. I wouldn't let him apprehend me. I would leap from atop the cathedral before I let them take me to prison.

"Or maybe," he went on, "Danny isn't really the Sweet Sixteen after all, and he's telling the truth about his source."

Something in his tone made me ask, "But you don't believe that."

"I don't," he said at once. "I think the other killer is someone who knows Danny. Someone who has a lot in common with him." His voice went ragged, husky. "Someone who gets rock hard when he hears about the blood."

My muscles clenched, a blinding wrath taking hold of me. I was a fool for not seeing it before. I'd been too paranoid, too guilt-ridden to recognize the obvious truth. Tyler Raines was just as much a monster as Danny.

He was going on. "Someone who fantasizes about ramming those honeys—"

"*Officer*," I warned, my fingers closing on the doorknob.

"—who almost comes in his pants when he thinks about those sweet bodies getting ripped apart—"

"*Murderer!*" I shouted, throwing open the door. I stumbled out. Raines was already flinging wide his door and wheeling toward the stairs. I gave chase, my mind a maelstrom of fury. Malephar was hurling invective at me, but the demon's words scarcely registered. Raines was agile, had nearly reached the stairs leading down, but my body was surcharged with a vigor and a clarity I had only experienced one other time, the moments when Sutherland and I were banishing the demon from Casey's body.

I barreled forward, already gaining on Raines as he descended the staircase. I had agreed to keep Danny's identity a secret, but I would not do the same for Tyler Raines. Somewhere, under the strata of rage, I realized that Raines's confession meant I was not the author of Julia Deveroux's gruesome death, and that knowledge filled me with an indescribable relief.

But my outrage eclipsed everything.

I clattered down the stairs after Raines. Below me, he rounded a corner, continued down, but I was leaping the steps four at a time, moving with an athleticism of which I wouldn't have believed myself capable. Raines scampered down the last few steps, nearly overbalanced when he reached level ground. Only fifteen feet behind now I vaulted from halfway down the last flight of stairs and landed nimbly on the carpeted corridor floor. Raines threw a terrified glance over his shoulder and kept running, but in moments I would ride him down. I hadn't thought any further than that, I only knew this was the chance for which I'd been craving to do some good in this world, to atone, if only a little, for my inexcusable complicity in last night's killing. I heard a shout from behind me but didn't spare a glance toward the person who'd uttered it. Because I was five feet away now, closing, closing. I leapt.

And crashed down on Raines. Together, we skidded to the floor in a flailing heap. The young cop was strong—I could feel his muscles writhing beneath me—but I was galvanized by rage. This monster had raped and murdered a child. Julia Deveroux would never breathe again, smile again, infuse the world with light again because of this depraved fiend.

Raines yelled for me to *Get off, get off.* He rolled over, but I straddled his bucking body, reared back, and swung. The blow caught him flush on the nose, eliciting a wet grunt and a cherry-colored spurt of blood from one nostril. Again came the shouting voice behind me, closer now, and to my right a door opened and a shape emerged. I knew they were converging on us, but I refused to relent. If I did, Raines might escape, and the crimes would continue in their new, two-pronged state. I couldn't allow that to happen.

Raines had raised his arms in an attempt to ward me off, but I swatted his hands aside, tore down with a looping fist, which smashed into his face just above the eye socket and whipped his head sideways. There were rough hands buffeting my upper body, but I was taking aim, meaning to unleash one last punch.

Then I was lifted away from him, someone with immense strength raising me as effortlessly as a child's doll. I was tossed aside, and as I scrambled to regain my feet and resume my punishment of Raines, the towering form of Father Patterson filled my vision.

Patterson's dark face was tinged with purple. "*Father Crowder!*" he thundered.

I glared at Raines, who was being helped to his feet by a secretary and a workman I didn't recognize. Raines was gawking at me.

I pointed at him. "He's a killer. He has to go to prison."

"He's lying," Raines shot back. "I told him some stuff in confidence and he took it the wrong way."

"You despicable—" I started to say, but before I could get further, Patterson seized me by the shoulders, drove me backward into another room. The women's restroom, I realized when an elderly lady at one of the sinks gasped at our abrupt intrusion.

"He's getting away!" I yelled.

"Shut up for a second," Patterson answered, his hands still clamped over my shoulders. He cast a glance at the elderly woman, who was clutching her chest in fright. "Please excuse us, Mrs. Merten. We have urgent business to discuss."

Mrs. Merten, whom I now recognized from her regular position in a third-row pew each Sunday, stood immobile.

"*Please*, Mrs. Merten," Patterson urged, a little hoarsely. "I wouldn't make such a request if it weren't of paramount importance."

"You can't let Raines go," I said.

"Just... shut... up," Patterson said through clenched teeth. He shoved me backwards.

Mrs. Merten glanced from the broad-shouldered priest to me, then evidently concluded she'd better escape while she had the chance. When she'd exited, Patterson bolted the door and rounded on me. "What in the *hell* are you thinking, Crowder?"

I wasn't to be intimidated. Not anymore. "It's *Father* Crowder, and you need to move aside."

Patterson opened his mouth to rebut me, but I stepped closer, jabbed a finger in his chest. "And don't give me this crap about privacy, Patterson. Our duty is to stop more girls from getting hacked to pieces!"

"Jason, listen," he started, but I made to elbow past. Without warning, he thrust out his arms, sent me skidding on my rear end into one of the stall dividers.

I scrambled to my feet, charged at Patterson, this time with my fists raised, but before I could swing at him, he growled, "*I agree with you.*"

He could not have surprised me more had he sprouted wings and fluttered around the room. "You never agree with anything I say."

"Drop the self-pity, it's one of your worst traits."

"And your relentless legalism is one of yours," I countered. "You want Raines to get away so you can preserve our reputation for good Catholic rectitude. While he's out there victimizing another child."

Something dangerous flashed in Patterson's eyes. "I'm gonna let that one go—the last one I do, Crowder—but if you say something like that again—"

"Then why not stop him?" I demanded. "If you believe he deserves punishment—"

"Do you have evidence?"

"I have a confession."

"That no one heard but you. And did he even come out and say it? Or just imply it?"

I balled my fists, my body trembling with pent fury. "Let's keep him here until the cops can pick him up."

"He *is* the cops," Patterson said. "Or have you forgotten? You think they're gonna arrest one of their own unless they're absolutely positive he's the killer?"

I thought of Liz's colored highlighters, remembered the light green one. "There's a theory the Sweet Sixteen is someone on the C.P.D."

"Oh there is, is there? Where'd you get that information, Crowder? The tabloids? Or do you have a criminology background I'm not aware of?"

"A cop would know better than anyone how to evade capture, how to hide evidence."

Malephar snarled, *I'll stop your heart, Crowder. The moment you utter the accusation, you'll fall dead on this floor.*

Patterson waved a dismissive hand. "If you go to the authorities with something a cop said in the confessional, you'll not only be ignored, you might very well lose your job."

I reached up, ripped off my Roman collar, tossed it at Patterson's feet. "Take it then. I'd rather get fired trying to do the will of God than keep my job by staying silent."

Patterson rubbed his temples. "Raines will have gotten away by now."

"Bet that pleases you, doesn't it? As long as we adhere to the very rituals Christ came to undo, you'll be satisfied."

Patterson gave me a stern glance. "That's heresy."

"Heresy is not using the brain God gave you. Do you really think a husband should have three wives, Patterson? Or that it's sinful to do God's work on Sundays?"

Patterson ignored that. "I suppose this Raines killed all of them, huh? And you'll be able to prove it in front of a jury?"

I stalked toward the sink, which dripped persistently. "He didn't kill the others."

Patterson made a scoffing sound. "There are different killers, huh? How many? Three? Four? Maybe we should accuse a whole basketball team."

I faced him. "There's only one other."

Careful, craven, Malephar warned.

"I suppose you know the other guy's identity too."

"I do."

If you DARE utter his name, Malephar began.

I couldn't hold it in any longer. "I'll tell you who the Sweet Sixteen Killer is. It's Da—"

A sledgehammer crashed into my breastbone. I dropped to my knees, groaning, straining for breath. A thunderbolt of pain rode all the way from my right shoulder to the tips of my fingers. Distantly, I heard Patterson shouting, rushing toward me, but I pitched forward, the world already going dim.

I told you I would do it, Malephar declared. *I told you I would stop your heart.*

Please, I begged, forgetting my pride, forgetting my loathing of the fell presence inside me. *Please let me live. Please forgive me.*

FORGIVE YOU? Malephar bellowed. And then the demon let loose with such a raw-edged spate of laughter that I was certain my life was forfeit. Though Patterson was supporting me, I felt as though I were floating above my body, the pain in my shoulder a howling dirge. Tears streamed freely from my eyes. *I'm sorry*, I thought. *I'm so sorry.* And in my extremity I had no idea whose forgiveness I sought. God or the demon's, Father Patterson's or Father Sutherland's.

Or was I trying to forgive myself?

I have no idea how long I lay slumped in Patterson's arms, but at some point I became aware of his steady breathing, the erratic drip of the restroom faucet. I opened my eyes, and at first Patterson's face was an unfocused square. Then, his features swam into view, and I saw his expression was one of relief.

"I thought you were gone," he said.

Then why didn't you call a doctor? I wanted to ask.

His stare was unblinking. "I need to make a confession."

"Don't tell me you're a killer too."

"I am," he said.

I looked at Patterson, saw the torment in his eyes.

"I killed my daughter," he said.

CHAPTER THIRTEEN

Sitting across from me on the floor of the women's restroom, Patterson asked, "You ever heard of a place called Turkey Run?"

"The state park in Indiana?"

Patterson's eyebrows rose. "Surprised you've heard of it. It's only about four hours south of here, but if folks in Chicago saw it they'd think they were on a different planet."

"I grew up in Indiana," I explained. Then gestured impatiently. "Are you going to let me call the police on Raines, or do I have to fight my way past you?"

"When I'm done, maybe you won't feel the need to call the cops."

"What the hell does that—"

"Listen," Patterson commanded, a measure of his intensity returning. "As your superior, I'm telling you to shut your mouth and listen. If you still want to go to the authorities when I'm done, I won't stop you."

"Who says you could stop me now?"

He chuckled. "Please. I'm twice your size, and meaner than you'll ever be. You don't want to get into a dick-swinging contest with me."

I was taken aback. I'd never heard Father Patterson utter such coarse language.

He grinned. "Don't look so affronted, Crowder. I'm a human being. And I wasn't always the urbane man of God you see before you."

"No?"

"Uh-uh. But by my late twenties, I'd gotten out of inner-city Gary. You been there?"

"Sure." I shrugged. "I've been through it."

"Good thing you didn't stop. Skinny white kid like you, they'd have gobbled you up and spat out the bones."

"Get to it," I said.

"I met a gorgeous woman, married her. She was white, not that that mattered." He scowled, rubbed his forehead. "I don't even know why I mentioned it. Maybe because it mattered to her family."

I knew Patterson wasn't married now, and I was surprised he'd been before. Then again, it wasn't uncommon for someone to enter the priesthood after a divorce.

"Laura loved nature. I swear, we hit every state park in the Midwest those years we were together. Potato Creek, Brown County. We had little Ariana one year after we got hitched and had a blast toting her around. A kid that young...she was pretty portable." He smiled. Then the smiled faded. "One time we went to Turkey Run."

I found it difficult to give him my full attention. It wasn't just the fact that a murderer had fled St. Matthew's and was about to start his shift with another, more prolific murderer. It was that nagging thought that wouldn't quite grab hold, that inchoate sense of urgency that wouldn't crystalize in my conscious mind. Something to do with those strobing thoughts I'd seen when Malephar grasped Danny... something about one of the faces...

Patterson continued, going over to the sink and washing his hands. "My wife called me the Safety Monitor. I guess I *was* obsessed with Ariana's safety. But I've always been a trifle paranoid, and when we had our daughter..." He shook his head. "...I guess that paranoia kicked into hyper-drive."

I listened, thinking to myself that, for the first time, I could relate to Joe Patterson.

He scrubbed his hands. "My wife, on the other hand, was a free spirit. Always talked about positive and negative energy. She claimed I emitted too much negative energy. Said my manias would stunt Ariana's emotional growth. I told her, 'If we don't take care of her physical well-being, her emotional growth won't matter.' She told me to stop being such a downer, and then we'd usually laugh a little. You know, marveling at how different we were.

"That made life an adventure. Her always telling me to lighten up, me telling her we had to be careful, that it only took one moment of carelessness for things to go wrong."

"How did your daughter feel?"

"She was young. She probably didn't think anything of the way her parents teased each other." Patterson sobered. "But some of the time I wasn't teasing at all. Some of the time, I was absolutely terrified of something happening. It's a scary world. You can do what you're supposed to do and be as careful as you want, but if someone else isn't paying attention..." He fell silent, regarded the sink. "It only takes once."

I didn't know what to say, so I waited for Patterson to continue. He came over, eased down, and leaned against a stall divider a few feet away from me.

Patterson smiled. "She loved the parks, though. Loved nature."

"Your wife?"

"Ariana. She got cranky when she was tired, but most of the time she just ran around and squealed with joy. God, she was a great kid."

His mouth twisted, and he looked away, collecting himself.

"We were at Turkey Run when it happened. If you've been there, you'll know about the river that runs through the park."

I frowned. "Sugar something?"

"They call it Sugar Creek, but it's bigger than a creek. A lot bigger." He shook his head. "Heck of a lot of water there. I was always nervous around water.

"But Laura claimed I was just being a downer. Told me to lighten up. So I did like I always tried to do, which was to lighten up. I mean, a guy doesn't want to be the one bringing everyone down, does he? Especially the two people he cares about most?

"We spent the night there. It was while we were looking at the brochures in our cabin that Laura learned of the falls."

"Wait, waterfalls?"

He nodded. "I was surprised too. 'In Indiana?' I asked her. Little Podunk park in the middle of the heartland? But there they were as big as life the next morning. Ever since Laura showed her the brochure, Ariana was obsessed with seeing the falls. According to the pictures, you could actually observe the waterfalls from inside the caves. So of course we just had to go there. If we hadn't, Ariana and Laura would've made me the bad guy."

He sounded bitter, haunted. I had little doubt something terrible had happened at the falls, but my desire to catch Raines was returning. He'd likely wait to do anything horrible until nightfall, but what if he didn't? He wasn't Danny Hartman, after all, and therefore might decide to kill on an entirely different schedule.

"I remember the smell of those caves," Patterson said. "Like the inside of a faucet. Cool and coppery and damp." He breathed in, as though scenting the aroma.

"They found a tunnel. Later on, I learned there were a dozen spots like the one we found ourselves in. Places where you could approach a waterfall from the inside and watch the curtain of water shimmering over the void." He glanced toward the single rectangular window, which was composed of frosted glass. "I remember the way the falls looked. About fifteen feet high and twenty feet wide. The water must've come from some large tributary, or maybe it had been raining a lot. Whatever the case, it was roaring something fierce when we approached.

"I was scared to death. Not for me, but for my daughter. The air was thick with moisture, and the ground was slick and mossy. I was afraid Ariana would fall and crack her knee, or worse, that she'd try to break away from me. Obviously, I was a lot stronger than her, but everything was slick. I held her back at first, told her we were close enough to the waterfall when we were actually about thirty feet away. But the way I looked at it, the falls were a hundred feet up from the creek, and if someone took a tumble from that height, there's no way they'd survive. But my wife, she tells me to stop being such a party pooper, and she goes right up to the waterfall. The ground there sloped a little, but not so much I worried about her falling. Laura was sure-footed." His mouth went tight. "But I'd be damned if I'd let my daughter walk right up to the edge with her."

He shook his head. "It caused a fight. A big one. Laura rarely used profanity around Ariana, though she used to cuss like a sailor before we got married. In any event, Laura started cussing me up and down, telling me I was worse than a Jewish mother. That made me mad. All stereotypes make me mad, but that one hurt not only because it was a religious one, but because it was her way of emasculating me. Laura was like that, though. Use whatever she could to her advantage. That became apparent during the divorce. But I already knew it from our time being married. If it suited her, she'd play the 'You should cherish me because I'm a woman card.' In the next breath, she'd accuse me of treating her like she was too delicate, say I was being a chauvinist. Then, she'd want me to be sensitive, but whenever I exhibited behavior she didn't feel was manly enough, she'd call me a Jewish mother or a Debby Downer.

"The fight got so bad—mostly it was Laura shouting, but I overreacted too—that she ended up getting between me and Ariana to prove her point. She took our six-year-old by the hand and hustled her right up to the edge of the cave. I was sure the both of them would tumble right into the water, but they stopped, and then it was like there hadn't been a fight. Laura told Ariana to look up at the waterfall, and then to hold out her hand."

Patterson faltered. "My daughter was little, even for her age. Laura was short, and Ariana took after her. So when Ariana held out her hand, she wasn't able to catch the stream of water the way Laura did. So Laura had her lean out farther. I was already sick seeing how close my wife had let Ariana get to the lip of the cave, and when I saw my little girl leaning on tiptoes over a drop of a hundred feet, I guess I lost it. I went to grab her...you know, snatch her back from the edge...but Laura stepped between us. We collided, and one of us must've nudged our daughter. One moment she was there, on her tippy-toes, trying to catch the spray with her fingers. The next she was just... gone."

340

Patterson took a moment to collect himself.

"She didn't even scream, least not that I could hear. The roar of the falls was so loud, it..." Patterson compressed his lips. He gazed down at his lap, cleared his throat. "They didn't find her until a diver went in. The water was deep, we found that out later. If I'd have known...but in my mind, I thought it'd be rocky. Shallow." He broke off, tears streaming down his cheeks. He'd clasped his hands, was staring down at them.

I said, "It was an accident. You loved your daughter."

He glared up at me. "No, Crowder, I *love* my daughter."

"What happened wasn't your fault—"

"Don't you *see*? It wasn't just that she fell. I know that if my wife had been smarter, less intent on proving she was right, Ariana never would've been in that situation." His eyes widened. "*It was the fact that I didn't jump in after my daughter.* If I had, I might've saved her life. I told myself I was being responsible, that if I died, she'd die too. So I sprinted through the cave and wound my way down to the water as fast as I could, but all the while I recognized the error in my thinking. If I'd have jumped, and if I died in the jump, that meant Ariana had already died too. But if she'd made it to the water alive, if the impact with the water didn't kill her, and if the water below wasn't too shallow, that meant there was still a chance. That meant I could have made the leap too, and I maybe could've saved her."

Though I dreaded the answer, I had to ask, "Did they ever determine the cause of death?"

"Drowning," he said flatly. "My daughter drowned because no one went in to save her. Not fast enough, at least."

We fell silent, the drip of the faucet our only companion.

I regarded Patterson's bowed head and finally understood why he was so cynical. And though I should have thought only of his emotional pain, I couldn't help but remember the eight murdered girls.

Kate Harmeson.

Mary Ellen Alspaugh.

Shelby Farnsworth.

Katie Wells.

Joy Smith.

Ashley Panagopoulos.

Makayla Howell.

Julia Deveroux.

Each girl had only been a decade older than Patterson's daughter, and though Ariana's death had been a tragedy, it hadn't been premeditated, hadn't been authored by someone's twisted desires.

But the Sweet Sixteen killings had been *choices*. None of those young women should have died. Yet they had.

Danny Hartman had claimed the first seven girls, and now he had an accomplice, or, to use Danny's own word, an *apprentice*.

I had to go, I decided. I had to stop Raines before he could kill again.

I rose. "Look," I said, "I'm sorry you lost your daughter. I'm sorry it ruined your marriage." Patterson got to his feet, looking ready to protest, but I cut him off. "I know that affected you, Father Patterson. It was probably the reason you became a priest. To save as many souls as you could to make up for Ariana's death."

He lowered his chin, his face taking on a threatening cast. "Don't psychoanalyze me, Crowder. And don't speak of my daughter."

"Fine. But if the story you told me was intended to coerce me into silence, I'm sorry, Father, but it didn't work. I'm going to put an end to this madness once and for all." I started past him. "I'm going to have Tyler Raines arrested."

Patterson's big hand shot out, clamped over my bicep. His grip made me wince, despite my efforts to appear impervious. "You won't get anywhere with that. You think you're the first priest to go to the cops? It's your word against his. It's a dead end, even beyond the morality of it."

"The *morality* of it?" I snapped. "How about the morality of killing—"

"Would you just *listen*?" he yelled, swinging me around. Six inches from my face he said, "We're gonna stop Raines together, you dumb shit. We're gonna catch the other guy too, the Sweet Sixteen."

He let me go, straightened the cuffs of his shirt.

"You believe me?" I asked.

He glanced at me. "You ever see an innocent man act the way Raines did?"

"I don't get it. What are you proposing?"

"We spend the evening watching him."

"And then?"

"Then maybe he'll lead us to the Sweet Sixteen." Patterson's eyes were hard, his voice flat. "I want both of these monsters, and I want them tonight."

◆ ◆ ◆

Malephar did not protest until I climbed into the shower. Then, as if the hot water roused him from some uneasy slumber, he railed at me. *You're shattering our covenant!*

We're following Raines, I answered. *Not Danny.*

Danny will be with *Raines, you cocksucker!*

I haven't told Patterson, I countered. *It was his idea to do surveillance on Raines.*

You led him to Danny.

If he discovers Danny doing something he shouldn't, that's not my fault.

Lying CUNT! Malephar roared.

There's nothing you can do about it, I said, soaping my armpits.

Is that what you believe?

I haven't broken our agreement. It's Danny's fault for making his butchery a group endeavor.

No answer from the demon.

Sharp needles of dread began to poke the nape of my neck. *Malephar?*

The pain was so sudden and exquisite it dropped me to my knees. On the way down my forehead smacked the temperature control knob hard enough to draw blood from my brow. I knelt under the boiling spray, shuddering and groaning at the pressure in my torso. It was as though someone had encircled my chest with a stout rope and was cinching it inexorably tighter. I pawed at my chest, my ribcage, but the invisible rope only tightened, stealing my ability to breathe. I fought for breath, actually embedding my fingers in the indentations between my ribs as though I could relieve the pressure there, but it was of no use. Panic set in. The base of the tub was a haze of steam, the moist air entombing me. My belly and torso leaden, I leaned over the edge of the tub until I flopped onto the floor. In the improved glow of the overhead light, I caught a glimpse of my bare chest, saw how it pulsed and twitched as though

344

giant centipedes teemed under my flesh. Yet that grisly sight scarcely registered because I was suffocating, my breath coming in shallow, labored sips. I heard a cracking sound and thought that one of my knees had broken a floor tile. Then two more cracking sounds erupted, and I realized I was hearing my ribs fracture. Instinctively, I pressed a hand over a spot where the pain was especially bad, and I was horrified to feel one of my ribs crunch outward, the jagged shard of bone poking me from beneath its tent of skin. Horrified, I felt scalding heat in the base of my throat and realized the violence being inflicted on my torso was causing severe internal bleeding. The hemorrhaging blood elevatored higher, slopping over my bottom lip and further clogging my airway. Blood splatted on the ivory tile. My body spasmed, racked with peristaltic waves of geysering crimson. Frantically, I thrust out a hand, hauled myself onto the sink, somehow made it to my feet, gazed into the mirror.

Saw the many spiky protrusions of splintered rib struggling to rupture the flesh of my torso. My sides swarmed with bobbing shards of bone, the agony of the ravaged tissue unendurable. I wailed, patting the undulating flesh as though I could succor the bones into lying flat, but the touch of my fingers only awoke greater violence, my entire ribcage spreading and contracting in a chorus of dull crunches and dreadful snaps. Just above my spleen, a rib fractured with such force that the flesh ripped open, the gory hole it made not unlike a bullet's exit wound.

In my extremity, I would not have believed it possible that my horror could wax any greater, but that was underestimating the ancient presence within me, was ignoring the myriad proofs of dominance Malephar had already unleashed.

My hands rose toward my face. My bloody mouth hinged open.

It wasn't until my eyes flicked downward that I realized I was grasping a razor blade.

As I've said, I had no father figure, and though my grandfather was a good man, I seldom got to see him. When I did, he would always give me little gifts, many of which I still possessed. One of my favorites had been an old-fashioned safety razor, the kind that weighed five times more than a disposable razor and felt good in one's hand. I still shaved with this razor and therefore made it a habit to maintain a supply of fresh razor blades. The night after Malephar had selected me as his newest host, I had awakened to find one of the razor blades pinched between my thumb and forefinger, the blade poised near my jugular. I had overmastered the demon, disposed of the blade, and resolved to rid my house of all lethal objects.

However, I had been so busy since then that I'd neglected to follow through on this resolution.

The razor hovered nearer my face, but this time I didn't possess the ability to stay the demon's terrible work. I watched in horror as my lips drew back to reveal my teeth and gums. I made a high humming sound, concentrated all my will on wrenching my face aside, on letting go of the razor blade. But my hand continued to rise, the blade creeping nearer and nearer my face. My eyes tracked the blade's progress until it ventured too close for my peripheral vision to see.

I glanced at my reflection and saw the blade floating an inch from my mouth.

I thought at first the demon would turn the blade sideways and, like some sick parody of dental floss, jam the blade into the tender skin of my gums.

Malephar had other plans. He kept the blade parallel to my front teeth, touched the cutting surface against the base of my right upper incisor, and slowly pushed the blade higher. A curl of off-white tissue formed above the rising razor, the demon shearing off the enamel of my tooth. The blade continued upward until it met my gum, at which point it sank in deeper, slicing off a section of pink tissue all the way to my inner lip.

The razor lowered to the bottom of the same tooth and began peeling off another layer.

The pain intensified.

My humming had become a moan, and my left hand was fluttering weakly at my side. I fought with the strength of panic, yet my face scarcely moved, the hand that wielded the blade moving even less. When the razor pierced my gum a second time, a syrupy gout of blood splattered on the mirror. I was sobbing, fully sensitized to the agony in my mouth, and as my eyes rolled around in impotent terror, I saw that the splintering of my ribs had spread to my clavicles and hipbones. Every part of my body from the neck down seemed to be twitching, cracking, the bones transforming into sentient creatures eager to explore their surroundings.

The pain was soul-shattering, yet the greater horror was the razor blade, which was shearing a third layer off my tooth. This time the cut was so deep that only a membranous layer of tissue still sheathed the dental nerve. I could glimpse the pinkish-purple matter beneath as the layer of tooth curled higher, and when the blade embedded in the gum this time, I felt it scrape the bone beneath. A sound unlike any I'd heard a living creature utter escaped my mouth, a shrill, ululating siren, one that went on and on.

But the demon wasn't finished.

When the razor punctured the inner layer of my tooth and the nerve was severed, I voided my bowels and vomited into the sink. So supreme was my anguish that I ceased to dwell in this reality, found myself entering a feverish nightmare world of pain. Malephar only chortled at me and continued his relentless onslaught. I was aware of my body changing, contorting, the bones breaking and rearranging themselves into pulsing, grotesque shapes.

Just when I believed the horror and the agony couldn't grow worse, Malephar repositioned the razor blade, grasping it perpendicular to my front teeth. Then, before I could register his intent, he thrust the razor blade into my savaged tooth, cleaving it into two pieces and burying the blade in my gum.

This time the furnace blast of pain was too great to endure.

I fainted.

Chapter Fourteen

I awoke in a pool of my own bodily fluids. Though it filled me with dread to do so, I brought a hand to my mouth, and though I gasped at how sensitive my gums were, the tooth seemed to be intact. Groaning, I managed to rise. My body felt like a bag of broken glass, but my reflection showed I'd been healing. There were bruises all over my chest, puncture wounds that hadn't fully knitted. But I knew Malephar had allowed me to live, having proved his point.

I spent an hour in bed, darkly fascinated at the gradual healing taking place in my body.

When I felt better, I set about cleaning up, wondering idly how much abuse one body could take. I was a danger, not only to myself, but to others. That was never more evident than now. Malephar could make me do anything. I wondered why he hadn't forced me to hurt someone I cared about.

I brushed away the thought. I had three hours before I was to meet Father Patterson so we could begin following Tyler Raines.

In the meantime, I wanted to see Liz.

Yes, I decided, purposeful now. I showered off the residual grime, got dressed quickly, and wolfed down a salami sandwich. Though I didn't want to examine myself in the mirror again, I knew it was a necessity. There mustn't be any sign of the gruesome self-mutilation that occurred earlier, any remnant of the rib-splintering episode in the bathroom.

I bared my teeth before the vanity mirror and detected no sign of trauma. I believed the emotional and psychological damage from that horrid episode would never fully heal, but outwardly, I appeared fine. I lifted my black t-shirt and assessed my ribcage. Totally intact, with no rogue bone splinters tenting my skin. Satisfied, I started out, then remembered the salami I'd devoured. If I was ever to kiss Liz, I didn't want my breath to smell like a garlic-tinged slaughterhouse, so I brushed my teeth thoroughly and scrubbed my tongue to fully rid it of any unpleasant odor.

I thought of calling Liz before I drove over, the way I usually did, but for some reason decided it would be better to show up unannounced.

As usual, my decision-making proved poor.

I knew that as soon as Liz answered her door. Her short blond hair was tousled, her eyes puffy. I realized with alarm she'd been crying, and my first thought was of Ron, who'd no doubt stirred up trouble by making some threat or ignoring the restraining order.

I was so sure this was the cause of Liz's angst that I bulled past her and began shooting furious glances around the foyer. I had saved Ron's life at that convenience store, and his manner of repaying me was to torment the woman I was growing to love? I would hammer that sarcastic smirk of his with my fists, would beat the arrogance out of him until he howled for mercy.

Liz said, "I don't think—"

"Where is he?" I growled.

"Who? Jason, you—"

"Ron," I answered. "I'm going to make him understand he doesn't have a place in your life anymore, that this isn't his house—"

"That's right," she said, spinning me around to face her. "It's mine. And the sooner you and my son acknowledge that, the better off everybody will be."

I stared at her in bemusement. She let go of my arm, blew a lock of hair off her forehead. "Casey found the room. You know, where I've been studying the crimes?"

I nodded.

"I keep it locked, but somehow he got in. It's not like it's that difficult, the kind of lock you can pop open with a paperclip."

"Why is this a problem?" I asked. "It's not like you're doing anything reprehensible in there."

She grunted a mirthless laugh. "You would've thought so, the way he reacted."

"How did he react?"

"He screamed at me, threw things. I've never seen him like that. At least...not while he was in control of himself."

We fell silent at the reference to Malephar's possession of Casey.

At length, I said, "Your son needs understanding."

She gave me a sardonic look.

"He's been through an incredible ordeal," I went on, "one that would have killed most people, or at the very least left their minds shattered."

"This isn't helping."

"What I'm saying is that he's resilient, Liz. He'll bounce back."

She crossed her arms, chewed a thumbnail. "I don't know."

"I *do* know," I said, cupping her elbows. "If Casey can survive that hell he went through, he'll return to his old self before long."

There was real heat in the look she gave me. "And you know that, I suppose? You know exactly how being host to a demon and enduring a violent exorcism affects an adolescent psyche?"

I opened my mouth to reassure her, then realized how hollow my words would sound. Sighing, I said, "You're right. I don't know. In fact, very few people do. Father Sutherland would have. He was one of the foremost experts on exorcism in the country. Maybe the world."

Fresh hope lit in her striking jade eyes. "You seemed to know a lot that night."

"More than the average priest, yes. I'm fascinated by the darker areas of the faith. By the supernatural." I shook my head. "But I know nothing compared to Peter Sutherland."

"Well, he happens to be dead."

"There's an alarming paucity of information regarding the psychological aftermath of demonic possession. You have to remember, science and faith have too often been at war. In the view of science, there's no such thing as evil, at least not of the otherworldly variety. And, unfortunately, those who do believe are often so eager to validate their faith that they leap to illogical conclusions. That's why there have been so many disastrous exorcisms. Only a sliver of them are situations that call for spiritual intervention. Far more often, the culprit is schizophrenia."

"Casey does *not* have schizophrenia."

"I was there, Liz," I said as soothingly as I could. "I know Casey was possessed. And our efforts to exorcise the offending spirit were successful."

"Then why is he so different now?" she demanded. "Why can't he be like before?"

"Liz...you're going through a traumatic time."

She pulled away. "Don't you dare patronize me."

"I'm not. I'm making a point. You're enduring a severe trial. In the space of a week, your son has been possessed by a demon, the spirit has attacked you and your daughter, two men have died in your house, and now your family has been fractured because of revelations about your husband."

"He's not my husband."

"To say there's been an upheaval would be to trivialize the scope of your difficulties."

"No shit."

I couldn't help but smile. "And hasn't it affected you? Haven't you lost sleep, found yourself acting differently? How much more pronounced would the effects be in Casey, the innocent child who was victimized by the demon?"

I could tell my words had sunk in. She gave me a strained look. "It's like he hates me now, hates Carolyn." She chewed her lip. "He despises you the most. It's like he blames you for what happened."

I lowered my gaze. "I see."

And I did, to a degree. Though fairness would dictate an appreciation of me, the priest who co-authored the exorcism, human emotions were more complex than that. Casey associated me with the worst night of his life, with all manner of pain and terror. I was sure he still bore the imprint of the cross on his chest, the place where the wood had sizzled into his flesh during the ritual. Add to that the fact that Casey's domestic life had been disarranged, his father cast out of the house as surely as the demon, and that I now seemed to be taking Ron's place, and you had a multitude of reasons why Casey should look upon me with resentment.

Liz said, "The only one he talks to is his uncle. For some reason, he sees Danny as his ally and you as his enemy."

Her words troubled me deeply, but I didn't dare say anything about Danny. Not ninety minutes ago Malephar had demonstrated what would happen if I dared challenge his will.

She said, "I might as well tell you, Jason. You're what we fought about today. He says you're not what you claim to be. He thinks—"

"Casey is deceived," I interrupted. I hardly knew what I was saying, but I couldn't allow her to give voice to the theory I feared Casey now believed. "He can't help but experience echoes of his time with the demon. That would include a mistrust of the clergy, would it not? A hostility toward the arch-enemies of the insidious presence?"

Her expression clouded, but now that I'd begun this train of thought, I was feverish to continue. "A demon is one of the foulest beings in the cosmos. Short of Satan himself, I can think of none fouler. The demon is distilled evil, an intelligence that has endured for eons, and in all that time has existed solely to further Satan's work and has dedicated himself to the destruction of the fragile links between man and God."

Liz watched me, interested. I went on, my voice echoing in the tall foyer. "Just think of all the terrible deeds a demon has wrought, Liz, all the monstrous things it has seen. I don't mean to cause you more suffering, but you need to understand this truth: Casey cohabited with this entity. And just as the demon's clairvoyance encompassed Casey's thoughts, so too did Casey glimpse its sinister history. Who knows what foul horrors Casey witnessed while possessed by that monster? Who knows what sick, depraved thoughts he was exposed to? You heard Father Sutherland. The being we cast out of Casey was the most powerful, the most diabolical he'd ever encountered. And this was after a career of doing battle with evil."

"So what are you telling me, Jason? That my son is lost? That he'll never be the same?"

I saw the pain in her eyes and knew some measure of comfort was needed. "I don't know what the long-term effects will be." I took her hands. "I only know we need to be patient with Casey. He loves you very much. And in time he might even come to view me as a friend rather than the man trying to take his father's place."

It was the most suggestive statement I'd yet made, but I didn't regret it. Nor did Liz look unhappy at my words. Our hands remained intertwined for a long, glorious moment. Then her expression grew troubled. "I need to check on Carolyn. Casey... he yelled at her a little while ago. She was trying to intervene...trying to get him to lay off me, and he really lit into her. The Casey I know would never be so cruel to his little sister."

I took in the strain around Liz's eyes, the seams in her normally smooth forehead. "Maybe I can talk to Carolyn. Do you know where she is?"

Liz nodded. "The basement. She always goes there when she's upset."

◆ ◆ ◆

I found Carolyn in a small playroom next door to Liz's investigation room. The incongruousness of the two spaces brought a wry grin to my face. Carolyn slouched on a red beanbag with her legs crossed and an iPad in her lap. On the wall above her there were movie posters for *The Incredibles*, *Tangled*, *Zootopia*, and *Beauty and the Beast*.

Carolyn didn't look up when I knelt before her.

"What are you playing?" I asked.

"I'm not playing anything."

"Ah." I endeavored to lean over and glance at the screen, where I saw plain black text on a white background. "What are you reading?"

"*The Princess Bride*," she muttered.

I nodded, impressed by her taste. "I recall reading that one. I watched the movie first though."

She continued to stare at the screen, evidently having no comment on the movie.

"I heard Casey was sort of hard on you."

"He's a jerk."

I stifled a grin. "I never had any siblings, so it's tough for me to say."

She looked up at me. "You don't know when someone's being a jerk?"

"I don't know what it's like to have a brother. Or a sister, for that matter. I imagine it's pretty difficult."

"It didn't use to be," she said, her eyes growing moist. "Casey didn't use to act like this."

I frowned. "I'm afraid Casey isn't himself right now."

"But he is," she said, setting the iPad aside. "He wasn't himself the other night...the night you and everyone else were here. In a way, that wasn't as bad. Even though he hurt me, I knew it wasn't really Casey doing it. But now..." She wiped her nose, sniffed. "Now it *is* Casey. Now there's nothing controlling him. Except himself. Now he's *choosing* to be mean."

I opened my mouth to respond, then fell silent, annoyed with myself. I'd been speaking to her like she was naïve, but I now remembered she was nearly ten years old. Clearly, she was a highly intelligent child, one who deserved to be treated as such. I eased down on the floor. "I know you've been through a lot, Carolyn, and I don't blame you for being frustrated."

Her eyes narrowed.

I went on. "Your whole world has changed. Your dad moved out of the house."

"He cheated on Mom," she said.

When I only stared at her, she explained, "Casey told me. He said Dad likes to pay women to do things to him. He said Dad does drugs and is a terrible person."

While I couldn't contradict any of those statements, I felt irritated at Casey for sharing such lurid details with his little sister. I wondered how graphic Casey's descriptions had been, then decided I didn't want to know. "Your mom will keep you and your brother safe."

"I hate Dad."

"I understand."

"Casey hates you even more."

I stiffened.

"He doesn't think you're a good man. He says you're worse than Dad."

"Carolyn, that's not—"

"He said the demon showed him what was inside people. He said he saw inside you, and you were thinking about Mom naked."

I blanched.

"He said you wanted to touch Mom and do things to her. Casey said you're pretending to be a good person, but you're really not. He says you're a fake priest. He says you..."

Carolyn went on in that vein, her words gushing out in a torrent. I'm not sure at what point the change began to come over me. All I know is that Carolyn's words enkindled in me an anger unlike any I had experienced. Was it too much, I wanted to demand, for me to pursue Liz without everyone, even her nine-year-old daughter, standing in judgment? We could develop a relationship if everyone would just get out of our way. Because if it wasn't Danny screwing things up, it was Ron. If it wasn't Father Patterson judging me, it was Casey. And now, even this sniveling whelp of a girl was deigning to pass judgment on me too, the girl too young and stupid to fathom all I had been through, too ignorant of men and women to understand how happy Liz and I could be if everyone would just fucking leave us alone!

"Father Crowder?" she asked.

I froze, my breath coagulating in my chest.

My hands were reaching for her throat.

Gasping, I yanked them away and scrambled toward the opposite wall. I was shaking all over, an inexpressible horror grabbing hold of me. I glanced at Carolyn, who had risen, her eyes staring moons. Her gaze shifted to the doorway, a few feet to my left. She was plainly terrified and wanted to escape. I couldn't blame her, and though I wanted desperately to reassure her, to demonstrate how harmless I was, I understood that such a demonstration would be impossible.

Moaning, I lurched toward the door.

Never in my life, not when I was being tortured by the demon, not when I was slashed from hip to hip by Danny Hartman, not even when I learned that I had killed an innocent man...never had I wanted to die more than I did as I fled that basement.

The only blessing was that neither Casey nor Liz saw me as I escaped up the stairs.

What use was I to the world if I could be manipulated to commit horrific crimes? I had joined the clergy out of a desire to do good. And that, I realized as I raced through the foyer and burst through the front door, was why Malephar had chosen me as his host.

It all came down to power. Control. The demon had possessed a helpless teenager and had wrought terrible deeds through Casey. Now the accursed entity was flexing his spiritual muscles, showing me that evil was the dominant power in the universe, that the devil could wield an instrument of God to inflict harm on others.

Whimpering with guilt and shame, I started my car and drove to St. Matthew's, where Father Patterson had instructed me to meet him. Would he read the guilt in my face? Would he denounce me as the fraud I was?

Was Carolyn even now informing Liz of my near-violence?

I clung to a faint hope that Carolyn might have misread my homicidal lapse as a show of concern. My hands had rested as much on her shoulders as on her neck, and it was possible she was now reassuring herself that I had merely attempted to soothe her, albeit in a spectacularly awkward way.

But it was doubtful, I decided as I motored toward the cathedral. Far more likely, Liz was listening to her daughter's story now, frowning and telling herself it couldn't be true. The man who helped save Casey couldn't have attempted to strangle Carolyn.

Would Liz suspect me of being possessed?

As central as it was, it was a question I hadn't pondered. I made a left turn, shaking my head grimly and marveling at how events were spiraling out of control. I sensed that things were reaching a breaking point. I would either lose my sanity or, manipulated by the demon, commit some detestable crime. Or Liz would tell the police what I'd done, and I'd be arrested. I signaled a left turn and imagined Danny Hartman—with Tyler Raines in tow—arresting me for the assault on Carolyn. How dreadful the irony would be!

A sick lump in my throat, I parked opposite the cathedral. Climbing out, I spotted Father Patterson's white Buick LeSabre sitting catty-cornered from me. The car seemed like something an older person would drive, but in his early fifties, I didn't think Patterson qualified for senior citizenship. I strode to his car, endeavoring to appear as calm as possible. He rolled down the window, eyed me from his seat. "I thought the bubonic plague had died out."

I mopped my brow, and my hand came away slick with cold sweat. I forced a smile. "Not enough sleep, I guess."

"You're green, Father Crowder. Like the inside of an avocado."

I glanced at the cathedral. "Maybe I'm coming down with something."

Patterson studied me. "Uh-huh."

"Should I get in?"

"You didn't happen to bring a breathing mask, did you?"

I mimed checking my pockets. "Sorry."

He sighed, started his engine. "Climb in, then. I've got a feeling this is gonna be nasty work."

PART THREE
REQUIEM

CHAPTER FIFTEEN

Locating Danny and Raines wasn't difficult. Their beat was near St. Matthew's, and they'd been working nights. We found them only ten blocks from the cathedral and proceeded to tail them through the nearby neighborhoods.

Father Patterson and I talked little, our silences brooding and uneasy. After having unburdened himself to me earlier, I had wrongly believed he might feel more at ease with me, but the converse seemed true. Patterson was a strong, proud man, and perhaps he didn't like the idea of someone knowing what was likely his darkest secret and the source of unimaginable emotional pain. I tried several times to lighten the mood by commenting on the Cubs and their prospects for the newly-begun baseball campaign, but after getting little response from Patterson, I asked him if he liked baseball at all.

"I'm a Sox fan," he explained.

It figured.

We rode on in silence, pulling over when Danny's cruiser stopped, hurrying to catch up when Danny drove on. The police car was an unmarked black Chevy, and though it was nondescript when compared to the cars with lights affixed to the roof, it was still noticeable enough to track with little trouble. Dusk approached.

Patterson broke the silence by saying, "Sister Rebecca thinks a lot of you."

I searched his face for signs of irony or disapproval. Seeing neither, I said, "Sister Rebecca is an angel. We're lucky to have her at St. Matthew's."

"You're playing dumb."

I hesitated. "She was patient with me the other day."

"You mean when you impaled yourself with my letter opener?"

I stared out the side window. "She helped me when I needed it."

"She claims she didn't do much of anything for you. Said she's never seen anyone heal that quickly."

I didn't answer.

"Neither have I," he said.

I nodded. "It looks like they're turning right."

I sensed Patterson grinning at me. "Not gonna give up your secrets, huh?"

"I don't have any."

"We *all* have secrets, Jason."

It hit me like a smack in the face, those words. They were eerily like the ones uttered by Danny on the sidewalk in front of Father Sutherland's house: *We all have our secrets, Father. I'll keep yours if you keep mine.*

"I say something wrong?" Patterson asked. "You look like an avocado again."

"It's nothing."

"Would you like to date Sister Rebecca?"

I sat up straighter. "You know that's against the rules. The impropriety... I couldn't possibly—"

"Maybe you're too attached to Liz Hartman?"

This time I turned in my seat to stare at him. I expected this type of clairvoyance from the demon, but from Father

Patterson... I had no idea how he could surmise such a thing.

He laughed. "You forget, we priests are perceptive."

My heart was thumping, but I didn't detect any malice in his face. I could never tell Patterson everything, but perhaps I could confide in him a little. After all he'd told me earlier that day, perhaps this sort of reciprocity was what he was seeking.

"Sister Rebecca is a breathtaking woman," I said. "But as we both know, it would be unseemly for us to embark on a romantic relationship."

Patterson's grin broadened. "You sound like a Victorian romance."

I scowled at him. "I'm just trying to be respectful."

"Be real," he answered. "It's better."

"Assuming she's interested in me—"

"She's interested. I could tell by the way she tended to you."

I tried not to show how pleased I was.

"I bet she's worried about the age difference, though," he remarked. He goosed the accelerator to get us through a yellow light so we wouldn't be separated from the cruiser.

"I'm not that much younger," I said.

"She turned forty-six in February."

I shrugged. "I'm more concerned with our vows."

"Smart boy," Patterson said. I flushed with pride. It was the closest thing to a compliment Patterson had given me. "But the one you really want is Liz Hartman," he said. "That about right?"

I had no idea how he knew about my affinity for Liz, but after a moment's debate, I concluded there was no reason to deny it. I didn't believe Patterson intended to use the information against me, which demonstrated how far our relationship had come in the past several hours.

"Liz is an amazing person," I said. And meant it.

He nodded, his eyes tracking the cruiser as it angled through another stoplight. Again, we made it through on yellow. "I've always liked Liz. Her husband, not so much."

"I didn't think Ron ever attended mass."

"He doesn't. I had an in-home visit with the Hartmans a month ago. They were going through a..." He made a face, appeared to debate.

I waited.

He flapped a hand in annoyance. "Oh, I don't suppose it'll hurt anything to tell you..."

"What happened?"

"I guess you'd say they had a family crisis."

"This was unrelated to Casey?"

He shook his head. "Casey was alright. The little girl too."

"Carolyn," I supplied.

"The kids were fine, and Liz was okay, but she was worried about her brother-in-law." He nodded at the cruiser we were following. "She said he was staying with them but wouldn't tell me why. Said she needed me to intervene because of the way her husband was treating Danny."

I listened, my mind racing. I knew Danny had been staying with Liz and Ron—Danny had been struggling with alcoholism and had holed up at his brother's house in an attempt to dry out in a supportive atmosphere. I was convinced that Danny's murderous rampage was the catalyst for the demonic visitation in the Hartmans' home.

"The reason I'm telling you this," he explained, "is that it might be germane to what's happening with Tyler

Raines." The cruiser halted at a stoplight, and three cars behind, we did too. Patterson looked at me shrewdly. "What do you know about Danny Hartman?"

Immediately, I felt the warning tightness in my chest, as though Malephar were grasping my heart and preparing to crush it to a meaty pulp the moment I broke our agreement.

Taking care to choose every word carefully, I said, "I knew Danny had been staying with his brother's family, and I knew about the drinking problem."

Ass-licking maggot, Malephar hissed. But I knew the demon wouldn't harm me. Though a diabolical, depraved being, he had thus far operated with an inexplicable species of honor, if such a word could be applied to one of Satan's emissaries.

"I assumed you did," Patterson answered. "I think the drinking was a poorly-kept secret, mostly because Ron told anyone who'd listen what a sad sack his kid brother was."

"What happened at the family meeting?"

"Fireworks. Danny and Liz tried to be diplomatic, Ron not so much. I could tell he held religion in contempt. And though I don't usually go hunting for racism, I'm pretty sure he disliked me because I'm black."

"Wouldn't surprise me."

"Ron's a loathsome person. I think he was cheating on Liz, and the fact that he's moved out sort of backs that up, don't you think?"

Careful not to let on I knew too much, I grunted noncommittally.

"Anyway," Patterson went on, "when I left that night, I had a weird feeling. You know that sixth sense we priests sometimes get about people?"

I nodded, though recent events had called into question the accuracy of my own perceptions. I hadn't a clue that Danny was the Sweet Sixteen Killer until he admitted it.

The light turned green, and we followed the cruiser through the business district, the brick row houses and lush spring foliage giving way to taller buildings and ubiquitous concrete.

Patterson laughed embarrassedly. "I don't know, Crowder. It's crazy, but I wondered then about Danny Hartman, and since you accused Raines earlier, I've been wondering even more."

I ached to say something, but that clenching sensation around my heart was intensifying. Perhaps Malephar was ready to discard all vestiges of honorable behavior and kill me on the spot.

Patterson said, "Do you suppose Danny could have something to do with the murders?"

The fist squeezed my heart, knocking my wind out and doubling me over.

"Crowder?" Patterson asked, alarmed. "You okay? I can pull over—"

"Follow them," I managed to croak.

"You sure? I can get you to a doctor…"

I gritted my teeth, gave a curt snap of the head. "Uh-uh. This is more important."

And it was. The pain persisted for several minutes, but by degrees, it abated. In its place entered the memory of what had happened with Carolyn. Patterson asked me a couple times if I was all right, and physically I was. Yet I couldn't get her frightened face out of my head, along with the self-loathing that came with being frail enough to be governed by the demon.

Patterson said, "Look."

The cruiser had slowed to a crawl. It was moving apace with a pair of pedestrians. One, I saw, was a woman of forty-five or fifty. The other looked like her daughter, a tall girl whose pink skirt and black tank top were a bit too snug. Something about her gait seemed familiar. Her dishwater blond hair was cut to a boyish shortness, but I couldn't see her face. The cruiser glided into a parking spot along the road, and thankfully, a space opened up just fifty feet behind them. Patterson parked there, and for a moment I mused on the peculiarity of the moment: We were watching Danny and Raines watch the mother and daughter. The women didn't seem aware of the officers, and I was certain the cops weren't cognizant of our presence.

"There they go," Patterson murmured. "Come on."

Indeed, the policemen were shutting their doors and merging with the milling pedestrians. As we climbed out, I noted that the women were perhaps twenty yards beyond the cops and moving at a leisurely clip. The mother and daughter spoke little to each other, and the cops didn't speak at all.

I didn't like the feeling I was getting.

I knew the killers wouldn't attack the daughter—who, upon further reflection, did appear about sixteen years old— with her mother in tow, but the fact that Danny and Raines were tailing the girl seemed too suggestive to be coincidence.

"Not too fast," Patterson said under his breath.

I realized I'd sped up considerably. I didn't know what would happen when we finally revealed ourselves to the policemen, but I knew I didn't want that discovery to occur yet. Patterson seemed to know what he was doing, and I was placing my trust in him. Not unlike, I realized, the

371

unconditional manner in which I'd placed my faith in Father Sutherland. Patterson didn't exhibit the same affection for me that Sutherland had, but at least he didn't seem to despise me anymore.

Or maybe he was just concealing it better.

"The Red Line," he said.

Frowning, I followed his gaze and saw mother and daughter entering a canopied walkway. It led to the train called the Red Line. Father Sutherland and I had often taken it to Cubs games.

Danny and Raines followed.

"You bring your transit card?" Patterson asked, his strides lengthening to keep up with the cops.

"It doesn't have any money on it."

He gave a rueful shake of the head. "We don't have time to stop at the teller. Pay me back tomorrow."

I nodded, but at that moment, all thoughts of money fled. The mother and daughter had turned right to descend the staircase that emptied into the underground loading area. I realized why the daughter looked familiar. I also identified another face in the montage of nightmarish images I'd glimpsed when Malephar had seized Danny's arm and I'd witnessed the Sweet Sixteen Killer's gruesome thoughts, both of his past and future victims. I had seen Liz, whom I knew was still in danger. I had seen Julia Deveroux, whom Tyler Raines had disemboweled.

And I had glimpsed a voluptuous blond girl who wore too much mascara, a girl who'd seemed familiar to me even at the time.

Now I realized who she was.

As we pelted toward the train, Patterson said, "What's on your mind, Crowder? You look spooked."

And I was. Because the girl we were following was the daughter of a man I'd watched blow his brains out, his hand controlled by Malephar.

The girl was Celia Bittner.

◆ ◆ ◆

"Celia *who?*" Patterson asked as we hastened after Danny and his partner.

"Bittner," I said. "Didn't you know Jack Bittner?"

"I know all the parishioners at St. Matthew's," he answered, a trifle defensively.

We clattered down the stairs. The light blue tiled walls amplified our steps, made me doubt our ability to remain unseen. And how long was that our goal? When did surveillance become action?

When the policemen attacked Celia?

There was no way she was in danger now, I told myself. For one thing, each killer worked alone. Add to that the public setting and the earliness of the hour, and I felt confident that Celia was safe.

For the moment.

What if, I thought as I reached the basement level and moved abreast of Patterson, they planned on following her home, waiting until Celia stepped out of the house so they could snatch her?

That made sense, I decided. Which meant it was imperative that we talk to Celia now, before she reached a more isolated location.

Patterson thrust out an arm, barring my way. I followed his gaze and discovered we'd almost revealed our pursuit to the policemen.

So? a part of me wondered. *Don't we want them to know they're being watched? What good will it do to hide in the shadows?*

"Careful now," Patterson said, and we continued on, remaining a safe distance behind the cops. Patterson got me through the turnstile, and I saw as I entered the waiting area along the tracks that the crowd size was just right for our needs. Populated enough to remain inconspicuous, but not so crammed with riders that we'd lose Officers Hartman and Raines.

"They're lining up for the next car over," Patterson murmured.

I followed his gaze and saw that Celia and her mom were waiting in the area directly ahead of us, while the policemen were part of a smaller cluster to their left.

"I'm going to speak to them," I told Patterson.

He gaped at me. "You're gonna *what?*"

"You heard me."

From the tunnel to our left came the distant rumble of the approaching train.

"What're you gonna say?" he demanded.

"The truth."

"You're going to walk up to them and announce that Celia's the next victim of the Sweet Sixteen Killer?"

"Her birthday's this week."

The rumble of the train amplified.

"You think Raines is just going to attack her here in the subway? With his partner right beside him? And Danny's just gonna stand there and watch?"

I looked away. "Who knows?"

"I thought you and Danny were friends."

"We went through hell the other night. That brings out the worst in people."

Patterson's gaze burned into me, and I prayed he wouldn't press me further. Perhaps providence intervened, because the train roared into view, its brakes squealing and its gears cranking to a halt. Moments later, the doors were whooshing open and people were disembarking from the opposite side.

Patterson and I moved into the wall of waiting people. This close, I realized that Celia was nearly five-foot-ten, and nicely built. Her skirt was short enough to reveal muscular thighs. By contrast, her mom was bony and not nearly as tall. I could only see part of her profile, but she looked like a hard woman, her hair bleached an unnatural blond and hairsprayed so thoroughly it scarcely moved. Her skin was tanning-bed brown, her nostrils large, and there were the beginnings of wrinkles at the corners of her mouth, perhaps from frowning so often. I thought back to what Danny had told me about her, about how she'd ripped out Jack Bittner's heart by taking away his daughter, about how she'd been a nightmare for Jack ever since she left him for another man. I hated to judge someone too harshly, especially when I didn't have the full story, but what I now saw of Celia's mother fit the precise profile I'd created for her, which wasn't at all flattering.

The train doors opened, and the crowd piled in. Patterson hunched over a little and looked askance at the policemen, who were in turn staring raptly at Celia and her mom.

The throng of passengers shifted, and Danny's eyes seemed to light on me. Then I passed through the double doors and hustled to the seat opposite Celia. Patterson opted to stand, gripping a vertical steel bar to my left, a spot I now realized that would shield me from the gaze of the policemen.

The train doors closed, the automated voice announced our next stop, and we started to roll.

I had no idea how much time I had to speak to Celia, but I remembered Danny telling me that Celia and her mom lived on the South side. If that were true, and if they were indeed headed home, I could have as much as thirty minutes, ample time to plead my case and to warn Celia to take the proper precautions.

But now that I gazed upon her, I realized the difficulty of my task. Just how did you tell a teenaged girl—one you'd never even met—that she was being targeted by a serial killer? It sounded ludicrous, even to me. How preposterous would it sound to Celia?

The memory of seeing her in Danny's mind recurred, and as it did I remembered how terrible it had been to inhabit the twisted psyche of the Sweet Sixteen Killer. In Danny's mind she had looked much as she did now, yet there had been a lurid, sexualized quality in Danny's head, a perverse filter that rendered her more alluring, more tempting than she actually was. To me, Celia was merely a girl who would one day become an attractive woman. Through Danny's eyes, she was a sex object. A temptress who teased him with her come-hither glances. Her eye shadow advertised plainly to Danny that she wanted sex, and her freckled cheeks, rather than reflecting innocence, expressed a wanton quality, a desire to be used and used roughly.

A woman said, "There are two policemen in the other car."

I looked over, startled, at Celia's mother, whom I discovered with alarm was glowering at me with her arms crossed.

She grinned nastily. "Didn't think I'd say anything, did you?"

I knew I was blushing, and I knew that made me look even guiltier. I took a breath, strove to maintain a level tone. "I don't know what you mean."

Her penciled-on eyebrows went up. "You know *exactly* what I mean. You don't think I notice all the men feeling my daughter up with their eyes?"

I began to sweat.

Celia's mom sat forward, her slate-colored eyes searing me. "She's a *child*," she said. "Do you understand that, you pervert? A child. Don't we parents have enough to worry about with all the horror going on in this city?"

Murmurs of approbation sounded from around us.

I shook my head, sweating freely now. "I feel as bad about the murders as you do."

"Oh you do, do you? And I suppose you're a parent?"

"I'm a priest."

"Then he's definitely a pervert," some man remarked, a comment that elicited mocking laughter. I looked up at Father Patterson for help, but he pretended not to notice me. I could see, though, how tight his jaw was, the way his neck muscles were twitching. He was furious, whether with me or Celia's mother, I had no idea.

We approached our first stop.

"You know what?" Celia's mom said, rising and grasping one of the support bars. "I *am* going to tell the cops. Who knows? You might be the killer after all."

"Asshole," someone muttered.

I felt the stares of a dozen people, every one of them hostile. Patterson didn't speak, perhaps preserving his anonymity with Celia and her mom.

Celia.

I turned to her, realizing I'd forgotten all about her during her mother's tirade. She was watching me, but her expression was unreadable. She hadn't defended me, but she hadn't joined in her mother's attack either.

Everything going on around me, all the taunts and laughter—even Celia's mother's strident condemnation—seemed to fade. I saw before me a child, a girl so beloved by her late father that his world was ruined when she'd been taken from him. Strangely enough, it was the memory of Jack Bittner, even with his flaws, that compelled me to address Celia.

"I knew your dad."

I heard a sharp intake of breath from Celia's mother. Celia herself looked liked she'd been slapped.

I hurried on. "I know you don't know me, but my name is Father Jason Crowder, and I was with your father when he died."

"It was you?" Celia said in a voice almost too faint to hear.

I slid forward in my seat. "He loved you, Celia. More than anything, he wanted you to be safe."

"Stop talking to her," her mother commanded.

"Which is why I'm telling you this. You're in serious danger. You're—"

Celia's mom interposed herself between us, brandished a threatening finger in my face. "You stay the hell away from my daughter, you son of a bitch!"

"—being followed," I went on, "and not just by me. There's someone after you."

"What are you saying?" Celia asked, her face pinched.

"Don't talk to him!" her mom demanded.

"The Sweet Sixteen Killer," I said, and then everyone in the car was talking over each other, many of them rising and staring at me. The city had been like an untended kettle over the past several months, and now it was shrieking, hissing, boiling over, and the train was rattling to a stop, the automated voice announcing our location. Yet I barely heard it, barely noticed anything save Celia, who was watching me with horror but also, I thought, belief. Her mom was shouting at me, maybe on the verge of physically assaulting me.

But I had to say all I could to her, had to impress upon her how real the peril was. "Don't go anywhere alone. Stay with a friend if you can, in a house where someone owns a gun."

"Stop talking to my daughter!" her mom shouted.

Celia ignored her. "My step-dad has a gun."

"Then stay at home. Sleep in your parents' room if you have to."

Several voices had risen to shouts. Commotion filled the train car as we shuddered to a stop. I stood, saw Patterson was peering into the car that contained Officers Hartman and Raines.

Who were, I realized with a sinking heart, standing at the exit doors and staring hard in our direction.

They'd spotted me.

They'd would be in our car in moments. And here was Celia's mom accusing me of accosting Celia, a dozen other riders whose faces reminded me of pitchfork-wielding peasants out for a good lynching. It was a sinister combination.

"I have to go," I told Celia. "Please believe me—I'm only trying to help you. Your dad wasn't perfect, but he loved you dearly. Honor his memory by keeping safe, okay?"

Awestruck, Celia gave a little nod.

The car stopped. All eyes were on me.

"You're not getting away," Celia's mom declared.

"He knows something about the Sweet Sixteen," a woman said.

Random hands pawed at me, but I swatted them away, muscled toward the exit. "I do know who the killer is," I said.

"Yeah?" a male voice asked.

"Bullshit," a pale, skinny guy said.

"Who?" a young woman demanded.

The doors opened. No one in our car moved, but people in the car beside us began to jostle out. Hartman and Raines were the first ones through the doorway.

I stepped onto the concrete, some of the riders following me, their expressions avid.

"Officers!" Celia's mom shrilled. "This man was threatening my daughter! He knows something about—"

"That's him," I blurted as the policemen rushed toward me. "The Sweet Sixteen Killer is Officer Tyler Raines."

CHAPTER SIXTEEN

The platform devolved into bedlam.

Passengers from the other cars were pouring out to get a glimpse of what was happening. The riders from our car were filling the gaps around us, all eyes riveted on me.

"Who's Tyler Raines?" someone asked.

Patterson's considerable bulk loomed between me and the approaching officers. "He is," Patterson said, indicating the younger cop. Raines cringed when Patterson identified him, perhaps realizing it would be more difficult to prove his innocence when there were two accusers rather than one.

"He's the Sweet Sixteen?" a woman's voice asked.

"Hell, no," Raines said. He had his cuffs out. Danny was stone-faced, his arms hanging loosely at his sides.

Before they reached us, Celia's mom pointed at me. "This man was leering at my child and should be arrested for lewd behavior."

"I'm about to deal with him, ma'am," Raines answered, gripping me by the bicep and directing me away from the crowd.

"But he didn't *do* anything," Celia said, and I felt a brief burst of happiness.

Danny was following us. Patterson stood outside the train, a look of pained indecision on his face. Celia took a couple steps after us, but her mom snagged her wrist.

"The priest is the killer," her mom said. "I hope they give him the death penalty."

"He's not a killer," Celia said, ripping away from her mom's grip. "He's just trying to help." Her face changed. "Is that you, Danny?"

Danny didn't speak, only continued to stride away from the crowd with me and Raines. I realized that Celia would have met Danny at some point, but the thought promptly scattered as Celia's mom shouted something unintelligible at her daughter.

Raines muttered, "So much for privacy, huh, Father? Thanks a lot."

A voice from behind us called, "Where are you three going?"

A backward glance confirmed it was a Red Line worker, an older, plump, bespectacled woman with steel wool hair and a kindly face. She couldn't have been more than four-foot-ten.

"This door lead somewhere?" Raines asked, nodding at a gray door inset in an alcove.

"Don't most doors?" the woman asked as she waddled closer.

"Open it," Raines growled. "By order of the Chicago P.D."

"Don't have to get all huffy," she said, plucking a key ring from her belt and selecting a faded gold key. "This man in trouble?" she asked.

Raines nodded. "He has information we need."

"Is he a suspect in the killings?" she asked as she keyed the lock and pushed open the door.

"Now what would give you that idea?" Raines asked.

"They're all saying it," she said with a thumb toward the still-gawking crowd. She peered up at me. "You don't look like a killer."

Danny spoke for the first time. "Looks can be deceiving."

"Move," Raines said, shoving me through.

The room we entered was a dingy gray and looked like a combination janitor's closet and storage area.

The woman began to move away, but Danny said, "Hey."

She stopped, gazed up at him through her thick spectacles. "Can I help you?"

Danny nodded at a door across the room, this one ancient-looking. Light green paint flecked off its bubbled surface. There had once been black text stenciled on it, but now it was illegible. "Where's this lead?"

The woman frowned. "You don't want to go there."

Raines was watching Danny apprehensively. "What's up?"

Danny gestured at the small room we found ourselves in. "This isn't very private. We need to make sure no one hears us."

The woman shook her head. "Nobody ever goes in here."

Danny looked at Raines. "We can't risk someone overhearing. Some people aren't too good at keeping their mouths shut."

I looked from one cop to the other, and in the thick silence charging the air I realized how furious Danny was with Raines. Maybe he didn't know exactly what Raines had said to me in the confessional, but he was canny enough to know Raines had let too much slip.

"There's a conference room upstairs," the woman suggested. "We have cookies."

Without taking his eyes off Raines, Danny strode over, tapped the door with his knuckles. "This one. Open it."

Brow furrowed, the woman riffled through her key ring. She finally settled on one, tried it. The lock wouldn't turn.

Her tongue sticking out the side of her mouth in concentration, she attempted another, which didn't work either. In the sallow light of the small room, I studied Tyler Raines, who looked like he might be sick. I couldn't blame him. He knew Danny was a serial killer. And now Danny was fuming.

Was Raines in as much danger as I was?

I hoped so. Julia Deveroux deserved justice. Her parents deserved justice. Prior to this whole affair I had been staunchly opposed to the death penalty, adhering instead to Father Sutherland's view that every soul could be salvaged, no matter how abhorrent its sins. Although I knew this view was a godly one, I found it more and more difficult to cling to. How could a man who raped, tortured, and disemboweled a child be salvaged? Did he deserve to be?

"Ah," the woman said, the lock finally snicking open.

Looking vastly relieved, she grasped the outer doorknob and made to go, but before she could, the door jerked out of her hand and a huge figure pushed inside.

"What are you doing with him?" Father Patterson demanded.

"None of your goddamned business," Raines snapped. He shot a glance at the short woman, who appeared ready to hyperventilate. "Why didn't you lock the door behind you? *Jesus.*"

"It's fine," Danny said. "He can come with us." A nod at Patterson. "How are you, Father? It's been awhile."

"Not that long," Patterson said. "How are you coping, Danny?"

Danny shrugged. "Not bad. You know, some days are better than others."

"You moved out of your brother's house?"

"Would you wanna live with my brother?"

"Danny, there's something you need to know about your partner."

Danny raised an index finger. "Hold on a sec." A look at the short woman. "The key you just used. Was it the master?"

She bit her lip uncertainly. "The closest thing we have to one."

"Give it here."

Her kindly face darkened, her internal struggle pitiful to behold.

"You'll only get in trouble if you don't cooperate with an official investigation," Danny explained. "If anybody gives you flak, I promise I'll take care of it."

Looking unconvinced, the woman removed the key from the ring and placed it in Danny's outstretched palm.

"And Miss?" he said.

She stopped at the door and looked at him, her comically magnified eyes plainly frightened. "Yes, Officer?"

Danny smiled. "Lock the door, all right?"

The woman nodded and scurried out. A moment later we heard the lock scrape closed.

Danny regarded Patterson. "We were just about to sort all this out. Father Crowder here seems to think my partner has been doing things he shouldn't. My partner thinks something's up with Father Crowder."

Patterson moved forward, his broad shoulders seeming to fill half the room. "Jason Crowder is a good man. He and I have clashed in the past, but my best friend, may he rest in peace, believed in Jason's character, and lately I've begun to understand why."

Maybe it was the sleep deprivation or the emotional roller coaster to which I'd been subjected. Whatever the case, Patterson's testimonial brought a thickness to my throat.

Danny nodded solemnly. "I've seen him in action too, Father Patterson. Which is why this is all so difficult. The other night, with my nephew Casey...I would've sworn Crowder would never harm anyone."

"I haven't," I said.

"I think I believe you," Danny said. "But we need to get somewhere secluded where we can hash things out."

Patterson spread his arms. "What's wrong with here?"

Danny grinned. "You think that little old lady's gonna be able to control the crowd? However big it was to begin with is only gonna double. They're gonna be right outside that door listening to every thing we say." He shook his head. "We gotta find a better place." He nodded toward the open door, out of which was emanating a rank, fetid stench. "That's more private."

Raines regarded the black doorway. "What's in there?"

Danny shrugged, his grin reassuring. "Just the tunnels, Tyler. The city's honeycombed with them."

The tunnels. Danny's words imbued me with dread. I looked at Patterson, who was eyeing the tenebrous doorway uncertainly.

Danny chuckled. "Don't worry, Father. I'll be there to protect you."

◆ ◆ ◆

Like I had on the night of the exorcism, I felt like I'd wandered into some ghoulish Grand Guignol performance, the kind where every actor's lines were tinged with sinister undertones. Danny used a powerful flashlight to illuminate our way. He went first, followed by me, Patterson, then Raines, whose right hand rested on the butt of his holstered gun. There were cobwebs all over the place and the furtive clitter of fleeing cockroaches, but the tunnel was tall enough even for Father Patterson to walk without stooping over. When we'd wandered down a narrow corridor for what felt like ten minutes, we encountered another door.

Danny said, "Let's see here," and fitted the key into the lock.

Unfortunately, the key worked. He twisted the knob, which screeched from disuse, and shone his light down an alarmingly steep flight of stairs.

Danny started down, called over his shoulder, "Close the door behind you, Tyler."

Knowing I could do little to stop our downward progress, I followed. Patterson, however, paused in the doorway. "Hey, wouldn't you say we're secluded enough? I don't have much interest in inspecting the city's sewer pipes."

Danny laughed but continued trudging down the steps. "That's a separate system, Father. Down here's where the freight tunnels are located."

Patterson started down. "I thought those were closed off."

"They were," Danny answered, his voice echoing up the cement throat of stairwell. "Too many indigents found ways to sneak down here. The city sealed up the tunnels in most places, but if you know Chicago like I do, you can still find a few ways in."

Raines made a remark, but I scarcely heard him. Because something I'd wondered about was clarifying, a comment Liz had made in her investigation room:

It was the Alspaugh murder that changed things, Liz had said. *Widened the net of possible suspects, so to speak. There were too many witnesses near the site of the murder for the killer to have simply walked away. There were security cameras everywhere. The killer had to have some secret way in and out to avoid being seen.*

I said softly, "You used the tunnels the night you killed Mary Ellen Alspaugh."

Four steps ahead of me, Danny froze, but I hardly noticed. Because that tightening around my heart moored me to the spot, made me lean against the wall in pain. I knew Patterson hadn't heard me—he was still at least twenty feet behind—but I knew I had come dangerously close to shattering my pact with Malephar.

As I stood there trying to breathe and hoping my chest wouldn't blow apart, I thought of Malephar for the first time in several minutes. I knew the demon would never harm Danny. He was, after all, one of evil's prized soldiers. Yet might there not be a way to utilize Malephar in this subterranean world? Could I somehow deliver Father Patterson and myself from the homicidal cops?

Careful, craven, Malephar warned. *If you transgress again, I shall simply kill you and leap into another body.*

If it were that easy, I thought, *you would have done so already.*

I was a coward—I knew it and despised myself for the deal I'd struck with the demon—but I remained horribly conflicted, and at some point our arrangement would become untenable. Malephar had to realize this as well, so if it were simply a matter of eliminating me and entering another, more appropriate host like Danny or Raines—hosts who would suffer no moral qualms—he would have already performed the transfer.

Danny began walking again, and when he did he muttered back to me, "Move up here, Father. We need to get a couple things straight."

I drew even with him and said in a low voice, "'Straight' is a funny choice of adjective. Abducting girls, raping them. Desecrating their bodies after taking their lives. Then taunting the police you profess to support. You're the very definition of a crooked cop."

Danny kept the flashlight trained on the stairs ahead, which fed onto a landing before continuing down. "I'm past the point of being mad at you, Father. I'm even beyond being freaked out by the way you survived that knife wound. Now I'm just fascinated."

I looked at him.

"Yeah, I know about the demon," he said, meeting my gaze. "It's the only thing that makes sense. You got that...that *thing* in you when it left Casey's body. And it somehow healed you up after I unzipped your belly." He frowned. "What I don't understand is why it chose you."

"It's a pestilence."

"I mean, why not me, right? Why not the guy who's killing all these succulent young honeys?"

I gritted my teeth. "I can't believe you're boasting about it."

"Keep your voice down, Father," he said with a backward glance. Apparently satisfied that Patterson was far enough behind us, he went on. "So Tyler spilled his guts to you. Man, what are the odds? A city this big?"

"It's not that surprising," I answered. "The cathedral is part of his new beat. He probably heard you say you're a member of St. Matthew's. Maybe, subconsciously, he wants you both to get caught."

"Oh, I'll admit he's got a nasty streak. Some of the shit he was saying about Celia even made me blush."

"You can't touch her now."

"Wanna bet?"

We reached the bottom of the steps and were immediately faced with a stretch of corridor so long and dark that it seemed to eat Danny's flashlight beam.

Standing side by side, staring into the darkness together, I said, "If something happens to her, everyone will know you're the killer."

Footsteps approached from behind. Patterson and Raines were almost upon us. "Guess you'll never know, will you?" Danny said in a low voice. He hunkered down and situated the flashlight on the crumbly floor, the cone-shaped beam illuminating his face from below. Lit up that way, like a camper telling a spooky story around a fire, he looked every bit as savage as I knew him to be.

I said under my breath, "You'll have to murder Father Patterson too. He's not going to keep silent about this."

"Oh yeah, about that," Danny said, turning to regard Patterson, whose face was sheened with sweat. "Father, you mind checking that fuse box on the wall behind you? I wanna see if it's still hot."

Patterson turned and looked at the wall, on which there was nothing but water stains and grime, and before I knew what was happening, Danny was taking out his gun and pistol-whipping Patterson in the base of the skull.

The large priest sank to his knees and pitched forward like a felled oak. Danny holstered his weapon, his face expressionless.

Raines gaped at Patterson's prone form. "Jesus Christ, Danny, what was that for? You can't go hitting a priest."

"I didn't hit him," Danny said, forcing his fingers under his waistband and coming out with a long, curved knife. "And I didn't do this either."

Before I could register his meaning, the knife was whipping toward Tyler Raines and slashing his throat. The slit was deep, the diagonal line opening like the crimson maw of some mutant catfish and spraying blood all over Patterson's unmoving back.

I stood immobile, my breath coagulating in my throat. Danny stepped toward me, wiping off the handle, and placed the knife in my hand. "Then you went for me, Father Crowder," he said, stepping back and reaching for his gun, "and I had to shoot you in self defense."

I lunged for him, knowing if he drew his gun I'd be dead. But Danny was too quick. My blade whickered past his face, and he pumped a fist into my stomach. My foot must have caught the flashlight as I stumbled forward, because the upraised cone of light suddenly danced about the corridor, licking the walls and coming to rest on Raines's alabaster face. Raines was slumped on his knees, still attempting to clutch his hemorrhaging throat, but I could hear Danny moving closer, no doubt aiming the gun at me or perhaps reaching for the flashlight.

I glanced back, saw it was the latter. Danny had bent over, his fingers almost to the thick black cylinder. I kicked backward at it and connected, the flashlight clicking off as it tumbled.

Danny and I were steeped in a darkness thicker than I could have imagined.

"You son of a—" Danny started, but I'd pushed to my feet, begun to scamper toward the steps, thinking to escape this shadowed tomb.

Before I reached them the corridor lit up with a fusillade of shots. Gasping, I jumped backward, slammed against the wall in an attempt to make the slimmest possible target. The dark hallway lit up with each concussive blast, the sparks from the slugs inching closer and closer as they sprayed chunks of concrete. I knew if I fled up the interminable staircase I'd make an easy target for Danny. Yet he was twice as strong as me, a cold-blooded murderer expert in doling out violence. If I attempted to physically best him, I knew I wouldn't last long. I could go for Raines's weapon, but I had no idea how to handle a gun, and what was more, the firearm was likely slimed in Raines's blood and might not even function properly. Which left only one option that I could see, an avenue that chilled my blood.

"Smile, Father," Danny said, and I knew he had zeroed in on me by the sound of my breathing.

I dropped to the floor just as he fired, the gunshot a blast of pale light in the stygian gloom. I clambered toward Danny on feet and hands, moving in a way I hadn't since early childhood. I was aiming for the space to Danny's right, where I thought the flashlight had fallen. Danny was cursing and crunching about on the gritty floor, no doubt searching for the flashlight as well. My probing fingers encountered an object that moved when I touched it, causing me to suck in surprised breath and shrink toward the middle of the corridor. It was Tyler Raines, of course, Tyler's breath now entering its death rattles, the gargling sound making my skin crawl. I clambered over Father Patterson, hoping the big man would rouse, but though he still breathed slowly and evenly, he was out cold, and I doubted he'd be awakening any time soon.

The flashlight should be about three feet away.

From almost exactly where, I realized with dawning horror, the sounds of Danny's movements were emanating.

I heard a soft sighing sound—Danny was pleased—and a moment later the flashlight beam lit up the tunnel. I was too late. Danny would shine the beam on me and put a bullet in my forehead.

It was at that moment that I realized I still carried the fillet knife Danny had handed me.

I lashed out blindly with the curved blade, and before Danny dropped the flashlight, I saw a dark stripe of blood open on his wrist.

This time Danny let loose with a guttural barrage of curses, but I had no plans to stick around to listen. Because Danny was already regrouping, turning, and aiming the gun in my direction.

I had no choice. He stood between me and the staircase, and anyway, the flashlight lay at *his* feet and not mine. But behind me there was darkness, and for the moment, it was my only ally.

I bolted into the shadows.

Danny fired once, the bullet pinging off the wall, and the gun clicked, its ammunition spent. Had I known Danny would have to reload, I might not have set off in a direction that guaranteed death. I might have chanced rushing past him and gaining the stairs while he was occupied.

But I had chosen my course and knew there was nothing but to follow it now. I sprinted as fast as I had in my life, knowing that Danny would fire upon me the moment he got his weapon reloaded.

I had to be out of range when he did.

I'd scampered maybe fifty yards down the narrow corridor by the time a dim glow appeared behind me. Instinctively I began to swerve right and left to make a more elusive target. But I needn't have worried.

Because the next moment, the light winked out and footsteps began to race after me.

Danny had decided to hunt me in the dark.

CHAPTER SEVENTEEN

I don't know how long I fled down that endless corridor. I only know that at some point I realized I needed to take caution not to slam face first into a wall. If I did, I might be knocked unconscious, and then Danny would be able to complete his ghastly scheme.

I imagined Danny's story in its stark, fabricated glory:

Officer Danny Hartman discovers that Jason Crowder is the one who murdered Father Sutherland. Crowder, knowing he's been discovered, strikes Father Patterson with a blunt object, produces a fillet knife, with which he slashes Tyler Raines's throat, before he's ultimately brought to justice by the brave Officer Hartman.

The symmetry of the lie sickened me. I had to find some way out of this, not only to save myself but to preserve what good reputation I still possessed in the eyes of those who mattered to me, even if I didn't deserve their regard.

I raced on through the black tunnel, completely unaware of how deeply I'd ventured or how far behind me Danny was. Sometimes I would slow, my ears straining to pick up Danny's movements. But he was a practiced murderer and was therefore adept at utilizing stealth. Each time I thought I heard a rustling from the corridor behind me, the noises would cease, and I'd be left with the labored sounds of my own breathing and my clumsy footfalls, which were growing increasingly heavy.

As I staggered forward, the ground began to drop away from my feet. I tried to slow down, but by the time I realized

I was descending, I had picked up too much momentum to halt my progress. I tumbled headlong, rolled, and grunted in pain as my shoulder crashed into some unyielding surface. Rocks and dust showered my upturned face. I coughed out chalky air. From behind me came the hurried tread of my pursuer.

It was enough to get me back on my feet. I groped in the darkness, touched the abutment into which I'd slammed. I'd reached a fork in the corridor. I had no idea which direction was the more logical choice, and the prospect of getting lost in what was likely an underground labyrinth suffused me with dread. Yet what choice did I have? Continue my flight or die.

I fled.

Taking the left prong of the fork, I set off at a trot, but immediately heard something that shocked me into silence.

The dull roar of water.

What was even more astonishing was the fact that I could make out a dim light emanating from somewhere ahead.

"*Father Crowder*," Danny crooned.

I gasped, halting. Moments later, the tunnel lit up.

"Now which one did you take?" Danny called. "The right lane goes into the freight tunnels, the left one heads deeper."

A pause, Danny's flashlight beam crawling over the concrete. I thought I'd advanced far enough to avoid detection, yet if he started down my tunnel, I'd stand little chance of surviving.

The beam went away. "I don't see you, Father," he said, his voice fainter now. "But something tells me..."

The light went out. His footfalls echoed. Was he approaching me, or had he selected the other tunnel? Noises down here were weirdly distorted. I thought he'd chosen the right prong of the fork, but I couldn't be sure. A desperate urge to bolt gripped me, but I forced myself to remain still, to confirm his position before giving away my own. I turned from the sound of Danny's steps and studied the meager light filtering toward me. It wasn't much, but I'd at least be able to see a little, and that was enough to get me moving again. I tiptoed forward, knowing any error on my part might bring Danny and his gun. He wouldn't scruple about shooting me—the story he planned to tell his superiors was perfectly plausible. He would be a hero. And go on killing.

Would he start with Celia Bittner?

Yes, the demon's voice answered. *He'll start with Celia, and he'll continue with a string of other delectable tarts. He'll rip them open and fuck their glistening wounds, and in time he'll graduate to Liz and her family. And he'll go on and on and on, you cocksucking coward. You've failed to stop him.*

"No," I whispered. I pocketed the fillet knife, its wicked surface sharp against my thigh.

Yes! Malephar answered. *Yes, you little bastard! You'll be anathema to Liz once she finds out what you tried to do to Carolyn. Why not simply die now and avoid her condemnation?*

"That was you," I muttered, "not me. I would never harm Carolyn."

Tried to strangle her.

I stopped you *from strangling her.*

Something sulky crept into Malephar's tone. *You didn't stop anything.*

Then why not kill her? I demanded. *You wanted to. I felt your hatred of her. Carolyn's goodness whipped you into a frenzy.*

You dare not challenge me, craven. Or have you forgotten the way I savaged you in your bathroom. You are nothing.

I moved forward, the light growing stronger.

"I am the light," I whispered.

What? Malephar demanded.

I didn't know why I'd uttered the words, but they'd perfectly captured the lifting sensation I was experiencing. Because I had remembered something I'd lost over the last several days, something more important than anything else.

I had defeated Malephar once.

You didn't defeat me.

I had vanquished him in Liz's house.

You became my host, craven!

By casting you out of Casey's body, I answered, my muscles seeming to swell.

You're mistaken! If any power existed in that house, it belonged to me—

I clenched my fists. *You only overcome those who believe in the supremacy of evil.*

—or to your murdered companion, the dead priest.

I will live out the rest of my days repenting for what I did to Father Sutherland—

—your days are finished, you insolent child—

—but you will not be the one to judge me, Malephar.

Your soul will roast, you simpering, cowardly—

"I rebuke you, accursed serpent, by the power of God," I said aloud.

WHAT? Malephar thundered.

I stalked forward, the light and the roar of water strengthening.

"And I demand that you depart from this body."

You don't have the strength *to cast me out, craven.*

From somewhere behind me I heard the clatter of footsteps. Danny had discovered his error.

He was coming.

"I order you by the might of the holy spirit and the name of Christ, to depart from this innocent flesh."

Innocent? The demon bellowed laughter. *You're a killer, a lecher, a ruthless—*

"The power of Jesus Christ compels you. Tremble before His mighty hand."

Tremble? You tremble before me*, false priest!*

"Jesus orders you to abandon this flesh. God demands that you leave this body."

I will not leave you, craven! the demon shouted, but the voice was shot through with uncertainty now, a plaintive note leavening the bestial growl to which I was accustomed. *I will use you to spread the devil's darkness!*

The tunnel tended right and downward, and I discovered from where the glow was emanating. There was an iron grate there, through which two-dozen bars of milky light poured. The grate looked solid, but it was also rusty, the bolts no doubt having been eaten away by age.

I began to run.

"Jesus Christ casts you out," I said.

What are you doing? the demon demanded.

I thought it fitting that now, when my powers had begun to wax—when my faith had begun to return—Malephar could no longer read my thoughts.

Or rather, he could only read them too late.

NO! he shrieked.

But I was already lengthening my strides, loping forward until I'd attained maximum speed, and diving forward, shoulder-first into the grate.

In the instant before impact I realized I might well die of a broken neck if the grate refused to give.

It gave. When my full weight crashed down on it at a sixty-degree angle the ancient bolts snapped, the grate swung open, and then I was plummeting into a shadowy expanse that was nevertheless brighter than the tunnel I had just exited. I dropped through the murk, the demon still raging within me, and landed, my lower back and buttocks hitting first and the back of my head smacking the ground. I tumbled, the slimy concrete verging downward, and eventually wound up a few feet away from an underground river.

A billion pinpricks of light bloomed in my vision, the pain formidable. Worse was the spiraling disorientation, the inability to gain my feet. I knew I had dropped out of the tunnel into some larger space, but I couldn't get my bearings and continue my flight.

Footsteps above me.

Danny was coming.

I finally got up, nearly overbalanced, but righted myself in time. Still dizzy, I jogged forward for perhaps fifty feet before going gray again and veering downhill. My feet sloshed into ankle-high water, and I realized I could see fairly well now. I also discovered where I was.

This slimy, vast concrete tube was part of the Deep Tunnel Project. And if the light I spied downstream was any indication, I wasn't far from the Jewel Reservoir.

The current was strong, and I knew if I waded deeper into the rushing water, I'd be swept through the tunnel and into the falls. I had stood around this reservoir on many Sunday afternoons and watched the excess water gush out of these giant tubes. The power they exhibited was awesome, the roaring of the runoff exploding out of the tunnels, pounding the reservoir below, and roiling like a storm-tossed sea.

No one could survive a fall into the reservoir. To follow the rainwater toward the mouth of the tunnel was certain death. My only hope was to hurry upstream and search for a way out.

I heard a whooshing sound and glanced up in time to see Danny sliding down the curved decline behind me, his gun drawn.

I was cut off. I fled in the only direction I could go, the direction of the reservoir. Danny's gun had been holstered, but I'd seen how quick he could be. I was sprinting toward the light, so his aim would only improve the farther we advanced through the tunnel.

"Where you going, Father?" Danny called. "Don't you wanna hear about my plans for after I kill you? You'll never guess what I'm gonna do to Liz."

Moaning, I loped on. Danny's words weren't idle threats. I knew it because I'd inhabited his mind, if only for a moment. But a moment had been long enough to glimpse the horrors there, the oozing darkness. Danny's soul was as black as pitch, and though there might have once been some good in him, that light had been extinguished forever. Danny was beyond saving.

The question was, was I?

Danny spoke again, closer this time.

"I can't tell you the number of times I wondered why Liz didn't leave that asshole brother of mine and climb into my bed. She never notices, but every chance I get I stare at her cleavage, peek up her skirt. You know, she once left her bedroom door ajar when she was changing out of her swimsuit, and I got the most glorious look at her ass." His voice was getting closer, the terrible words echoing off the curved walls and becoming clearer over the roar of the river.

"She had tan lines, you know, because it's risky to lay out naked around here. But that snowy-white ass of hers... God, it was curved and firm and not a bit dimpled from cellulite. I can't tell you how often I've thought of carving it up and eating it like jerky."

I cringed, my limbs feeling leaden, my nerves frayed. Danny, on the other hand, seemed totally at ease. What was more, he didn't sound a bit out of breath. I recalled how strong he was, how physically fit. He was a specimen of raw power, agility, and animal cunning.

And all his considerable talents were focused on ending my life.

The vast tunnel trended left, the way ahead gradually brightening. I could see now that the river of runoff was perhaps eighteen feet across, and I guessed it to be about six feet deep in the center. I flirted with the notion of leaping into it, but even as I slipped and slid on the curved, scum-slicked floor, I was still making faster progress than the water was. If I jumped in and allowed the current to carry me, I might not be able to climb out of the river before the tunnel emptied into the churning reservoir far below, and worse, I'd be an even easier target for Danny, who'd simply jog alongside me and fire at my head whenever I breached the surface. I wasn't a terrible swimmer, but I wasn't an accomplished one either. My only hope was that an exit presented itself between here and the end of the tunnel. If not, I'd either be swept into the reservoir to drown, or Danny would end my life with a bullet to the head.

"So what's it like?" Danny called, his voice closer.

I didn't answer, but I knew what he was asking about. Demonic possession was intriguing to many people. How much more tantalizing would the subject be for a depraved monster?

"I said what's it like?" Danny repeated. "You're about to die, you know. Might as well confess your sins to somebody."

Sins, I thought, frowning. *Sins*.

My body was failing me, Malephar doing nothing to help. Perhaps he wanted me to die. But something about that word, *sins*, was dredging up a memory.

The night Danny had attacked me in the cottage, the night Malephar had seized his arm and shown me the identities of Danny's former and future victims, I had glimpsed a great many faces. Faces of the dead and the living both, and all but one of them had been identified.

We were nearing the mouth of the tunnel. I pushed forward and saw the vast, staring eye of the tunnel's terminus, beyond which lay the deepening dusk, sunset having taken a stranglehold on the city.

I shot looks left and right, but there was nothing but concrete, nothing but rushing water. Eighty more yards to the mouth of the tunnel and no exit in sight.

But something else was gnawing at me. Moments ago, during my recitation of the rites of exorcism, Malephar had struggled violently. I believed myself capable of finishing the exorcism and vanquishing Malephar again. Yet now I wondered why Malephar would cease struggling. Was it merely because of the momentary stoppage of the rites, or was there something more sinister at work here, Malephar again plotting to best me?

Danny was gaining. "You know, I've been thinking a lot about the little friend inside you, Father."

Friend, I thought, a chill squirming through me. *Agent of my damnation is more like it.*

"And I came to the conclusion that you're not really fit for the job."

My energy was flagging, the stitch in my side like relentless knife strokes. Only fifty yards to go. I realized that this tunnel was positioned beneath at least one other tunnel, because there was a continuous sheet of water flooding over the circular opening.

I couldn't help but recall Father Patterson's story of Ariana. Of how she'd been lost forever by tumbling into just such a waterfall.

And I had the feeling that the reservoir falls were far more violent than the ones in the state park.

Thirty yards.

"Now take a guy like me," Danny went on, his tone conversational, "a guy who's not afraid to do the grunt work. Who's able, and more importantly, *willing* to get his hands dirty."

I shivered, twenty yards from the opening, a large magenta circle on a tar-black tapestry.

"Wouldn't I be a better vessel for your passenger?" Danny said.

An electric jolt sizzled through my body. I realized exactly what it was that Malephar wanted.

He wanted Danny.

"No," I breathed, slowing as I neared the terminus.

An image flickered in my mind, a girl's face.

"Stop, Father. Put those hands up high."

I stopped. I had no choice. Three feet from where I stood the tunnel plummeted into an abyss. At a glance, I saw the drop was at least half a football field, maybe more. The roar of the falls was earsplitting.

"Hands *up!*" Danny shouted.

I raised my hands.

"Now face me."

I turned and saw Danny striding toward me. His expression was easy, genial as always. He looked like he'd hardly broken a sweat. If not for the gun pointed at me, you would have thought we were getting ready to share a beer together.

"I heard that stuff you were saying back there," Danny said. "You were trying to get rid of the demon, weren't you?"

I said nothing, but I was thinking hard. That face in Danny's mind... that face...

"And it makes me wonder," Danny went on, continuing to display the same uncanny perceptiveness that had allowed him to murder seven girls under the noses of his colleagues and an entire city, "why you'd be so gung-ho to do that. I knew from the 7-11 incident, you know, piecing together what Ronnie and everybody else told us, that it wasn't you acting alone against those assholes in masks. You had help."

Danny stepped closer, the gun aimed at my chest. "So I wondered, 'Why doesn't he use that power to fight me?' I felt it that night in your house, you know. That thing inside you could've ripped my arm off if it had wanted to. But it didn't. And it doesn't want to help you now."

I looked into Danny's soulless eyes, asked, "Why do you think that is?"

"I think you know, Father. And I think you know what I need from you."

I did. God help me, I did.

He wanted Malephar. This sick, demented killer craved the demonic infestation that was plaguing me. Danny wanted Malephar to inhabit his body rather than mine.

And I knew the demon wanted the transfer too. Malephar realized I wouldn't acquiesce to his ghoulish wishes any longer. He needed someone more tractable to manipulate.

Or in this case, someone eager to execute the devil's will.

"So you're gonna do one more thing, Father. And the best part is, you're not gonna have to lift a finger. All you have to do is stand there, and I'm gonna put a bullet in you, and as you choke on your own blood, the thing inside you is gonna relocate to a proper home, a place where it'll be more appreciated."

I paled, imagining how lethal Danny would become with the demon girding his actions. He'd already proved equal to the task of carrying out his atrocities and eluding capture. Now, with the demon aiding him, he would be unstoppable. His reign would last for decades.

One thought, one image kept intruding on this bleak possibility. The one girl I hadn't yet identified.

It doesn't matter, Malephar snarled. It was the first time the demon had spoken in several minutes. That told me I was near the mark, that the girl's identity really might matter.

Danny gestured with the gun. "The demon went into you at the end of Casey's exorcism, right? So finish *this* exorcism."

Finish it, Malephar echoed.

Danny was right. If I exorcised the demon now, both Malephar and Danny would get their wish.

"Say the rest, Father," Danny commanded, his amiable smile going tight.

But Malephar couldn't continue if both of us were dead.

"I won't do it," I said. "If I die, the demon dies too."

A flicker of disappointment played across Danny's face. Malephar raged within me.

Danny shrugged. "Well, fuck it, you know? You die, it'll be like this never happened. I've done fine on my own so far. I just thought it'd be a kick to wield the kind of strength you showed at that convenience store."

He raised the gun. "Any last words, Father? What do they call it? A benediction?"

"Valediction," I said, turning toward the sheet of falling water.

"Face me," Danny ordered. "It's gotta look like I shot you in self-defense."

"What if I drown?" I asked softly. I closed my eyes, sought for the name Malephar had discovered when he'd glimpsed the face in Danny's mind.

"Not as good," he said, splashing closer. "The story doesn't work as well, and who knows? You might live. Stranger things have happened."

"The last face," I said, staring at the falling water. The sky beyond it was violet, the day writhing in its death throes. I probed for the name, and though Malephar struggled to conceal it from me, it was crystalizing in my mind.

"Turn *around*, Father," Danny demanded. "Don't make me ask again."

Something Liz said about the killer echoed in my brain:

I hate him, but… I think he's in terrible pain. Something from his past. I think that can be used against him.

I lowered my hands as I spoke. "I made a mistake. I thought the people I saw were all your victims, the ones you'd killed and the ones you were planning on murdering."

Danny's voice was uncharacteristically tense. "Shut up."

"But there was one face that was separate from the rest. She had a different…" I paused, licked my lips, and imagined her features. "…a different aura than the other faces. A different color."

"Shut your *mouth*, Father."

"The others, there was a reddish cast to them. They were the ones who incited your bloodlust, who you'd carved up and tortured. Or the ones you planned on raping and disemboweling."

"Mother*fucker*," he growled, right behind me now.

"But this one was a solemn blue. A sorrowful memory."

"I'm not just gonna shoot you," he said, his voice raspy, "I'm gonna make you suffer. Who knows, they might not even find your body."

"She was the one who broke your heart. She was the girl you loved when you were sixteen."

"Keep talking, Crowder, I'm gonna enjoy this. I'm gonna carve you up worse than any of my honeys," he snarled.

"You were in love with her. You told her so. You believed she'd marry you, raise children with you."

His voice became a husky growl. "Gonna rip out your *spleen*, Father. Gonna eat it while you beg for mercy."

"And then she left you for an older guy, a college student."

"Get ready, you worthless motherfucker. Get ready to know pain."

I took a breath. "Her name was Jill Kelly."

"YOU SON OF A BITCH!" he bellowed, grabbing the back of my neck.

I whirled, the fillet knife flashing in the sundown light, and opened a blooming red gash in his stomach. But in the same instant something exploded between us, my right side set aflame, and I knew Danny had shot me. He fired again at point blank range, but I'd seized his wrist, shifted it just enough that the slug went wide. He staggered against me, and I slashed down with the knife, yet at the last moment he caught my forearm, held it in place with his terrible strength.

For an endless moment we struggled against each other, our feet inches from the edge of the tunnel. The water roared by us, disappeared into the dying light. I glanced down, saw our blood streaming into the rushing surf and washing away into the reservoir.

Danny grinned into my face. "I might get my wish after all, Father. If you die before I do."

I returned Danny's rabid grin.

"It's not gonna happen," I said.

He showed his teeth. "Why not?"

"Because we're both gonna die."

And gripping him, I launched us into the falls.

CHAPTER EIGHTEEN

I wasn't prepared for the hammerblow of the water. In the split second between deciding to drag Danny out into the gushing runoff and actually executing my plan, my only misgiving was a simple one: falling from a great height. My fear of heights had never been debilitating, but it had frequently troubled me. Climbing ladders. Traveling in planes. Even gazing out the windows of tall buildings. So other than ending the Sweet Sixteen Killer's reign of terror once and for all, the only thing on my mind was how terribly high we were and how very long it would take us to reach the thundering surf below.

When the powerful falls walloped us, we were both sent cartwheeling through the air. Miraculously, we did not lose hold of one another. It was a testament not only to my desire to prevent more murders, but of Danny's lunatic hatred of me, the one who had learned his secret and dared to confront him.

Because I was grasping the fabric of his police uniform so tightly, the fillet knife was pinned between my palm and his shoulder. We had toppled end over end perhaps three times before our vertiginous revolutions began to slow, and I was able to think clearly. The pressure of the waterspill was so colossal that we had been taken into the gush only momentarily before being belched inward, deflected toward the outcropping tunnel perhaps ninety feet beneath the one out of which we had fallen. I saw Danny throw a panicked glance downward at the huge concrete cylinder, his eyes vast with terror, and in that moment, I knew my chance had come. His guard was down, his superior strength nullified by his fear of dying. As we gained speed in our final descent, I gripped the knife handle, pulled it back, and jabbed it straight at Danny's left eye. In the last moment he glanced up at me, and in his eyes I saw a flicker of fear, a last, feeble remnant of his humanity. It occurred to me in that moment, as the wicked point of the fillet knife zoomed toward his eye, that Christ wouldn't do what I was doing, that Danny was still perhaps capable of being saved.

But I wasn't Jesus. I was just a man, and a deeply flawed one at that.

This was the best I could do.

The fillet knife sank into his eyeball, popping it like an overcooked egg.

He released me, and though our fall was still accelerating, my brain swiftly registered the worry that he might yet survive. If the knife hadn't sunk in far enough and if the impact with the water didn't kill him and if he somehow managed to navigate the pounding water beneath us, all my efforts would be for naught.

Then his head collided with the outcropping tunnel, and I knew Danny Hartman had breathed his last.

The force of my knife blow had thrust his head backward just enough to align it with the unforgiving rim of the tunnel. The base of his skull slammed into the concrete rim at an ungodly speed, snapping his neck like a stick of chalk and transforming his body into a boneless, flailing rag doll.

That much, I thought as I plummeted into the maelstrom, was done. The Sweet Sixteen Killer—Killers, I amended—would terrorize the city no longer. Millions of

Chicago-area parents could rest easier knowing their daughters would cease to be hunted.

But what of me?

I was mere moments from entering the seething cauldron of water, the throaty boom of the upracing reservoir nearly deafening now. And though it was selfish, though I knew the city would be better off if I died too, and the demon were trapped inside my lifeless shell, I wanted nothing more than to live. I deserved punishment, I thought in those last moments. Maybe I even deserved death.

But I didn't want it.

I plunged into the tumult, my body immediately sucked under and forward by the unimaginable weight of the gushing water. Thousands of gallons pummeled me lower, punishing me, battering my body deeper into the sable depths. I had swallowed a good breath before I'd hit, but now, several seconds underwater, I could feel my lung capacity beginning to struggle against the immense weight bearing down on me. It was as though pitiless giants were kneading me and tossing me about like a lump of clay, their merciless fingers wringing, releasing, flicking, pushing, and at some point I opened my eyes and saw, far above me, a lighter shade of water. It was faint, diffuse, but I knew it was the sky. If I could only reach it, only summon the reserve strength that must surely reside deep within my body, I might stand a chance of deliverance. I spread my arms, pushed backwards, gathered my hands together and then stroked as hard as I could. Bolstered by the titanic force of the churning water, I moved away from the tumult, and what was more, I still had sufficient air to rise through the water, to make steady diagonal progress upward, upward, until the indigo sky above me appeared within reach. I stroked, stroked, and then I breached the surface, spluttering and gasping, unwilling yet to believe I had survived, that I had escaped the terrible drowning that only moments before had seemed inevitable.

As I bobbed in the water, my good spirits disappeared.

If I had survived, that meant Malephar had survived too. My noble aim—taking my own life to rid the world of the demon, had been usurped by my frantic desire to live.

Elated yet troubled, I began to tread water, moving slowly away from the thundering surf and into the comparatively placid waters of the semicircular reservoir. I was perhaps sixty yards from the retention wall, and though it might prove difficult climbing out of the water on my own, I knew help would come eventually. The reservoir was rimmed by a fitness trail that would almost certainly be populated by joggers and other Chicagoans at this time of night. I pictured them helping me out of the water, marveling at my good luck at surviving the ordeal, or perhaps bristling at my stupidity for risking death. I imagined them taking my hand, smiling down at me...

...Malephar leering up at them. Malephar attacking them.

My throat tightened. I couldn't allow the demon to strike again.

My voice low, hoarse, I resumed the recitation: "By the power of the saints, I cast you out."

No! the demon growled. *You're alive, damn you! Have you forgotten about your gunshot wound? Why do you think it is healing?*

I had completely forgotten about the wound, and though being reminded of it revived my pain, I strongly suspected that Malephar's incredible powers had already repaired much of the damage in my side.

But I continued with the rites anyway, my voice strengthening. "Depart, seducer. Depart, transgressor."

And what of your remarkable survival back there? Do you think you possessed the power to escape the rapids alone?

That made sense, I thought as I treaded water, but it changed nothing. Malephar's actions had nothing to do with helping me and everything to do with perpetuating his own malign existence. "Be gone, you foul pestilence! Depart from this flesh!"

I saved you, you sniveling weakling! You would have died without me!

I knew this was true. But I was grimly intent on bringing this to an end. Either the demon would be driven from my body, or I would be killed in the process. Either way, the world would be safer without Malephar, even if the respite were only for a year or two.

Something told me it would be a good deal longer.

I began the Lord's prayer.

It acted on Malephar like a livewire. My whole body began to judder, to thrash, the demon wild to prevent me from continuing the prayer. But I pressed on.

You will never defeat me! Malephar screamed. But there was pain in the sound.

"Thy kingdom come," I said between gritted teeth. "Thy will be done..."

I will visit untold tortures upon you, craven! the demon bayed.

"On earth as it is in heaven."

I felt the same kindling of pain I had experienced in the bathroom earlier. Malephar was attempting to snap my ribs, to splinter my bones and pierce my entrails.

Yet gone was the feeling of helplessness. Gone was my impotent fear.

I continued the prayer.

Sensing my resolve, Malephar redoubled his efforts to assault me from within. New pain ignited in my chest, sharp hooks of agony ripping through my shoulders.

But I said, "For thine is the kingdom..."

Malephar roared.

"...and the power..."

The demon's voice became a squeal of pain—

"...and the glory, forever and ever..."

—and then of horror and disbelief.

"Amen," I breathed. A weight pressed in on me, as if my core were imploding, and in the next moment the pressure reversed itself, rushing away from me in all directions. Soothing air filled my lungs. Water droplets peppered my face. I had a momentary worry that the demon had manipulated me all along, that it had somehow jumped to Danny's body and fulfilled the terrible coupling I had strived so desperately to prevent.

Then I remembered the way Danny's neck had been broken, the limp tumble of his body after it connected with the tunnel's rim.

Yes. Danny was dead. The terror was over. I needed only to swim the remaining expanse of water and call for help, and in short order I would be safe, my body and my life free of the demon's infestation, the city liberated from both Malephar and the killers.

Almost sobbing with relief, I set off in a series of leisurely strokes toward the nearest portion of the reservoir wall. In the past minute or so, the surge of the churning water had nudged me closer to the perimeter of the large pool, so that now I was maybe thirty yards away, an easy enough distance even for an average swimmer like myself.

I thought of Liz, of Carolyn. I would have to explain myself to them, perhaps going so far as to tell them the horrible truth. How else could the child ever trust me again? Then, if they—and Casey—found it in their hearts to forgive my concealment of the demon, we might begin our hesitant attempts to build a new family. I wondered if Casey would hold his uncle's death against me. I was now Danny's killer, after all. Objectively, I had murdered a serial killer, one that would go down in the annals of true crime with John Wayne Gacy, Jack the Ripper, and the Zodiac as one of the worst in history. Surely Casey would see that. Surely he would understand—

Something seized my ankle and yanked me underwater.

I didn't have time to suck in breath before I was dragged under, and immediately my throat was flooded with icy water. I kicked my leg to free it from my attacker, and in my frenzy to escape I imagined Danny Hartman grinning at me, my assumed victory over him simply an illusion. But as the fizzy water around me cleared, and I gazed into the face of the one who'd seized me, I realized Danny had nothing to do with this. His capacity to harm others had ended.

But Malephar's had not.

Red-eyed, his face a sanity-shattering abomination, the demon leered up at me in triumph.

◆ ◆ ◆

In all my readings, in all my late-night discussions with Father Sutherland, even in my nightmares, I had never entertained the notion that a demon could take the form of physical matter. Not without a host.

But Malephar had. The accursed vision with which I was now presented, my mind scrambled to explain, was not really the demon; it was merely a projection of my worst imaginings. For what now loomed closer—its dark, pulsing face; infernal red eyes; and gaping, fanged maw—was the villain of a child's darkest nightmare, the sort of phantasmagorical djinn conjured by a deadly fever or a severe illness. Though the shadowy water made it impossible to discern completely, the figure hauling me nearer was humanoid in shape, though unquestionably larger. The limbs were slender, yet sinuous... and alive with vicious energy. The face was venomous, exultant. And something else.

As Malephar's red eyes bathed me in their lurid glow, as his tapered, serrated teeth roared laughter I could feel in my bones, I realized what I read in the demon's expression was relief. Had he not grabbed me before I could exit the reservoir, he would have been consigned to a watery grave. I had the feeling that the strain of becoming physical matter was too great to be sustained for long.

Water trickled down my throat. A horrible acquiescence began to drowse over me.

The demon's face was only a foot from mine, the eyes slitted in obscene longing. I flinched away, choking on the cold water. I flailed against the monstrous face, my strength ebbing. In my head, Malephar's laughter intensified and caromed about, the demon's celebration drowning me as surely as the water. I lashed out, struck the demon a strengthless blow to the face, and was appalled at the manner in which the creature's skin abraded my hand. Bloody whorls curled upward like smoke. Something about the vision reminded me of Casey's mangled body the night of the exorcism, the smoke that had plumed from Casey's flesh when—

—with a convulsive movement I thrust my hand into my pocket, seized the crucifix, and stabbed at the demon's left eye. The orgasmic, half-lidded look departed Malephar's face, and the lids disappeared, revealing red, lambent irises. The crucifix, though small, cleaved through the eye, and for the briefest moment I saw a burst of fire where the crucifix had struck the demon. Malephar instantly released me, the demon sinking, his Klaxon roar loud enough to tremble the water, the demon's bellow of pain emitting a power so awesome it compelled me backward, upward. But I knew it was too late for me to regain the surface of the pool. I had taken in too much water.

But I had finally completed my sacrifice, my act of love. Though I knew myself to be a sinner, a wretched soul who didn't deserve grace, I wondered if perhaps God might appreciate my attempt to become something greater than I was.

The demon's corporeal form descended into blackness, the remaining red eye fixing me with a look of fiercest loathing. The momentum of Malephar's hateful paroxysm having spent itself, my upward movement ceased. I floated at a level that I now saw was only five or six feet beneath the water's surface. If I had only used the crucifix sooner. If I had only fought evil with God's power a moment or two earlier, I might have lived.

A bone-deep frigidity iced my veins. Cold fingers caressed my limbs. My body grew heavy. I opened my mouth, the last breath of air escaping my lips...

And in that moment of dying I fancied I saw something that made no sense at all, a large, thrashing figure plowing through the water toward me. A pang of fear shot through me, a vestige of the horror from my encounter with Malephar.

The figure clarified and I recognized the face. A large, dark hand grasped mine. Pulled me higher. Not yet convinced this wasn't some dream, I allowed myself to be towed along, the water around me changing to a light brown, then a greenish yellow. And then I was jerked upward, my head breaking the surface, my lungs assailed by sheets of flame.

Father Patterson gripped me in a bear hug. Before I could so much as cough, his great, muscled arms squeezed me in a movement far too violent to be one of kindness. My stomach and chest were frozen in an agonizing approximation of a broken machine, one so old and gummed with dirt and corrosion that coaxing it into working order is a fool's errand. But Father Patterson repeated the movement, slamming my body against his once more. We bobbed on the surface of the water, Patterson manhandling me in a way that would have been comical had my terror not been so consuming.

My desire to live returned, my dogged, irrational need to keep on breathing. When Patterson's interlaced fists slammed into my back, pinning my body against his, I vomited up what felt like fifty gallons of brackish water. He turned his face sideways but was still painted with the contents of my stomach and lungs. I spluttered, gasped, not quite able to breathe, but my lungs at least making the effort to suck in air now.

As I coughed and gasped for breath, I realized that Patterson had saved my life.

CHAPTER NINETEEN

Father Patterson rode with me in the ambulance, and for the second time in a week I found myself in the hospital. The doctors were perplexed by the wound in my side. It looked, in the words of a Korean doctor whose last name was Kim, "like I was shot a month ago, and the wound has mostly healed."

That was about right, I thought. For once, I felt grateful to Malephar, monster that he was.

I had no illusions about the demon being dead. I hadn't seen Malephar dissolve or explode into a million pieces. He had simply sunk to the bottom of the reservoir, his uninjured red eye gleaming measureless hate.

I asked Patterson, as he sat by my bedside nursing a steaming mug of tea, what he believed had happened to the demon.

He regarded his mug, shivered, and said in a subdued voice, "I don't like to think about it, tell you the truth."

I waited, noticing how deeply seamed his forehead looked. It was early morning, maybe a little after six, and he hadn't yet left my bedside. I had slept off and on for much of the night, but as far as I knew, Patterson hadn't. He remained in the same green vinyl armchair, a few feet to my right.

"This thing shook me, Jason," he said, his voice lower still. "Like every man, I've questioned my faith at times... especially after Ariana died. There are things I'm still not sure about. Like how can you hold it against somebody that he was born in a third-world country? If someone's never heard of Jesus, how can we expect a person to believe in him? And then we..." He made a pained face, ran a palm over his stubbly cheeks. "...we put distance between ourselves and others. We pick out differences between people and we amplify them and act like they're lost and we know the answers, and the truth is, we're *all* lost. We've all sinned."

My nerves stretched taut, listening to him. I had always thought of him as one of the sanctimonious ones, one of the priests most prone to judging others. Like I had in other matters, I now realized, I had misjudged him.

He sighed. "And now this. I can tell you this now, Jason, and your mentor was the only other man in the world I've admitted it to... I never believed in demonic possession. I'd keep quiet when my superiors would talk about it, but inside I always thought it was superstition. Overreaction. I never believed..."

"Was the incident with Casey Hartman what changed your thinking?"

He looked at me then. "You really want to know this?"

I nodded, though I wasn't totally certain I did. The medicine they'd administered was nauseating me, and I was in dire need of a drink. I wanted to ask Father Patterson for one, but I sensed there was something in his words I needed to hear, whether I wanted to or not.

Still looking at me, he said, "I thought you killed Peter Sutherland."

Oh my God, I thought. *Oh my God.*

A smile played at his lips. "Didn't expect that, did you?"

"No," I said. With an effort, I stopped shy of screaming.

"But now... now it all makes a weird kind of sense. The demon goes into Casey, Sutherland exorcises the demon. The demon enters Sutherland, and he leaps through the window to put an end to it." He paused, frowning. "The demon then entered the nearest body," he went on. "That was you. You tried to keep it a secret, but in the end, it became too much. Things came to a head in the tunnels, and then..."

"Did you see Malephar?"

He scowled and looked at the door. "Don't call it that. Don't give that thing a name."

I sat up in bed, little beads of sweat breaking out on my skin. "You did, didn't you? You saw—"

"I suspected strongly when you skewered yourself with that letter opener," he said. "I wasn't sure until I was in the reservoir."

"What did you see?"

"Not a lot, thank God. It was way under the water by the time I reached you. But..."

"You still saw it?"

He hesitated. "I saw something. It was really big. Bigger than me, at least." He looked at me for confirmation. I nodded. "It had... what, glowing red eyes?"

I nodded again.

He barked out a harsh laugh. "See, it's crazy stuff. Horror movies and monsters and..." He frowned, sipped his tea. "And yet I saw it. I know I did."

My throat was bone dry, but I had to get his opinion. Now that Peter Sutherland was dead, no one's opinion mattered more.

Well, maybe Liz's.

I hadn't spoken to her yet, and as far as I knew, she hadn't called or visited, which I took for a very bad sign.

I asked, "Do you think we're in danger?"

When he didn't answer straightaway, I asked, "Do you think Chicago's in danger?"

"I don't know, Jason. I know I'm scared to death of what they'll find if that reservoir ever dries up. Or... what if a workman goes down there? Some poor scuba diver trying to make repairs?"

The prospect chilled me. I imagined the black depths of the reservoir, the oppressive weight of the water. Then a pair of vermilion eyes flashing huge and triumphant at the unsuspecting diver.

"One thing I do know," he said, "is that the Sweet Sixteen will never kill again."

"There were two killers," I reminded him.

He gave me a wry look, studied his tea. "You're right. I forgot about Raines." He looked up. "Danny really cut his throat?"

"Does that surprise you?"

He looked like he'd tasted something bitter. "No, I guess not."

I searched his face. "You jumped in after me."

He averted his eyes.

"How did you find me?" I asked. "You were out cold."

"Raines had a flashlight. I got all kinds of blood on my hands, but I found it. Then I just followed your voices and used the flashlight when I had to."

"You jumped out of the tunnel after me."

He flapped a hand. "Let's not make a big thing of it."

"It *is* a big thing," I said, my voice thick. "I would've died if you hadn't saved me. And then you squeezed the water out of me—"

"You didn't have to puke in my face, you know."

I laughed, but my eyes were wet. I cleared my throat. "Thanks, Joe."

He gave me a small smile. Then he sighed. "I should've done the same thing for my daughter." His eyes filled with tears. He gazed out the window across the room. "God, I wish I'd saved her."

I leaned over, grasped his hand. "You saved me."

"I'm glad of that, Jason, but..." He closed his eyes. "I wish that were enough." Then, in a voice almost too quiet to hear, "I miss my little girl."

He wept then, silently. I kept hold of his hand. We stayed that way for a long time.

◆ ◆ ◆

It was Saturday, and Father Patterson was scheduled to conduct Mass. But the events of the night before had taken their toll on him, as had his sleepless vigil by my bedside, which didn't end until noon that day.

So with Father Sutherland gone, and Father Patterson too weary to speak, it fell to me to lead Mass. It was my first time, reason enough to send my nervousness into high gear. What complicated matters more, however, was the reverence and adulation my peers accorded me. After being discharged from the hospital, I had thought to sneak into my office that midafternoon to collect myself and devote some quiet time to prayer. My faith had grown a great deal over the past week, and I knew I had much to be thankful for.

But I hadn't even closed the door of my Civic before Father Richards materialized before me, exhibiting twice as much vitality as I'd seen him show in all my years of working with him. "Jason!" he said, his basset hound face alight with joy. "It's so good to see you well!"

When I didn't answer, he licked his lips, clapped his hands together and said, "Quite a week, huh? A successful exorcism. A robbery foiled. And then not one, but two murderers brought to justice?"

I gazed up at the cathedral. "Each of those came at a great cost, Father Richards. I don't think you're celebratory tone is entirely appropriate."

Richards frowned, crestfallen. Then, he seemed to pep up again. "Are you all ready for tonight?"

"Tonight?"

"Your sermon," he explained. "Ever since we changed the name on the sign—you know, 'Tonight's message will be provided by Father Jason Crowder'—there's been a buzz at St. Matthew's. After what you did at that 7-11, people were practically begging for you to give the Mass." He bounced on his heels. "Now I guess they get their wish, huh?"

I gave him a surly look and moved up the steps to the cathedral, where I saw the words he had alluded to in the glass-encased sign. The white letters on the black background read exactly as Father Richards had said. Where there was ordinarily a specific message listed, the space was blank.

It occurred to me I had no idea what I was going to speak about tonight.

Meaning to scurry down the hallway so I could hole up in my office for the next several hours, I pushed through the heavy double doors and found myself face-to-face with Sister Rebecca.

I stared at her, at a loss.

She nodded toward the road out front, gave an embarrassed little shrug. "I watched you pull up from my window."

Though the lion's share of my affection was still reserved for Liz, I have to confess to being pleased by the girlish way Rebecca was acting. I once heard someone say that age was just a number, and looking at Sister Rebecca's lovely face, her good-humored grin, I'd never agreed with the sentiment more.

Because I could think of nothing else, I said, "How are you?"

Her face stretched into an incredulous smile. "How am *I*? My goodness, Jason, the question is, how are you holding up? What a terrible week this has been."

Her words assuaged my nerves dramatically. Unlike Father Richards, Sister Rebecca wasn't talking about the events of the past several days like the exploits of some ecclesiastical superhero. She could see the weariness and stress in my face, and she regretted that I had to endure all of it.

"I'm managing," I said. "But I'm alive. I owe everything to God. And Father Patterson."

"I'm thankful you both survived."

"Where is he?" I asked. "His office?"

"The red room," she said. "He was falling asleep on his feet, so I ordered him to get some rest. He's been snoozing for a couple hours now."

"Mind if I check on him?"

"Only if you don't wake him up."

Chuckling, I moved past her toward the staircase, but she stayed me with a hand on my shoulder.

"You're sure you're okay, Jason?"

"Why wouldn't I be?"

"You were shot in the side," she said. "And you nearly drowned."

"You make it sound more impressive than it was."

"You stopped them," she said.

I started to protest, but she squeezed my arm. "You did, Jason. They were stalking Celia Bittner, they were going to do to her what they'd done to the others."

I shook my head. "Where did you—"

"It's all over the news," she said, and I was surprised to see that her eyes were glistening. "Your name hasn't been released yet, but everybody knows it was you and Father Patterson who followed the killers." Her voice was thick with emotion. "I know it was you who killed Danny Hartman."

"I didn't want to kill anyone."

"I know," she said, smiling. "And that's why I'm so proud of you."

And before I knew what she was doing, she leaned in and kissed me firmly on the cheek. For a moment, I could smell her breath. Sweet and laced with peppermint. My whole body grew warm.

Then she pulled away, smiled, and released me.

We went our separate ways, a pleasant heaviness weighing me down.

I made my way to the long basement corridor. When I reached the red room door, I carefully turned the knob, not wanting to awaken Father Patterson if he was still sleeping.

He was. I moved into the room and gazed down at him. His color had improved. He didn't look quite as hardy as he had before our encounter with Officers Hartman and Raines, but he would recover.

I decided it was a good thing that the city didn't know our identities, at least not yet. It would allow Father Patterson to rest, and I could reestablish a sense of normalcy if given more time.

Yet, inevitably, I realized, the truth would come out. The police had warned us of this in the hospital. The media would descend on the cathedral. Our parishioners would be confused, perhaps even alarmed.

Maybe it would be better if they heard it from me first.

I nodded, realizing exactly what I would speak about tonight. Closing the door noiselessly, I hurried down the hallway and locked myself in my office, where I wrote out my entire sermon.

CHAPTER TWENTY

"Brothers and Sisters in Christ," I began. It was the way Father Sutherland always opened. "I want to start out by setting the record straight on a number of counts, the first of which involves the rumors about Father Peter Sutherland's death."

The pews of St. Matthew's were filled to capacity. Folding chairs had been added wherever possible to accommodate the parishioners, but even so, there were numerous people crammed in the corners of the sanctuary, standing shoulder-to-shoulder in the back, even peering from the chapel doorway to my right. The choir loft looked so packed that I feared it would collapse on the crowd below. I was nervous, yes, but I knew what I wanted to say, and no amount of jitters would prevent me from speaking the truth.

Or at least most of it.

"Father Sutherland," I continued, "was an amazing man. A bastion of faith and a pillar of this church."

Nods and murmurs of assent. Several older ladies in the front pews looked misty-eyed. They had probably harbored secret crushes on my friend, I thought, smiling inwardly.

"And he died in service to God, in service to members of this wonderful congregation."

A ripple of movement from my left drew my attention, and when I looked that way I saw Liz Hartman seated in the front pew, her children flanking her. I had been so intent on delivering my message that I hadn't even noticed her presence. I tried to read Liz's face for signs of malice, but gave up after a moment. There would be time to address matters later. If she was still willing to speak to me.

I couldn't even meet little Carolyn's gaze.

I took a breath. "Therefore, when you hear a rumor about Peter Sutherland that portrays him as something other than what he was—kind, loving, patient, brilliant, brave, steadfast, a true fisher of men—crush that rumor for the lie that it is, and in doing so, honor the man who gave his life for Christ, who sacrificed everything to serve Him."

A smattering of applause and a general wave of approbation.

I continued, my voice growing stronger. "Speaking of rumors." I paused, swept the crowd with my eyes. "I gather there are a great many rumors about me being bandied about. I would like to set the record straight about those as well."

Another ripple from the crowd, this one not as boisterous, but even more electric than the prior ones had been. As I studied my notes, I felt the hungry eyes crawling over me, weighing me, comparing what they'd heard about my actions to the man who stood before them.

I muttered a breath prayer and went on. "Concerning that dark night, the night on which our beloved Peter Sutherland lost his life, I did assist in an exorcism, and though Father Sutherland perished as a result of the ceremony, the offending spirit was driven from the host."

Shocked gasps followed this, a reaction I had expected. After all, why wouldn't an adherent of the Catholic faith react strongly to the news that a supernatural evil had preyed on a child?

"As I have said, Brothers and Sisters, I was only an assistant in the rite of exorcism. Father Sutherland was responsible for saving the host, and it is to him—and to God—that we should give our thanks."

More murmurs of assent. My eyes happened upon Sister Rebecca, who was watching me from a side door. I winked at her, eliciting a brighter smile. She nodded and went out.

The murmurs died down. "What happened this week at a local 7-11 is another matter entirely."

As one, the crowd seemed to lean forward expectantly.

"What occurred in that store was a nightmare and not something I wish to relive."

A disappointed sigh from some corners of the cathedral.

"But I will say this," I continued to a quickening of excitement. "The three perpetrators of the convenience store crimes were lost souls who needed, at some point in their lives, someone to intervene. They needed Christ's love, and though I don't regret doing what I did to stop the sexual assault of a young woman and what would almost certainly have been further violent crimes inflicted on the innocent people present that night, I do regret that the perpetrators' hearts were so closed to Christ that they resorted to sadistic behavior rather than seeking shelter in love."

I could tell that the parishioners were surprised by my direction. Perhaps they had expected a vengeful condemnation of the criminals or a tearful apology for the deaths I had caused, but they clearly hadn't expected me to express sorrow for the criminals' waywardness.

"This is why, Brothers and Sisters, I urge us all to renew our dedication to *loving* our fellow man rather than to despising him. I encourage us all to destroy the barriers that divide us, rather than thickening these walls as though we're inhabitants of some medieval keep instead of a house of God." I allowed my eyes to strafe the crowd for emphasis.

"The House of Christ is not an elite club. It is open to *all*, regardless of any differences, whether they be real or perceived."

A restless muttering here and there.

I frowned, peered down at the lectern. "Unfortunately, friends, evil does not discriminate either. I am referring, of course, to the unthinkable turmoil that has gripped this fair city during the past several months. I am referring to the Sweet Sixteen Killer."

All sound in the sanctuary ceased.

I had begun to sweat, not due to the size of the crowd and the avidity of its attention, nor because of the spotlight focused on me. I had selected my words about Danny Hartman and Tyler Raines with care, especially in the case of the former individual, who after all had been a longstanding member of this congregation, as well as a highly respected police officer in the neighborhood, and who had now been unmasked as a serial killer.

Yet I hadn't considered the fact that Liz and her children might be present. What would she make of this portion of my sermon? Just as importantly, how would Carolyn and Casey feel? To them, their Uncle Danny had been a foundational element in their lives.

My eyes flitted toward the Hartmans, and again I toyed with the notion of scrapping this section. Hadn't they endured enough already? Liz had suffered through the demonic possession of her son, physical abuse at the hands of the demon, heard terrible revelations about her husband, seen her entire existence irrevocably altered. And now one of the few people in whom she'd placed her trust had proven to be the fiend responsible for seven savage murders.

But Liz was strong. And there was the central issue of my involvement with the case. As selfish as this sounds, I knew I could never move forward with my life if the shadow of the killings still hung over me in any way.

I had to tell the tale.

Tensing my muscles, I began to speak again. It didn't take long. I omitted several crucial facts. Had I revealed to the congregation that I'd known Danny was the killer for the past several days, I would have either faced the prospect of explaining Malephar's possession of me or worse, confront the possibility of jail time for concealing the Sweet Sixteen's identity. I did tell them about Tyler Raines's confession booth admission, and at this there were audible gasps and a great deal of talking. I had to raise my hands for silence.

My newfound confidence surged. "After I confronted Officer Raines about his confession, I worried Father Patterson would prevent me from doing my duty as a citizen in bringing Raines to justice."

I paused, permitted myself the slightest of grins. "I need not have worried."

I continued, making sure to paint Father Patterson in a heroic light. It wasn't difficult. The congregation knew nothing of his failure to save Ariana, so in their minds, his dive into the churning waters of the reservoir was motivated exclusively by a desire to do good.

I could tell that my account was having the desired effect. The crowd looked pleased, respectful, appreciative. Even edified. Their faith in God's redeeming love had been restored. As I spoke, my eyes were repeatedly drawn to the Hartmans. Carolyn's expression was inscrutable, but not, I thought, closed to me. Casey seemed preoccupied by other thoughts, examining his fingernails and perhaps mourning his uncle. I couldn't blame him. To Casey, Danny had been a family member and a friend. I couldn't imagine how difficult a time his young psyche must be having trying to reconcile the Danny he knew with the beast that had rampaged through the city.

But it was toward Liz that my eyes were most often drawn. Earlier, I'd been unable to discern the emotions on her face. Now, however, as I brought my narrative to a close, I understood that what I saw in her eyes was nothing more complex than powerful, unwavering affection. She was grateful I had survived, and she wanted to be with me. It was similar to the expression she'd worn after I had helped save Casey, only this time there existed a greater hunger in it, a maturity that made me both giddy and lightheaded. If we continued down this path, our relationship would become physical. Would I be able to love her the way a man should love a woman? Would my inexperience disappoint her? Make her yearn for someone else, someone without the insecurities that plagued me?

That issue was for another time, I decided. Now I had to bring my oratory to a close, to cinch the matter for these people whose faith had been tested, whose exposure to depravity had darkened their view of mankind.

"In a perfect world, Brothers and Sisters, we would not have to worry about our neighbors coveting our possessions, spreading lies about us." I lowered my voice. "Even preying on our children."

The emotion was thick amongst my parishioners. Joy Smith, after all, one of the Sweet Sixteen's victims, had lived only twelve blocks from St. Matthew's and had occasionally attended services here with her aunt. She had known Casey, which had likely led to Danny's interest in her.

My eyes shifted to Casey, who was still studying his hands.

A tremor of disquiet shook me.

I reached up, adjusted my collar. "Man is capable of incredible love, friends, it is true. We need only look toward the courageous and selfless acts of Father Joe Patterson yesterday to discover evidence of man's goodness. The fact that I am standing before you today is proof that we can transcend our baser natures.

"But never doubt for an instant, friends, that man does possess a shadow side, a tendency toward darkness that necessitates an honest, unblinking assessment of ourselves as a species. We are selfish. We desire control, and though we have been given free will, we seek to exert our will over others.

"The two murderers—Danny Hartman and Tyler Raines—are examples of the depths to which people can sink. Neither of these men, Brothers and Sisters, suffered from mental illness. These men, like those all over the world who kill for power, who inflict pain for the sheer thrill of it, demonstrate why we must transform love into an active force, why we must strive to emulate Christ's example, why we must..."

I trailed off, unable to speak, unable even to think. Because my gaze had returned to Casey Hartman. Or more specifically, to something he was studying.

He wasn't examining his fingernails.

No, I thought. *It's not possible.*

I shook my head, forcing myself to end my sermon and thereby quelling the surge of unrest now beginning to take hold of the crowd. I muttered something about loving one another, stumbled through the benediction as coherently as I could, then escaped the lectern. I slipped out the side door and stood leaning against a pillar, my breathing quick and shallow, my body doused with sweat.

The service ended moments later, and to my surprise, a slender figure made its way down the little-used hallway toward me. I thought at first it was Liz. In the pooled shadows, it was difficult to tell. But when the figure emerged into the jaundiced light spilling from the sanctuary, I realized it was Liz's son.

Casey's head was cocked to one side, his expression hostile. "That was a pretty selective speech, Crowder. Left out an awful lot, didn't you?"

I noted the disrespectful way he addressed me, felt a flicker of annoyance, then reminded myself of how much he had endured.

I said, "I saw no reason to delve too deeply into recent events."

"Hung my uncle out to dry but made yourself look like a big hero."

It wasn't what I'd expected. Maybe I should have anticipated Casey's rancor after our interactions at his home, but the heat of his tone still caught me unprepared.

"Casey, you need time and rest. None of this is your fault."

But he seemed not to have heard me. "You think you're a big man, don't you? Uncle Danny was worth a hundred of you."

"I know you're hurting—"

"Maybe you'll be hurting soon."

I stared at him. His eyes looked sludgy in the wan candlelight. I felt a chill, remembering how his face had looked before we'd chased Malephar from his body.

"What are you saying, Casey? I know you'd never threaten anyone."

"Oh no?" Casey asked, dark eyes gleaming.

I thought of the demon's hellish form sinking to the bottom of the reservoir. It wasn't possible he'd already escaped his watery tomb.

Was it?

I swallowed. "Casey, you haven't experienced anything strange at your house, have you?"

"You're talking about Malephar, right?" he asked. "When you showed up at my house the other day, I knew the demon had chosen you."

My head was spinning. I cleared my throat. "Have you experienced anything supernatural—"

"Supernatural my ass," he said, snorting laughter. "I promise you, Father, what happened to me the other night was perfectly natural."

I reached for the crucifix in my pocket. "It wasn't your fault the demon took control of you. And if he has attacked you again—"

"I'm not talking about the night of the exorcism, Father. I'm talking about the murders."

I froze, staring. "What do—"

"Uncle Danny told me all about them," Casey said. "He told me he was gonna commit suicide, or turn himself in. He said you'd go to his superiors, that it was only a matter of time before he got caught."

I couldn't feel my legs beneath me, couldn't breathe. "Casey, your uncle was a sick man—"

"He was a *great* man!" Casey shouted. He took a step toward me, his eyes flaring. "He did amazing things. And he would've been fine if you hadn't—"

"He was murdering *children*, Casey. He had to be stopped."

"Nothing has stopped, Crowder. You've only made things worse."

"Casey, you need to—"

"It wasn't Tyler Raines."

I stared at him.

Casey nodded, reveling in my surprise. "Uncle Danny told me all about what you did to Sutherland. You're a killer too. Don't deny it."

But I barely heard this last. Because he had extended a hand toward me, palm up.

I stared in numb horror at Julia Deveroux's emerald-lined crucifix.

My eyes rose to meet Casey's. His smile was ghastly. "Uncle Danny coached me. He told me exactly what to do."

The floor had fallen away beneath me. "*No,*" I whispered.

"Yes," Casey answered. "And you know what else, you son of a bitch? I enjoyed it. Losing my virginity and stopping her screams—"

"I don't believe you."

"I *enjoyed* it," he repeated. "For the first time in my life, I didn't feel like a pussy. I wasn't afraid anymore. You understand that, Crowder? I wasn't afraid!"

I extended my hand toward the emerald-lined crucifix, but he snatched it away, shook his head. "If you tell a soul about what I did, Crowder, I'll tell everyone the truth about you."

"No, Casey," I pleaded. "Let's talk about—"

"There's nothing to talk about, Crowder. Fuck you."

I could only stare at him, the innocence I'd beheld only a week ago gone. Replaced by a pitch-black hatred.

He nodded. "I'd watch the news if I were you. See you soon, Father."

He walked away.

♦ ♦ ♦

My chest burning, my cheeks tingling with salty tears, I fled down the stairwell to the basement corridor, which was blessedly empty. The regular employees had either gone home, or were now milling with the rest of the parishioners in the sanctuary or the narthex. I was grateful that none could see my tears of sorrow at Casey's terrible admission. I had again erred in my reasoning, again believed an innocent man to be guilty of murder.

But at least I hadn't killed Tyler Raines. Danny had done the honors for me.

Thinking of Raines, I shambled down the long, nearly lightless corridor toward the red room. Raines had harbored unsavory thoughts, it was true, and given time, he may have allowed those desires to cross over into bloodshed. But Danny had killed him because Raines *wasn't* a killer, because Raines could identify Danny.

While the true murderer of Julia Deveroux was living with his mother and sister in a luxurious house on Rosemary Road.

I couldn't believe it. Casey, of all people, had become his uncle's sinister heir.

Nearly swooning from the revelation, I opened the door of the red room and prepared to unburden myself to Father Patterson. The couch on which he had lain earlier, however, was empty, and my catharsis was delayed.

Not bothering to close the door, I proceeded down the hallway, thinking of Liz, who had already lost a husband and might now lose a son. Was Casey already lost to her?

Yes, I realized. He'd either keep on killing, be apprehended, or die in an attempt to flee justice. It all came to the same thing: Liz would no longer have her boy.

Moaning, I blundered up the stairs at the end of the corridor, only the wooden handrail preventing me from collapsing. Father Sutherland and I had exorcised the demon from an adolescent body only to see that young man commit an unspeakable atrocity the same week. Had Casey somehow been afflicted with Malephar's evil emotions in a permanent, irreparable way? It made sense, I decided, as I moved up the final set of steps to the administrative wing of the cathedral. How could such a deep, complex—though unwanted—union with such a ferocious entity not leave an indelible stain?

Or had Casey harbored such unwholesome cravings all along, and only, through the realization that his uncle was the serial killer terrorizing the city, been given the opportunity to unleash his darkest urges?

It was a possibility too horrible to contemplate, one that bore a hideous resemblance to the sermon I had just delivered. Was man, in his tendency toward sin, irretrievably doomed? I didn't think so, yet the notion that Casey had always possessed the potential for such wickedness troubled me to the marrow.

Enervated, desperately longing for a friendly face, I moved through the reception area and opened the door to Father Patterson's office. Closing it behind me, I turned and was surprised to find Patterson in his big chair, looking at me. The overhead light was off, and the lamps were dark, but there were several candles glowing on the corners of his desk and on the end tables that lined the perimeter of the office.

My shoulders sagged with relief. "Hey, Father. I was hoping you'd be awake."

Good humor twinkled in his eyes. His expression seemed very warm in the candlelight, his demeanor more relaxed than I'd seen since this ordeal began. Though it didn't erase the shock of learning what Casey had done, it did ease my jangling nerves somewhat.

He gestured toward the chair opposite him. "Take a seat, Jason."

Shooing away a greenbottle fly, I did as he bade.

"Sister Rebecca told me the service went well," he said.

I smiled what I was sure was a dopey smile, but I was unable to restrain my pleasure at receiving Father Patterson's approval. After Sutherland died, I never thought I'd enjoy the same mentor-pupil relationship, but now that Father Patterson and I understood one another better, I suspected that was exactly the sort of dynamic we were establishing.

"Were you nervous?" he asked.

"Very," I admitted. "But my preparations were thorough enough to get me through the jitters."

"That's fantastic, Jason. I'm proud of you."

I beamed down at my lap, feeling better than I had since...

...since finding out about Casey.

My good spirits vanished. I felt terrible about taxing Father Patterson with such a weighty issue so soon after the trauma he'd endured, but I knew this discussion couldn't wait.

"Father Patterson..." I started.

"Yes, Jason?"

"Tyler Raines didn't kill anyone."

His smile slipped a little. "Then why would Danny kill him?"

"He knew Danny's secret. Danny killed him out of self-preservation."

Elbows on his desk, he spread his hands in a puzzled gesture. "If Raines didn't kill the Deveroux girl, who did?"

I told him. I thought for sure he would scoff at the revelation, or at the very least attempt to dissuade me of Casey's guilt, but he seemed to accept everything I said.

He made a pained face. "What should we do?"

I realized I'd backed myself into a corner. I could never tell him the complete truth, that I was hesitant to turn Casey in because he knew my secret, knew I'd murdered Father Sutherland.

I said, "There's no good solution. If we go to the authorities, we stop the murders, but we break Liz's heart."

"Father Crowder," he said, lowering his forehead and holding me with his profound gaze. "It's better to let Liz begin the healing process now if it means no more dead children."

I nodded. He was right, of course. If Casey told the police what I'd done after they arrested him—which he was certain to do—I would simply tell them the truth, that I'd

446

murdered Sutherland in error. I would go to jail for a long time, but at least the mayhem would end.

It would be better if I told Patterson now. He would likely despise me for killing his best friend, but there was a small chance he might respect me for confessing the truth. And who better to bare my soul to than a priest?

My lips began to form the words, but before I could utter them, Patterson said, "Sister Rebecca has certainly taken a shine to you. I don't mind telling you, there have been moments when I've felt attracted to her myself."

I tried not to show my surprise. She and Father Patterson were closer in age than she and I were, but the notion of Patterson harboring romantic feelings for her was one I'd never considered.

Perhaps he read the worry in my expression, for he said, "Don't worry, Jason. You're the one she pines for. Not me."

Too bad I'll never be able to enjoy a relationship with her, I thought. *Her or Liz.* I imagined Liz's lovely face, imagined her horrorstruck expression at learning that I had murdered Sutherland. I shivered, became aware of a dripping sound.

Father Patterson noticed my frown, said, "The sink's been doing that for days. I haven't gotten around to having it fixed."

"Ah," I said. "By the way, where is Sister Rebecca? I saw her in the sanctuary earlier, but she disappeared."

Patterson smiled. "She's right here in the office, Jason."

When I only frowned at him, he nodded over my shoulder. I turned, expecting to see Rebecca's kindly face smiling down at me in that beguiling way of hers that was somehow motherly and bewitching at the same time.

But Sister Rebecca wasn't standing at my shoulder.

She wasn't smiling.

She was nailed to the back wall with foot-long spikes, her limbs spread apart, her naked body flayed open from her throat to her vagina.

Gagging, I stumbled out of my chair and sank to my hands and knees, unable to endure the ghastly sight.

"Is something troubling you, Jason?" Father Patterson asked.

"What's..." I managed through a series of choking coughs. "What's... wrong with you?"

"Death is perfectly natural," Patterson said in that same serene voice. "I would think you'd know that better than anyone."

I brought a forearm to my mouth, realized where the flies had come from. They were buzzing around Sister Rebecca's corpse, supping of her congealing blood. I ventured a glance at Rebecca's feet, saw how they'd been skewered with Patterson's cruciform letter openers. I didn't need to glance at her hands to confirm they'd been impaled in the same brutal manner.

I was aware that Patterson had stood up behind his desk, was waiting for my reaction.

"Why did you do this?" I moaned.

"Because you killed one of my servants, Jason."

Only he hadn't used my name. I turned slowly and stared up at Patterson, who leered at me in triumph.

"What did you call me?" I whispered.

"*Craven*," he answered in a guttural, buzzing voice.

I fell back and landed on my buttocks and elbows. I scuttled away from the huge figure, who tracked my movements with that same, unblinking leer.

"*Fortunate Patterson came along when he did*," the voice growled. "*He makes the perfect host.*"

"No," I said in a strangled voice. I was shaking my head, but the figure only watched me, the eyes seeming to change now.

To emit a lurid red glow.

"*I entered his body as you were being helped out of the reservoir,*" the voice said. "*When you grasped Patterson's hand at the hospital, I showed the priest your secrets. It shattered his faith, craven, knowing you'd murdered Sutherland.*"

I was weeping, thrashing my head in mute horror. Sister Rebecca's blood continued to drip steadily, the flies buzzing and flitting over her mutilated carcass.

"*Your fingerprints are all over this office, craven. The virgin's blood will bathe your quivering flesh.*"

The Patterson-thing stalked around the desk, my friend's body seeming mountainous now, misshapen. The elbows and knees stretched the fabric of Patterson's clothes, their knobby joints threatening to burst the seams. Patterson's stout neck, too, pulsed and hopped, as if the muscles there were trying to escape the Roman collar that bound them. For the first time I noticed the clear plastic gloves he wore.

"*You will be anathema, Crowder. The city will howl for your arrest. The priest who mutilated the nun!*"

I tried to crawl backward toward the door, but the Patterson-thing loomed over me, bent unnaturally at the waist, and brought his face close to mine. The red eyes gleaming, the fanged teeth bared, the Patterson-thing said, "*You will be apprehended. You will languish in prison while I slaughter Liz, while I slay her whelp of a daughter.*" The leer expanded, stretched the demonic face wider. "*But not Casey. He and I will revel in our butchery. Together, we will make the Sweet Sixteen Killer look like a child's fairy tale. We will redefine horror.*"

The Patterson-thing's slaver dripped onto my cheeks, the bloodcurdling face mere inches from mine. "*And without my strength,*" Malephar said, "*you will be helpless to stop us.*"

He seized me by the hair. I writhed in his grip, battered at his hand, but the powerful fingers were implacable. "What are you doing?" I asked. "Let me go!"

The Patterson-thing dragged me toward Sister Rebecca's sagging corpse.

I bucked against the Patterson-thing, but it towed me steadily closer, closer. Then it was shoving my face toward the mangled hole between Sister Rebecca's legs. I shrieked, knowing finally what Malephar intended. The ultimate degradation, a befoulment so profane it would shatter my sanity.

"No!" I implored. "Don't make me!"

But my face entered the glistening, flyblown cavity, my screaming lips moistened by the gore.

"*Taste of the virgin's blood!*" Malephar bellowed. "*Drink from her holy womb!*"

ABOUT THE AUTHOR

Jonathan Janz grew up between a dark forest and a graveyard, which explains everything. Brian Keene named his debut novel *The Sorrows* "the best horror novel of 2012." *The Library Journal* deemed his follow-up, *House of Skin*, "reminiscent of Shirley Jackson's *The Haunting of Hill House* and Peter Straub's *Ghost Story*."

Since then Jonathan's work has been lauded by writers like Jack Ketchum, Brian Keene, Edward Lee, Tim Waggoner, Bryan Smith, and Ronald Kelly; additionally, *Booklist*, *Publishers Weekly*, and *The Library Journal* have sung his praises. Novels like *The Nightmare Girl*, *Wolf Land*, *Savage Species*, and *Dust Devils* prompted

Thunderstorm Books to sign Jonathan to an eleven-book deal and to give him his own imprint, "Jonathan Janz's Shadow Side."

His most recent novel, *Children of the Dark*, received a starred review in *Booklist* and was chosen by their board as one of the "Top Ten Horror Books of the Year" (September 2015-August 2016). *Children of the Dark* will soon be translated into German.

Jonathan's primary interests are his wonderful wife and his three amazing children, and though he realizes that every author's wife and children are wonderful and amazing, in this case the cliché happens to be true. You can learn more about Jonathan at www.jonathanjanz.com. You can also find him on Facebook, via @jonathanjanz on Twitter, on Instagram (jonathan.janz) or on his Goodreads and Amazon author pages.

Look for these titles by Jonathan Janz:

Novels

The Sorrows
House of Skin
The Darkest Lullaby
Savage Species
Bloodshot: Kingdom of Shadows
Dust Devils
Castle of Sorrows
The Nightmare Girl
Wolf Land
Children of the Dark

Novellas

Old Order
The Clearing of Travis Coble
Witching Hour Theatre
A Southern Evening

Coming Soon

The Dismembered
The Dark Game

COMING SOON

We Are Always Watching by Hunter Shea

A Soundless Dawn by Dustin LaValley

Just Like Hell by Nate Southard

Find these and other horrific books at
www.sinistergrinpress.com

Made in the USA
San Bernardino, CA
02 May 2017